INTRODUCING...DANIELLE ROSS
and an exciting new mystery series
by acclaimed author Gilbert Morris

Young, beautiful, and intelligent, Danielle Ross is a female detective, who along with hired sleuth Ben Savage, takes the world of crime by storm in a new series of novels that offer suspense, intrigue, and romance with a Christian perspective.

In *Guilt by Association,* the first of the Danielle Ross Mysteries, Dani's faith is put to the ultimate test as the threat of death at the hands of a deranged captor looms over her and twelve others. As tensions rise and despair fills the hearts of the prisoners, Dani races against the clock to solve the mystery behind the strange abductions.

Here is the first in a series of entertaining, unforgettable books that will keep you on the edge of your seat from the first page to the last.

GUILT BY ASSOCIATION

GILBERT MORRIS

Fleming H. Revell
A Division of Baker Book House Co
Grand Rapids, Michigan 49516

Library of Congress Cataloging-in-Publication Data

Morris, Gilbert.
    Guilt by association / Gilbert Morris.
       p.   cm.
    ISBN 0-8007-5395-X
    I. Title.
PS3563.08742G85   1991
813'.54—dc20   90-26028
                                                 CIP

Fifth printing, December 1994

Printed in the United States of America

In the life of every writer there is always that one person who gives the first boost that makes the whole thing possible and who's always there to prop up the ego when things look a bit grim.

So here's to a man who is that rare mixture of Christian zeal and scholarly mind, my first booster and my continual propper-upper:

Wendell Hawley

Contents

Contents

GUILT BY ASSOCIATION

1
Homecoming

"Ladies and gentlemen, this is your captain speaking. We'll be cruising today at thirty-five-thousand feet, en route from Atlanta to New Orleans. Just to give you a brief update on the weather in New Orleans, the temperature is seventy-eight degrees, with clear skies, winds light and variable out of the southeast. Our time en route today is going to be one hour and twelve minutes. We're expecting a smooth ride, so sit back and let your flight attendant give you our good service."

The captain ended his speech, and Danielle Ross settled back in the comfort of her seat in the Delta Boeing 757. Picking up the brochure from the pocket in front of her, she noted that the aircraft held 178 people and wished that the passenger on her right had been assigned to sit by someone else. Even as her thoughts turned to him, the man's elbow pressed suggestively against her arm. He was a type she had learned to despise—a flashy dresser, crudely good-looking and with the mistaken impression that all he had to do was turn on his charm, and any woman would be captivated. She gave him a quick glance, taking in the cream-colored slacks, the expensive suede jacket, and the ostrich-leather boots. A smooth tan made his teeth look very white as he grinned boyishly at her. Dani wondered who his hairdresser was, for Apollo's thick, blond hair fell across his brow in studied carelessness.

His name she knew, for immediately after boarding in Atlanta, he had introduced himself as Lance Apollo. She had nodded, refusing to give her name. Now, however, he seemed determined to bring her around.

"Say," he said quickly, leaning close enough so that she could smell the strong odor of his shaving lotion. "I've got this deal with the mayor to wind up, but I'll have it in the bag in a couple of hours." He leaned closer, pressing his arm against hers, and lowered his voice to what he no doubt considered a sexy tone: "Now, it just so happens that the manager of the Sanger is a friend of mine—owes me a favor. You heard about that hit musical *The Phantom of the Opera?* Sure you have! Well, I can get a couple of good seats—no problem! Whaddaya say we take it in, then have a late snack at Antoines?"

The pressure of his arm increased. Dani shook her head firmly. "Sorry, I have some business I have to take care of."

Apollo gave her a closer look, then bared his teeth. "Hey, let me guess your line!" He inspected her closely, sweeping her from head to foot.

What he saw was a tall young woman with a square face, perfect complexion, and fair coloring. He admired the wide mouth and noted the unusual gray-green of her large almond-shaped eyes. Her mouth was too wide and her chin too square and her nose just a trifle short for a beauty. He also noted the small, white scar on her right cheek, below the level of her earlobe. *Most dames would have that taken care of with plastic surgery,* he thought. *Wonder why she never did?* A mass of rich auburn hair fell across her shoulders, and one small mole stood out on her right cheek—a beauty mark of sorts. She wore a beige linen suit with a soft pink blouse and matching pink shoes.

After a careful look he said, "You're in show biz, I bet."

"No."

"No? Well—a model then?"

"No."

He ignored her curt answers and shook his head. "Nah—you wouldn't be a model. They're all skin and bones. No, you wouldn't be a model with those curves!" He pressed against her and demanded, "What *is* your line?"

"I'm a minister of the gospel."

Dani's broad lips turned up at the corners as Apollo's face revealed his shock. Sensing a movement on her left, she turned her head to see that the muscular middle-aged man who'd sat wordlessly beside her all the way from Boston had lifted his head from his book and now stared at her with a startled expression in his faded blue eyes.

Dani spent a great deal of time fending men off, and it had been a relief to make the flight from Boston without a problem. At the same time, this man had puzzled her. Ordinarily, people speak when they are side by side, just inches away, even if only of superficial things—but her companion had nodded slightly as she sat down, then had drawn a cloak of silence around himself. For the first hour,

Dani had paid him no attention, yet as she had read the flight magazine, she had studied him without a deliberate effort. Watching people had become second nature to her, and she knew almost at once that this man was troubled. His unsteady hands betrayed him, and instead of reading his book, he stared blankly at the page, not turning it for fifteen minutes. Although she could see only the right side of his face, she noted how the lips would tighten, then droop, lapsing once into a tremble that he shut off by quickly biting his lower lip. His eyes were vague, but once, when he turned to take a soft drink from the stewardess, Dani saw fear in his expression, and he blinked too rapidly.

At once she sensed that her words "I'm a minister of the gospel" had shaken him. As Dani started to speak, from her right, Apollo's big hand closed on her upper arm, and she was pulled back to face him. Irritated that she had turned from him, Apollo shook his head. "A preacher? Hey, that's cool!" He had her attention, or so he believed, and she could almost read his thoughts: *This broad is a preacher? All right, so that's what I work on!*

"I'm sort of religious myself. . . ." He nodded, and, holding on to her arm firmly, began telling some story about how he went to church when he was a boy.

Dani looked at him, wondering how to get free of his attention. Obviously if she was to have any opportunity to speak to the man beside the window, ordinary methods would not work. A thought flashed into her mind. At first she rejected it, but as it came back, her lips thinned and her eyes narrowed.

"Stewardess?" she called out as a red-haired girl in a

wine-colored uniform was approaching. "Could I have a cup of black coffee—a *large* cup, please?"

"Surely! I'll get it right now."

As she waited for the drink, doubt flitted through Dani's mind. *Even if he is second cousin to a gorilla, do I have the right, Lord . . . ? After all, I don't really want to* hurt *him.*

At that moment Apollo laid a hand upon her knee and accompanied the action with crudely sensual words even a gorilla would know never to apply to a minister of the gospel.

Well, what's sauce for the goose is sauce for the gander, decided Dani stubbornly. *And I'd say this gander has it coming to him.*

The stewardess arrived with the coffee. "Careful—it's hot!" she warned as she handed it over.

"Oh, I'll be careful." Dani nodded as she took the cup, tasting it carefully. Good, it was scalding hot. Placing the cup on the small fold-down table before her, she half turned in her seat, leaning as close as she could get to the man. Her eyes widened so that they seemed enormous to Apollo, and when she whispered in a throaty voice, "Can you *really* get tickets for that musical?" he almost jumped out of his skin.

He grinned, triumph in his greedy eyes, and he lifted his right hand to touch her cheek, saying, "Baby, you'd better believe it! Just you and me, and after the show— Ow—!" Apollo leaped out of his seat, brushing at the front of his slacks, which were stained with the coffee. Dani's hand had struck the cup as she reached to pick it up.

"Oh, I'm so sorry! Let me help you!" she cried and

pulled a tissue out of her bag. "I can't think how I could be so clumsy!"

"You dumb broad!" Apollo leaped to his feet, brushing at the front of his trousers, doing a jig in the aisle. His face had turned crimson, and he looked down at the brown stain that spread out over the front of his cream-colored slacks. Moving toward her, he uttered a curse, and for one instant Dani thought he was going to hit her. When she repeated, "I'm so sorry!" he snarled, jerked open the door of the overhead compartment, yanked out his flight bag, and dashed down the aisle toward the rest room, almost upsetting the red-haired stewardess in his blind rage. She regained her balance; a smile creased her lips. She came to stand beside Dani and, looking down, murmured, "Romeo got his ice-cream pants all spoiled?"

"I'm afraid I was very clumsy!" Dani said with a straight face. She shook her head. "Better stay close to me when he gets back. I may need a bodyguard."

"No problem. The copilot of this plane was a wrestling champ at Notre Dame. I'll put him on the case."

As soon as she left and made her way down the aisle, Dani turned to the man beside her, saying, "That was very clumsy of me, wasn't it?"

"Oh, I guess we all spill things once in a while." He was in his mid forties, Dani guessed, and his sandy hair was getting thin on top. His clothes were inexpensive, and the heels of his scuffed wingtips were badly run over.

"My name's Danielle Ross," she introduced herself quickly when he turned to stare out the window.

Encouraged by her attention, he nodded, saying, "I'm Frank Wilson." He hesitated, and she saw that he was looking at her with interest. "Are you really a minister?"

He gave her a slight smile that made him look younger and continued shyly, "You sure don't *look* like a preacher?"

Dani smiled and shook her head. "Tell me about it!" A sober look swept across her face, and she added ruefully, "I used to think about all the problems I'd have if I ever went into the ministry—but the one thing that never occurred to me was that I'd have trouble convincing people that I actually *was* a minister." A thoughtful look crossed her face, and she added, "To tell the truth, I felt out of place at the seminary. I really want to go as a missionary to Africa. I felt so—so unfitted for the job that I decided to go get some training. I could never really be a *pastor* or anything like that."

"Guess most of us never saw a preacher who looked so good." He stopped abruptly, a slight tinge of red touching his cheeks, and he said hurriedly, "I don't mean—!"

"Oh, that's all right—" The plane took a sudden dip into an air pocket, and both of them grabbed at their armrests and gave a little involuntary gasp. "Wow! I never get used to that!" she said with a nervous laugh. "I think, every time it happens, *Well, this is it, Dani! Get ready to meet the Lord!*"

Wilson smiled, then sobered instantly. "I guess that wouldn't be so bad for some people." He looked down at his hands, appearing to study them as if they were some strange, wonderful objects he was pricing for a sale. When he spoke, it was in a whisper so faint that she almost missed it. "There are worse things than going out in a crash."

Dani waited, but a sudden convulsion swept his pale face, and he abruptly swiveled his head away from her.

Quietly she asked, "You have some big trouble, don't you, Mr. Wilson?"

For an instant she didn't think he had heard her. He sat beside her, his head rigidly set, his hands twitching in his lap. Then he made fists of them and turned to face her. His moist eyes filled with fear as he whispered, "I'm going to die. That's what the doctors said. I'm going to die." An involuntary shiver drew his heavy shoulders together; then he reached back and hauled out a handkerchief and wiped his eyes with it. Blowing his nose, he deposited the handkerchief back in his pocket and attempted a smile that was a failure. "Sorry to be such a crybaby, Miss Ross—but it's so—well, I'm just not—"

Dani said, "Will you tell me about it?"

He began to speak haltingly, telling her the story—how he'd gone to see the doctor about what he'd thought was a minor problem and discovered that it was the most major of all physical problems. "That was only last week," he said jerkily. "My wife made me get a second opinion, so I did. The new doctor told me the same thing, but he said I needed to get the best there was—so he sent me to the Mayo Clinic. That's where I've been." He clasped his hands in an attempt to control them; then he looked at her with such fear in his eyes that meeting them was painful. "They said I only had one chance in a hundred."

The jet engines droned, and strips of cloud flew by as Dani sat there, looking into his eyes. Then he said, "I'd never been much for church, miss. Looks like that's been a bad mistake."

He stopped, but she knew this was a cry for help, for comfort, for a soul in agony.

As he waited for her response the hope in his eyes began to dull. Desperately Dani searched for an answer, frantically reviewing the long hours of seminary lectures, given by some of the world's most distinguished professors of theology—but nothing surfaced.

Then came just a wisp of memory. When it first touched her consciousness, she reject it summarily, but it returned like a ghostly hand.

On a cold, blustery day in downtown Boston, icicles had hung from the eaves of the shops, like glittering daggers. She had emerged from shopping at Jordan Marsh, meeting with bitter gusts that sucked her breath from her. Turning to the right to make her way to her car, she had found a small cordon of people blocking her way. They were listening to a man dressed in a thin, worn overcoat, and she had grimaced with irritation as she realized he was preaching in a loud voice. One glance revealed the rough boots with thick soles, the brown toboggan cap pulled down to his eyebrows, and the worn knees of a pair of khaki pants. The broad face was raw with the cold. She had swiftly turned to press her way through the small crowd. But she could not avoid the carrying voice. Poor grammar, yes, but he had that forceful intensity that makes it seem of little importance. As she walked rapidly away his words had followed her: "Look unto me and be ye saved. . . . Jesus is the way the truth and the life!"

Dani relived that moment in one instant, and she thought, with a sudden flash of bitter impatience at herself, *That poor man probably never saw the inside of a high school—but he'd know what to say to a dying man like this one—and here I am, with all my seminary training, shaking like a leaf!*

She *was* trembling, but this inward battle had not been

observed by Frank Wilson, though he had kept his eyes fixed on hers. Taking a deep breath, she threw out all her academic training in one sudden flash of determination. Unconsciously she drew instead on the years she'd spent listening to sermons by her childhood pastor. He had been such a plain man—so basic that unconsciously, at seminary, she'd come to look down on him as being simplistic—the worst charge one could make at Hayworth Divinity School! But his fundamental approach had rooted itself in Dani more deeply than she'd thought. Suddenly she pulled the Bible out of her purse and with one quick, silent prayer began speaking simply.

"I'm so sorry all this has come on you, Mr. Wilson. And I wish there were some sort of magic formula I could give you to make everything all right. But we both know that it's not quite like that, don't we?"

He shook his head sadly. "No, I don't reckon there's anything like that." He clasped one big hand into a fist, and a streak of anger stirred his voice. "Why did it have to happen to me? What's God mad at me for?"

Dani said, "God isn't mad at you. That's not the way to think of it—though we all do, when we get in serious trouble." She paused, then said, "Remember the first book of the Bible? 'In the beginning God created the heaven and the earth.' Then when He was finished, it says in the last verse of chapter one, 'And God saw every thing that he had made, and, behold, it was very good. . . .' " Dani smiled and said, "But it didn't stay good."

Wilson nodded. "No, I remember that from Sunday school, when I was a kid. Adam and Eve got kicked out of the Garden, didn't they?"

"Yes. And the world went bad." Dani explained, "God

put a curse on the earth and on man—and ever since that time, people have lived in a world that doesn't work. There was no death in the Garden, but as it says in Hebrews 9:27, 'It is appointed unto men once to die. . . .' There was no sickness or pain for Adam or Eve, until they broke God's law and were driven out—but now we all live in a world that's filled with disease and death."

Wilson nodded, and bitterness turned his lips down. "Not much of a world, is it?"

Dani said quickly, "But this isn't the only world, Mr. Wilson—and even in this world there's hope."

He looked at her uneasily, and there was doubt in his simple face. "I guess you mean Jesus, don't you, miss?"

"Yes. He's my hope. And I'll face death myself, won't I? Maybe this plane will go down—but if it does, I'll face death with Him on my side." She hesitated, then asked, "Mr. Wilson, may I read from the Bible what Jesus can do for you?"

He sat there, unmoving, and for one instant she thought he meant to refuse her request. She feared rejection and for that reason had never been able to press people to accept God into their lives. Even as she waited, she knew that she had stepped over some sort of boundary. Never again would she be able to sit silently, for God seemed to be saying to her: *This is the way for you—to declare My Name to those who need it.*

"Well, sure you can, miss," Wilson said suddenly. Dani began turning from Scripture to Scripture, reading carefully and marking them, watching his face as she read. At one point she became vaguely aware that Lance Apollo had returned and had taken his seat beside her. Ordinarily that would have embarrassed her, but she took no note, for there was a certainty in her that she had never known in her efforts to serve God.

"But it seems like such a poor thing to do. I mean, I've been ignoring God all my life—and now to come runnin' to Him, when I'm finished—" Wilson objected.

"Don't think of it like that," she said. "In the first place, He's never yet refused anyone who asked in faith. We just read about the thief on the cross. And in the second place, you may not be finished."

"You mean God might heal me?"

"He might. He's done it before." Dani thought quickly and said. "Did you ever hear the story of the three Hebrew children who were about to be thrown into a fiery furnace?"

"Think I did."

"When the king threatened them with death, they gave an answer that I've loved all my life. It's my own motto, I guess."

"What did they say?"

Dani found the place in her Bible and read it carefully: " 'O Nebuchadnezzar, we are not careful to answer thee in this matter. If it be so, our God whom we serve is able to deliver us from the burning fiery furnace, and he will deliver us out of thine hand, O king. But if not, be it known unto thee, O king, that we will not serve thy gods. . . .' " She looked up and said, "They said, 'God is able to deliver us, if that is His will'—but then they said, 'if not,' and that's what I live by." She closed her Bible and laid her hand gently on his arm. Her voice was warm as she added, "I believe that God is able to do anything for me, to deliver me from any trouble. But *if not*, that is, if He chooses not to do so, why, that doesn't change what He is or prove that He loves me any less. Can you see that?"

"Fasten your seat belts, please. We will be landing in five minutes."

Dani looked up with a start at the announcement that had come over the speaker, then quickly said, "Mr. Wilson, we'll be landing soon. Will you let me pray with you?" She had never done this before, and she was intensely aware that Apollo, on her right, was listening—but there was no way that she could do anything else.

"I—I don't know how to pray," Wilson whispered, shaking his head.

She took a few minutes to instruct him. As the plane dipped forward she began to pray a simple prayer for him. She took his hand, and just as the wheels struck the ground with a sharp thump, he lifted his head and looked at her with blank astonishment. The brakes caught, throwing them forward slightly. As they settled back, he took a deep breath and said, "I—I don't know what it is—but I'm not afraid anymore."

Her heart seemed to leap for joy, and tears filled her eyes. She whispered, "That's what Jesus does, Frank!"

They sat silently as the plane turned and began taxiing down the long strip that led to the low buildings in front of the flight tower. "But—am I healed?" he asked as passengers got up and began pulling their baggage down.

Dani said, "I don't know. But you've got Jesus on your side now. I'm going to pray for you to be healed—but *if not*, you're a child of God." Again she prayed for God to give him health. Aware that the passengers were filing off, she took a card out of her purse, wrote a number on it, placed it in the Bible, and handed it to him. "Take the

Bible and study the verses I marked. Call me if you like. I'll be in New Orleans for a few months."

She got to her feet, noting that Apollo had pulled down his suitcase but was standing back, watching them. Frank Wilson pulled himself up, took a worn, brown vinyl suitcase out of the compartment, then stopped to look at her. "I'll never forget you, Miss Ross!" Tears came into his eyes, and he put his hand out, giving hers a firm shake. "God bless you."

He turned, and Dani said, "Call me if you need help."

She stood there, watching him leave, and heard Lance Apollo say, "That guy—he's bought it?"

Dani faced him and asked, "Bought what?"

Apollo's eyes were thoughtful, and he shook his head. "Going to die, is he? Did I pick that up right?"

"That's what the doctors have said."

"And now he's on a religious trip." He shrugged his heavy shoulders. "Well, can't blame him much. I might do the same, if my number was about to be called."

He stooped and picked up his flight bag and started to leave, but she said quickly, "I'm sorry about that coffee."

He gave her a sudden grin. "Aw, what's the diff?" He looked at her carefully, shook his head, and said in wonder, "Preacher lady, you are a *trip*! Gimme one of your cards, hey? Maybe I'll need a preacher myself, sometime."

She reached into her purse, took out a card, and wrote her number on it. When she handed him the card, he stared at it, then read aloud: "Danielle Ross. CPA. Office of the Attorney General, State of Massachusetts."

He gave her a startled look, his eyes narrowing suspiciously. "Wait a minute! What's this attorney general stuff?

I don't see nothing about a preacher. You some kind of fuzz?"

"Used to be, Lance, in a way. That's an old card. I worked with the attorney general's office for a while before I went to seminary. That's my parents' number I've written on it." She smiled at him. "Who knows? Maybe we'll have dinner together sometime—and you can go to church with me."

The idea amused him, and he slipped the card in his pocket. "Maybe so, Ross—but it sure seems as if the good Lord made a mistake with you."

"Mistake?"

"Yeah, wasting those big eyes and all those curves on a preacher!" He laughed, put out his hand, and when she took it, he nodded. "See you in church."

He left the plane at a swift walk, and Dani retrieved her flight bag from the overhead compartment, then moved along the aisle. She smiled at the red-haired stewardess, who returned it with a sly grin, saying, "Watch out for the big, bad wolf, honey!"

"Not to worry," Dani answered. "My house is built out of bricks."

A blast of hot air struck Dani as she left the airport, after collecting her luggage. Somehow she had almost forgotten the oppressive, humid heat of Louisiana. It had been cool in Boston, and she wore clothing suited to that weather, but by the time she got into the cab, perspiration was already gathering on her face.

"Take me to Mandeville," she instructed the driver. "I'll tell you which way to go when we get there." He pulled out with alacrity, handling the cab with a touch of daring. As he turned onto Lake Pontchartrain Causeway she watched the gulls wheeling and screaming and felt a brief gladness at the thought of seeing her family—but that faded as the cab sped along the ribbon of concrete that spanned the lake.

Dani hadn't been in New Orleans for nearly a year, and this trip was not of her choosing. She sat back, looking out the window, thinking of the letter in her purse. "If you could come and work with the agency for just a few weeks, it would be a great help." Not a very urgent request, but from her father it was the equivalent of a desperate scream.

Her father's heart attack, the previous July, had come without warning, and she had flown to Houston for his triple-bypass surgery. Her mother, usually strong in a crisis, had been unexpectedly devastated by her husband's illness, and she'd turned to Dani, as had Rob and Allison, Dani's younger brother and sister.

Her father had recuperated well, but even after she returned to Hayworth, Dani had felt the grasping tentacles of responsibility at home. At first nothing had been said about her coming back, but she read between the lines that things were not going at all well. Her father's business, Ross Investigation Agency, was so firmly built around the integrity and drive of Daniel Clark Ross that the hired help could not do. In his letters hints of trouble had come in the form of brief statements: "The new man didn't work out." "We lost the Adkins account this week; they demand a great deal, I suppose."

Dani looked out at the lake, thinking of the heavy feeling that had come the previous Wednesday when she'd received the letter asking her to come home and help "just for a few weeks."

There had been no choice, of course. She had dropped

all her courses, said good-bye to all her professors (who'd done all they could to encourage her to stay), sublet her apartment, and stored the furniture. Common sense told her to sell it, that she'd be in New Orleans a long time; however, she'd lifted her chin and told herself that she'd be back again someday.

The cabbie wheeled off the Causeway, catching Highway 22, and sped through Mandeville. Dani leaned forward to say, "Take the first left—by the gas station." He made the turn, and as she looked at the familiar landscape, she stirred herself, thinking: *Brace up, Dani—you're crying like a baby! What about all those Scriptures you're always spouting? "In every thing give thanks. . . ." ". . . All things work together for good. . . ."* She forced her shoulders back and glanced out at the beginning of the oaks, bearing their loads of Spanish moss, that lined the road.

"That's it," she said and leaned forward to gesture at the two-story house on the left. The cabbie pulled up in the circular driveway.

Dani got out and paid the fare, adding a five-dollar tip. "Just put the bags on the porch, will you, driver?" She didn't wait for his answer, for she was running awkwardly, in her four-inch heels, to the fence that ran parallel to the house; a rust-colored quarter horse behind the bars was bowing and throwing his head up at the sight of her.

No trace of sadness in Dani's face now! She reached the fence and took the long Roman nose of the horse in both arms, laughing and crying out, "Biscuit! You son of a gun!"

She stood there stroking his nose and laughing as he nudged at her neck, nibbling at her gently with his velvet muzzle. "You just wait until tomorrow!" she threatened. "You've been soldiering long enough! I'll run that fat off you—why, I'll bet you couldn't run the barrels in half a day!"

As she turned and moved back toward the house, Dani felt happier than she'd been since she'd gotten the letter. She had always loved horses and at one time had cared for nothing in the world but running the barrels in high-school rodeos. She thought of the joy that had been like heaven when she and Biscuit had won the National Championship in Tulsa. She smiled ruefully and thought, *We're a little too old for that now, aren't we, Biscuit? But not too old to do a lot of riding.*

Her mother and sister stood on the porch, waiting for her, and as she trudged toward them, Dani thought how she loved the old house that had been her home until she left for college. It was only ten acres, but it looked much larger, for it was a long rectangle facing the road for a quarter of a mile. It was a restored planter's house in the Louisiana style—plain enough, except for the eight pillars that rose in front to the roofline. It had been cheap enough, back in the day when Daniel Ross had bought it, and he had spent many hours restoring it.

At the foot of the steps Allison, age fifteen, tackled her with a force that almost brought them both down. "Hey, you're getting to be a little large for that!" Dani laughed and looked down at her sister. Allison was a slow bloomer and showed only traces of Dani's beauty. She was painfully shy and now stepped back, embarrassed at having shown so much emotion. Quickly Dani embraced her and kissed her soundly. "It's so good to see you, Allison." She smiled warmly. "We're going to have lots of time to do things together, aren't we?"

The words brought a glow to the youngster's cheeks, and she nodded quickly. Dani gave her a squeeze, her conscience gnawing at her. *Should have written her more,* she thought as she turned to her mother. *I think she's had a hard time—and I haven't done much to help.*

"Dani, you're looking tired," her mother said as she took her kiss then had a long look at her daughter.

Dani looked at Ellen Anne Ross, who was only forty-four and looked even younger, and said, "I'll make you wait on me until I get rested up, Mom." But she was thinking that her mother looked exhausted and worried. In Dani's eyes her mother was the most beautiful woman in the world. She had been one of those tall, ash-blond Texas beauties who never seem to lose the battle to old age. But the brow was lined now, in a way Dani had never seen before, and she knew that she hadn't come home too soon.

They moved into the house, all three of them talking at once. "Your father is asleep," Ellen said finally. "You go lie down for a little while; then we'll have dinner." She smiled and embraced Dani, saying, "What you need is about two yards of boudin and a bowl of crawfish étou-fée!"

Dani noticed just a trace of clinging in her mother's embrace and understood that it was part of the relief Ellen felt at having her home. They would all be expecting her to take the strain off the house, bringing the agency back to full efficiency and standing in the gap. *Well, that's what I came back for,* she thought.

The three of them took her bags up to the second floor,

to her old room, which had not been changed at all: a big room with a heart-pine floor, a ten-foot ceiling, and a huge oak bed with a canopy that seemed to fly.

It was nearly dark outside, and Dani soon dozed off, looking out the large, mullioned window, avoiding the thoughts of difficulties that lay ahead. She awoke when Allison's voice came through the door: "Time for dinner, Dani."

She rose, stretched, brushed at her hair, then went down the curving staircase. Her father was waiting for her, and she went to him, putting her arms around his neck and kissing him with a loud smack. Then she stepped back and said saucily, with a gleam in her gray-green eyes, "Why you fraud—you look healthy as a horse! You're just playing sick to get me to do all your work!"

It was the line she'd decided to take, but in fact her father looked better than she had expected. He was one month over sixty and with his beautiful white hair and classic features, was one of the handsomest men she'd ever seen. He had always been strong, and the first sign of his illness she had seen was the pallor that lightened his usually tanned skin. Closer contact had revealed a certain weakness in his grip and a loss of some of the dynamic strength in his face.

"I'm sorry I had to ask you to leave school, Dani," he apologized.

"Oh, don't be silly!" She laughed and, linking her arm with his, added, "I was getting too bookish anyway. Besides, I won't be here all that long. You'll be back in harness again in no time."

"I hope so, Dani," he said, and she noted that the heart attack had taken more optimism out of him than she had thought. The illness that had reached out and struck him flat had taught her father to feel his mortality.

They went into the long dining room, and she gave a pleased cry. "Why, look at this! The good china and everything!" The table was set with the white damask linen, and silver, crystal, and china gleamed in the pure light of the antique chandelier. She sat down in the chair on her father's left and looked around. "Rob's not here?"

"He'll be in before we're through, I hope," Ellen said, and a slight hesitation in her voice caused Dani to ask no more.

"I made the crawfish étoufée, Dani!" Allison piped up. "I can make it as good as Mama now."

"Well, let's bless it and see if you're boasting," Daniel commented. They all bowed their heads, and he said quietly, "Thank You, dear Lord, for this food. Thank You for our family and for all the blessings You have poured out upon us in the name of Jesus."

They all began filling their plates, and Dani felt a lump in her throat as memories of a thousand meals just like this came to her. She shook her head and plunged into the étoufée, stuffed crabs, red beans and rice, and boudin— the hot, spicy sausage she loved—all with spicy Cajun seasoning.

They laughed at her stories of the seminary, but Dani noticed that nothing was said about the problems at the agency. *That'll come soon enough*, she thought. She listened to the list of Allison's accomplishments and made much of the girl, happy at how easy it was to bring pleasure to her sister.

Finally the meal was finished, including strong coffee with chicory to wash down the lemon icebox pie that was her mother's specialty. Then Ellen said, "You have some more coffee with Dad while Allison and I do the dishes— no, you go on," she urged as Dani protested. "We'll join you soon."

Dani and her father walked down the hall to the living room, which was filled with the antiques that were her parents' hobby. She sank down in one of the overstuffed chairs, waited until her father was seated, then asked, "How are you feeling, Dad? You look so good."

"Not bad at all," he admitted, leaning back in his chair. "The doctors are happy, but—" He paused and shook his head. A streak of doubt shadowed his face. "I can't do what I want to do. You know me, Daughter, always going full-speed ahead."

"I know you, all right." She smiled at him fondly. "That's why I came home, to keep you from doing just that."

"It's not good at the agency," he said slowly, biting his lower lip. "I hadn't realized how much of a one-man outfit we had until I had to step back."

He may not have known it, but Dani had known it for a long time. Daniel Ross *was* the agency. He employed two or three investigators, mostly to do the legwork, but his clients came to him because they wanted Daniel Ross— and that was the way he had liked it. Now that he was unable to meet that demand, inevitably business would fall off, Dani realized. She only said, "Well, Dad, I can't take your place, but I have some ideas about how we can get some new business until you're back full time."

He looked at her and smiled, saying only, "You're a good girl, Dani. I thank the Lord for you every day of my life."

She shrugged uncomfortably under the praise. "Oh, fuzz! Now, tell me what's wrong with Rob."

"You saw that, eh?" he said heavily. "He's not doing well, Dani. I guess seventeen is a bad age for kids these days. Somehow I hoped that Rob wouldn't get involved in the usual trouble—drinking and so on. But he has."

"How bad is it, Dad? Is he into drugs?"

"Don't know. Not the hard stuff, but these kids today think nothing of smoking pot." Daniel pulled his shoulders together and shook his head. "I've not done a good job, Dani. Should have spent more time with him."

Dani shook her head. "That's wrong. You've been a good father to all of us."

Awakening with a start, Dani sat up in bed, totally confused. Loud voices came from the hall, and the sound of a thump against the wall brought her out of bed. She threw on a robe, ran to the door, and stepped out into the hall.

A dim light was on, and she saw her mother struggling with her brother, Rob. He was obviously drunk or high and was talking loudly in an angry voice. "Lemme 'lone! Don't—need your help!"

Ellen struggled to get him down the hall, but he was pushing at her, striking the wall with his fist. As Dani moved toward the pair, he suddenly fell to the floor, almost pulling his mother down with him. Dani grabbed his arm, and the two women pulled him to his feet.

"Whose zis?" he asked thickly, peering at her face. A rank smell of whiskey came to her as his eyes focused, and he mumbled, "Dani? Zat you, Dani?"

"Yes, now come on to bed," she commanded. The two women moved down the hall, propping him up until they got him to his room and Allison, who had come out of her room, opened the door. She had a frightened expression on her face, and Dani said, "You go on to bed, honey. It'll be all right."

She and Ellen shoved Rob into the bed; his tall, gangly body sprawled wildly, and he went out like a light. Ellen pulled his shoes off, loosened his belt, said, "He'll sleep all night," then led the way out of the room. "I'm sorry you had to come home to this, Dani," she said heavily.

Dani took her in her arms and murmured, "Go to bed, Mom. We'll talk about it tomorrow."

Ellen went without protest, and Dani returned to her own room. She was wide awake and stood at the window, watching the yellow moon, shaped like an up-ended Cheshire cat smile, move across the sky.

She stood there for a long time, so long that the thin gauzy strips of clouds veiled the yellow moon. A fog was rising over the lowlands, covering the brown, dead stalks of grass like a soft blanket, and the only sound she heard was the occasional lonesome cry of a night bird.

Her shoulders slumped as if her thoughts weighted them down. She thought of Rob, wondering if he were one of the many she'd known who seemed to be beyond anyone's reach; of Allison, with all the fears of adolescence; of Ellen, with the marks of strain on her smooth face; and of her father, whose unprecedented weakness frightened her.

Finally she went back to bed and lay there, seeking sleep, but it was long before it came.

2
Savage

September faded into October, which brought little relief from the muggy heat. Dani tried to ignore her longing for the crisp New England fall she loved, and for three weeks she rose at dawn, spending long hours at the agency. She attacked the problem typically, throwing herself into it with an efficiency that almost frightened the staff.

She completely overhauled the financial system, installing a Macintosh computer with appropriate software and training Angie Park, the secretary, on it. Every client the agency had served for the past twenty years received a full-color brochure, setting forth the services of the Ross Investigation Agency, and most of them received a personal call from Dani.

Angie was young enough, at twenty-seven, to fall in with the new urgency that Dani brought with her, but the male operatives were a problem from the beginning. Larry Maitland quit two days after Dani took over. He left cursing women in general and Dani Ross in particular, and

Angie sighed with relief, saying, "I've fought him off for three years. Never could understand why your father kept him on." She ruffled her blond hair, adding, "He was good at prowling around Bourbon Street, in the joints, finding out things."

"Now he can do it on his own time," Dani remarked tersely. The two women were sitting in her office, after Maitland left. She studied Angie carefully, then asked, "What about Monroe?" Tom Monroe, a man of almost seventy, was thin and moved slowly, coming into the office only when called for.

"Oh, he's got lots of connections with the police and the state troopers." Angie shrugged. "Your dad never used him for much more than that. He's retired from the police and doesn't want to work regularly."

Dani nodded, having seen that much for herself. "He doesn't cost us much." Then she frowned and tapped her teeth with the pen she was holding. "Then there's Al."

Al Overmile was thirty, an ex-cop. He was handsome in a heavy way—a weight lifter going to fat. He had blond hair, blue eyes and a wide, sensuous mouth. In some way he reminded Dani of Lance Apollo, perhaps because he had tried to take her out from the day she first came to the office. She had refused him coldly, but he seemed totally insensitive. Every time he came to the office, he pursued her with his eyes and usually found some excuse to touch her. Soon she knew he would try to step over the line.

Angie's cheeks flushed, and she said tonelessly, "Oh, Al's all right in his way."

Dani gave her a quick look. "You been dating him, Angie?"

"Well, I used to—but Al's restless. Likes to play the

field." Angie was attractive, with her large blue eyes and fair skin. But Dani saw at once that her memories of Overmile were not pleasant. Angie shifted restlessly in her chair, then added, "Some jobs take a man, Miss Ross— and I guess Al's no worse than most of the others."

"I suppose," Dani said slowly, but she was unhappy with the man. To her knowledge he had lost them at least two highly desirable clients. She had contacted them almost at once, and one, the Melton Oil Company, had been firm. "We like your work, Miss Ross," the vice-president had said, "and we'd use you—but not as long as you employ Al Overmile." He refused to be more specific, but Dani knew that if she had turned up two unhappy clients, there were bound to be others.

That afternoon Dani left the office discouraged. She had done all she could. When she spoke to her father that night after supper, she startled him by bursting out unhappily, "I wish I were a man!"

They were in his study, where they went every evening to review what she had done. He stared at her, then smiled, "Well, I don't. I like you just the way you are."

She threw her head back, and her eyes were angry. "It's not *fair*, Dad!"

"Dani, there's always going to be some who will be able to see you only as a woman, and they think investigative agencies need a man—which in some cases they do."

"Oh, I *know* that, Dad."

"Well, what's the problem."

"I lost that job with Oliver Hackman." She sighed and let her head fall back on the chair. "It would have put us in the black, too!"

"I'll talk to Oliver," he said quietly. "But if I understand the job, we don't have the personnel to cover it." He hesitated, then asked, "Are you getting along any better with Al?"

"Oh, it's all right—but he's not a top-flight operator, Dad."

"And we're not paying him what a top-flight investigator would demand."

Dani laughed and got to her feet, stretching hugely. "Oh, I know that. I'm just ornery tonight."

"You've worked too hard, Dani." Her father considered something for a long moment. "I've been thinking about this a lot. Dani, it may be a long time before I come back to work—no, don't argue with me!" he said sharply. "Even when I do come back, it'll be on a reduced basis. So, we've either got to step up—or close down."

Dani slowly nodded. "I've been thinking that way, too. We get adequate help and gamble that we can pay the tab. That's the only way we can make it, I think."

"I'll see who's available. I can do that much from here with a phone. But you'll have to do the hiring. You're the one he'll have to work for."

"I think we can do it, Dad—but you'd better get somebody who can do more than strong-arm people. Some clients insist on talking to a man, so be sure he can carry on a sensible conversation."

"I'll get on it in the morning." Looking relieved, he asked, "What are you up to tonight?"

"Going to a rock concert with Rob."

"Allison going?"

"No, she's got a practice for that play at school." She made a face and added, "I hate rock."

"You always did," Daniel smiled. "Even when you were

a little girl, you hated it. The other kids thought you were perverted somehow. I'm glad you're going, though. Maybe you can find out what's going on in Rob's head."

"I hope so—but I'm antediluvian to him. He thinks I'm a square—and he's right." She laughed and kissed him on the cheek. "I'll give you a report tomorrow."

She didn't know exactly how to dress for a rock concert, so she wore black cotton slacks, a long-sleeved red blouse, a black plaid jacket, and black ankle boots. When Rob saw her, he groaned, "You're not going to wear *that* getup, are you, Sis?"

"What's wrong with it?"

"If you don't know, I can't tell you." He looked at her with a gloomy expression. "Well, let's go. I can tell them you're a distant relative I have to show around."

They left in his car, a red Corvette, and on the way to the concert she teased him, "Did you know this car has the highest frequency-of-repair record of any American car?"

"I don't believe that!" He snorted indignantly. "You just made it up!"

"Fact. And did you know that if you're driving a red car, your chances of getting stopped for speeding are three times greater than with any other color?"

"I believe *that!*" He nodded. "Next thing, the fuzz are gonna give me a speeding ticket when I'm backing out of the driveway!"

She carried on with him in a joking fashion, and when they got to the concert, it amused her to see the reaction she got. All his friends looked like escaped refugees, in their baggy clothes and wild hairstyles. Though they all gave her a hard time at first, before the evening was over, most of the girls hated her, for the young men couldn't keep their eyes off her. She stood out in the crowd like a beacon, and Rob whispered to her once, grudgingly, "You're a hit, Sis."

She gave him a quick smile and said, "It's our fatal charm. All us Ross kids are irresistible."

She endured the cacophonous roar of the various groups with the calmness of a social scientist watching the rites of a savage tribe, then afterwards accompanied them to the apartment of one of the boys. It was soon filled with the same clanging music, and the air was thick with smoke.

One of the boys, a short, muscular type named Tim, who had been drinking, kept trying to make her lose her cool. He said loudly, "I hear you're a preacher. That why you don't smoke dope or drink?"

Dani gave him a smile and raised her eyebrows in surprise. "No, that's not the reason."

"Why not then?"

"Dope is illegal, and alcohol ruins your liver." A laugh went up, and she added, "Besides, I like to do things well, and you can't do things well if you paralyze your nerves with drugs."

"Well, I can do *one* thing well!" Tim said and fell against her, pawing at her. "I can . . ., hey!" He found himself plucked up, for Rob had grabbed a handful of his thick hair and hauled him to his feet.

"Cut it out, Tim," Rob said, and his craggy face was flushed with embarrassment.

"Look, *you* were the one who dragged her here, so she gets no special treatment," Tim shouted. He reached out for Dani, who had come to her feet, but Rob hit him on the side of the neck with a wild swing. It didn't do more than rock Tim, and he caught Rob in the mouth with a wicked right hand, knocking him down instantly.

Everyone started to scream, and Rob got to his feet, his face pale and blood running down his chin. Dani said, "Come on, Rob, let's get out of here," but before she finished, Rob took another swing at Tim and succeeded in knocking him down. Tim got to his feet at once and threw a punch at Rob—but it caught Dani on the cheek.

The world exploded, and she was driven backward, hitting the floor with her head. This sent a shower of stars in front of her eyes, and for a brief time she knew nothing. She was not exactly out; it was very much like the time she had fallen off Biscuit, while riding the barrels. The world seemed to be spinning, and all the sounds of the room were muted.

Then she came out of it to find out that Rob and another boy were half carrying her out to the car. "I can walk," she protested, but they held on to her and put her inside without more ado.

"Better have her see a doctor, Rob," the other boy called as he pulled out.

"No, I don't need a doctor," Dani said quickly. Her face had been numb, but now the pain was coming, and she reached for her purse. Taking out a small mirror, she said, "Turn on the overhead." He snapped it on, and she saw with relief that the skin was not broken. "Looks as if I'm going to have a whale of a shiner tomorrow."

"Never should have taken you," Rob said between gritted teeth. He added angrily, "That guy is no good."

"Oh, he's all right." Dani shrugged. "Just a little physical. Anyway, you hit him first."

"Well, I like that!" Rob said in an outraged voice. He

gave her an injured look, then swerved to miss a car. "I get into a fight to protect you, and you—!"

"Oh, Rob, don't tell me it's the first time one of you guys ever made a pass at a girl at one of your orgies. You've done the same thing, I bet."

He straightened up in shock, then shot her another outraged look. "That's *different!*"

"I don't see why," Dani said calmly. She began to comb the mass of hair, adding, "If you'd taken Allison along, the same thing would have happened to her sooner or later."

"Hey—I'd *never* take Allison to a party like that!"

"Wouldn't you, Rob?"

"No!"

"I'm glad to hear it. Allison, in case you haven't noticed, is having a hard time."

Rob risked a glance at her, then paused to think about what she had said. "What kind of hard time?"

"She's not beautiful like me, and she's not smart like you," Dani said in her logical voice. "In a few years she'll be better looking than I am—but she doesn't believe that. Right now she thinks she's dumb and ugly."

"Why, that's crazy, Dani!" Rob said incredulously. "She's not either one."

"You ever tell her that?"

A long silence fell, and finally Rob said, "No." Quickly he added, "But I'm having sort of a hard time myself—in case you haven't noticed."

"Sure. You're dumb and ugly, too."

"Don't be cute!" Rob shifted in his seat and said nothing, nor did she try to urge him to speak. Finally he burst out, "Look, Dani, you're off in your own little world.

You're a CPA, and you've been a cop, and now you're off into this seminary thing. What have *I* ever done? Nothing."

"And you're already seventeen years old," Dani said mockingly. She softened her voice. "What do you *want* to do, Rob?"

"I don't know, Dani. The whole world's falling apart, and by the time I get on the scene we may all blow up, who knows? I can't even decide whether or not to go to college. . . ." He went on for a long time, talking fiercely, and Dani realized it was probably the first time this hurting, quiet boy had said those things to anyone.

His words ran down about the time they pulled into the driveway. Just before they walked in the house, she said, "Thanks for telling me, Rob. And thanks for socking that nerd!"

Rob suddenly smiled and gave her a hug. "I'm glad you're home, Dani." Then he wheeled and ran ahead of her, embarrassed at the gesture.

The next morning Ellen took one look at her and gave a scream, crying, "Dani! What in the world . . . ?"

Dani had tried to use cosmetics to cover up the purple and green bruise under her eye, but nothing had worked. "It's a lovely shiner, isn't it?" She grinned. "But it's an honorable wound. Sit down and let me tell you about it. I think you may see a little different Rob from now on—at least we've got a chance!"

During the next three days, Dani interviewed three men, all from the local area. It had seemed a simple enough matter; she had done many more complicated things. But before she was through, Dani was shaken.

Whatever made me think I could handle this job? she asked herself in desperation. *Dad thinks I can run the agency—and I can't even hire the help!* She became so nervous and irritable that she considered giving up on the whole thing.

None of the three came close to being what she needed, and in desperation she called Dom Costello, a captain in the Boston Police Department. They had worked together on several cases, and he was one of the few men who'd treated her with absolute fairness—hard, at times, but always fair. He listened carefully as she described what she wanted and said almost at once, "I got a guy you can look at, Dani. He just got kicked off the force in Denver—but I guess that won't mean much to you."

"What did he get booted for, Dom?"

"Insubordination was the charge. I checked into it a little, and it means he wouldn't go on the take, so they rousted him."

"You recommend him?"

"Well, he's a pain in the neck most of the time—but if you can put up with him, he's smart and tough."

"Where is he, Dom? I'd like to talk to him."

"I got a number. Let me give him a call."

He had hung up, and the next day he called. "Finally got hold of Savage."

"Savage?"

"Ben Savage—the guy you want to talk to," Costello said impatiently. "He'll be around to see you."

"Wait a minute—I can't pay his expenses for that!" Dani protested.

"He's got his own plane. Just about all he *has* got, I guess. But he likes to fly all over the place, so look for him any time. Hope it works out—but like I said, he can be a pain in the neck." He stopped and then said, "Hey, I left one thing out."

"What's that, Dom?"

"Well, he don't like women much. Don't have much trust in them, seems to me."

"If he can do the job, that's all I ask. Thanks, Dom!"

"Let me know how it comes out."

Thursday afternoon she was sitting in her office, thinking of Oliver Hackman. He was one of the biggest businessmen in New Orleans and had used the agency several times in the past. Now he had a problem, but had stated flatly that only a man could deal with it. Dani had gone to see him, and he had been affable but firm, "With no disrespect to you, this is a man's job. I'll use you when we need your skills—which are impressive—but this time you can't handle it."

Dani was tired and about ready to go home for the day, when her buzzer sounded. "Someone to see you, Miss Ross. His name is Ben Savage."

"Send him in, Angie."

The door opened, and a man came in. He seemed small at first, and he had Slavic features in a squarish face, with deep-set eyes protected by a shelf of bone that beetled over them. These hazel eyes seemed cold as he looked at her. His hair was very black and unruly, cut unfashionably short. "I'm Ben Savage," he said.

"I'm Danielle Ross," she answered. "Have a seat." As he moved across the room she noted that he was graceful, but he wore a pair of jeans and an aged suede jacket over a blue sport shirt. On his feet were a pair of dirty white running shoes.

It offended her that he wouldn't take the trouble to dress for the interview, and she spoke coolly, "Dom Costello recommends you—with certain reservations."

A grin suddenly broke across his wide mouth, which had a thin upper lip and a fish-hook scar at the right corner, but he said nothing.

His silence offended her. The other applicants had been vocal, if nothing else, and now this—this *tramp* sat there and said nothing!

"You were fired from your last job, I understand," she said, watching his eyes.

"Yes." No explanation. No excuse.

"Well—*why* were you fired?" she demanded.

"I was insubordinate. It says so right in the report." He sat in the chair squarely but was somehow relaxed as a cat. His eyes were taking her in, she saw, and a smile pulled at his lips as he focused on the remains of the black eye.

Somewhat rattled and more than a little inclined to tell him to leave, Dani forced herself to be calm. "I'll look into it—if we get that far." Such a possibility seemed unlikely, but she continued, "You'll have to fill out an application."

He reached into his jacket pocket and handed her a legal-size envelope. "There it is."

She took it, opened the sheets of paper inside, and glanced through them. It was a well-done resume, and she remarked, "You didn't do this typing yourself."

"Yes, I did."

He had a habit of saying only the necessary, and after hearing so much talk, it rattled her somehow. She covered her brief moment of confusion by running down the first sheet, reading aloud: "Twenty-eight years old, not married. Born in West Virginia—the Marine Corps from eighty to eighty-four—honorably discharged. Denver Police from eighty-five until last week."

She shuffled through the other sheets, filing them, and finally put them down on her desk. "Did Dom Costello tell you about this agency—what we're looking for?"

"Not much. Just said you needed an investigator."

"My father started this agency and ran it up until his heart attack a few months ago. It was a one-man affair, because he wanted it that way. Now I've got to keep it going until he comes back—if he ever does." The last phrase slipped out, and Savage's hazel eyes betrayed that his brain had recorded the words. She hastened on, "I need a man who can handle the rough stuff—and that's not hard to find. But I need someone who can talk to clients as well. Just looking at you, I'd say you can't handle either chore."

She said it to shake him out of his composure, but a light of amusement touched his eyes, and he responded, "You'll never know until you try me, Miss Ross."

She walked across to the window, thinking hard. He looked terrible—but Dom Costello was a sharp cookie, and he said Savage could cut it. And she *had* to have a man. She turned again. "You're not very big. How much do you weigh?"

"One hundred and seventy-five pounds," he said promptly, then he asked politely, "How much do *you* weigh, Miss Ross?"

"That's not the issue!" she snapped. "I'm not going to have to handle some tough who's trying to wipe out a client. And I can do without the humor, Mr. Savage."

He raised one black eyebrow and asked innocently, "Is it all right if I smile vaguely, if I'm struck by a humorous thought?"

She stared at him, then smiled grimly. "If you can do the job and carry your weight, you can laugh like a hyena, Savage!"

That pleased him. "Look, Miss Ross, I'm no good at applying for jobs. Never was. Never applied for but one, come to think of it—aside from the corps. I know I'm not dressed right, and I know my mouth is too big. I've got better clothes, and I can watch my mouth with clients. I need a job—but not all that bad. I can see you don't like me, so I can walk out. Or you can give me a shot at the job—say a week. If I don't suit, you pay me enough gas money to get to Miami, and we're square."

Dani bit her lip while she thought it over. "How about this," she offered. "You go see a man called Oliver Hackman. He needs some help—but he'll only give the job to a man. Go tell him you're with the Ross agency. If you can get the job out of him, we'll see."

"Sounds all right."

She wrote Hackman's number and address on a card and handed it to him. "He's a sharp operator. You won't charm him into anything."

He took the card, nodded, and turned to leave. When he got to the door, a perverse impulse to shock him came to her, and she said, "Oh, Savage . . . ?" She waited until he turned, then smiled and said, "I weigh one hundred and thirty-four pounds."

He blinked. "Sure." His eyes ran over her, and he said, "I'd say about a size twelve."

He turned and left the office, and Dani stared at the door, her cheeks burning—and then she giggled! "What a showboat!" she murmured. Before turning back to go over his references, she looked at the door and shook her head, thinking, *He got it right, though!*

Savage walked into the expensive-looking suite and moved directly to the receptionist. "I'm Ben Savage. Ask Mr. Hackman if I can see him."

The secretary, a fortyish lady who was trying to be thirtyish, looked up in surprise. "Why, you'll have to make an appointment to see Mr. Hackman, sir."

He leaned down and whispered, "I think he'll see me. Most people see IRS investigators without appointments."

Her eyes widened, and she punched nervously at her intercom. When a voice said, "Yes?" she responded quickly, "Mr. Hackman—there's a Mr. Savage here to see you. He doesn't have an appointment—but I think you'd better see him. He's with the IRS." There was a brief silence, then the voice said, "All right, send him in."

"Thanks," Savage said and walked through the door on the secretary's left.

"What is it?" Hackman asked gruffly. "If it's a tax thing, see my accountants. That's what I pay them for."

"I'm not with the IRS," Savage confessed. "I just told your secretary that most people see IRS inspectors."

Anger jumped into Hackman's eyes. "I don't have time to play games, Savage. What are you selling? And I don't want it."

Ben Savage spread his hands wide. "I had to see you, Mr. Hackman, and I'd guess you don't give appointments easy. Miss Ross hired me, and she wanted me to see if I could convince you to give us the job you spoke about."

Hackman hesitated then asked, "She hired you?"

"Well—" A grin broke across his broad lips. "I'm hired if I can talk you into giving me a shot at the job."

Hackman suddenly laughed loudly. "Well, you've got the brass for the job, Savage." He stared across the room at the smaller man, then nodded. "All right, I'll give you a crack at it. I like initiative—and I'd like the Ross agency to have the business. I like Daniel Ross."

"What's the problem?" Savage asked.

"Sit down and I'll lay it out." The two men sat and Hackman lit a cigar. "You know what a hacker is, I suppose?"

"Heists information off computer files."

"Sure. Well, one of them got into our files and grabbed some information that I don't want another firm to have. Now this crook is holding the stuff for ransom. If I don't fork over twenty-five thousand dollars, he'll give it to my competitor. And *that* . . . ," Hackman snorted, "will cost a whale of a lot more."

"Maybe he'll take your cash and have a copy made."

Hackman stared at him. "Ah, *that's* why I wanted a man to do the job. It could get nasty." He stared at Savage and said, "You don't look tough to me—but if you can get the stuff back—*and* make sure there's no other copy, no negatives or prints, I'll pay the agency five thousand."

"I'll take care of it, Mr. Hackman."

The older man shook his head. "I haven't told you all of it yet. This guy is a wimp—but he's got two tough friends. They live in a high-rise building, and nobody can get in without being searched. Most people never get by the door, I'm told. They're expecting me to send somebody, and they're sitting there like cocked guns."

"Sure." Savage looked almost bored. "Just give me the

dope—what the thing looks like and how I'll recognize it."

Hackman stared at him. "Savage, you can get killed in a thing like this!"

"Well, they can't kill me but once, can they? Now if you'll fill me in . . . ?"

Morey Borntrager, a small, pale accountant accustomed to a regular life, liked things all nice and orderly—but nothing had been that way for the past few days, and it made him nervous. Beside him, the big hands, broken nose, and muscular frame of Jack Rimmer seemed neither neat nor nervous. Borntrager's second companion, Terry McGuire, lacked Rimmer's height, and his black hair grew low on his forehead.

The three were sitting around the living room of their suite, when the doorbell rang. Instantly Borntrager moved to the bedroom, and both McGuire and Rimmer headed for the door. McGuire pulled a .38 from his belt and nodded. Rimmer opened the door and faced the delivery boy, who stood there with a box. "Three orders of pepperoni and bell peppers?" he asked.

"Yeah. How much?"

"Fifteen dollars and twenty cents."

Rimmer pulled some bills out of his pocket and shoved them at the boy. "Keep the rest," he commanded and took the boxes. McGuire put the gun back inside his belt and said, "Let's eat."

Borntrager came out of the bedroom and looked at the boxes. "You didn't get pepperoni *again!*" he moaned. "I'm sick of that stuff!"

"Tomorrow you can eat what you want, Morey," Rimmer reminded him, sitting down and opening one of the boxes. "Either we get the dough from Hackman, or we get it from the other side. Either way we're in clover."

"I wish I'd never told you about this thing!" Borntrager said angrily. He took the box and opened it, then complained, "I've got to have some beer to go with this garbage!"

He rose to go to the refrigerator, but stopped as if he had run into a wall.

McGuire noticed his abrupt halt. "What's the matter . . . ?" His words broke off, for a man had come out of the bedroom—a man with a sawed-off shotgun aimed right at him.

Rimmer looked around to see Borntrager and McGuire frozen and got to his feet so suddenly that the pizza slid to the floor.

"I wouldn't move so quick, if I were you," Savage advised pleasantly. He moved forward, the shotgun in his hand not wavering from the bodies of the two larger men, though he ignored Borntrager. "Take that gun out very carefully, by the butt."

McGuire wanted to do something else—but the muzzle of the shotgun was trained relentlessly on his middle, and the hazel eyes of the gunman did not blink. He took two fingers and pulled the gun out.

"Toss it to me." McGuire tossed the gun, and Savage plucked it out of the air and stuck it in his belt. "Now your gun," he said.

"I ain't got no iron," Rimmer said.

"Let's not play games. Give me the gun, or I'll cut you in two—quick!"

Rimmer jumped and cried out, "Be careful with that thing, will you?" Reaching into his pocket he pulled out a small .32 and at a sign tossed it to Savage, who caught it and placed it next to McGuire's weapon.

"Very good. You two have a fair chance of getting out of this alive—and even without going to jail. Lie down and put your hands behind you."

They both did so instantly, and Savage stepped beside Rimmer. He reached into his pocket and removed a short piece of wire. Bending over, he wrapped it three times around the man's thumbs, then did the same for McGuire. "Now—you just lie there like good men and true while I have a little talk with your friend. Come along, Morey."

Borntrager had watched all this with staring eyes. Now he began to tremble. "Let me go! Don't kill me!"

"Nobody's going to hurt you, Morey—not if you do the right thing." Savage moved to take the smaller man by the arm and walked him into the bedroom, saying over his shoulder, "If you fellows get nervous, I'll come back and calm your nerves for you." He shut the door and turned to face Borntrager.

"How'd you get in here?" the man whispered. "We're ten floors up. Nobody could climb up to that window! We checked!"

"I don't think they could, Morey." Savage nodded. "It's all sheer glass. But this building is only twelve floors high. Not much of a job to come down just two floors."

Borntrager looked at the rope that hung down outside the window, and his face collapsed. "I know what you want. It's in that briefcase by the bed."

"Very nice, Morey." Savage put the shotgun down on the bed, picked up the case, and opened it. A brief inspection was all he needed. "This is it. Now, Morey, if you'll give me the copy, I'll be gone, and you can get out of town."

"Copy?" Borntrager cried. "That's all there is! I swear it!"

Savage moved across the room so quickly that the other man could not even attempt to escape. He forced Borntrager's arm behind his back, marched him to the open window, and shoved the small man out so that his feet cleared the floor. Leaning into the cold air, he said, "It's a long way down, Morey. See how little the people look? Almost like dolls. Morey, I don't have it in me to hurt people. Some I could name would pull you to pieces a little at a time—and you'd give them the copy. But I can't do that. All I can do is drop you to the pavement down there. And I'll ask you only once—only once, you hear me, Morey?"

Morey stared at the sidewalk, his stomach heaving. He had always been afraid of heights, and when the strong hands loosened and felt himself slipping, he screamed, "It's in the kitchen—in the coffee canister!"

"Good man!" Savage said enthusiastically. "Let me pick it up, and I'll be on my way." He moved out of the bedroom, crossed to the kitchen, and found a roll of film at the bottom of the canister. He walked back to the bedroom, dropped the film in the case, and snapped it shut. Ben slipped the shotgun into a loop on his belt, then paused to look at Morey. "Hey, it's been a real fun thing, Morey—but I'd seek out new worlds to conquer, if I were you, hey?"

He attached the briefcase to a clip on his belt, sat down on the window, and grasping the rope, began to pull himself up. He didn't use his legs, Morey saw, but moved up the rope as easily as a flyer in the circus. Morey didn't go on watching. He threw his clothes into a bag and left without stopping to unwire his former associates.

Dani had hardly begun her paperwork when the door opened and Ben Savage walked in.

She glanced at him, startled, and asked, "Well, have you talked to Hackman about the job?"

Though she expected him to say no, he nodded and reached into his pocket, pulling out a slip of paper. It was a check for five thousand dollars made out to the Ross agency and signed by Oliver Hackman. She looked at it, then asked with surprise, "He paid in advance?"

"No." Savage shrugged his shoulders. "It wasn't a very hard job. I took care of it yesterday."

Dani looked at the check, then back at him. Finally she said, "Well, Benjamin Davis Savage, it looks as if you're our new investigator. Welcome to the Ross agency." She smiled and put out her hand. Ben took it and nodded.

"Let's have coffee, and you can tell me about it," she offered.

"Not much to tell, Miss Ross. Guy stole something, and I persuaded him to give it back. Case closed."

Her eyes narrowed, and she demanded, "How did you 'persuade' him?"

He looked at her innocently. "I said, 'Pretty please with sugar on it.' "

Dani was happy with the check and strangely pleased that he'd made a place for himself, but she saw some danger in Ben's attitude. "Look, Savage, you've done well—but keep in mind that this is *my* agency. When I ask for a full report, you'll give it to me. I know you don't like women—Dom Costello told me that. I'm not all that crazy about you, for that matter."

Savage answered evenly, "It sounds like the beginning of a beautiful relationship." He turned around and said, "I'll write up the report. You probably won't like it."

He left the room, and she sat down, angrily, noting that her breathing was a little rapid. *He can stay—as long as he delivers the goods*, she thought, drumming her fingers on the table. Then she looked at the check and muttered, "I don't care what the blasted report says—as long as he gets the job done, we can survive!"

For some reason Dani rose and walked to the mirror over the lavatory. As she stared at her face a thought came to her: *I wonder why he doesn't like women?*

3
A New Client

"Blast!" Dani slammed down the phone with a look of indignation, which caused Ben to look quizzically across the desk at her. Shaking her auburn hair with irritation, she added, "I put my car in the shop, and they *promised* me it'd be ready by five—now they say it'll be tomorrow."

It was almost five o'clock, and for an hour the two of them had been struggling with the Tellerman case. Virgil Tellerman had been injured on the job at Case Bearings Company, and when the company refused to pay up, he had sued—and lost. Though Tellerman had no money, after listening to him, Dani had decided to take the case because he was being cheated. She had covered all the paperwork and sent Ben out that morning to check out the witnesses. He had returned to the office at three, and they had gone over the case from every angle, with little success. The phone call was just an extra aggravation.

"You need a ride home, Miss Ross?" Ben asked.

"Oh, I hate to bum rides! But Dad wants to see you

anyway." Dani got up and stretched her aching muscles. "He wants to talk to you about some of the cases you've been working on. We might as well go now."

They left the office. When they got to the street, Savage said, "Car's in the lot down the street." As they walked along, he commented, "You know, on the Tellerman thing, I got a feeling the witnesses were all bought off. All three who testified against Tellerman have been with Case Bearings since before the Flood."

"They were bribed to lie on the stand?"

"I guess no cash changed hands—but it wouldn't surprise me much if all three didn't get a promotion pretty soon—or a big Christmas bonus."

As he turned in to the parking lot she shook her head. "Case Bearings is a multimillion-dollar business. Why would they swindle a small working man out of compensation?"

He gave her a glance and shrugged. "Total depravity, I think they call it." He stopped by a car and with no expression said, "This is it."

Dani stopped and looked down at the old Pinto. Originally the car had been one color, but it was nearly impossible to guess which one. All four fenders and one door had been replaced with wrecking-yard parts, none of them painted to match, so it resembled a patchwork quilt. "You'll have to get in from the driver's side," Ben said, opening the door. "That side is jammed."

Awkwardly she climbed in and scooted across the seat, giving a little cry as something punched her bottom.

"Watch out for the broken springs," Ben warned belatedly.

The inside was a wreck, mostly held together with silver

duct tape. Some of the instruments had been removed so that the panel resembled some battered pug with most of his teeth knocked out.

Ben reached under the dash and pulled out two wires; when he touched the ends together, the battery cranked the engine, which caught at once. Putting the wires back, he shifted to low and moved the wreck out of the lot. "Which way?" he asked.

"Go right. We'll take Highway 61."

The interior was stifling, and he announced. "That's the air-conditioner switch." Dani saw he was pointing to the window crank and rolled the window down. He did likewise, and hot air blew in, offering some relief.

"You're probably wondering where I got my car," he said, moving easily through the traffic, changing lanes and barely missing pedestrians.

"From a wrecking yard?"

"Right the first time! Paid fifty bucks for this little hummer." Ben seemed proud of the thing and added, "Engine is good, but the body is a little rough."

When they got to the turnoff and hit the potholes, the jar nearly shook her teeth out, but he only commented, "Guess it wouldn't hurt to fix the shocks."

"Why'd you buy a thing like this, Ben?" she gasped as he swerved from side to side, dodging the worst of the holes.

"Wanted a heap I could just walk off and leave with no regrets," he answered. Then he explained. "Better that way. I don't like to invest too much in things you can lose."

All the way down the lane, she thought about his words. A dark streak of fatalism ran through the man, and she thought *I don't like to invest too much in things you can lose* might be the key to that side of him. Suddenly she thought, *Maybe I'm a little bit that way myself.* The thought disturbed her, so she tuned it out.

Dani pointed out her parents' house, and when he stopped, she asked suddenly, "Did you mean cars—or people—what you said about not investing too much?"

He gripped the wheel with his square hands. "Both," he said, getting out. Dani dodged the broken spring and asked no more questions.

Leading the way, she found her father in his study, reading. "Here's Ben, Dad. I made him bring me home, when my car wasn't ready. You two can talk until dinner."

After blessing the meal, they all began on the roast that Ellen had cooked. Ben said almost nothing, but he ate hungrily, and once he commented, "I haven't had a meal like this in a long time, Mrs. Ross. You're a wonderful cook."

As the meal ended Rob said, "Dad, I've *got* to have someone look at my car. It's running rough."

"Mind if I take a look at it?" Ben asked. "I've tinkered with engines quite a bit." The two left the dining room as the boy explained the misbehavior of the engine.

"He certainly doesn't have much to say, does he, Dani?" Ellen commented. "Hardly said a word all through the meal."

"He's the kind who doesn't talk unless he has something to say," Daniel responded as he began to help clear the table. "I was a little apprehensive about him, Dani, but he's sharp as a knife! We went over several cases, and he knows them better than I do."

Dani had leaned over to pick up the gravy bowl. Now

she looked at her father and nodded. "Oh, he's good, Dad. But he runs ahead of things sometimes." She related how Ben had cut corners on an office procedure and concluded, "He was fired for insubordination in Denver. That's not a good sign."

Daniel shook his head. "Every really good man—or woman—I ever knew wanted to get things *done*! That means more than keeping a record of it or running to the boss every time something has to be done." He paused and wiped his forehead. "It's hot in here, isn't it?"

"Yes," Ellen agreed. "I think the air conditioner is off again."

"Oh, no!" Daniel groaned. "Not another repair bill on that blasted thing!"

They finished the dishes and adjourned to the patio, where they found Ben and Rob in a deep conversation about engines. Rob jumped up and exclaimed excitedly, "Dad, Ben fixed the Vette. Just turned a screw or something, and it hums like a sewing machine!"

"Just out of time." Ben got to his feet, and they all sat down.

"I'd ask you to stay the night, Ben," Daniel said. "But the central air is out. We'll all roast tonight, I'm afraid."

"I worked for a heat-and-air outfit once," Ben said. He got to his feet, and proposed "Rob, if you'll show me where the thermostat and the units are, maybe we can jury-rig something that'll last the night."

"It's an old unit," Ellen called out as Rob led him into the house. "It would cost a lot to get it all replaced, but you can't live in Louisiana without air."

Shortly, Ben and Rob came out of the house. Ben went

to his car, came back with a toolbox, and the two of them disappeared around the side of the house.

Fifteen minutes later they heard a sound, and Daniel said, "There's the compressor. He got it going."

Ben came back with Rob. He put the tools back in the Pinto, saying, "Not too bad. The circuit in the outside compressor is shot. I'll pick one up tomorrow. Cost maybe twenty dollars."

"Thank God!" Daniel laughed. "I was thinking of a couple thousand at least!"

"Most things can be fixed." Ben smiled. Then the smile faded, and he shrugged. "Most mechanical things, that is."

"Have some tea, Ben," Ellen offered. "You've earned it. Sometime you'll have to come out and just visit—instead of fixing all our broken-down machinery." She was pouring the tea into his glass when Allison came out wearing a gymnastics outfit—a hot-pink bodysuit over gray tights with black leather ballet slippers. She almost turned and went back, when she saw them all seated there, but Ellen said, "Come on, Allison. You won't bother us with your practice." She looked at Ben and explained, "Allison's taking gymnastics at school."

"Oh, Mother, I don't want—"

"Aw, come on, little sister," Rob urged. "Show them that new stunt you showed me yesterday."

"Oh, I'm no good!" Allison protested, looking at Ben in embarrassment, but when the others urged her, she finally moved to an open spot of concrete, pulled open a pad and spread it out. Putting her hands over her head, she lowered them quickly and went into a handstand—but she went too far and fell with a thump. She got up and tried again but failed. Her face turned red, and she cried, "I'll *never* learn to do a handstand!"

Dani was sorry they were there. Obviously Allison was too shy to perform. She decided to get the others to go in the house, but before she spoke, Ben said, "You're trying to stand on your palms. Try standing on your fingers."

They all looked at him in surprise, and Allison asked, "Stand on my fingers?"

"Sure." Ben got up, walked over to where she was, and held his hand out to her. "When you kick up, Allison, you have to let your weight rest here." He indicated the underside of his fingers. "If you try to bear your weight on the palm—right here—you'll never get up. So roll up just far enough so that your weight falls on the fingers. It'll hurt a little at first, but when you start falling over, you can *push* with your fingers, and it'll stop you from going over. That's what a handstand really is—a controlled fall. Your body is overbalanced and wants to fall, but you won't let it. You keep it up by pushing with your fingers."

Allison stared at her hands. "I don't know. . . ."

Ben said, "Let me show you. Stand close, and watch my fingers when I kick up. They'll turn white because they're pressing hard to keep my body from falling. Watch now . . . !"

He suddenly bent at the waist, his legs went up, and he held his body still in a perfect handstand. "Look at my fingers," he said, and when Allison looked with big eyes, he added, "You can't hold your body straight, either. Put an arch in it—like this."

"It looks so easy when you do it!" she exclaimed.

"Anything is easy after you learn to do it." He grinned

from his upside-down position. "As young as you are, you'll learn to do *this* in no time. . . ."

He drew out of his arched position, suddenly threw his legs forward, and his body performed a perfect forward flip, so that he landed on his feet as easily as a cat. He turned to face Allison and was suddenly conscious that the rest of the family was watching him in amazement.

"Good night!" Rob breathed. "You must be an acrobat!"

"Easier than it looks," Ben explained uncomfortably. "Now, Allison, just try a kick up, and I'll stop you until you learn to hold yourself with your fingers."

She looked dubious but took a deep breath and kicked up. He stopped her from falling, saying, "Now, hold it there by pressing against the mat—see? It's easy, isn't it? Now try another kick." She tried another, and this time, though she swayed precariously, she did not fall. "That's it!" Ben encouraged quickly. "Now, arch your back and throw your feet forward—keep your legs together and point with your toes like a ballet dancer. Good!"

Allison kept her balance for what seemed like a long time, then came to her feet, her face shining. "Ben! It was easy!" She reached out and grabbed his arm demanding, "Teach me some more!"

As he looked at Allison, Dani saw an unusually gentle cast to his face, but when he glanced toward the others, the tough expression came back. "Well, you work on that; then I'll show you how to stand on *one* hand. That'll dazzle your gym teacher!" He dropped his gaze and said abruptly, "Well, I'll have to get along."

"Oh, stay and visit for a while!" Daniel invited instantly.

Though they all urged him, he refused, offering instead, "I'll pick up the part for the compressor tomorrow. Then if it's all right with the boss, I'll run out and install it."

Dani nodded. "It'll be a great help, Ben."

"Good night—and thanks for the dinner."

As he pulled away in the Pinto, Ellen asked, "What sort of place does he live in, Dani?"

"I have no idea," she answered slowly, adding, "I didn't know he was an acrobat, either." She turned to watch the car disappear in the gathering darkness and said so quietly that no one heard her. "I'm beginning to think there are quite a few things about Mr. Benjamin Davis Savage I don't know!"

The next day, after the office closed, Savage went home with Dani and installed the part in the compressor. Ellen pressed him into staying for dinner, and afterwards Rob and Allison almost came to blows over him. Rob wanted to talk cars, and Allison wanted Ben to help her with gymnastics. He did both, and several times over the course of a few days, Dani was pressured into asking him home.

She said once to her father. "Dad, maybe it's not wise to have Savage here so much."

"Keep the hired hands in their place?"

Dani flushed but shook her head stubbornly. "You know what I mean, Dad. Business is business—and it might give him the wrong impression."

Daniel looked at her with speculation. She had always been smarter than most people, and she had handled it well. But something in her could not accept Savage, and he thought he knew what it was. "Ben gives you problems, doesn't he?"

"Why, no!" Dani gave him an indignant look, and the

lift of her square chin revealed the stubborn streak in her. "Why would you think that, Dad?"

"Because you keep him at arm's length. Either you're a little snobbish—or you're jealous of him."

"*Jealous!*"

"Well, maybe *you're* not, but *I* am!" Daniel said emphatically. "He's good with people. Look how he's got Rob and Allison eating out of his hand! And he's a good cop— maybe better than I am. Maybe he's smarter than you."

"He's *not* better than you!" she objected too loudly.

He rubbed his chin and cocked his head to one side. "Well, maybe you're attracted to him—and afraid of that."

Dani laughed and shook her head. "Oh, Dad, don't be silly! The *last* thing I need is a romance with a roughneck like Ben Savage!"

She had laughed, but later the conversation would come back to her.

As the weeks went by, something else happened that was hard to take. Calls kept coming in, clients wanting to speak to Ben. At first it amused her—but when she tried to ease herself into a few of the cases, she discovered it could not be done.

Al Overmile was in the office with her, once, when such a call came. A woman named Lucy Benton had retained the firm to run a check on one of her relatives, and she insisted on speaking to Ben.

"Mr. Savage is out of the office, Mrs. Benton, but he's filled me in on your case. Couldn't you talk to me about it?"

Overmile lit a cigarette as Dani finally concluded, "Very well, Mrs. Benton. I'll have Mr. Savage call you as soon as he comes in. Good-bye."

She put the receiver down with more force than was

necessary, and Overmile said, "Wouldn't talk to you, eh?" When she shook her head silently, he sent a blue smoke ring out of his lips, then advised sourly, "Bad business, Dani. Savage is not a team player."

"He does all right."

"Maybe—but he's building up his own little kingdom." Overmile walked over to where she was sitting. He placed his heavy hand on her shoulder and said, "Best way I know of to start your own agency. Get in with a firm; convince the clients you're the best; and when you hang out your sign, you've got clients."

Dani moved away from his touch, stood up, then shrugged. "No. Ben's not thinking of that." She bit her lip, and a frown came to her brow. "But he *is* too independent." Al started to argue, but she cut him off and sent him out of the office. She stared out the window, watching the traffic, but thinking of the agency.

Things *were* better, and she knew that she had done most of it. Still, it rankled that clients preferred Ben Savage. Dani was a logical thinker—but something inside her kept upsetting her judgment of the man. She thought again of her father's opinion—either she was jealous of him, or she was attracted to him. She gave her shoulders an angry shake, picked up the report on the desk, and forced herself to work on it.

That was on Tuesday, and more by chance than anything else, she got another "I'll only speak to Ben Savage" call on Wednesday and two more on Thursday.

The second Thursday call came at two in the afternoon, and Dani's eyes glinted as she came out of her office, pulling on a tan jacket. "What's Ben's address?" she asked Angie.

Angie looked at a sheet taped to her desk. "He lives at 4312 Hickory Street," she said. "Is something wrong?"

"Yes, something is wrong!" Dani snapped. "I'm sick of clients who'll only talk to Ben. Darrell Simmons just called, and he wants to talk to Ben. So I've got to run him down! What's he working on today?"

"Well, I'm not sure—"

"Never mind. I'll leave him a note, if he's not there." Dani stamped out of the office, got into her car, and roared out of the parking lot with a screech of tires. She was so angry that she had started driving before she realized she had no idea where Hickory Street was, so she had to pull over and locate it on the city map.

Dani drove up to a two-story white frame house in one of the older sections of town. It had once been fashionable, but the professional men who'd built the big houses had gone out with the tide, and now almost all the homes were boardinghouses. Most had signs, FURNISHED ROOMS FOR RENT, and a slightly sinister air hung over the decaying neighborhood. It was the sort of place where drugs flourished, and Dani made a note not to come back after dark.

She went up the steep steps, rang the bell, and waited until a heavy woman with blue hair toddled down the hall. She glanced at Dani's expensive clothes and asked warily, "You ain't looking for no room, are you, dearie?"

"No. Does Ben Savage have a room here?"

The woman opened the door. "Sure. Room 202—top of the stairs. Hey!" She called out abruptly as Dani walked quickly by and went up the stairs. A sour grin lifted her lips, and she muttered, "He's already got a girlfriend up there—but you look like a better bet." She turned and padded back to her room, her worn slippers whispering as she moved. At the thought that there might be trouble—even a shooting—excitement brightened her eyes. She looked upward toward the second floor with hopeful interest, then shook her head, saying "Nah!" and went into her room.

Dani found the numbers 202 over one of the four doors and knocked on it firmly. She heard nothing and had just raised her fist to knock again, when it opened, and Ben stood framed in the door. He was barefooted, wearing a pair of faded jeans and a thin cotton T-shirt. She brushed past him, saying angrily, "Where have you been? I can't take time. . . !" Abruptly she halted, for a woman was sitting on the couch, staring at her. One look was all it took for Dani to recognize her trade. She wore too much makeup, and there was a sullen, sensuous quality in her features. Her mini skirt was hiked up, and her overblown figure was plainly revealed beneath the sheer cotton blouse. A bottle of whiskey, half-empty, sat on the coffee table, along with a glass; the woman held another glass.

"Who's this, Ben?" the woman asked harshly.

"Just a friend," he answered. He didn't shut the door but gave Dani an inscrutable look. "Maybe you can come back later, Dani," he said quietly.

It was a dismissal, and a streak of raw anger ran through Dani. It was all so cheap—so tawdry! Her chin went up, and she forced herself to say evenly, "I don't pay you for this kind of thing, Savage! Angie will send you your severance pay. You don't have to come back." She turned and left the house, letting the screen slam loudly, got into her car, and forced herself to drive away at a reasonable speed.

She drove automatically for ten minutes, then gave her shoulders a shake and tried to think. The violence of her anger shocked her, and for the first time in her life Dani understood how a person could commit a violent act.

Back at the office, Angie took one look at her and stood. "What's the matter?" she asked.

Dani stared at her, her face paler than she knew, and said, "I just fired Ben."

Angie gasped. "But—what did he do, Dani?" Neither of them noticed that she used her employer's first name.

"He's holed up with a street woman instead of doing what I'm paying him for." The scene rolled back before her mind. Dani whirled and wordlessly went into her office. Angie didn't dare to ask for any detail. She left at quitting time, and an hour later Dani left the office.

Next morning, when she got to the office, Dani went at once to the file and pulled out the folder of the applications she had taken before hiring Savage. The longer she looked at them, the more hopeless it seemed.

Angie came in, and a subdued silence lay between the two women. Neither mentioned Ben.

At noon Angie stuck her head in Dani's office and said, "I'm going to get a salad. Can I bring you something?"

"No, thank you, Angie. Transfer the calls to me while you're gone."

At twelve thirty-five the phone rang, and Dani answered, "Ross Investigations. This is Danielle Ross speaking."

A man's voice said, "Ah, Miss Ross, I was hoping to speak to your father."

Dani explained the situation and asked, "I'm in charge of investigations. May I help you?"

"Well, I doubt it. It's a rather complex affair—a financial problem. Actually I was calling your father to ask him to recommend some firm with the expertise to handle such a thing, but—"

"I am a CPA. And I've worked on such things with the attorney general of Massachusetts."

A note of respect came into the voice. "Ah? Well, that is different. My name is Roy Lovelace. I live in Houston."

"Are you calling from there, Mr. Lovelace?"

"No. This problem is quite—sensitive. I don't want anyone from Houston even knowing about it."

"Why don't you come to the office, Mr. Lovelace? I'd like to hear about this situation."

Following a slight hesitation, Lovelace said, "I suppose I'm a little paranoid about this thing—but I'd rather not be seen in New Orleans—especially going into a detective agency." He paused, then asked, "I flew myself down in my own plane. I'm calling now from a gas station about a mile from the landing strip. It's just outside a small town called Kenner. Do you know where that is?"

Dani took down directions and replied, "I'll be there in an hour."

She picked up her purse, slipped on her coat, and went through the door into the outer office. She hesitated, then stopped at Angie's desk and wrote: *Gone to talk with a client at Kenner. Be back by 3:30.*

As she propped the note up where Angie could not miss it, she noticed an envelope exactly in the middle of the desk. Her name was written in the center, and the name *Savage* was in the upper left-hand corner. She picked it up, stared at it, then grabbed a letter opener and slit the paper. Inside was a single sheet of paper, and she scanned it quickly. When she had finished, she took a deep breath and made a curious gesture—she doubled up her left hand and placed the forefinger in her mouth, biting it with her teeth. It was an action she had not used for a long time—a holdover from her childhood days, something she would do when she was hurt or frightened or guilty.

Realizing what she was doing, Dani snatched the hand away and lifted the letter again. At the top it said, *Report on the Tellerman Case.* It was handwritten in strong, squarish letters, and in effect it said that a woman named Della Markham had witnessed the accident that had injured Virgil Tellerman. She had been promised a great deal of money *not* to come forward and testify, and she had agreed. The formal report ended: "Della Markham is now ready to testify that the accident that injured Virgil Tellerman was entirely the fault of the Case Bearings Company." Then the last sentences were heavily underlined: *This witness is highly defensive. She must not be pushed. It has taken a great deal of time and effort to bring her to the point of giving her testimony, and it would not take much to make her unwilling to testify. I suggest that you do not contact her, Miss Ross. Use another operator if possible.*

It was signed *Ben Savage* and dated November 29, 12:30 P.M. Dani looked at the door with a startled expression. "He must have brought it after Angie left for lunch!"

She stood there, her hands not steady, and knew at once what had happened. *He worked on the woman, brought her to the place where she'd tell the truth—and then I blundered in and wrecked it all*! A bitter taste was in her mouth, and she knew at once what she had to do.

Quickly she locked the office, hurried to her car, and pulled up in front of the boarding house on Hickory Street in record time. She was dashing up the steps, when a voice called out, "He ain't there no more, dearie!"

Dani stopped and turned to see the manager, the same fat woman she'd talked to the day before. Coming back down the steps, she asked, "He's out?"

"He's *moved*, dearie!" The small eyes examined her with interest. "Packed his stuff and moved out today. Sold his car to a young guy who rooms here, for twenty-five bucks."

"Did he leave any forwarding address?"

"Sure—*Miami, General Delivery.*"

Feeling sick, Dani turned and left the house. She got into the car, started it, then drove down the street, thinking, *He's got a plane. It must be at the airport.*

Glancing at her watch, she saw that she had only thirty minutes to get to her meeting with Lovelace. As she stepped on the gas she decided: *I'll meet Lovelace, then go to the airport. They have to file flight plans, I think—I'll have them radio him a message!*

She drove recklessly through the city, turned off the main highway, and five minutes later came to the sign that said MABLEVILLE. The airstrip was four miles out of town, exactly where Lovelace had indicated, and she saw a two-engine plane pulled up at the end of the strip. A man was standing under the wing, and he waved as she drove up.

She stopped the car and got out as he moved to meet her. "Miss Ross? I'm Roy Lovelace." She took his thick, strong hand, and he added, "I know you're in a hurry, so if you'll step into the plane, I'll explain the situation and give you the papers you'll need."

He was tall, six feet at least, with heavy shoulders and a strong neck. His eyes were light blue, and though his face was unlined, his hair was completely gray. Something of a military air hung about him, and for one instant she thought he looked familiar, but she could not place him.

The plush cabin smelled of new leather. He climbed in and passed behind her, saying, "The papers are back here. Just one moment. . . ."

Dani sat there, looking out over the fields of sugar cane that flanked the landing strip, thinking more about Ben than about Mr. Lovelace's problem. The she shook her head and forced herself to put Savage out of her mind. One problem at a time.

"Do you think it'll be necessary for me to come to Houston, Mr. Lovelace?"

His voice came from right behind her—and it sounded different somehow, though she couldn't say why. "You've got a long trip to make, Miss Ross—but not to Houston."

Suddenly his arm came around her breast, holding her like an iron bar, and terror flooded her so completely, that for a moment she was paralyzed. She began to fight, to struggle with all her power, but she was like a child.

He's brought me out here to kill me! she thought frantically and at that same instant felt a sharp pain in her left shoulder. Dani cried out sharply and twisted her head to see a large hypodermic needle held in Lovelace's large hand, piercing her flesh. She tried to butt him with her head, but only hit the back of the chair. As she watched in horror, he carefully pushed the plunger with a steady pressure, until the clear fluid was gone, and he pulled the needle out.

"Just sit there quietly, Miss Ross," he said in a conversational tone. "You'll be going to sleep now—very soon."

4
The Silo

The blackness was not absolute. Once a shattered ray of light broke through, and a faint, muffled voice filtered to Dani's mind: "Better give her another shot—she's waking up." An almost imperceptible pricking sensation touched her arm, and she plunged again into the world of cotton-soft oblivion.

Pyramids might have been built while she floated in the ebony night that muffled all sound and sight. Or it all might have been a flicker of time, taking no longer than the *click* of a rifle being cocked.

Finally she became vaguely aware of being picked up like a child; an engine started up, whirring smoothly. She was swaying in space, the same sensation she'd had as a child, when her father had swung her in the tire swing he'd made for her, in the backyard. One rough jolt clicked her teeth and jerked her out of the velvet darkness—a summoning intensified by a light that shone suddenly like a dozen suns. Instinctively she squeezed her eyelids tight—sending brilliant showers of red and blue sparks dancing in front of her brain.

A hand touched her face, and a voice said, "Stop crowding! Give her room to breathe!"

It was a woman's voice, but a heavier voice with a slight accent said, "Lonnie, carry her to her bunk."

"Sure, Commander." Strong arms lifted her, and her face pressed against rough cloth smelling of strong soap. Heels clicked, and the sudden motion made her slightly nauseous, but very quickly, it seemed, the woman's voice said, "Put her on this bunk, Lonnie."

"Sure, Doc."

Dani opened her eyes to thin slits, guarding against a bare light bulb that burned to her left. A man's face hung over her—a round face with a pair of bright-blue eyes that regarded her intently. Then the other voice: "All right, Lonnie. You can look her over later."

"Hey, she's coming around!" It was a new voice, more shrill than the first woman's, and as her eyes grew accustomed to the light, Dani opened her eyes more widely and tried to sit up.

Firm hands held her shoulders, and the first voice commanded, "Don't try to sit up for a few minutes. Rachel, will you bring some cold water and a cloth?"

Soon a rough cloth moved over Dani's face, and the cold water sharpened her senses. She realized that she felt so thirsty that it was almost painful. Her lips were dry, and when she tried to ask for a drink, nothing came but a dry rasping sound. Then the cloth disappeared and an arm under her shoulders lifted her. "I know, you're thirsty," the woman said. Dani opened her eyes and saw an oval face, large blue eyes, a shock of blond hair tied up in a bun, and a generous mouth that now smiled.

"Drink a little of this—slowly." A cup was held to her lips, and Dani drank eagerly. She tried to take the cup in her hands. "No, just a little now. You can have more later," the woman said firmly. "Do you want to lie down?"

The cool liquid had lubricated her lips and throat well enough so that Dani could whisper. "No, let me sit up."

"All right, but you don't want to do too much at first." The woman lifted Dani's legs and shifted her around in the bunk so that her back was against a hard surface. "My name is Karen," she said. "Better put your pillow behind you."

"Thank you." Dani's face felt stiff, but she managed to smile. "I'm Danielle Ross—*Dani* for short." Her words sounded hollow, and she realized that they echoed the tone in Karen's voice.

"Welcome to the Hilton." Several other women had been standing back, and now one stepped into the circle of light thrown by the light bulb. "I'm Candi Cane—your next-door neighbor." She was short, not over five three or so, wearing a pair of tight jeans and a T-shirt. She had very blond hair and a heart-shaped face accented by large blue eyes.

"Hello." Dani nodded, then asked, "Neighbor?"

"Sure," Candi laughed. "I got the bunk next to yours. Hope you don't snore!"

Dani's cleared vision took in the room—although *room* was not the best description of the large area. Several bare light bulbs were burning, attached to heavy white wires strung overhead, but when she looked upward, it gave her a dizzy sensation.

There was no ceiling! She peered up, trying to see past the murky darkness just over the light bulbs, but the dim light faded, shading off into an inky blackness. She had the sensation that she was in the bottom of some sort of shaft and drew her eyes quickly down to avoid the sensation.

She saw that the large space was roughly a half circle. Across from her bunk a concrete block wall about eight feet high ran the length of the area. At the end to her left it was broken by a door through which a faint glow broke the dim light. From each end of the flat wall, the room curved in a wide arc. The wall was, she guessed, no more than thirty-five feet or so, but a sense of openness resulted from the sweeping, circular walls. She reached back and touched the wall behind her, finding it to be chilly metal, slightly moist with condensation.

"Have another drink—just three or four swallows," Karen said, and Dani drank it down more slowly than before. "How do you feel?"

Dani handed back the glass and was suddenly aware of several pains. "My arms are sore," she said, moving them cautiously. Then shifting carefully, she added, "And my bottom, too."

"That's from the shots." Karen nodded and asked, "Any other symptoms?"

"No, don't think so." Dani's mind was clearing rapidly. "What is this place?"

"That's the big question we debate." A third woman moved to stand beside Candi. "I myself think we're all in hell."

"Oh, don't start with that garbage!" Candi said angrily. "Give the kid time to get her act together before you drive her crazy like you have the rest of us."

The woman she addressed was, Dani saw, very attractive. She wore a pair of loose-fitting slacks, a red blouse, and white sandals. Her hair was dark, as were her eyes, and only an oversized nose kept her from being a real beauty. "I'm Rachel Gold," she said, and as she spoke a smile replaced the bitter twist that her wide mouth had borne. She came forward and put her hand out, saying, "Pay no attention to me, Dani. I'm not at my best, you might say."

"For cryin' out loud!" Candi said loudly, "Not at your best? I'd like to know when *that* is!"

Dani looked at the three women, then at her watch. A surprised look came into her eyes, and she shook her head. "It's only the thirtieth!"

"When did he get you, Dani?" Rachel asked.

"Just yesterday, but it seems like a lot longer."

"Where are you from?" Karen asked.

"New Orleans."

Karen shook her head. As she handed Dani the glass of water, she commented thoughtfully, "New Orleans? He got you here in twenty-four hours. He got me in Minneapolis, and it took a little longer—almost two days."

Dani drank the last of the water, then said, "I think I want to stand up." She accepted Karen's helping hand under her arm, swayed slightly, then asked, "Who is this *he* you're talking about? Is it a man named *Lovelace?*"

"A very tall man—over six feet?" Rachel questioned quickly. "With gray hair and blue eyes—something of the military in him?"

"Why, yes."

Rachel nodded. "His name was *Roberts* when he sucked me in."

"It was *Masters* when he talked me into going with him," Karen chimed in. "He changes his name, but it's the same man. He kidnapped all of us."

"But—why?" Dani asked in bewilderment. "If he's looking for ransom, he won't get any from me!"

Candi laughed suddenly. "Me neither, Dani."

"Almost none of us have any money." Karen shrugged. "As for why we're here, I guess that's the question that's driving us all up the wall."

Dani studied the women, then asked pensively, "Why would anyone kidnap four people who don't know each other and who have no money for ransom?"

"Not four," Rachel said quickly. "*Twelve* is the number." She smiled at Dani's consternation, then nodded toward the straight wall. "We're in the women's quarters—the seven men are over there. Either next door or out through that door in the rec room."

"Seven men? But that's only eleven?"

"Betty Orr is cooking dinner," Rachel nodded. "You ought to try to eat something—but first you need a warm bath."

"Oh, that *does* sound good." Dani felt grubby. She looked around for a bathroom.

"Come along, Dani," Karen said. "I'll show you. Candi, will you try to find her something more comfortable to wear?" Dani followed Karen on legs that felt rubbery. Passing through the door in a second flat wall at the top of her bunk, she discovered a pie-shaped room with a commode and a lavatory on the shortest of two flat walls, the one on her left, and another door beside the lavatory. Inside, she found herself in another room, this one approximately eight by ten, where a large, old-fashioned bathtub sat. Some sort of aluminum ring overhead supported a shower curtain and a shower head that had been installed on the end of a six-foot iron pipe. To one side stood a large medicine cabinet against the wall and beside it a straight chair. Two of the walls were flat, while one was of metal and curved. Set in one of the straight walls was another door, and Karen walked over and slammed a bolt home, locking it.

"That's the door to the men's quarters," she said. "Lock it when you come in, and unlock it when you leave. If you'll get out of your clothes, I'll run you a warm bath." She bent over and turned on the water. As the tub filled, she walked over to a wooden box fastened on one of the walls and took out a large plastic container filled with pink liquid. "Here's some bubble bath, and there's some shampoo and soap." Her eyes smiled at Dani, and she added, "I hope you like the brand, because it's all we have."

"Anything will be fine, Karen." She took the bubble bath and poured some into the water. When she peeled off the last of her undergarments, Karen said, "Let me see those bruises." At Dani's surprised look, she grinned and said, "Never argue with your doctor!"

"Are you a *real* doctor?" Dani asked as the other woman looked at her arms and checked her carefully.

"Yes." Karen nodded as she looked at the needle marks. "The drugs may have some sort of aftereffect. He uses such massive doses on his victims, it's a wonder some of us haven't OD'd." Then she stooped and picked up the soiled clothing. "I'll see these get in the wash. You jump in and soak for a half hour. I'll have Candi bring you something to wear."

She left the room, walking briskly, and Dani stepped into the hot foamy water. With a sigh she let herself down and lay there until the water covered her. She turned it off and relaxed, letting the hot water wash away some of her tensions as well as the accumulated grime.

As Dani lay in the bath, staring up at some sort of a

wire-net screen that served as a ceiling, her restless mind began going over the bizarre events that had brought her to such a strange prison. First, she went back to the call from Lovelace. It almost seemed as if she were listening to a tape recording, so clear was her memory of it.

He didn't take my name out of a hat, she realized. *He wanted me specifically. But why?* She ran through her memory, trying to identify the voice. Nothing. Then she thought of the name *Lovelace. No good thinking about that—he changes it with every victim. Probably takes it out of a phone book.*

What of the brief encounter at the airstrip? She called up her first glimpse of him standing under the airplane. She willed herself to see the plane, and slowly the numbers on the fuselage seemed to appear—*122454.* It was a blue Beechcraft with a white stripe down the side. *When I get out of here,* she thought as she sat up and began to soap herself, *it won't be hard to trace that plane.*

Engrossed in the problem, Dani gave a start when a voice called, "About ready to get out?" She sat up with a great splash to find Candi before her with a stack of folded towels. "You can rinse off with that shower ring, if you like."

Dani turned on the water, gasped, for it was cold after the hot tub, then stepped out and took a large blue towel. She dried carefully as Candi laid out some clothing on the chair, saying with a shrug, "You won't like the clothes much, but there ain't a lot of choice."

As Dani slipped into the underwear, she said, "Where is your home, Candi?"

"Oh, no place in particular. The Creep got me in Los Angeles. I was the featured attraction at the Melton Theatre."

"Really?"

Candi handed Dani the tan linen slacks, watched her slip into them, then said with a gloomy tone that pulled her shrill voice down to a lower level, "I guess you maybe don't know that one—and it ain't as fancy as it sounds." She shrugged and added, "I was one of the strippers there."

Dani let nothing show in her face as she took the pale-blue blouse from the other woman. She slipped into it, and as she buttoned it up the front, she asked, "Have you been in show business a long time?"

Candi wore a great deal of makeup, applied artistically, but a cynical light darted into her blue eyes as she nodded. "Longer than I should have." She stepped back and picked up a pair of white crew shoes from the chair. "I hope you can keep these on. The Creep thinks we're all a bunch of elephants down here."

The slacks were a bit too small and the blouse too large, but Dani said nothing. Sitting down, she slipped on a pair of white socks, new ones just out of their wrapper. Then she slipped her feet into the shoes and smiled. "I see what you mean, Candi."

"Too big, huh? I think he buys our clothes by the *pound*!" Candi snapped. "There's enough to wear—but he sure don't spend no time on style or sizes!" Then she said, "I found an extra brush, and you can use my comb until the Creep sends another one."

Dani took the brush and moved to a large mirror fastened to the wall on the opposite side of the room from the medicine cabinet. Her hair was tangled and needed washing, but later would do. *I guess I'll have plenty of time, for once*, she thought ruefully, then turned to smile at Candi. "I'm ready now."

"You look swell," Candi nodded. "The guys will pop their eyeballs." As she turned and led the way out of the bathroom, into the sleeping area, she added, "Come along and meet your new playmates."

Stepping inside the next room, Dani blinked, for the lights that were strung over the area were numerous and of larger wattage than in the room she stepped out of.

"Well, our newest addition has arrived! Welcome!" A white-haired man with a strong Nordic face and electric-blue eyes had been sitting at one of the four round tables grouped in front of what appeared to be a kitchen. As the man came forward to greet her, with his hand out, Dani saw that the room was a true circle, with half the area devoted to the kitchen–dining area, while the other had two couches, several upholstered chairs, and a few wooden tables with magazines and books on them.

"I am Karl Holtz." The face was not young, but the hand Dani took was muscular and strong. "And you are Miss Danielle Ross—or is it Mrs.?"

"It's Miss."

"So. Then come and take your place. We have been waiting for you." He led her to one of the tables, where Karen sat with a man. Pulling a chair out, he nodded as she sat down, and he smiled. "Suppose we all have dinner, and then you can get better acquainted." Turning to a thin woman in a flowered dress, he asked, "Betty, is the soup ready?"

"Everything's ready." Betty was about forty-five years old and very thin. She had a scowl on her thin lips and a mop of carelessly combed gray hair. "I hope you like chicken-and-rice soup. It's all we have right now."

"Oh, that will be fine."

"Let me serve you," Holtz said. He picked up a dish and a plate, went to the stove, and spooned out a generous helping. Returning to the table, he added, "Now, the rest of us can be served."

At Holtz's words, a thick-set chunky man with pale skin and washed-out blond hair moved quickly to the serving table and picked up a platter in one hand and a large bowl in the other. Betty followed suit, and the two began to carry food to the four tables. Dani waited for the others to be served, but Holtz said, "Oh, eat your soup while it's hot, Miss Ross!"

Dani felt suddenly awkward. All her life she had disliked people who made a display of their religion, but one circumstance had brought her into a commitment that gave her problems. It had to do with asking a blessing over a meal. Her parents always took praying over food for granted, but when she had left the isolation of that dining room for the college world, and later the world of business, she had given up the process. Then she had met a man who had insisted on the ritual—and after a long skirmish, she had adopted his ways.

"It's one way of telling the world who you are," Jerry had said the first time she'd criticized him for bowing his head and praying over a meal. The scene came to her, sharp as an etching. On their second date, they had been with two other couples at an exclusive restaurant. Dani had felt as embarrassed as the other four when he had bowed his head silently, but she had waited until they were alone to say, "You ought not to insist on asking a blessing, Jerry. It's ostentatious, and it insults some people."

"It's one way of telling the world who you are. It's become sort of a test with me," he had added, his dark hair mussed and his grin crooked. "I really am grateful to God, and it's little enough to ask a simple blessing. If the Muslims can bow down and face Mecca with their faces on the floor, I guess I can bow my head for ten seconds to honor God."

They had argued about it for weeks, but in the end, she had made the same pact. It was never formulated, but she had always bowed her head before a meal—and now it was hard!

Her stubborn streak surfaced, and Dani refused to be intimidated by the stares of the others. She bowed her head, shut out the world by closing her eyes, and asked a simple blessing. When she looked up, she noted that the room had gone silent, the two servers had paused, and Holtz had his blue eyes fixed on her with interest. He nodded slightly but said nothing, and the big man and the woman continued to serve the food.

Holtz said, "I will introduce the others later, but the man next to you is Alex Morrow, from Houston. You have already met Karen. Now, we will eat."

Dani tasted the soup, and when Holtz saw that she ate it all, he said, "Ah, you could have something heavier? Is that all right, Doctor Sanderson?"

"A little roast will be all right, Commander—but only a little." Karen began to talk as Karl got up and walked to the table to get the food. "The food is good, Dani. We put in an order for what we want, and sooner or later we get it—more or less."

Alex gave her an irritated look. " 'More or less' is right!" He was of average height, Dani judged, but somewhat overweight. Nervous movements betrayed him as a highly motivated man, and she guessed that he was efficient and impatient with others less so. He had slightly thinning brown hair and brown eyes that moved restlessly over the room. He took a bite of the roast from his plate, chewed it, then looked at Dani. "Don't pay any attention to me, Miss Ross. I'm spoiled."

"You shouldn't eat that roast, Alex," Karen said quietly. "You know it won't agree with you."

"So what?" he snapped. "I can't eat milk and toast *all* the time."

Holtz came back carrying a plate with small portions of meat, English peas, and mashed potatoes. "Our physician will monitor your diet," he commented.

Dani ate hungrily. The voices of her companions came to her, somewhat hollowed from the expanse overhead. The woman named Betty and the man who helped serve moved around the tables, keeping the others supplied with tea and coffee, as well as with food.

Noticing her watch them, Karen said, "Don't feel sorry for Betty and Lonnie, Dani. It's their turn to serve—but in a few days you'll be serving, and they'll be sitting down." She glanced across the table and said, "It's Commander Holtz's system. At first we were all falling over each other, getting irritated with the way the food was cooked and served."

"Better a servant once a week than every night." Holtz nodded. He caught Dani's sharp look of inquiry and grinned at her. "Oh, yes, *I* become a busboy and waiter, along with the rest."

Surprised that he read her thoughts so easily, Dani decided, *He's a sharp cookie. I'd hate to have him against me in a case!* But she laughed. "I waited tables most of my life, Commander. At home, then working nights, while I was at college."

"What field?"

"Accounting." Dani took a sip of her tea and explained, "I got my CPA a few years ago."

Morrow looked at her with fresh interest. "You don't look like any CPA I ever had." He snorted. "I hope you've got more sense than mine."

"I don't do much of that any more. I left the field for another one a little over a year ago."

"What are you doing now?" Karen asked.

"Until a couple of months ago, I was enrolled as a student at Hayworth Divinity School."

"Ah, a theological student!" Holtz said with a smile. "That should be useful in our situation!"

"I'd rather she were an escape artist," Morrow wished sourly. "Religion won't get us out of this hole."

"Oh, I don't know, Alex," Holtz said. "I seem to remember that it got the prophet Daniel out of a lion's den."

"You don't believe that fable any more than I do!"

"I haven't decided yet whether or not I believe in miracles," Holtz said, and his face grew serious. "I have seen some strange things in my time."

He would have said more, but the thin black man who sat facing them at one of the farthest tables called out, "Hey, Commander! How about letting us meet the lady?"

Holtz nodded and got to his feet. "Yes, Rosie, I think you are right. It is time for our guest to be introduced. Her name, as you know, is Miss Danielle Ross. She is from New Orleans. Have any of you ever seen her—or heard of her?" He waited, but no one spoke, and he shook his head, "I did not think so. But in any case, I will introduce each of you. Then if she would be so kind, perhaps she will tell us a little about herself.

"The gentleman who insists on meeting you is Roosevelt

Andrew Smith," Holtz said, indicating the black man, who grinned at Dani. He was very thin, with a smooth face and a pair of small, brown eyes. He had a thin mouth, and his hair was slick and black. Though she had difficulty gauging his age, Dani discovered later that he was fifty-five.

"Rosie is from Alabama originally, but from just about everywhere recently. His profession is serving, and he has been a waiter on ships and on shore almost everywhere. He has a wife, three children, and seven grandchildren from whose bosoms he was abruptly snatched five weeks ago. He is a gentle man," Holtz said with a sudden quirk of his strong lips. "However he makes no secret of the fact that he has a straight razor and will give the man who abducted him a free shave at the earliest possible opportunity."

"I will indeed!" Rosie nodded. He continued in a high voice. "I would say it's good to have you here, miss—but I guess that's a little wrong." He had, Dani realized, largely moved away from the black English he had grown up with, but traces remained. She smiled at him, and he grinned back.

"And sitting beside him is Sid Valentine." Valentine sat straighter and looked directly at Dani with a pair of hard, black eyes. He had a pale, sharp-featured face, coal-black hair, and appeared to be around forty. "Sid is from New Jersey, Miss Ross," Holtz continued. "He came here less than a week ago, and we're still getting acquainted. Would you like to greet Miss Ross, Sid?"

Valentine gave Holtz a sharp look. He had an air of covert suspicion in his lean face, and he only shook his head silently.

"No? Well, perhaps you'll have something later. Sitting beside Mr. Valentine is Mr. Bix Bently. He's the youngest member of our little group, in years, if not in experience. Bix is a musician. Unfortunately we have no instruments here, which is a source of disappointment to him."

Bently was no more than eighteen or nineteen, Dani guessed. He had a full head of blond hair, a rather good-looking face, and pale-blue eyes. When he placed them on Dani, she saw in him some of the same reckless spirit she'd seen when doing investigations for the attorney general among some rockers. He was not much older than her brother, but a weariness in his eyes made him seem so. He'd tried everything, she guessed, and nothing had brought any satisfaction. Burnt out by twenty—and absolutely convinced that the values held by his elders were false.

He was wearing an oversized sweatshirt and a pair of faded cutoffs and sported a Fu Manchu moustache. "Hey, pretty lady," he said lifting a thin hand. "Awesome!"

Holtz shook his head, saying, "Later on, Bix. You'll have plenty of time to convince Miss Ross that the world is a terrible place." He nodded at one of the two men who sat at a table close to Bently. "Mr. Vince Canelli lists Detroit as his hometown and is in business there."

"Hi!" Canelli nodded. "Sorry you got sucked into this, Dani, but you'll add a little class to the joint."

Canelli looked very much like a younger version of Dean Martin—only much harder. Swarthy skin, curly black hair, and the sturdy neck of a lineman complemented his straight nose and wide mouth, along with a tough-looking chin and a pair of large, dark eyes. All went together to give him a raffish look, like a buccaneer, Dani thought. Most of the others, except for Holtz, seemed subdued by their plight, but there was no fear in the eyes of Canelli, and he smiled at her in the practiced way of a man who has had almost unlimited success with women. The man might be handsome and even cultivated in a rough way— but he had the eyes of a carnivore.

"And finally, we have Mr. Lonnie Gibbs of Corning, Arkansas." Holtz smiled, indicating the thick-set young man who had served the food.

"Aw, I guess we done met, ain't we, Dani?" Lonnie said. "It was me that carried you to your bunk."

She smiled and said, "Thank you very much."

"Anytime!" He was, she saw, no more than five ten, but he had thick shoulders and a chest that filled his thin, blue sport shirt. A large stomach spilled over his belt, and light-brown pants encased a pair of short, heavy legs. His light skin would sunburn when subjected to the weather, and his face was round and cheerful. He had a set of large ears, light-blue eyes and tow-colored hair.

"That's all of us, I think," Holtz said. "You met all the ladies?"

Dani said, "All except this one. Betty, is it?"

"Ach!" Holtz said, shaking his head. "This is Mrs. Betty Orr, the most important person in this place. She is our cook." He gave the woman an affectionate look and said, "If not for her, I think we would have been in terrible shape."

Betty Orr was in no way outstanding, Dani saw, unless her large, light-brown eyes, filled with a warm intelligence, could be so designated. But a pair of gold-rimmed glasses shielded them. She was no more than five foot three or four and thinly compact. When she spoke her voice was flat, with a Midwest twang. "I come from Saint Louis—and I hope you can cook!"

Dani laughed and nodded. "Not as well as you, I am sure. But I will do my best."

Betty smiled then, and it made her look almost pretty. "Well, that'll be a blessing."

"Now, Miss Ross, would you care to introduce yourself?" Holtz asked.

Dani slowly stood, feeling the weight of their eyes. She was an accomplished public speaker, but never had she felt so awkward. "I'm still confused about all this," she said slowly. Looking around at the circular walls that rose up into the murky darkness, she shook her head. "If there were an easy way out of this place, you would have found it by now. I might as well tell you that I'm scared stiff!" She heard the small laugh that went around and nodded, "But as that famous American philosopher Yogi Berra once said, 'It ain't over, till it's over.' " She saw Vince Canelli's lips curl upward in a smile, and Lonnie laughed out loud. "So I don't have much to say. I have a family and things to do in the world. All of you do. And I believe that somehow, someday, I'll be out there doing them."

She sat down, and Karen said, "Good, Dani. It's what we need to hear." Then she got up and said, "Our turn to bus tables, isn't it, Alex?"

He rose, and the two began to clean the tables. Dani was surrounded at once by the men, and Rachel took note of it. She smiled grimly, and said to Betty, "Just what we needed, Betty. A glamour girl!"

"She's not that kind," Betty shook her head firmly. "Very attractive, but not a chaser." Then her lips tightened, and she added, "I've seen enough of that kind to know!"

"Doesn't matter," Rachel insisted. "With looks like hers,

there'll be trouble. Look at Vince. He's like a fox in the chicken house, isn't he? I wouldn't be surprised to see him lick his chops!"

"Maybe now he'll stop pestering you, Rachel." Betty gave the younger woman a knowing look.

Rachel shook her long, black hair in an impatient gesture, then walked away without answering. Candi had come up in time to hear the last of the conversation, and said, "Don't be too sure she *wants* Vince to leave her alone, Betty." A sharp, triumphant light touched her eyes, and she nodded. "He lost interest in her when I came along."

"I guess we all know that." Betty's mouth became prim, and she turned and walked away from Candi, her back straight.

Dani was kept busy for nearly an hour, and by the time Holtz came to rescue her, she felt tired.

"Come, now, let Miss Ross have a rest!" he exclaimed. "We'll smother her, if we're not careful.

"I know you're tired, but may I show you one thing?"

"Of course, Commander." She followed him and saw an angry expression on Vince's face, though he made no comment. *He hates to be crossed*, Dani thought.

The hour had given her time to study her new acquaintances, and of them all, Holtz was the most interesting. "Commander of what?" she asked as he took her to the comparative privacy of a table set along the wall just opposite the kitchen.

"I was commander of the *Triton*, a German submarine." He watched her face. When she said nothing, his tense expression relaxed. "You are not still fighting that war, I see." When she looked at him in astonishment, he added with a gesture of his head, "Rachel Gold *is*, I'm afraid.

93

She's Jewish, of course, and anything German is anathema to her."

"But she wasn't even born until that war was over!"

"No, but some of her relatives died at Buchenwald."

"I see."

"Well, you'll hear about that from her, I'm sure," he said brusquely. "Here is what I'd like you to do. . . ." He took a sheaf of paper out of a notebook that lay on a small table and gave it to her. "This is a little experiment of mine. If you would fill it out, I would appreciate it." Dani saw that it consisted of long lists of items—cities, occupations, relatives, and many others.

"You're trying to find the common denominator?" she asked.

"Ah! You are very fast!" He smiled and added, "An accountant is what we need. Someone who has the determination to go through long lists with no impatience."

"Well, actually, Commander, I'm now a private investigator." His eyes flew open in surprise as she told him of her new work, and he looked pleased.

"That is even better!" he exclaimed. "We can now work together. The others do not see the importance of this. Some of them will not even take time to fill out the papers."

She looked at the people and then around at the steel walls. "What *is* this thing we're in, Karl?"

Warming at her use of his name, he said, "It is what is called a grain elevator. Here, I will show you."

He took another folder off the table, which evidently served as a desk, and found a notebook. Opening it, he said, "You've seen grain elevators, I'm sure. They're called silos in some parts of the country. Most of them are like this, huge round tanks as much as ten or twelve stories high—and usually in groups of five or more, all side by side."

He put two sheets of paper in front of her and said, "This one has been made into a prison—an escape-proof prison, one is tempted to say. Looking at Drawing A. . . ." He pointed out the features of the neat drawing of two circles with the furnishings and inner walls.

"As you see, two of these silos have been made into one by cutting a door. One silo is for sleeping; the other is for cooking and lounging. We call this the rec room."

Dani stared at the drawing as he went over the features. Finally she said, "It's odd, isn't it? The way he's provided separate sleeping arrangements—for men and women— and the bathroom door can be locked."

Holtz nodded with approval. "You *are* a detective, Miss Ross! It tells us something about whoever it is. He may have kidnapped us, but he has some sort of morality. It would have been much simpler to have put all the bunks in that one sleeping area, but he did not do that."

"A strange sort of morality," Dani mused.

"There is something else strange," Holtz said. He pointed out the bunks with a thick forefinger. "There are exactly twelve of them. Seven in the men's quarters, five in the women's quarters. They are all welded to the bulkheads—the walls, that is—and I will prophesy that you are the last arrival."

"You're saying whoever it is *planned* for us specifically?"

"Yes! Nothing was left to chance."

Dani touched the second drawing. "What's this? A horizontal view of the silo?"

"Yes. I cannot say how high this structure is." He

95

Drawing B

Remains of Steel Ladder

Vents

Camera

Supply
Box

Winch

Rec. Area

Slot

Kitchen

36'

100 ft.
(approx.)

Drawing A

Stove

Sink

Cabinet

Ref.

Table

(Tables/Chairs)

Rec.
Area

H-W Tank

Women's Sleeping
Quarters

Men's Sleeping
Quarters

Bath

36'

96

tapped the other drawing marked *Drawing B.* "At least one hundred feet high, I would say, and there is no way in or out, except through the roof."

"No doors?"

"Not now. There were two small ones, but they have been welded shut." He looked up into the dark overhead space. "You came down from up there in a large supply box." With a short laugh he added, "The supply box looks almost exactly like a coffin, about two by six. It's made that size so that our unknown captor could send us down in it. We all came here the same way you did. Every bite of food, everything, must come the same way."

He motioned toward the wall. "There's a slot in the wall over there—the only opening of any kind in this silo, except for the door at the top, which the supply box passes through, and those four vents." He pointed toward the small openings, about thirty feet high, through which the sun shone in bars of light. "We put messages through the slot, orders for food, clothing, medicine—things like that."

"Do you *get* the things you ask for?"

"Sometimes exactly what we request—sometimes nothing. I have the idea that someone takes the orders, gets whatever's handy, and ignores the rest."

"What about that camera?" Dani indicated one fastened to the wall by a steel framework. It was about ten feet from the floor and was aimed at the center of the silo. "Are they watching us?"

"I suspect they are, but we've had no message at all."

She leaned back and the sound of music drifted across the room. It was what musicians contemptuously call "elevator music." She looked at the table and noticed a number of magazines and several books. "I see we have some entertainment."

"Not much, I'm afraid." Holtz shook his head sadly. "We have a tape player, and from time to time they send some new tapes, but it's all very—unsatisfying. Most of it is music from the forties, big-band sound, or else light popular music. No jazz, which drives Bix crazy, and no country-western, which Lonnie keeps ordering. And the magazines are no better. They're all quite innocuous— *Saturday Evening Post* type of thing. But there are many right-wing magazines, most of which none of us had ever heard of. You know—keep America pure, that type of literature."

Dani sat there silently, thinking, then looked across at the German. "What have you deduced, Karl? About our being here?"

He dropped his head for a moment, as if the weariness of time had suddenly pressed against him. Finally he lifted it and said evenly, "I have had one experience with a madman named Adolf Hitler. Now I think there is another such in the world—and we are completely at his mercy!" He rose slowly and added quietly, "I think you will find out very soon, Miss Ross, how strong your Christian faith is. As for me, I am an old man and have little to lose, but I would hate to leave this world from such a place as this. I would like to think," he said very quietly and with a hopeful look in his blue eyes, "that there is more to life than dying like frogs in the bottom of a well!"

5
All the Guilty

"These are real good, Dani," Betty Orr remarked. She was standing beside the twin stacks of golden pancakes that Dani had made from scratch. She had picked up the last one, a small cake no more than three inches in diameter and tasted it critically. "I never was much good at pancakes myself. I made a batch a while back, out of a mix, but they weren't anything like these!" She gave a sudden smile, adding, "You'll be taking my job away from me, if I'm not careful!"

Dani had been turning the sausage patties that sizzled in the huge iron skillet, but at Betty's words she turned and patted the older woman on the shoulder. "No chance of that!" She laughed. "You're the best cook I've ever seen, Betty."

That was not true, strictly speaking, for her own mother was at least the equal of Betty Orr, but it was close enough. After only three days in the silo, Dani had learned much about her fellow prisoners. Food and meals were of paramount importance, far more important than on the outside. The boredom of the place magnified any activity.

Karen had told Dani, "We nearly had civil war before Betty came! None of us could cook worth a darn! We fought over who was going to cook, then complained about the meals, *whoever* cooked them. But when Betty came, she took over, and it's made things a lot easier."

Rachel came in just at that moment and stood there, waiting to serve the breakfast. She was wearing the outfit that Dani had worn when she was brought in, and it looked very good on her. Dani commented, "You look lovely, Rachel! That looks *much* better on you than it does on me!" Then she warned, "You'd better put a coat on over it, though. It's getting colder."

Rachel moved over to pick up the platter of pancakes. "Thank you for letting me wear it, Dani."

She moved away toward the tables, and Betty said quietly, "Better be sure she doesn't put strychnine in the commander's syrup. I wouldn't put it past her." She caught Dani's surprised look, and shook her head, adding as she turned to pick up the coffeepot, "I mean it, Dani! Rachel is hard as nails. She told me once that she'd like to give Holtz what he gave the poor Jews in that concentration camp—and you should have seen those black eyes of hers! She'd do it in a minute!" Then she added, "And he feels about the same way toward her. Look at his eyes sometime, when he's looking at Rachel!"

Dani became accustomed to the gossip, for the close confinement intensified frictions between various inmates. Trivia that would not have mattered outside became magnified when they could never get more than a few feet away from one another.

Lonnie and Rosie, for example, had almost come to

blows over a tube of toothpaste. She had not seen it, but Vince confided that Lonnie had been ready to stomp the other into the concrete when he suspected that the slender black man had used his "personal" tube. " If I hadn't been there," Vince admitted with a grin, "Lonnie would have broken his neck. Those two are sure out of step!"

Dani noted that the two never sat at the same table or played any of the group's interminable games together—if they did, Lonnie's slurs nearly always ignited Rosie.

She put two sausages on Alex Morrow's plate, and he gave her a quick smile. "Thanks, Dani. I'll have to take a pint of Maalox, but it's worth it!" He was very polite, though short tempered, she quickly discovered. According to his version, he was a wealthy man, and Dani believed it. Morrow seemed accustomed to getting his own way in things, and it irritated him to have to do menial chores.

As she served Sid, Karl, and Karen, who were sitting at his table, Dani thought of the awful row Morrow had started. It would have been comical, if he had not been so furious.

The hot water was inadequate for all their needs. A forty-gallon tank had to provide enough to wash clothes and dishes for twelve people, in addition to twelve baths or showers. So Holtz had finally worked out a rigid bath schedule.

On the night after Dani's arrival, a practically hyperventilating Morrow had come raging into the rec room, his face red with anger. "Who used up all my hot water?" he had screamed. Alex had reserved the hour of eight in the evening for his shower, because that gave the hot-water tank time to catch up after the dishwashing. He liked to stand under the shower as it dripped on him slowly for a long time—until the hot water was all gone, Holtz told

Dani. When he discovered Candi had slipped in before him, Alex had cursed her thoroughly. Such outrage did little good, however, for she stood toe-to-toe with him, giving as good as she got—and even a little better!

"They sure are good cussers, ain't they, Miss Dani?" Admiration had covered Rosie's dark face. "Kind of professional, you might say!"

Dani served the rest of the sausages, put the frying pan back, then went to her seat. She was at a table with Bix, Betty, and Lonnie, and to her surprise Lonnie got up and pulled her chair out. "Thank you, Lonnie," she murmured. She heard Betty say clearly, "I never noticed you giving me that kind of attention!" but paid no heed.

She bowed her head and said a silent prayer of thanksgiving, noticing that the others fell into three categories: Rosie and Betty bowed their heads with her; Alex, Vince, Karl, Lonnie, and Karen sat there quietly until she lifted her head. Candi, Rachel, Sid, and Bix plunged into their meals at once, Sid and Bix making as much noise as possible to make sure she didn't miss their meaning.

When she lifted her head, they all began eating, and soon they were calling out their praise for the pancakes. "All *right!*" Vince said enthusiastically. "You are the greatest, baby!"

Most of the others commented on the excellent meal, and Karen said, "A change is good." She gave Dani a close look, her calm blue eyes missing nothing, and finally stated, "You've adjusted more quickly than the rest of us, I think."

Dani flushed and shook her head. "That's because I was the last, Karen. You had all gotten the system working by the time I dropped in."

"Well, *that* ain't right, doll!" Bix said, speaking around a mouthful of pancakes. "Ain't no system in this world gonna make *me* adjust to this creepy joint!" He swallowed convulsively, and before the food went down his throat, he had stuffed another huge bite into his mouth. "All my life I been fightin' against the system. Then just when I found the way to do my own thing, I get thrown into a nutty jail where I even have to go to the bathroom on schedule!"

Dani tested the pancakes critically, found them good, then answered mildly, "Oh, Bix, I don't think any of us are ever really free from a system. As far as I can see, the only freedom we have is to choose which system is the best for us."

"Now don't you start in preaching at me!" Bix shot in angrily. "It's bad enough in here, without having to put up with a lot of phony religion."

"Shut your yap, punk," Lonnie said conversationally. He turned to lay his gaze on Bix. Lifting a heavy forearm, he added, "One more crack like that to the lady, and you won't have no choppers to eat these here fine pancakes with." Then he turned to Dani and nodded. "You gotta excuse Bix, ma'am. He ain't had no proper raising, you see."

Bix's jaw dropped, and he said loudly in an outraged voice, "*Proper raising?* Why you ignorant redneck! If I didn't have . . . !"

Dani placed her hands on both their arms, saying, "Please don't fight." She felt the thin arm of Bix, which contrasted with the muscular swelling of the Arkansan's mighty bicep and added, "Let's just enjoy the meal."

They both subsided, but when the meal was over and everyone was sitting back, talking, over coffee, Rosie asked suddenly, "Miss Dani, seeing you are a preacher, why don't we have us a service, this bein' Sunday and all?"

Instantly, a protest went up, Sid Valentine slapping the table and saying with a profane oath, "No! I had enough of that when I was—" He didn't finish, but slapped the table again, saying sullenly, "I say let them that's religious keep it to themselves."

A sharp debate broke out, with Betty saying, "Those of us who are Christians have a right to have a service," only to be challenged by vociferous, sharp objections from Candi and Bix. Rachel's face tensed, and she said firmly, "What about me? Will you have a Jewish meeting for me?"

Distressed, Dani finally stood up and picked up her plate, then Lonnie's. The argument suddenly stopped, and she found everyone looking at her, waiting for her to urge a service on them. She picked up Rachel's plate silently. When she looked around, seeing the anger, she said quietly: "This is wrong. We're in enough trouble without fighting over God." She picked up Bix's plate, which made a loud sound as she let it drop on the others, then turned to face them. "Would it be all right if all of you give those of us who would like to meet together a time? Just an hour, while the rest of you are taking a nap or something. Perhaps in the women's quarters."

"That wouldn't do, Danielle," Karl objected at once. "Rosie wants to be there." He looked around and said, "Most of us aren't too lively after lunch. I think we might let the service take place from one until two." He looked around and asked, "Any objections?"

Valentine looked up with an injured air. "The phonies ain't running me out of no place, but let them play their little games!" Rachel and Bix wore angry expressions, but neither spoke. Holtz looked around and nodded, "Very well. From one until two, Miss Ross, you have the floor."

All morning Dani dreaded the time Holtz had secured. She offered to help Betty prepare lunch, but the older woman smiled and patted her arm. "No, honey. You work on your sermon. I know preachers like to do that. There's a Bible over there on the coffee table."

Dani picked up the plain, black Bible and smiled at the inscription inside: *Placed by courtesy of the Gideons.* "I'll bet they'd be surprised at where this one has ended up," she murmured to herself. All morning she sat around reading and trying to pray. Her sermons to congregations of well-fed and self-satisfied church members had not proved difficult. She had spent a great deal of time extracting choice quotations from the better class of theologians, added some pertinent statements from poets and philosophers, then read the manuscript in a clear voice.

Today she could call up enough quotes, but the stark reality of the circular prison clashed with her polished discourse. The cold air that seemed to settle on her like a blanket was no colder to her body than to her spirit, and when lunchtime came and departed and Rosie walked over with a beaming, expectant smile, she was quietly desperate.

A quick look around showed that only Rachel was not present. Breathing a frantic prayer, Dani nodded and assumed a smile that might have quivered slightly. "Thank you all for staying," she began and turned to nod at Sid, saying, "especially those of you who are opposed to a service. I'll be very brief, I promise." Sid snorted and picked up a copy of *National Geographic* with a picture of a snow leopard on the cover. Bix settled down defiantly, with his feet on the table and his arms crossed over his chest. "Get it over with!" he muttered angrily.

Dani opened the Bible. "Let me read you a poem that I've loved for a long time." Slowly she began to read the Seventy-eighth Psalm. What she would say when she had finished reading, she had no idea. *God, give me something!* she was praying as she read, feeling weak with fear at the thought of trying to preach without notes—without even an *outline!* The first eighteen verses spoke of the mighty works that God did in the history of Israel, and when she got to verse nineteen and read the words: "Yea, they spake against God; they said, Can God furnish a table in the wilderness?" something happened to her.

That is my word: The thought came to her so suddenly and with such clarity that at first she almost thought it was something audible. After a second, she realized that it had not been spoken aloud, but had come into her spirit. Never had anything quite like that happened before, but at once Dani lifted up her eyes and began to speak. Each sentence was like throwing herself off a cliff into a dark pit, for she did not know from one to the next what would come. It was almost as if she herself were listening to some speaker, though her own voice fell over the silence of the room.

"Can God furnish a table in the wilderness?" she repeated softly. "Anyone can furnish a table where there is plenty of food, but the children of Israel were trapped in a barren desert. Even the animals in that howling wilderness lived on the razor's edge of existence, fighting over the scant food. And here they were, over a million people, some say, with nothing to eat. And they cried out in their fear, 'Can God furnish a table—*in the wilderness?*'"

She went on to speak of the stark conditions, the lack of water, and the peril of starvation, in such bold vivid terms that even Bix forgot to look antagonistic.

"Those people had no place to look but to God. There was no McDonalds, with a million quarter pounders, down the street. It was God or else. Sooner or later, with *all* of us, it comes to that. It may not be food, but *something* will catch up with us—something so big that we can't handle it. Maybe sickness—or the death of a loved one. Things that can't be 'handled' or ordered on a telephone."

As she spoke Karl looked around cautiously, noting that everyone in the room was listening—even Sid. He could see Valentine's face, which was hidden from Dani behind the magazine, and momentarily the tough expression had faded as he listened. Rachel had come to the door of the women's quarters and was standing in the shadow, her face hidden. But she stood there, poised as one who cannot decide whether or not to retreat. Candi's face was set in an angry scowl, but both Karen and Betty were listening intently, especially Betty, who nodded emphatically from time to time.

Rosie was the most enthusiastic, saying, "Amen!" loudly and grinning broadly. Lonnie, from across the room, was nodding also. An unhappy look covered Alex Morrow's face, and he shook his head slightly as Dani came to the end.

"God *can* furnish a table in the wilderness. I don't think we are a bunch of 'cold carbohydrates headed for destruction,' as one writer has said. I think we are special to Him." Then she said very quietly, "I believe God has furnished a table for us. Jesus Christ is the answer for our troubles—all of them."

She spoke a little longer, sharing her own conversion, and ending, "I'd like to close with a hymn and a prayer. Rosie, do you know 'Amazing Grace'?"

Rosie nodded happily and began to sing in a fine tenor voice, "Amazing grace! how sweet the sound—That saved a wretch like me." Dani joined in, as did Lonnie, Betty, and surprisingly, Bix Bently. He added a harmony with a baritone that made the music somehow blend. The others sat there, looking a little uncomfortable, but as the song went on, it seemed that the room lost a little of its frigidness.

Then Dani prayed simply, and when she was through, she gave a short laugh. "I guess you know now that I'm not much of a preacher. Thank you so much for joining me."

"Ain't you gonna take a collection?" Sid asked acridly. "Never knew a preacher who didn't have his hand out for money!"

But Lonnie said, "That's good preaching, Miss Dani. I've heard lots of preachers, but never no lady ones. Yet that was as good as any I ever heard!"

The following night, after supper, Dani joined Karl and Alex at what Holtz called his office, a single table, separated from the rest of the furniture, with neat stacks of papers and a shelf for books. As she sat down Holtz smiled, commenting eagerly, "I have tried to organize a systematic study of our condition, but no one is very interested—except Alex."

"Well, it's something to do," Morrow said. "But we're not going to *think* ourselves out of this, Karl."

"We'd better," the German responded grimly, his lips suddenly a thin line. "Because we're certainly not going to escape through that hole up there!

"The prime target is to find out what we all have in common," he explained. He picked up a folder and drew out a sheet with hand-lined rules and a list neatly drawn up on the left side. At the top were the names of the captives, and he said, "I'll have to add your name, Danielle. Now, look, category one is *location*."

Dani looked at the sheet and said, "Not much there. We come from all over the place."

"Ah, but when we tie that with the dates that we were brought here, it may mean something. Look at this sheet." He found another sheet of paper and put it on the table. It also listed the names, with a date beside each name:

Sept. 30	Karl Holtz	New York, N.Y.
Oct. 8	Rachel Gold	New York, N.Y.
Oct. 8	Sid Valentine	Newark, N.J.
Oct. 14	Karen Sanderson	Minneapolis, Minn.
Oct. 24	Bix Bently	Miami, Fla.
Oct. 24	Roosevelt Smith	Palm Beach, Fla.
Oct. 29	Vince Canelli	Detroit, Mich.
Nov. 11	Alex Morrow	Houston, Tex.
Nov. 12	Candi Cane	Los Angeles, Ca.
Nov. 15	Lonnie Gibbs	Corning, Ark.
Nov. 15	Betty Orr	Saint Louis, Mo.
Nov. 30	Danielle Ross	New Orleans, La.

Dani studied the list silently, thinking hard. "Three times two people came in together—and at least two of these three were from the same area."

"But it doesn't work." Alex frowned. "Karl, you were in the New York area, along with Rachel and Sid. If he'd been nabbing people from one place he'd have gotten you at the same time, wouldn't he?"

"I was different." Holtz shrugged. "I was in Berlin and had trouble with my reservation. I was originally scheduled to come to New York a week later, but I had to change my plans."

"Why did you come, Karl?" Dani asked curiously.

"I was to write a book and become famous," Holtz said with a sharp irony in his voice. "I'd been contacted by a man who called himself Eric Johnson. He was going to do a book about the *real* life of a German submarine commander in World War II—not the Hollywood version. It was going to be profitable, but that was not why I came. I wanted to set the record straight."

"He suckered you, just like the rest of us." Morrow groaned and put his head in his hands in despair. "He was going to let me in on a bunch of United States government leases, with oil bubbling out of the ground!"

Dani was looking at the list. "I can see that he got Rachel and Sid from the same area, and Bix and Rosie from Florida. But what about Lonnie and Betty? He's from Arkansas, and she's from Saint Louis. Not very close."

Holtz shrugged and said, "I know. Maybe it's all some kind of coincidence. But if we ever make any sense out of this, we have to get all the information we have *collectively* and try to find a pattern. Maybe geography has nothing to do with it." He leaned back and gave Dani a sharp look. "Tell me your impressions. I'd like to see how they match up with what the rest of us have thought."

Dani shook her head doubtfully, "It's like nothing I've ever heard of, Karl. I know groups of people are kidnapped, hijacked, at times—but they are all a *unit*—they all have something in common. We don't seem to have that unity."

She paused, then wondered, "What sort of person would do such a thing? Well, a *rich* person, obviously. It cost a lot of money to set this all up—fixing up this prison—and he had to spend a lot of money getting our backgrounds—" A thought struck her, and she gave a short laugh. "I wish *my* agency could land a big job like *that!*"

"What else do you think about this man?" Holtz asked.

"He's mad, of course." Dani shrugged. "But there's such *method* in his madness! Just the details of getting us all here prove that. He *knew* what he was doing."

"Yes, I have thought of that," Holtz nodded. "And he could have killed all of us, but did not." He leaned back and closed his eyes. "I do not understand it. It's like some crazy world out of one of Kafka's novels."

Dani sensed his depression and said quickly, "Don't go to sleep. Show me what all you've done. Maybe something will click for me."

They worked on the papers for several hours, with Morrow getting bored almost at once. He left, and Dani and Holtz talked for a long time. He was a fascinating man, she discovered, and just as he got up wearily to go to bed, she said warmly, "Karl, I'm glad you shared this with me. As a matter of fact, I'm glad you're here—oh, I didn't mean that!"

He smiled and took her hand. "I know what you mean, Danielle. We will have to lean on each other, yes?" Then he turned and said, "Good night. I will see you in the morning."

Dani was not sleepy. There was little sensation of night and day inside their prison. The small vents high overhead allowed only narrow shafts of sunlight to come down to their level, and on gloomy days such as this there was little sense of time having passed.

She went to fix another cup of coffee and saw that she was alone in the rec room. Dani got her coffee, returned to

Holtz's office, and began to go through the papers. An idea struck her, and she grabbed a pencil and began writing furiously.

It must have been five minutes later when she almost jumped out of her skin as a hand touched the back of her head! She gave a muffled cry, leaped to her feet, and turned to find Vince Canelli standing by her.

"Didn't mean to scare you, Dani," he said instantly. "Guess these crepe slippers are quieter than I thought."

"That's—that's all right," she said, trying to control her shaking hands. "Just give some kind of a warning next time, okay?"

"Sure." He moved closer. "Mind if I join you for a cup of coffee?"

"Oh, I've had about ten cups already, Vince," she excused herself quickly. "It's pretty late."

He took her arm and smiled, and his grip became almost painful. "Aw, come on, Dani. You been holed up with the German all night. How about a little equal time?"

"Well, maybe for a few minutes, but I'm pretty tired."

"Sure, sure." He nodded. "Come on over here. I been wanting to find out how a chick like you got into the preaching business." He pulled her over to one of the couches, and when he sat down, she found herself pressed against him. He took his hand off her arm, but before she could move, he put it over her shoulder in what seemed to be a careless gesture, but the look in his eyes told her it was not.

She began to talk rapidly, trying to think of some way to get out of the situation, but he held her so tightly that she had no chance to pull away. Finally she said, "Vince, don't hold me so tight. I won't run away."

He laughed and slid his other arm around her. Before

she could say a word, he kissed her, holding her in his powerful arms, and began to push her back on the couch.

She tore her mouth away, crying out, "Let me go!"

He ignored her and laughed at her struggles, but suddenly a voice interrupted, "Pretty late for the lady to be up, Vince."

Canelli gave a start and loosed his grip. Dani took that moment to break free and stand up. Vince rose, anger deforming his handsome face, and said, "I'd butt out of this if I was you, Lonnie!"

Lonnie had walked halfway across the room and stood there looking mildly at Vince. He said nothing, but at that moment Vince's face revealed his murderous emotions. He stepped toward Lonnie, then whirled to his left, where Candi had come out of the sleeping quarters, wearing a wool robe, and a strange expression on her face. "Doin' a little homework, Vince?" she asked tautly.

Canelli hesitated, then laughed and threw up his hands. "This place is turning into some kind of Bible school," he said. "Never saw so much fuss over a kiss."

When he left the room, Dani said in a voice that was not as steady as she'd have liked, "Thanks, Lonnie—and you, too, Candi."

"Aw, he didn't mean nothing." Lonnie yawned. He went to the sink, got a glass of water, and after drinking it noisily, said, "G'night," and disappeared through the door.

"Yeah, he meant something," Candi said bitterly. She stood there, staring at Dani, her eyes hollow, and she was a pathetic figure. Her story was all written in the pretty face that had begun to show the marks of hard living and in the flesh that had begun to lose its youthful tone. Candi turned and went back into the other section. When she walked past Candi's bunk, to go to bed, by the faint light of the small bulb, Dani thought she saw tears running down the other woman's cheeks. She wanted to stop, to say something, but Candi turned her face to the steel wall, leaving Dani no choice but to wordlessly go to her own bunk.

The next morning, at breakfast, Vince said little to anyone else, but Dani noticed he sat beside Candi. She ate very little, but he kept talking to her, smiling and laughing, and by the time the meal was over, she had offered him a watery smile.

Dani had gotten to her feet to begin clearing the dishes, when a sudden loud voice broke through the table talk: "I wish to speak with all of you."

Dani looked around wildly, for the voice was hollow, artificial somehow. Karl, who was standing close by, said, "The speaker!" She looked up, following his nod and saw again the large speaker and the camera that she had ceased to notice.

Everyone was standing mutely in place, staring at the speaker, when the voice came again: "Come and stand in front of the camera—all of you."

They all moved reluctantly forward.

"I don't like this," Bix muttered. "It don't seem right, not seeing whoever that is."

"Be quiet!" Karl ordered sharply. Then he looked up and said, "We are all here. What do you wish to tell us?"

"Ah, Herr Holtz," the voice responded at once, "Always in command, eh?"

"I am in command of nothing!" Holtz snapped out, a trace of the seething anger that lurked deep inside him making his voice harsher than normal. "I protest against this thing you have done to me—to all of us."

"Your protest is noted," entoned the unbodied, ghostly, impersonal male voice, seemingly devoid of age and emotion. When the voice spoke again, Dani thought it belonged in a training film.

"I will not exhaust your patience with a long speech," the voice droned on. "We live in a world in which justice has almost ceased to exist. Murderers are routinely set free. Even a man's home is no longer his castle, for he may be murdered with his family in his own living room. It is a day in which every man does that which is right in his own eyes—and justice hides its head."

After a very slight pause, every one of the prisoners felt as if the speaker was looking right at him: "It is every man's duty to see that this condition is dealt with. That is why you have been brought to this place. You are guilty, and you will be punished."

"Guilty of *what*?" Lonnie burst out angrily. "I ain't done *nothing* to be put in a hole like this!"

"Nor have I!" Rachel spoke up. She shook her fist at the camera's blank eye and said, "You are a tyrant! A tyrant!"

"Rachel, Lonnie! Be still!" Holtz spoke up. "One of the first laws of justice is that a man must be informed of his crime. If you are intent on justice, what crime are you holding us for?"

"That will come—it will come!" For the first time a trace of emotion touched the toneless voice, and he added, "You will all know the charge against you, but if you will confess of your own free will, it will go much better for you."

"How can we confess, if we don't know what we have done?" Alex cried angrily. "Be reasonable, man!"

"I am reasonable," the voice went on tonelessly. "It is reasonable for men and women to lead decent lives. It is reasonable for them to have the protection of the law and the armed forces to watch over their lives. And it is reasonable, when men and women violate those laws, to bring them to trial and justice."

An angry cry went up, and they all began to try to talk at once, but the voice said, "I will give you exactly forty-eight hours to step forward. If you do not admit your guilt, I will know what course to follow. Remember—forty-eight hours."

The speaker went dead, and the red light on the camera blinked out. They all stood there, struck dumb, until Alex said heavily, "Well, we've got a real kook out there, friends."

They all began to mill around, speaking rapidly. Each wanted to talk, and no one wanted to listen. Finally they broke up, and Karen paused to say, "What do you think, Dani?"

"I'm afraid," Dani answered honestly.

"Who isn't?" Rachel had heard the question and gave a shiver. "This is much worse than I thought—and I thought it was pretty bad."

"I guess I was hoping it'd be money." Dani said. "Even though that didn't make much sense." She shook her head slowly, and an almost palpable heaviness came into her breast. She sat down and stared at the floor. "Money is one thing, but this man is neurotic. And as far as I know, there's no way to satisfy a neurotic."

Rachel nodded, then suggested bitterly, "Well, we all

better be thinking up some nice juicy confessions. That's what we've got to come up with by Friday morning!"

Dani asked, "Commander, may I have some writing materials? I want to write down what he said."

"Of course!" Karl ushered her to his desk and furnished her with paper and a ball point pen. She began to write as he busied himself with another task. Five minutes later she said, "Will you look this over for accuracy?"

He took the paper and read it carefully. Surprised, he exclaimed, "Why, this is almost word for word, Dani!"

"Oh, not really, but pretty close, I guess. I've always had a good memory for things like that." The two of them went over her text carefully, studying each word. Finally Dani said, "It's not enough but I'll get down everything he says, and sooner or later he'll give something away."

"You have a fine mind." Karl smiled. "I trust you'll be free again soon to use it."

All day long the message seemed to hang in the air, like an invisible fog, dampening their spirits and carrying grim foreboding. They all seemed inhibited, even to the point of ignoring it, until finally the thing would not be contained, and they dissected every word and quarreled over its portent. The idea of guilt seemed ominous, and Sid broke out once, crying, "Why, *everybody's* guilty of something! Everybody in the whole world! What does this nut want?"

Wednesday passed, creeping by slowly. They ate three meals, read, and exercised; Lonnie and Sid even played their favorite game, Monopoly. Alex took a quick shower—for the first time in anyone's memory—and went to bed at nine o'clock. The rest followed shortly.

Dani lay awake, her mind humming like a hard disk,

but she got nowhere at all. After what seemed like an eternity, she finally drifted off, only to awake with a start as people moved across the floor, talking excitedly.

"What is it?" she cried out in sudden fear.

"The box! It's comin' down!" Candi cried. "Come on!"

By the time Dani got to the rec room, everybody else was already there, staring at the roof. A high-pitched whine came to her ears, and she asked, "What's that, Lonnie?"

"Winch—lettin' something down."

"Never got anything this late," Betty said doubtfully. "Be like the scum to send our supplies down in the middle of the night."

"And it wouldn't be another prisoner," Karen said. "The bunks are all filled." They all watched carefully as a large, rectangular, ghostly box slowly descended into the lighted area of the silo.

"Stand back!" Vince commanded, reaching up and guiding it down. At once the whine stopped, and they all crowded in closer. "We got a new playmate," Vince said. "Anybody know him?" He asked the question perfunctorily, and Dani saw from the faces of those in front of her that the answer was no.

She stepped from behind Bix, who had crowded in front of her, and looked down at the face of the man strapped firmly inside the box. The shock she got reminded her of a time when she had been struck in the pit of the stomach during a volleyball game.

Standing there, she felt lightheaded for a few seconds. Quietly she answered Vince, "Yes. I know him." She looked up into the startled faces around her and said, "His name is Benjamin Davis Savage."

6
The First Confession

As soon as Dani had identified Savage, Holtz asked sharply, "How do you know him, Danielle? Who is he?"

"He's one of my investigators," she explained, not missing the suspicious look in Holtz's eyes. "We can talk about that later. Karen—"

Karen Sanderson bent over, lifted one of Savage's eyelids, and peered carefully at the eye. "Concussion," she said tersely. "I don't know how bad—but that cut has got to be sutured. Get him out of this thing and put him on the table, while I get my bag. Put a pad of some kind over the table, and be careful when you move him."

While Vince removed the straps, Betty ran to get some blankets. She came back quickly and arranged them deftly. Vince directed, "Give me a lift, Lonnie. Holtz, you and Rosie take his other side." Carefully they lifted the injured man to the table, and Betty eased a pad under his head. "He took a pretty bad beating," Vince observed as he looked down at the bloody face. "But I

119

guess he got in a couple of licks, from the looks of his hands."

As Karen hurried back, stepping up to Ben's head, Dani noticed that his hands were raw, the knuckles scraped and bleeding. Then Karen said, "I'd be afraid to give him any kind of anesthesia, with that concussion—which is a good thing, because I don't have any. Vince, you'll have to hold his head steady. I don't think he'll feel anything, but just in case."

"Well, okay, Doc," Canelli said uneasily.

"All of you, move back," Karen said. "The rest of you men take one of these couches into the women's room, close to the heater. Fix up some sort of light by it, so I can see. I want to be close to him until he wakes up, and it gets too noisy out here. Somebody get some water; boil it and put it in a pan."

"I'll do it," Dani said quickly. She had a queasy feeling as she looked down at the gaping wound in Ben's forehead. Scurrying off, she boiled the water. Just as Karen was straightening up, she brought it to her.

"Put it down here, Dani," the doctor commanded tersely. Taking a sterile pad from her kit, she dipped it in the water and began sponging the wound.

Dani kept her eyes averted, but asked, "Is it very bad?"

"Not unless he's got some internal damage. We'll check for bruises when we get him moved."

She worked quickly, and ten minutes later Dani was in the women's quarters, standing over the couch that the men had set up. Holtz had rigged a light, which hung to one side. When the men had left, Karen said, "Now let's see if he's got any bad bruises. If his body is as bad as his face, we've got problems." Moving to the end of the couch, she unbuttoned the worn suede jacket and commanded, "Lift him up, Dani—you and Rachel. I'll try to keep his head from moving too much."

Dani and Rachel, one on each side of the couch, lifted Ben and, being as gentle as they could, pulled the coat off. "Now the shirt," Karen said, and they removed that. "Ugly bruise over his kidney," she muttered, shaking her head. "Let him down easy."

They carefully put him down, and Karen released her grip and stepped to look down at his chest. Rachel said softly. "What a *mensch!*"

"If that means 'What a man!'" said Karen with a faint smile, "I agree with you." She indicated the swelling muscles that rounded out the chest of the unconscious man and shook her head. "You find that sort of development in swimmers or gymnasts." Carefully she ran her hands over his side. "I don't think he has any ribs broken." Then she ordered, "Pull his slacks off."

Dani stared at her, and a flush rose to her cheeks. Karen saw her expression and laughed. "Guess that sounded a little rough, Dani. I forgot I wasn't talking to a hardened medical student. Let me do it." She stepped forward, removed Savage's trousers skillfully, and after a quick look said, "All right, get him covered up—lots of cover!"

Rachel and Dani found extra blankets and placed them on the unconscious man.

Karen said, "We'll have to watch him. He could kick that cover off and get pneumonia. We don't need anything like *that!*"

Dani said, "I can watch him, Karen."

"All right. If he comes out of it, wake me up." Karen and Rachel went to bed at once, for the clammy cold bit at the flesh. Dani pulled two of the straight chairs over in front of the couch, made herself a facsimile of a bed, and wrapped up in her blankets.

Betty and Candi came in, took a look at Dani at her place by Savage, then quickly went to bed. Rachel said, "Give me a call when you freeze out, Dani. I'll take a turn."

"All right, Rachel."

Dani shut her eyes and pulled the blankets under her legs as tightly as she could, then spent half an hour trying to convince herself that she was going to sleep. But minute noises kept jarring her awake. The wind rose and fell, seeming to travel around the silo, brushing at the sides with ghostly fingers, making a very low and quite unnerving keening noise. A deep groaning startled her as the entire structure seemed to give under the power of the wind, but she shook her head, knowing it had to be her imagination. The sounds of a man coughing came to her; then one of the women—she couldn't tell which—uttered a muffled cry that rose and then broke off abruptly. Worst of all were the faint *scurrying* noises, for Betty had informed her that rats inhabited the silo.

She shifted from side to side on the hard chairs, keeping a close guard on Savage, but he never seemed to move. Once he moved his head from side to side and mumbled something, but he stilled when she went to him. As she tried to relax, she kept thinking of how inadequate she was. *What made me ever think I could be a missionary—or even a detective? I'm a hothouse flower!* Finally she dropped off into a fitful sleep.

". . . Timing isn't right. . . . Florrie? . . . Didn't make it! . . ." Ben spoke in muffled tones, and had thrown off all his blankets. Awakening with a stab of fear, Dani got up quickly, nearly collapsing on legs that had no feeling. She snatched up the blankets and tried to keep them on Ben, but he kept thrashing, throwing his limbs about and moaning. A wild swing of his hand caught Dani across the mouth, and the pain made her bat her eyes, but she captured the hand and managed to get his arms under the cover. She kneeled beside him, holding him down. Suddenly he turned his head toward her, and his eyes opened. "Florrie?" he asked thickly. "Florrie?" His face was only inches away from her, and she saw that his eyes were not clear. He called for Florrie again, and this time his voice rose in what sounded like fear. "Florrie . . . ?"

"Yes," Dani whispered. "It's Florrie. Now, try to rest, Ben."

At the sound of her voice, he lay still. His eyes were fixed on her, but she saw that he was not awake. As he said, one more time, "Florrie!" the eyes closed, and she felt his body relax.

Sitting there, watching his face, Dani wondered how he had found her—and *why*. Ben had simply dropped into her life, and she'd been terribly unfair at their last meeting. The memory came to her sharply, and she bit her lip, aggravated for she disliked being wrong. *He could at least have told me what he was doing*, she thought bitterly. *What else would anyone think—seeing him half dressed in his room with that woman?* Somehow that did not comfort her, and she shifted uneasily on the hard chair. How would she face him when he came out of unconsciousness?

He grew quieter, and she sat there in the hollow silence, looking down at the tough face on the pillow. The faint light highlighted the stark planes of his features, darkening the deep-set eyes and emphasizing the pale scar by his mouth. His coarse black hair had fallen over his broad brow, and she reached out unconsciously to brush it back.

"I guess you know him pretty good, huh?"

Dani started, jerking her hand back, and turned quickly to see Candi, who stood back a few steps in the darkness, watching. She came forward, clutching a blue woolen robe to her chin, and sat down in the other chair. The dim light softened the hard lines of her face, making her look much younger and somehow more gentle. "You in love with him?" she asked, when Dani didn't answer her first question.

Dani shook her head quickly. "No. Nothing like that."

Candi studied the still face of Savage, and a wistful quality entered her voice. "He's got kind of a tough face." She leaned closer and after a while added, "But he don't look *mean* tough—you know?"

"Maybe I do." Dani studied the face of the other woman. "You're right, Candi—there's no meanness in Ben. He's stubborn as a bulldog, and he talks tough, but underneath all that, he's gentle." She did reach out then and smoothed the unruly hair from his forehead. "You must know men pretty well, to see that in Ben."

Candi flinched slightly, and a trace of bitterness crept into her tone as her low voice went on, "Yeah, I wish I didn't know them so good!"

Suddenly Dani felt the same helplessness she'd experienced when she'd talked to Frank Wilson. As she looked at Candi's weary expression, she wanted to reach out and comfort her, but, *What do I know about her kind of suffering?* she asked herself. *She's no older than I am—but she's been stripped of every precious thing a woman ought to have! How can I understand that kind of pain?*

The silence grew heavy, and finally with a desperate effort, Dani cleared her throat and said carefully, "Candi, have you ever been to church?"

"Don't talk to me about *church!*" Candi's head went back, and her eyes glinted with anger. "You want to know who got me started living the way I do? It wasn't some fast-talking, wild dude—it was a member in the church my folks went to!" She got up and ran toward the door, her slippers making a rapid tapping on the hard concrete.

Dani sat there, tears of frustration welling up in her eyes. Karen was there beside her. She had heard the harsh words of Candi and remarked quietly, "You can't win them all, Dani."

"I can't win *any* of them, it looks like." Dani wiped her eyes quickly, then got up and went to her cot. She lay down, covered herself with the blankets, and waited for a morning she dreaded.

"He's coming out of it!"

Karen bustled out the door and came over to where the others were eating lunch. Her face wore a slight smile, as if she'd won some sort of victory. "Dani, he knows you, so it might be better if you were there when he wakes up."

Dani tossed her ham sandwich on the table. As she hastened toward the door, Karen directed, "Don't let him get up right away, and don't be surprised if he acts peculiar."

"All right." She passed into the women's quarters. Ben was moving restlessly, and his eyelids fluttered. Sitting down on the chair beside him, she took his hand and said quietly, "Ben? Ben—can you hear me?"

The eyelids blinked, opening wide, and she saw at once

that they were far more alert than they had been the previous night. It was typical of him, she thought as she held his hand firmly, that he would stare at her steadily, concentrating on her features. She saw recognition come to him, and asked, "How do you feel?"

He gave his shoulders a tentative shake, then looked around and licked his lips. "I'm okay," he answered in a husky voice. She dropped his hand and poured him a glass of water.

"Drink some of this—in little swallows."

He pulled himself into a sitting position, closing his eyes for a moment; when he was upright, he opened them and took the glass. He took a few sips, wet his lips, and studied her. A small smile touched his mouth, and he spoke in a clearer voice, "We've got to stop meeting like this."

His spirit lifted her own, and she smiled briefly, "Ben, I want to say something. Are you awake enough to understand me?" He nodded, and she blurted out, "I—I was wrong—about firing you." Her cheeks burned, and she went on very rapidly, "As soon as I read your report, I knew what a fool I'd been. I went right to your room, but you were gone. I was going to find you . . . , but I got into this mess." She swallowed and almost whispered, "Please, forgive me!"

His dark eyebrows went up slightly, and he studied her thoughtfully. Then he shrugged. "Why, I didn't think too much about it, Miss Ross." Her words seemed to have caught him off guard, and he dropped his eyes, studying the glass in his hand as if he hoped to find some sort of explanation there. Finally he took another sip of the water, paused, and added, "I guess I'm so used to things fouling up, I just expect the worst. Guess that's why I like machinery better than people. You can figure out what a machine will do."

"I know. When you told Dad about the air conditioner, you said, 'Most mechanical things can be fixed.' "

He stared at her and asked, "You ever *forget* anything? Have to be careful what I say around you." He looked around the silo carefully. "Well, are we all alone in here?" She explained the situation, and he said, "Yeah, give me my pants and you can take me in to meet the folks."

Dani handed the slacks to him and turned her back as he put his feet on the floor. "Are you sure you feel strong enough?" She handed him his shirt, and while he put it on, knelt and guided his feet into his loafers. As she rose, he stood up swayed slightly, and nodded. "Sure."

Dani held onto his arm. As soon as they walked through the door into the rec room, Karen came toward them, looked carefully into Savage's eyes, then smiled. "All clear," she pronounced. "Come and sit down."

"This is Karen Sanderson," Dani said. "*Doctor* Sanderson, I might add. Come along and meet everyone."

As soon as he was seated, Rachel brought a steaming cup with a spoon in it and put it before him. "Chicken soup," she explained with a smile. "Guaranteed by my mother to cure anything that ails you."

Savage nodded, took the spoon, and sampled it. "Thanks."

Dani addressed them all: "This is Ben Savage. He's on the staff of my father's firm, Ross Investigation Agency." Sid Valentine straightened his back at that, and Vince seemed to find that information interesting, for he gave Savage a hard look. Dani went around the circle, naming names, and Savage's hazel eyes fastened on each face. She ended, "While Ben finishes eating, Karl, would you give him a rundown on this situation?"

Holtz nodded and began to go over the details of the silo, pointing out the difficulties of escape but giving his view that the most pressing thing was to find out why they were there and who had abducted them.

"I can tell you who—but not why," Ben announced when Holtz finished. A murmur of surprise broke across the room.

Dani asked instantly, "Did you run into him, trying to find me, Ben?"

Savage reached up and touched the stitches on his forehead. Nodding and smiling slightly he corrected her, "I guess he ran into me, would be closer to the way it was."

"Who is it, Savage?" Vince burst out, and Holtz said, "Yes, what is his name?"

"Maxwell Stone." Ben's words made little impression, and he nodded. "I never heard of him either, but he's quite well-known in some circles."

"Did you talk to the maniac?" Alex Morrow demanded.

"Never saw him." Savage looked around and requested, "If I could have some milk. . . ." When Betty placed the glass in his hand, Ben took a long pull at the drink, then said, "It was like this. Miss Ross disappeared, and the law wasn't making much headway. I'd gone to Florida, but Miss Ross's father has connections down there. He got a message to me, so I flew back to look into it.

"Her note said that she'd gone to Kenner, but the police found her car at another town, twenty miles away. I started snooping around, and after talking to half the population of Kenner, I found a kid who said he'd seen her car at the old airstrip. He also said he'd seen the aircraft that landed there."

He took another sip of milk, and a smile touched his lips as he added, "I've been a cop for a while, and one thing always goes: You never *stumble* onto a good lead; you dig it out a piece at a time, and usually it takes forever. But that kid lived right across from the strip, and he'd gone up to look at the plane. The guy flying it gave him a cussing and ran him off. But the boy took one thing with him."

"Let me guess," Dani said. "Registration number 122454 on a blue Beechcraft."

"Got it the first time!" Ben exclaimed. "Well, that was it, really. Once I had that number, all I had to do was trace the plane. It was registered to Alpha Financial Corporation, located in Little Rock, Arkansas, and it turned out to be a front for Maxwell Stone. I never heard of him, but a friend in the FBI told me plenty. Stone's a real right-wing political radical. Made a bundle in patent medicines years ago and invested it all pretty well, so now he's got millions—maybe even billions."

"Wait a minute!" Alex exclaimed. "I've read about him, I think. There was a news story, about two years ago, about paramilitary groups in this country. Most of them have gone back into the woods—and Stone was one of them."

"That's your man." Ben nodded. "My friend said they had several filing cabinets filled with information, but Stone's clean. No violations." The detective shrugged and leaned back in his chair. "Stone has what amounts to a private army in the Ozarks, up north in Arkansas. I guess he doesn't have tanks yet, but any other weapons, you can bet he's got—and a highly trained bunch of mercenaries who know how to use them."

"What does he want an army for?" Bix asked.

"Who knows?" Ben shrugged. "A lot of guys like Stone sign up for the Rangers in the corps—or go fight in one of the hot little wars down south. A magazine or two caters to them, filled with stories about weapons, along with the latest news of a nice war where a Rambo type can get some action. But Stone has got the money to play soldier in a big-time way."

"I guess you rushed into that without bothering to wait for help?" Dani asked.

"Well, I was a little impulsive." Ben looked sheepish and shook his head. "I was just going to snoop around, but when I flew over Stone's camp, I spotted a blue Beechcraft parked on the landing strip. So I landed at a little town forty miles away and sneaked back." He shook his head again, saying sadly, "I've lost a step, I guess. Once I could have walked through the lines of Stone's patrols with no problem, but they caught me."

"They treated you pretty rough," Canelli spoke up.

"Well, I had about five of them covered, but they called up reinforcements."

"Now that Dad knows all this—about Maxwell, I mean—he'll raise the roof!" Dani's eyes were bright, and optimism lifted her mood. Savage, however, said nothing, so she asked sharply, "Ben? You *did* tell him about all this?"

"I was going to pin it all down first—but it didn't work that way."

"And you had the agency card in your billfold." Dani moaned. "So they knew you were looking for me!"

"Oh, *great!*" Morrow groaned. "Just what we needed—a dumb cop to throw away the only chance we've had!"

"Aw, lay off, Morrow!" Lonnie snapped. "The guy was tryin'!"

"That's enough talk, anyway," Karen ordered firmly. She looked at Ben and said, "You can stay up for an hour, if you feel like it, but no more." She would hear no argument, but took Ben's arm, guided him to one of the upholstered chairs, and plumped him down on it. After she'd directed the men to put the couch in the men's section, she stood guard for the hour.

As they moved the couch, Ben asked Karen, "No extra bunks?"

"Just the twelve. I guess you're unexpected company." She shook her head. "Sorry you got roped into this mess." She shot an inquisitive look at him. "How much chance do we have, Ben? Of somebody finding us?"

"Not much." He shook his head. "Stone is smart, and I've made matters worse. He'll shut all the doors now, and I guess the plane was his only slipup."

Karen said, "We'll be all right. You must think a lot of Dani, to risk your life for her."

Savage's lean face revealed little. He only commented, "I work for her."

At breakfast the next morning, Karen told Ben, "You look much better."

"Feel better." Savage looked around and asked, "Is everybody always this tense at breakfast?" Most of the inmates seemed jumpy, and few were talking much.

"No. We're all a little keyed up this morning." She told him about the ultimatum and admitted, "I guess we're all hoping someone else will confess—but nobody will, of course. Who could know what that madman wants?" When Lonnie brought their food and Rachel followed with the coffee, they began to eat. But before they had finished, the loudspeaker blared loudly, "All of you will take your places!"

Holtz whispered to Ben, "Maybe it would be better if Stone doesn't realize we know his identity."

"He settled that when he put me in here. *I* know him, and he'll know I'd tell you."

That proved accurate, for as soon as they moved in front of the camera, Stone said, "Mr. Savage is with us, I see. I trust you are not feeling too bad after your—ah, *encounter* with my security force?"

"Just peachy," Ben answered evenly. "How's the tall guy with no front teeth?"

After a momentary break, Stone replied, "He is being taken care of." Then his voice grew stronger, and he entoned, "I will now hear the confession of anyone who has the wisdom to make one."

No one moved. Alex coughed abruptly, but otherwise everyone was very quiet.

"Very well, if we cannot do it one way, we will do it another." Stone said. "Eileen Patterson, come to the front of the group!"

They all looked around, and Holtz said in a puzzled tone, "Eileen Patterson? There is no one here by that name."

Dani had heard a small gasp to her right. She turned to see that Candi's face was pale and her lips were trembling. Dani said quietly, "You don't have to say anything, Candi—"

But Candi bit her lower lip, then threw her shoulders back and spoke loudly, "That's my real name! What about it?" She took several steps forward and defiantly stared up at the blank eye of the camera. "Why don't you come out like a man, from wherever you are? Are you scared?"

"Give Miss Patterson a chair," Stone commanded. "This may take some time." Sid moved to get a chair, and Candi sat down at once, as though her legs had given way. Beneath her heavy makeup lay a dead pallor, and Dani whispered to Karen, "She can't take much of this!"

What followed sickened Dani and the others. Stone began, "All you have to do is confess to the crime you *know* you are here for."

"What crime?" Candi cried. "I ain't done *nothing*!"

"What about the night of June the twenty-sixth, two years ago?" Stone asked. "You were arrested, tried, and found guilty on charges of prostitution, according to the record."

"I—I was framed for that!" Candi said. She pulled a handkerchief from her pocket and began twisting it. "I was an actress in a show, and they pulled us all in—"

"An *actress*, you say? Then give us a few lines, say, from *Romeo and Juliet*." He paused, but Candi could only look down helplessly. "While you try to recall a few lines for Romeo, I have here a list of similar charges," Stone droned on. "Sixteen, to be exact. You cannot expect me to believe you were framed for *all* of them?" Stone waited, but Candi could not answer. "And you did serve a year at Louisiana Correctional Institute for Women, on the charge of selling a controlled substance. Is that correct?"

"Yes! But that's got nothing to do with you!"

"And several years ago, you were found guilty of assault with a deadly weapon, I understand?"

"I—was just fifteen," Candi whispered, and the tears of anger and shame rolled down her cheeks, making rivulets in her makeup. "Two guys caught me on my way home. They dragged me into this alley, and I—tried to get away. One of them held a knife to my throat—said he'd kill me—I grabbed his hand, and while we were fightin', he got cut in the face! The law came, and he said I'd cut him with it—that it was *my* knife!" She began to sob, until Dani could barely hear her words. "And they sent me to reform school—"

Stone ignored her sobs. He went over every sordid detail of a hard life, and by the time Karen stepped forward and exclaimed, "That's enough!" Candi was in hysterics. Karen took her arm, saying quietly, "Come on, Candi." She led the woman away, without a backward look.

Stone said at once, "Eileen Patterson was not brought here as a result of any of the things I have brought out. It was my hope that she would realize that there is nothing that can deliver her from this place except the truth." His voice began to rise to an oratorical pitch; he spoke rapidly and even eloquently about liberty and the price that must be paid to keep it.

He ranted on for ten minutes about the men who fought for America, then added, "This country must survive, and it will! Unlike Alexander, who grieved because he had no new worlds to conquer, this nation of ours had a destiny! And it will not stop until we are the most powerful nation on the planet!"

"Stone!" Karl Holtz cried out loudly, "I have heard all this before—back in 1939. It was Adolf Hitler telling Germany we had the right to *Lebensraum*, to conquer other nations who stood in our shadow. Germany was going to rule the world. That Third Reich was to last a thousand years; where is it now? I need no new mad tyrant!"

Suddenly Stone's voice grew almost hysterical, as he screamed, "You are guilty, Holtz! You are *all* guilty. Guilty as Judas! All of you!"

He paused abruptly, and when Stone spoke again, his voice was calmer, but no less deadly. "I will give you twenty-four hours. If you do not confess, judgment will fall. Twenty-four hours!"

The speaker went dead, and once again silence blanketed the silo. Finally Rachel Gold stared at Holtz and said, "How do you like it, Commander? How does it feel to have a big Nazi type jam you in a concentration camp?" She laughed bitterly, and her voice crackled with anger as she said, "It's almost worth dying for—to see you suffer as you made the Jews suffer at Buchenwald!"

"Well, *I* don't think it's worth dying for!" Vince announced bitterly. "*Nothing* is worth dying for!"

"There had better be something worth that, Vince," Betty Orr said in a voice that wasn't quite steady. "Because, unless I miss my guess, dying is what that man has on his mind!"

7
"It's Never Too Late!"

"Hey, Rachel, when we get out of this tin can, why can't you and me party together?"

Rachel looked up from the sink, where she was scrubbing the grease out of the big frying pan, and gave Bix a scornful look. "I can't think of anything that would give me less pleasure," she answered, grunting as the ironlike clusters of dried fat resisted her efforts. "We have absolutely *nothing* in common."

Bix grinned leisurely as he dried a glass, held it up to the light critically, as if it were a precious jewel, then placed it carefully on the shelf. He was drawn to Rachel's dark beauty and intrigued by her intelligence and stubborn independence. Although he made a great show of scorning material gain, the fact that this attractive older woman had been a successful writer impressed him. He edged closer to her, put his arm around her waist, and whispered, "Aw, come on, baby! We got a lot in common. Both of us are good-looking and like the better things of life—things like this, I mean. . . ."

He leaned over and planted a kiss on her neck, and she turned to give him a freezing look. "If I ever do something really *evil*, Bix, I'll look you up and go out with you—as penance for my sin!"

Bix laughed and pulled at the corner of his droopy moustache. "Come, on, now, baby. That's another thing we got in common. You don't believe all that religious stuff about sin and hell any more than I do."

Rachel gave up on the frying pan in disgust and handed it to him—then she suddenly paused. Her expressive, dark eyes grew thoughtful. She turned suddenly and glanced across the room to where Dani and Holtz were sitting at his desk, going over a paper. She nodded at them and said, "I give you points for that one, Bix. Look at them, the Nazi and the Christian! They've got one thing in common—they both pushed the Jews around, down through history."

"Ah, the German's not so bad, and the preacher lady is luscious!" Bix gave the pan a careless swipe with the dish towel and stowed it in the lower cabinet. Then he asked curiously, "Aren't all Jews religious? I sort of had the idea they were."

"The older ones maybe," Rachel said. "But not all of us younger Jews are. Many of us are nationalists.

"I remember," she said softly, "when I went to Jerusalem. The one thing I remember best was a soldier walking down the street, and a friend of mine, an old man who'd escaped Hitler's gas chambers, said, 'Look at that!' " I asked him what he saw, and he just said, 'A soldier with a gun—but it's a *Jewish* soldier!' " Rachel arched her back and stretched her arms high. "The new Jews have a saying, Bix: 'Never again!' "

137

"What's that mean?"

"It means that we will never be conquered again—by *anyone*." She laughed, reached out, and pulled his shaggy hair. "We do have one thing in common, Bix. We're both rebels. You against society—me against the world!"

Bix reached for her. "No," she shook her head, fending him off. "The difference between us is that one day you'll shave off your beard, take a bath, and become a respected member of the establishment—a genuine WASP. But you see, Bix, it's not so easy to stop being a Jew." Rachel sobered, and her lips grew tight. "As a matter of fact, the only way to do that, is to die." She turned and walked away from Bix, who stared at her in consternation. Finally he shrugged and moved to the table where Vince and Sid were playing poker with a deck of worn cards.

"Hey, you dudes will never believe this," he said, falling into a chair. "But I offered first rights on my body to Rachel—and she turned me down."

Canelli grinned at him, his white teeth gleaming against his olive skin. "Maybe I better give you lessons in how to handle a broad," he said. "Or maybe a demonstration. That's a good-looking dame. Just needs to loosen up."

Bix shook his head. "Nope, I don't think even *you* could break that one down, Vince. She ain't like Candi and most other women. All she wants is to enjoy being a Jew—and maybe knock off the commander."

"I ain't too keen on Holtz myself." Vince shrugged. "But he's good at gettin' things done. I give him that."

Bix looked over toward the camera and shook his head. "I don't like the way the looney talked about judgment. What'd you reckon he meant by that?" Since neither Sid nor Vince bothered to answer, Bix went on, "I don't like it! It's like living on death row!"

Valentine suddenly threw down his cards, his sharp-featured face white with anger. He rasped out, "Shut your face, you lousy punk! What do you know about anything?"

Vince watched carefully as Sid suddenly clamped his lips shut and began to pick up the cards with trembling fingers. The big man's eyes narrowed, and he said softly, "You got to watch yourself, Sid. You give yourself away."

"What's *that* supposed to mean?"

Canelli leaned back in his chair and considered the older man, then shrugged. "You been in the pen, Sid. I've always known that. Now I know you were on the row." Valentine opened his mouth to answer, but Vince said impassively, "Nothing to me, Sid. I don't care what you've done. But maybe you ought to tell Stone about it. Might be the confession he's looking for."

"You'd like that, wouldn't you, Canelli?" Sid snapped. "Throw me to him in a minute, if it'd save your hide, wouldn't you?"

"Sure I would, Sid." Vince grinned wolfishly, "And you'd do the same to me—and so would the punk here," he added, nodding at Bix, who was staring at them with big eyes. "That's my philosophy—look out for number one. And anyone who says he's different is a liar." There was no doubting the callous cruelty in the eyes of Canelli, and he laughed suddenly. "Come on, let's go tell the commander your big secret."

"Wait a minute—!" Sid cried out in alarm. He scrambled to his feet and ran to grab Canelli's arm, but the big man just grinned at him and pulled him to where Holtz sat.

139

"Hey, Commander," he said loudly. "I think I might have a clue. You two private eyes might give this a listen. Sid here has just confessed he was in the row—and you don't go to the chair for parking violations, do you now?"

Valentine tried to break free, but Vince held him easily with his massive hand and laughed. "I been in the pen, too, so I'm confessing. But I had better sense than to draw murder one! Maybe this is our boy, do you think? Maybe we can throw ol' Sid to Stone, and he'll let the rest of us out."

"That wouldn't bother you—sacrificing a friend?" Holtz asked, giving Vince a steady look.

"Not a bit—and don't any of you get so pious, because you'd do the same thing." Vince looked straight at Dani and grinned. "Even *you*, Reverend. You'd do whatever you had to do to save that pretty hide of yours!"

Dani returned his gaze but refused to argue. "I guess one never knows about a thing like that—until he has to make the choice. But you're wrong about Stone taking Sid in exchange for the rest of us. He'll never do that."

"How can you know that?" Vince demanded.

"Don't you know the penalty for kidnapping in this country, Vince? A capital offense—and capital punishment is coming back into fashion," Dani said clearly. Out of the corner of her eye she saw that Vince's loud voice had drawn every ear, and she wanted to make a point. "If I got out of here, I'd go straight to the feds, Vince, and I'd do my best to put Mr. Maxwell Stone in the chair. Probably I couldn't do it, because it's hard to put a billion dollars on death row. But for a man like Stone, it would be better to die than to lose his power, to become just one more number in a prison."

Vince nodded. "You got that right, Ross—money talks!" Then he cocked his head and asked, "You saying that we're never going to get out of this place?"

Dani nodded slowly. "I think you know that, Vince. We *all* know it. We've just been whistling in the dark, trying not to mention it—the way we don't mention a terminal disease in the presence of someone who has it." Dani swung her head around and saw that her words had touched a nerve in most of the listeners.

"It's not *fair!*" Alex Morrow yelped. His round face had turned pale, and his voice was high and unsteady as he leaped to his feet. "I've worked like a dog all my life, and now this maniac comes along and ruins it—it's not *fair!*"

He sounded like a child who'd lost his favorite toy, and Lonnie snapped at him, "You want a guarantee, buy a refrigerator!" Then he looked at Dani, his simple face filled with doubt. "If he don't want *one* of us, what *does* the nut want, Dani?"

They all waited for her answer, and Dani looked to Holtz. "The commander's been trying to tell you that for days. Stone doesn't care what we've done as individuals. He doesn't care if Sid's been on death row or if I've killed twenty people." She took a deep breath and said, "It's something that we've *all* done—done as a group."

"We've never even *seen* one another!" Alex insisted. "How could we all have done something together?"

"That is what we have to find out, Alex," Holtz said quickly. "We've got only one chance—and that's to find out what Stone thinks we've done. Then we can talk about it with him."

An argument broke out at once, ending only when the group separated. Savage had said nothing, but now, as he

141

sat with Holtz and Dani, he spoke, "Karl, we're not deal-ing with a rational man. No matter what anyone *says*, he'll never let us out of this place. Unless someone traces us here, our only hope is to bust out." He got to his feet and stared around the silo, his muscles tense.

Holtz dropped his head, then lifted his eyes. "Ben, dur-ing the war I had a friend named Leo Horstmann. He was in the submarine service with me. But Leo is now at the bottom of the North Atlantic. He went down in his vessel the *Swordfish*. It was his coffin." Then Holtz looked at the two and said quietly, "Leo Horstmann has as much chance of escaping from the *Swordfish* as any of us have of break-ing out of this place!"

"We'll get out," Savage insisted. There was a stubborn set to his chin, and he stood there poised, his eyes defiant as he stared up into the darkness. "There's always a way."

"This isn't a movie," Holtz commented sadly. "It's life."

"Any prison one man can invent, another can find a way out of!"

"Miss Dani, if you get a chance, try to talk to Alex. He's in pretty bad shape." Rosie's dark face was filled with concern, and he shook his head as he handed her the coffee she sought. "After Stone made his little speech, seems like all the starch went out of him. He went to his bunk, and I tried to cheer him up, but he won't say noth-ing."

"I guess we're all a little stunned, Rosie."

"Sure—but I reckon a little Christian encouragement is what the man needs. I sure am glad we got us a preacher in here!"

Dani shook her head as he smiled and left. She was

exhausted and felt grimy. The very thought of trying to reach out to Alex rose up like a mountain, and she rebelled inwardly. *I'm so tired! How can I help anyone when I'm practically wiped out myself?* Dim and indistinct at first, a thought formed, then focused in the form of a verse—one that had never meant much to her: "And the whole multitude sought to touch him: for there went virtue out of him, and healed them all."

Dani suddenly thought, *Why, that's why Jesus grew so tired at times! Helping people did it! Every time He healed a person, it drained him of strength—and that's what real ministry is.* Now the wry thought came to her as she sat in the cold silo, wrestling with her feelings, *Well, Danielle Ross—I think this cold hunk of steel—not Africa—is your mission field!*

Friday night passed, and Saturday morning slowly moved into the steel cylinder. Dani got up early, shivering in the cold, and washed her face. After brushing her hair quickly, she dressed in an electric-blue running suit with a huge yellow lightning bolt across the chest. It looked tacky, but was the warmest thing she had found. She pulled on heavy wool socks, donned a pair of Nikes, picked up her Bible and notebook, and moved past the others, who were still asleep.

After grabbing two doughnuts, and pouring a cup of coffee, she started for the table. Alex, slumped in a chair, stared at the wall. She had not seen him all day Friday, and it was one of the few times all day when privacy would be possible. A strange feeling came to her, for before falling asleep, she had offered God a half-defiant prayer: *Lord, I will try to talk to Alex, if I have a chance to do it alone.* That seemed unlikely at the time, and she had felt

143

the burden leave her—but now she had no choice but to go and try.

"Hi, Alex," she said cheerfully as she moved to stand beside his chair. "Let me get you some coffee." He shook his head, but she said firmly, "I hate to eat alone!" Quickly she went to get another cup of coffee and two doughnuts.

Listlessly, he began to nibble at a doughnut, not seeming to listen as she sat there making light conversation. Alex looked wan and drained in the dim light, and Dani realized how little she knew about him. Slowly the rare privacy and the intimacy of their talk caused him to open up. He was divorced and spoke bitterly of his wife, insisting she had turned the two children against him. His business life had been very successful; he had built a small furniture factory into a large one that had expanded sales all over the Southwest. But material benefits had not satisfied him.

Finally it came out that he had alienated his wife by his extramarital affairs. He added bitterly, "They weren't really that much fun, Dani.

"I guess you've got the picture. I've made a mess of my life, and there's no way to fix it."

Dani said carefully, "I think everybody hits the place where they feel like that, Alex. I know I have."

He looked at her in surprise, then shook his head. "You say that, but it's not so." His eyes were bleak, and he looked old and defeated. "You've got religion, and I'm glad for you. But it's too late for me." Tears welled up in his eyes, and he averted his face, pulling a handkerchief out of the pocket of his robe. Wiping his face, he cleared his throat and said, "No, I've missed it, Dani."

"It's *never* too late, Alex!" Dani said quietly. "Would you just let me read some Scriptures?" He paused so long that she thought he was about to refuse, but he shrugged and nodded.

She opened her Bible and began to read, choosing Scriptures from the gospels, which presented Jesus meeting the needs of people. As he listened, she read of the Lord opening the eyes of the blind, healing the sick, and even raising the dead. She thought a spark of interest lit his eyes. Then she began to read a few verses from the epistles of Paul, setting forth the doctrine of Jesus as the Saviour of the world. He stopped her once, asking what a verse meant, and she explained it carefully.

Finally Lonnie came out of the sleeping area, followed by Vince. As the two broke the silence, Alex seemed to withdraw. "We'll talk some more, Alex," Dani said quickly. "Maybe you'd like to read my Bible awhile."

He refused, but she knew that it was because he didn't want the others to see what he would consider a weakness. Nevertheless, she felt a thrill of joy as she went to help Betty with breakfast, for she felt that somehow Alex had been touched and helped.

The day passed slowly, and finally at noon, Vince looked around the tables and said loudly, "Well, it's twenty-four hours since Stone threatened us, and nothing's happened yet. I guess he was just talking." A crooked grin crossed his face.

Nobody challenged him, but an air of restraint hovered over the group all afternoon. More than once, Dani caught herself glancing at the silent speaker on the wall. She spent most of the afternoon with Holtz, going over his endless lists, and was glad to stop when dinnertime came.

"We don't have to wonder what's for dinner tonight," she said as the two of them moved to the table. The smell of frying fish was strong, and going to the kitchen, she saw that Rachel and Betty had prepared hush puppies and French fries to complete the fish supper.

Karen came to the table and frowned. "Betty, Alex doesn't need to eat fried fish. His stomach is in terrible shape. . . ."

Betty gave her a look of irritation. "Why didn't you say so earlier?"

"I'm sorry, but I just forgot—and he won't police his own diet. Could you fix him something light?"

Betty shook her head, then said grumpily, "He can have an omelet—but he'll have to wait until I have time to fix it."

Karen said, "You go on with the fish, Betty. I can't cook much, but I can make an omelet."

Rachel said, "Karen, make that omelet big enough for two. I don't want fish tonight. My stomach's been upset."

Karen plunged in, banging bowls and breaking eggs, and by the time Dani had served the others their fish, she had mixed the omelet and given it to Betty, who cooked it quickly and slid it onto a plate. Karl had come to the serving bar, and picked it up saying, "It looks good, Betty. I'll take it to Alex."

"Put half of it on a plate for Rachel," she ordered. He divided it and carried out the two plates.

After supper, the conversation at each table made a pleasant hum. Alex complained about not getting any fish, and Rachel patted his hand. "I've got two candy bars left from those we got three days ago, Alex. I think we deserve them."

"Oh, I wouldn't take your candy, Rachel!" he protested.

She laughed and said, "I'll bet you will! Everybody

knows about that sweet tooth of yours!" She got up and left the room, and when she came back, gave him a Snickers bar, which he began to unwrap at once. She stood there with an odd look on her face, then said, "I had three left. Here, Herr Holtz, you take this one."

Everyone stared at her in amazement, and she looked around at their faces. "The Bible says to love your enemies, doesn't it, Dani? And if I remember right it says if you give to them, it'll pour coals of fire on their heads." She tossed the candy bar to Holtz, saying, "There's your coal, Holtz. I hope it burns your brains out!"

Holtz caught the bar, gave her a long look, then said, "Sometimes it's more blessed to *receive* than it is to *give*. Thank you, Rachel." He told Dani later, "I wanted to throw that bar in her face, but that was what she expected me to do! So I ate it to spite her."

Dani and Rachel did the dishes. When they moved out of the kitchen, they joined the others, who were listening to Lonnie and Bix engage in an argument about animals. The two got louder, and it was obvious that neither of them knew much about the subject. Basically Lonnie was saying that animals are stupid, and Bix vehemently insisted that they were *not*. None of the others cared much, but after a heavy supper, they were all sitting back and listening lazily.

"Why, you dumb redneck!" Bix shouted at Lonnie. "Didn't you ever see a sheepdog work?"

"No, and you haven't either, you hippie punk!" Lonnie snapped back. "I been around animals all my life—and you ain't never been out in the woods once!"

"Well, maybe not, but I've seen movies, and those dogs

147

are smart! And what about how they train all kinds of animals, like at a circus? Why, all those animals, even elephants, keep time to music! That's not dumb! I'm a musician, and it's hard enough for humans to keep time, I can tell you! So if animals can do it, they're not dumb!"

"You've got that wrong, Bix." Savage spoke so seldom that everyone turned to stare at him. He was sitting at the table with Holtz, Valentine and Canelli, and he was smiling as he said, "I know it *looks* like that, Bix, but it doesn't work that way. You'd freak out if you saw how they train those big horses the equestrians ride. They tie a can to the horse's tail, they fire off guns, rattle a ratchet—anything to make a lot of noise—and the reason for all that is time."

"I don't get that, Ben," Canelli said.

"The circus lives on time and by split seconds. Every performer spends years developing that beat, and the people on the horses have to have the same beat as the horse, or they'd break their necks. A good ring horse is the performer's platform, and he has to keep a steady beat. And that beat never changes."

Ben's face was pensive, and he seemed not to notice that he was talking to an audience. "The tent may fall in, a bomb may go off, a flyer may fall from the top—but if that rosinback is the right kind of ring horse, he'll keep plugging away until his man says to stop." Then he halted abruptly, glanced around the room, and seemed embarrassed. "Well, anyway—it's the band that keeps time to the horses, Bix, and not the other way around. And when you see the elephants do the hootchy-kootchy, why, they're *leading* the band. Those animals will do their thing, no matter if the band plays or not."

Vince stared at him and voiced what they were all thinking. "You worked in a circus, huh?"

The answer came slowly, reluctantly. "For a little while."

Holtz said sharply, "That's not on your list of jobs, Ben."

Savage shrugged, and a stubborn look came over his face. "I guess I forgot."

It sounded weak to all of them. Holtz looked angrily at him and said in a harsh tone, "I don't see how you can forget a thing like that—"

At that moment, a cry of pain interrupted him, and Holtz looked around to see Alex, who had staggered into the room. He was holding his stomach, and his mouth hung wide open. "My—stomach!" he cried. "It's on fire! Help me . . . !" He suddenly fell to the floor, curving in a fetal position, and Karen rushed to his side.

When she tried to get him to straighten out, Alex's scream made Dani's skin crawl. "Get him on the couch!" Karen ordered, and it took four men to do it, for he refused to uncoil, and they could not move him easily.

As Karen tried to get him to answer her questions, Morrow writhed on the couch in such agony that he would have fallen off if Ben and Vince had not held him. All the time he was screaming in long, womanish cries, taking in breath only to utter another scream.

"What's wrong with him?" Holtz demanded.

Karen gave him an angry look. "How should I know?" she snapped. "He's got a bad stomach—but I've never seen anything like *this*!" She stayed beside him. Finally when his screams grew fainter, she whispered urgently, "Alex, tell me where it hurts!"

He gasped and tried to speak, but could only get out,

"Stomach!—like a knife—cutting me in two!" He sobbed and doubled up again, with a fearful groan.

The next hour was a nightmare for all of them. The sick man would cry and beg for help, clutching at Karen. Then he would double up and his cries would fill the space.

"It could be appendicitis," Karen said once. "But none of the books describe it like this. Might be a gallstone, but he's not grabbing the right spot."

"He's got an ulcer, hasn't he?" Betty asked.

"Yes, but I've never heard of an ulcer—" She broke off to ask, "Rachel, are you all right?"

Rachel was standing to Dani's right; turning, Dani saw that Rachel's face was pale and her lips were blue. A fine perspiration beaded her forehead, and even as they all watched, she suddenly bent over and said, "I—I'm awful sick!"

"Put her on the other couch!" Karen said. When she was supine, the doctor asked, "Rachel, what is it?"

Rachel stared at her, pain drawing down the corners of her lips.

Karen made a quick decision. "It has to be food poisoning. They both ate that omelet and the candy bars."

"Can't be the candy bars," Karl said. "Not unless I get sick. I had one, too."

"We'll have to give them both an emetic."

"Is it in your bag?" Savage asked quickly.

"No—warm soapy water," Karen answered. A bitter expression on her lips, she shook her head, saying, "It won't be pleasant."

An hour later, Dani was sitting at one of the tables, her head buried in her arms. Karen's words had been a masterpiece of understatement! They had forced the emetic down both patients, until they gagged over and over again, yet it had had little apparent effect. Morrow had slipped into a half coma, while Rachel lay on the couch, her face like putty, but not unconscious.

Dani wanted to run into the other room and bury her face in her pillow, but nobody had left the room. She tried to shut it out of her mind, but could not. Finally she heard Karen say, "Dani . . . ?" and looked up. Karen was standing there, her eyes defeated. "Alex is dying. He's conscious—and he wants to see you."

Dani whispered, "Karen, I *can't!*" Her hands were trembling and her throat was so full she could not speak properly.

Then Rosie came to stand beside her, and putting his hand on her arm, he said gently, "Why, course you can, lady! Come along. You and me, we can pray, can't we now?"

Without Rosie, Dani would never have gone to the side of the dying man, but she got up slowly, and with his thin hand guiding her, she made her way to the couch. They both knelt by Alex.

Morrow looked frightful! His lips were pulled back from his teeth, and his eyes were sunken so that his face resembled a skull. His eyes were shut, but when she whispered his name, the eyelids slowly lifted, and he gazed at her, blindly for a moment. "Dani?" he gasped.

"Yes—yes, Alex!" she whispered. "I'm here!"

He tried to lift himself up, but a sudden spasm of pain caught him, and he fell back. He rolled his head, then looked at her. "I'm dying—help me!"

She shut her eyes, almost ready to faint, but Rosie's grip on her arm tightened, and she swallowed hard. "Remember the verses we read, Alex?" He nodded faintly, and she began telling him of God's love. Her speech was broken and faltering. More than once Dani had to choke down the sobs. Alex's hand grasped hers, and his eyes were locked on her face. Finally she said, "Remember what I said yesterday, Alex? It's never too late to ask for forgiveness. Would you ask now?"

"I—don't know how!"

"We'll help you, Rosie and I," Dani said. "Think of your children, Alex, if they'd hurt you, then came and said, 'We're sorry, Daddy, please forgive us!' you'd forgive them, wouldn't you?"

"Yes—yes!"

"God loves you better than you or I could love anyone. Remember that verse in John, 'For God so loved the world, that he gave his only begotten Son, that whosoever believeth in him should not perish, but have everlasting life.' "

The breath of the dying man seemed to grow more shallow, and his voice grew even fainter, but he nodded. "I—'member—help me!"

Dani's tears rolled off her cheeks on to the man's feeble hand, and she said, "Let's just pray, and we'll ask him to forgive you and take your pain." There was a pressure in the fingers, and she and Rosie began to pray. Soon Dani heard Alex begin to sob, but she also heard him gasp, "O God, O God, forgive me . . . !

How long she prayed, Dani never knew. She finally became aware that Rosie was pulling at her, saying, "Come on, Miss Dani. It's all right. He's done gone to be with Jesus now!"

She opened her eyes and saw that Alex's face was still

and the signs of pain had faded. There was the mark of a struggle, to be sure, but the lips were relaxed, and Rosie said, "Gone to be with Jesus—gone to his rest!"

Dani tried to rise, but her legs would not seem to work. Strong hands lifted her, moving her across to a chair, and she looked up to see that Ben was lowering her. Then she put her head back and closed her eyes, as drained and exhausted as she had ever been in her life.

Hours later, Karen lifted her head and said with a note of victory, "Rachel's pretty sick, but she's going to make it!"

Dani went to her bunk and fell on it without undressing. Even as she pulled the blankets up and was falling into a heavy slumber, the question came to her, *How could food poisoning work so quickly?*

8
Second Warning

"O death, where is thy sting? O grave, where is thy victory? The sting of death is sin; and the strength of sin is the law." Dani's voice sounded thin and hollow as she read the Scripture—the cold, damp air of the huge drum that towered over the small group muffled her words. She glanced down at the blanket that covered Morrow's body, in the rough pine box. Shivering slightly, she completed the reading: "But thanks be to God, which giveth us the victory through our Lord Jesus Christ."

Dani bowed her head, noticing that the others reacted typically. All were there except Rachel, who was too ill to get out of bed. Rosie and Karl bowed their heads at once, as did Karen and Betty—and Lonnie yanked off his green toboggan cap and shut his eyes. Vince and Sid stared straight ahead, stubbornly refusing to do more than stand in front of the body, as Dani had requested. At the very back of the circle, with her face fixed stolidly, Candi had listened to Dani's brief remarks and the Scriptures. Now, as she met Dani's gaze, something changed in her eyes, and she bowed her head. Bix tried to look unconcerned, but the strain in his smooth face had not been there before, and after glancing quickly toward Vince, he awkwardly bowed his head slightly and stared at the floor.

When Dani said, "Amen," she stepped back and turned to look at the camera. At once the distant whine of the winch came to them, seeming more ghostly than ever in the heavy cold. The line that supported the box slowly tightened, grew tense, and then the box left the floor, swaying from side to side like an enormous pendulum. As it rose to eye level, a thin shaft of light from one of the high vents fell across the body, highlighting the red checks of the wool blanket. All eyes fixed on the swaying burden as it passed out of that light and ascended slowly into the murky air of the cavernous darkness.

Eerily the body of their companion faded away, lifted into the heights, a chilling counterpoint to the usual practice of placing a casket deep in the earth. Once again a shiver ran through Dani as she stood there with her head tilted back, watching the tiny rectangle of light that marked the opening through which containers were passed. As it went through the opening, the box blocked out the light and the sound of a heavy door clanging shut followed.

"I guess that's all," Dani said quietly, and the group hastily moved away, as if fearful to remain in the area. *Like people leaving the cemetery after the ceremony*, Dani thought soberly. *Except we can't go home and get the tragedy out of our memories.*

For the next hour she tried to read her Bible, but it seemed incomprehensible. Finally Dani moved toward the door leading to the women's sleeping quarters, where she found Karen standing beside Rachel, taking her pulse and temperature. She loosed her wrist, took the thermometer out, and read it. "Well, you're back to normal," she announced. "Temperature and pulse, anyway."

"I feel pretty chewed up," Rachel responded in a small voice.

Karen stared at her, considering her words. Karen had, Dani thought, lost much sleep, and it showed in the lines around her eyes. "Try to rest, if you can't sleep."

"I'll sit beside you for a while," Dani said, and Karen nodded. She sat there for only a few minutes before Rachel drifted off, saying, "Thanks, Dani!"

She took the girl's hands and placed them under the blanket, noting how strong they were, then moved outside to the rec room, where she found Ben and Karl deep in conversation.

"How's Rachel?" Ben asked. "I thought she was going to croak, too."

"Nicely put, Savage!" Dani snapped. "Nothing like a well-turned phrase!"

He lifted one eyebrow, saying, "Sorry. I must be losing the keen edge of my highly polished urbane manner."

"Oh, shut up!" she commanded crossly. Then she laughed abruptly, adding, "I'm losing mine, too, it seems."

He remarked without emphasis, "May have found a way to bust out." They stared at him, and he continued, "You know that little wedge-shaped space to the left of the refrigerator? All filled up with mops and brooms and stuff?" They both nodded. "There's a section of the floor in there, right by the wall, that was poured out of a different batch of concrete."

Holtz considered that, then asked, "What does that mean, Ben?"

"Maybe nothing—but that mix wasn't too good. That section is pretty flaky. Maybe we can get that concrete out and tunnel under the bulkhead."

"But we have no chisels," Holtz protested. He was correct, for there were no tools at all in the silo—a deliberate omission, they all realized.

"I've got this." Ben held up a section of angle iron about a foot long. "It's part of my cot. Not very sharp, and won't hold an edge; but we've got twelve bunks, and every one of them's got four of these braces. I'll rig up something to use for a hammer, and we can start tunneling through."

Dani looked at the piece of steel and shook her head. "It'll take a long time, Ben, and you don't know what you'll hit beneath the concrete. We're in the mountains; this whole thing might be built over a rock."

"It's the only game in town, boss. If the count of Monte Cristo did it, so can we! We'll call it the 'Jericho Project.' Maybe, like Joshua, we can get these walls to fall down— even if we don't have any trumpets!"

Savage wandered away, and Dani spent most of the day with Holtz. He told her about his days as commander of a German submarine, and for the first time she understood how he stood the confines of the silo so much better than the rest of them. The silo was huge compared to the space of a submarine packed with a large crew.

Finally he grew sleepy, and she walked with him as far as the door. He paused and said, "Thank you for taking care of an old man, Danielle! God will bless you, too, for what you did for our poor friend, Alex."

"Oh, Karl, I didn't do much!"

"Yes. You helped him from this world to the next, and that is a wonderful thing." Embarrassed at the emotion he had allowed her to see, he turned away quickly.

Dani spent the rest of the day ironing clothes, reading a little, and taking a nap before dinner. The group was strained as they sat down, because the memory of Alex's death was strongly linked to the evening meal. After they finished, Karen came from the serving table saying, "No dessert tonight—just oatmeal cookies."

She passed them around. Bix took one, stared at it, then said, "I hope this is all right."

"All right?" Rachel asked. "What does that mean?"

"Well, I guess we've all been thinking about Alex," Bix said defiantly. "It wasn't no accident, the way he died."

Vince stared at him, then nodded. "The kid's right." His gaze switched to Karen, and he asked abruptly, "How about it, Doc? It was poison, wasn't it?"

Karen returned his look, and there was a stubbornness in the set of her back. "I'm not a coroner, Vince. That's what it would take to prove that he died of poison."

"But you *suspect* something of that sort, don't you, Karen?" Dani prompted. "We might as well face up to it." she added realistically. "We had a warning, and then a man died—and it was nearly *two* people."

Betty nodded emphatically. "Of *course* it was poison! What else would kill a man that quickly?" She shuddered and added, "And he didn't even know which one of us it would be!"

Dani stared at her. "What do you mean by that, Betty?"

"Why, it's obvious, isn't it?" She looked around in surprise, her plain features animated with anger. "Two people ate the omelet, and they were the only ones to be affected. The poison had to be in something that was in that omelet. It could have been the milk or cheese, but I think it was the eggs."

"Why the eggs?" Dani asked quickly.

"Because the rest of the ingredients have been here all the time, but the eggs came in that morning—three dozen."

"Did anybody get a look at the omelet that was left?" Vince demanded.

"No, because the dishes were all washed by the time Alex got sick," Betty said.

"Rachel and I washed the dishes," Dani said thoughtfully. "I don't think there was much of the omelet left, was there, Rachel?"

"No. Just a few bites that we put with the garbage."

Suddenly Sid said loudly, "Well, maybe it wasn't Stone. Maybe someone in here done it." A chorus of voices instantly rose to protest, but he insisted, "It could have been one of them women. They were all messing around in the kitchen."

Betty immediately began to argue with him, insisting it could have been somebody at the table with Alex.

"I suppose it was me!" Lonnie snapped. Then Karen, who had sat at the table with Alex, pointed out, "No way any of us could have done it without everybody noticing."

"That's enough!" Holtz's face was pale, but his voice was strong. "What a bunch of fools! I'm sure Stone is enjoying all this. We are all overwrought and devastated by the tragedy—but we must not fight among ourselves."

Holtz paused and said, "Now, was the omelet poisoned? And if so, how? We have two trained investigators with us; let's hear what they think."

Dani saw that Ben would not speak, so she shrugged, saying, "It wouldn't be too hard to put poison in an egg, would it? Just remove part of the egg with a hypodermic needle, put the poison in to take up that space, a little glue over the hole, and who would ever notice? As Betty says, Stone didn't care which one of us died. We all eat eggs, and it was just a coincidence that the poisoned one got in the omelet."

Candi cried out, "But, he could do it again—anything we eat could kill us!"

She had voiced the fear that had touched all of them, but Rosie said, "Well, my daddy was a hard-shelled Baptist preacher. He believed that whatever is gonna happen is gonna happen. He went through World War II as an infantryman, and he told me he never ducked his head once. 'If a bullet got your name on it, ain't no tree gonna save you!' he always said. So I guess I'll just do like Daddy did. If Old Man Death comes looking for old Rosie, why, he's gonna find me. So I'm gonna eat my vittles without worrying all the time about what's inside."

Dani smiled at him, saying, "I'm not sure about your thinking, Rosie, but it's better than some I've heard."

After dinner, Holtz explained Savage's plan, but the idea met with less than a groundswell of enthusiasm. Most of them looked dubious, but Vince nodded, his eyes manifesting a new hope.

Early the next morning, after breakfast, Ben took Dani and Holtz to the spot and showed them a hammer. "I took some wire and tied a bunch of these supports together."

They saw that he had run wires through the bolt holes in the supports. He had six on one side and six on the other, with one brace between them, extended about three inches. He'd wound some adhesive tape around the rough steel to protect the hands. He knelt down on the floor, looked over his shoulder, and murmured, "One small blow for mankind!" Then he lifted the tool and let it fall on the cement. It struck the line between the old and new batches, and a fragment of cement flew off. He paused, stared at it, then began raising the hammer and letting it fall with a dogged regularity.

Dani and Holtz left, but she returned an hour later to find Vince taking over. "Going to be slow," Ben muttered as he got to his feet and flexed his stiff fingers. He looked at the blister on the inside of his palm and then at the small irregular crevice represented by his labor. "Don't ruin your hands, Vince," he said. "Lonnie will take a shift."

Off and on all day, the men worked at it. The next day, late in the afternoon, Dani went back to check the progress. Karen was standing beside Ben, putting tape around his hand. Looking up, she said in exasperation, "Talk to your employee, will you? He's grinding his palms to hamburger!" She pushed one hand down, and when she said, "Now the other one," Dani saw that the palm was raw. "This crazy idea will never work, anyway," Karen complained, slapping something out of a tube onto his palm. She put a cotton pad over it, expertly wrapped the hand with tape, then said, "I don't think Stone will have to poison anyone else. If he leaves us here like this, we'll all go crazy and kill each other!"

Ben cocked his head. "There's our master's voice—let's go."

They quickly filed out and joined the others in front of the camera. Maxwell Stone was saying, ". . . Death of your fellow prisoner. No one regrets any more than I do that such stringent measures must be taken. I am hopeful that you will see how serious this matter is and decide to cooperate. Those of you who do so will not be released, of course. The matter is too serious for that. But I promise you that you will be taken from this silo and placed in a comfortable prison. And while no prison is pleasant, neither is death."

The raw threat ran along Dani's nerves, and she spoke up at once. "Stone, you talk a great deal about justice and freedom. Can't you see that what you're doing to us negates everything you claim to stand for? You love this country, but it was to guard against such things as you are doing now that George Washington and his peers risked everything they had. And the wars that you mention, they were all fought by men who would fight against *you* for robbing us of our liberty!"

She spoke at length, as if she were pleading before a jury, and Stone made no move to interrupt. Finally, however, she stopped, and he said, "Miss Ross, you are an eloquent speaker. You are a brilliant young woman, and I take your words seriously. But our country is filled with brilliant people—yet we are losing *everything*!"

"Here it comes again," Karen whispered to Ben. "How many times have we heard what a rotten generation we are? He's like a broken record! But that's the way his form of megalomania works."

For nearly half an hour Stone rambled on about the

162

decadence of modern Americans. "The so-called 'hippie,' who has thrown decency and honor to the dust, those pseudo-intellectuals who take more pride in their beards and unwashed bodies—they are not *fit* to be Americans."

After branding the youth and the modern media (straight out of the pits of hell!), he began on the politicians. "Roosevelt sold our country out to Stalin at Yalta—and he was not the last who has fallen into Communist hands. The Supreme Court of the United States sold out to Russia and China!"

Finally he paused, "But despite all this, there is hope. Some of us are aware of the critical danger America faces. We have no intention of standing by, of being drained of our liberty by the forces that would destroy us. And I am giving you one opportunity to redeem yourselves." He paused, and his voice dropped into a more intimate—and somehow more enticing tone—than any of them had heard. "If you will decide to confess to the evil that has destroyed you, it is not impossible but that one day you will be invited to join with us. There would have to be a long period of indoctrination, of course, but I would help you. Think of it carefully. You have been a part of the forces that are destroying this great land, but with time, you could come into the truth."

Holtz had listened to this with a deepening scowl on his face. "I believe another word for that is *brainwashing*, Stone. And if what you're doing for us is a sample of your ways, I'll rot here before joining you!"

All of them were startled when Stone gave a low laugh. "Ah, Commander, you are offended by what has happened to you? But you have done worse!"

Holtz blinked, then nodded. "I presume you refer to my

service in the German navy. Well, I confess that we were wrong. Most of us didn't know about Auschwitz and Dachau—and all those terrible places—and you would be shocked to know how many Germans were revolted by Hitler's insane cruelty. But I make no plea for forgiveness—not from you!"

Stone's voice somehow contained a note of triumph as he answered quickly, "Oh, I was not referring to that part of your past, Commander, as terrible as it is. There is something else that you have done. I refer to your family."

Dani saw a sudden reaction pass over Holtz, as if he had been touched with a live wire. His eyes blinked rapidly, and he shook his head abruptly. "I have no family but my sister, Anna."

"But you did have a brother, didn't you? A brother named Wilhelm?"

Holtz's mouth flew open, and when he spoke, it was in German: "*Ja, er war mein junger Bruder, wer in Berlin geboren wurde—*"

"In *English*, if you please, Herr Holtz!"

Holtz seemed to shrink into his chair. His shoulders slumped, and when he spoke it was in a hoarse whisper. "Yes! I had a brother. He was the best of us all, I think. He left Germany and came to America when he was a very young man. Many times he wrote me, and he always said, 'Hitler will destroy you, Karl.' But I would not listen. He—did well in America. He joined the merchant marine and rose to a high place—a captain. I—I never saw him after he came to America."

"Herr Holtz," Stone demanded. "It is time for the truth!"

"All right! All right, I will tell you all of it." Holtz's face

164

was ashen, and his eyes were filled with pain. "He was captain of a ship called the *Republic*. She carried fifteen hundred soldiers. She was part of a convoy, and our U-boats attacked one afternoon. I was too far away to be in on the attack, but I took my boat there to—to pick off survivors."

He licked his lips and looked blindly around, seeming not to see anyone. "We got there at dusk, and I saw one ship, waddling along, carrying all those men. Then I saw the name on her stern—the *Republic*! And I *knew* that my brother Wilhelm was at the helm. My brother, Wilhelm!"

He broke off, tears running down his face, but Stone continued implacably, "And what did you do, Commander?"

"I sank her!" Holtz whispered. "She went down with all hands!" He got to his feet and stumbled away, disappearing into the sleeping quarters.

Stone let the silence run on, then said, "That is a good beginning. It is not the real crime that burns into the commander's soul, but that will come. That will come!"

Then the red light blinked out, and the camera went dead.

9
A Glimpse of the World

Wednesday brought a break in the cold weather, but Lonnie warned them after breakfast not to get too excited. "Old man winter's just foolin'." He nodded. "We're in for a hard winter."

"How can you know that, Lonnie?" Karen asked from the kitchen.

Lonnie gave her a surprised look. "Why, the caterpillars was extra fuzzy this year, and the acorns had thick shells." He nodded sagely, but when Karen laughed, he said in an insulted voice, "Go on and laugh! But when the *real* winter hits this sardine can, you'll see!"

She apologized, but he stalked away to join the poker game Sid and Vince pursued languidly at the table. Putting her dish towel away, Karen paused, then moved over in time to see Ben straighten his back and look up. "You've been chipping away at that floor off and on all morning," she scolded. Going to lean over his shoulder, she saw that an area no more than a foot square and about two inches deep had been removed. Shaking her head, she asked, "Ben, do you really think there's a chance to break out?"

"Always a chance, Doc," he said. His inner toughness intrigued her, and she studied his face, wondering what had put such dogged purpose in his features. It was the face of a fighter, the bridge of his nose showing a small break, and the fresh scar on his forehead giving him a tough look. The hazel eyes, which regarded her, seemed relaxed, half hooded by his eyelids; those eyes and the rounded muscles in his body gave the impression of a large cat. Perhaps, she thought suddenly, behind his toughness was also a weakness.

"Come along!" she commanded, but a smile curved her generous mouth and touched her eyes. "You can play at being the Count of Monte Cristo anytime."

He dropped the chisel onto the floor with a sharp clanging and got to his feet. She walked like a farm girl, he noted as they moved through the kitchen and across the recreation area, with big steps and swinging her arms more actively than most women. She sat down in a chair, drew her feet under her, and nodded at the other chair. When he dropped into it, she asked at once, "What do you make of all this, Ben?"

He regarded her carefully. She wore a man's shirt, open at the neck; it fell carelessly away from her throat and showed the smooth, white shading of her skin. Her features seemed sharp, but he knew that this was an illusion dispelled by the room's light. Her lips were long, and her light-blue eyes were wide spaced and steady. The strongest impression she left with him was of a woman who kept herself under strict control at all times. She was, in a way, almost mannish in her driving energy, but there was nothing masculine in the rounded figure that was not concealed by the loose-fitting shirt and the long, full skirt.

"You want the conclusions of a trained investigator, I guess." He touched the scar on his forehead pensively, then shook his head. "I guess it's going to take more than a few hints from Crime Stoppers to figure this one out. One thing, people are going to start breaking pretty soon. All these interviews—they're wearing people down—and they're going to get worse."

Karen nodded. Ever since his encounter with Holtz, Stone had summoned various individuals for his attention. He had grilled Sid for over an hour, and by that time Sid was a bundle of quivering nerves. "I know. It's like an interrogating room, isn't it? Wear people down until they can't stand it. Who's next?"

"No telling," Ben shrugged. "He's already had a shot at Vic, Holtz, Candi, and Rachel. Sooner or later he's going to do the same to all of us. Morrow was just about ready to go over the edge, and that was a rough jolt Holtz took yesterday. He's a pretty hardy specimen, but he's not rolling with this one so well."

"I know. He's been covering that guilt for a long time, I'd guess. Candi isn't going to make it. I'm giving her antidepressant tablets, but she's not responding well. As a matter of fact, Ben, I'm not too sure *any* of us are going to make it."

He studied her closely, then nodded, "You'll make it, Doc. You may bend, but you won't break." He leaned back, laced his hands, and covered his eyes. "You got a family out there?"

She shot a quick look at him, then shrugged. "No." The

brief reply sounded curt, and she added, "I had one once, but it got away from me." She waited for him to ask for details. If he had, she would have broken off at once. But he lay there, relaxed, with his eyes hidden behind his hands, so she went on speaking.

"I always wanted to be a doctor—always! No matter what else, *that* was the one thing I never let go of. I worked as a waitress to pay my way through college; then I learned how to get grants and loans to get through medical school." Her voice changed subtly as she added, "My third year I met Pete Sanderson. It was his first year, and he was having a hard time with money. We started going together and fell in love, got married. I got a good appointment as soon as I finished and was able to make enough to get him through."

She reached over and pulled his hands away from his eyes, asking, "Are you pumping me, Savage?"

"Certainly." He nodded. "Like I said, I'm a trained investigator."

Again, she would have stopped, but his relaxed attitude seemed to encourage her. She was not a big talker, but the tensions of the silo had drawn her nerves fine, so she leaned back in the chair and continued: "Pete specialized in surgery, and when he finished, we both got good positions. More money than either of us had ever seen. Why, Pete made more for one operation than most men make in six months! And I had a baby the first year we were married. We named him *Charles*, after my dad." Karen's voice grew tight, and she said, "There were eight good years—and one bad one before the end. We had everything money could buy, and we lived at a terrific pace. I thought I had the perfect marriage—then one day Pete came home

169

and said he wanted a divorce. He'd met a socialite, and said he had to have her—and he did. It was a messy divorce, fighting over Charlie. We hated each other by the time it was over, and Charlie was a nervous wreck." Her voice suddenly trembled, and she looked away from him quickly.

"Always hardest on the kids," Ben said quietly.

Karen nodded and whispered, "I'd like to go back—do it all over. But it's too late for that, Ben. It's way too late!"

He handed her a handkerchief, then sat there looking at the wall while she wept silently. Finally she handed him the handkerchief back, and when he reached to take it, she said, "Sorry, Ben." A look of surprise came to her face, and she said in wonder, "I didn't mean to unload all that on you!"

"It's my honest face." He nodded, then gave her a sudden smile. "You're going to make it, Doc."

She stared back at him, then laughed shortly. "Yes, I'll make it. Thanks for not offering all kinds of advice!" She said suddenly, "Let me see your hands." She held them and looked carefully at the half-healed blisters. Neither Ben nor Karen was aware that Dani had come out of the sleeping area and was watching them. Just as Karen said, "They're healing nicely, just don't work without protection," Dani turned quickly and went back to the kitchen.

He got up and said, "Most women can't throw straight. Can you?"

She stared at him in amazement, then shook her head. "You've got a mind like a butterfly, Savage! What in the world makes you ask a question like that?"

"Wait here, and I'll show you." He headed for the sleeping area and came back at once carrying something. "See that vent up there?" He indicated the small rectangle, thirty feet up. "I want to get a look out of that thing." She stared at him, and he held out a foot-long piece of steel with a rope tied to the center. "Got just enough rope to reach that far, but getting the thing through that little hole is going to be hard. Want to try?"

She got to her feet, looked up at the small square, and shook her head. "I can sew up your head, but I can't throw for sour apples."

He grinned and gathered the thirty-foot length of rope in a coil. Holding it in his left hand, he measured the distance to the vent and threw the piece of steel in an overhand motion. The line played out well enough, but his throw fell short. The steel clanged against the wall four feet below the vent, then dropped to the concrete with another loud clatter.

"Hey!" Lonnie yelled. "What in the cat hair are you doin', Ben?" Savage didn't answer, but after he tried twice more and failed, the three men came over to watch.

"You don't plan to get out through that little hole?" Vince asked curiously.

"Nope, but if I could get a look out that vent, we might learn a little more about this place."

Sid stared up at the vent then shook his head. "That's a long drop. You'll break your neck if you fall."

They watched as Ben failed time after time to get the steel through the vent. Finally Lonnie said, "Lemme try, Ben!" He took the rig and made a shot. It hit the vent, but sideways, the ends of the steel striking the edges of the opening.

He tried again, and soon everyone had gathered to

watch. It was a game that went on for a long time, everyone laughing and insisting on a chance to try it.

"That is good, Ben," Holtz said once. He had come in to see what the noise was about, and Ben had gone to stand beside him. "We need a little fun, yah?" Looking up at the vent, he shook his head. "A long way to climb a rope, but it would be good to have a report on our situation. Can you climb that far?"

"Is George Bush a Republican?" Ben grinned. Then he shrugged and said, "Was a time I could, Karl. But I've lost a step. Come on, let's have a cup of coffee."

The two went to the kitchen, got coffee, and talked for twenty minutes. Suddenly a cheer went up from the crowd. Lonnie's loud voice rattled the walls: "I done it! I done it! Hey, Ben, I got it!"

"Let's take a look."

Lonnie was beaming. "I got 'er in, Ben!"

Ben grinned at the big southerner, clapping him on the shoulder. "Good job!" He took the rope, holding it tense and then put his weight on it. The end of it came within a foot of the floor, and he lifted his feet, waited, then jerked at the rope, but it didn't move.

Dani watched this, then tilted her head back, peering at the vent. "Ben, that piece of steel might be just barely holding. It's too dangerous."

"I'm fully insured, boss," he said, then he went up the rope. All of them had expected him to put his feet to the wall and walk up in the manner of a mountain climber, slowly, hand over hand. But he extended his legs, holding them together at a right angle from his body; as fast as his hands could move, he hauled himself up in a series of movements that were so smooth that his body seemed to *float* upward, without hesitation or strain. Ben went up the rope with no more apparent effort than a man would expend walking up a flight of stairs.

"Wow!" Bix gasped as Ben reached the top and peered out. "He wasn't lying about bein' in a circus!" Then he asked, "What's he doing now?"

"Looks like he's tying a knot in the rope," Rosie said.

Letting go with one hand, Ben had reached down, pulled up a short length of the rope, and working slowly, fashioned a loop. He looked down, laughed, and said, "Should have practiced up on my knot tying before I got up here!" But he got the knot made, lowered it, and carefully inserted his foot. He put his weight on it, and free from the strain of holding on with his hands, he steadied himself and gazed out the vent.

"What's it like?" Vince called out. "Can you see anything?"

"Tell you about it in a minute," Ben answered. His eyes swept the horizon, and the sight of something other than the blank walls of his prison was soothing. He searched the landscape, putting his head out and turning to look both ways. Finally he pulled his head back, kicked his foot out of the noose, and came down the rope, hand over hand. "Better tie something around the rope so the bar won't move so much," he said.

Rachel pulled a chair forward, and he anchored the rope firmly, then turned to face them, his square face thoughtful. They crowded around him, and he said slowly, "It's mountain country—the Ozarks. We're in a valley, between two ridges. I think this was a town at one time—at least a whistle stop. A set of tracks comes right by the silo, and over to the left I can see some old deserted houses."

"Lots of places like that, all over Arkansas," Lonnie put in. "When farming went to pot, people put their fields into timber, and the towns died off."

"Well, there's some sort of clearing over to the left, with a few metal buildings," Ben went on. "I keep trying to remember if I saw this place when I flew over it, but I can't. My guess is that this is part of Maxwell Stone's military kingdom. I could see fresh tracks in the muddy road that comes by here—probably from some kind of four-wheel-drive truck. It looks like there's six of these silos in this group, and we're in the two in the middle."

"No sign of life?" Holtz asked.

"Nobody stirring. But there's got to be a room somewhere where he watches us with that camera. And I could see the box down there, where we put out the list for supplies. I'll be able to get a good look at whoever comes for it." He looked thoughtful and added, "I could even talk to him; he'd only be thirty feet away."

"Offer him a bundle?" Vince murmured. His dark eyes gleamed, and he nodded, "I'm in for a hundred grand—and we can promise him anything."

"I don't think Stone would send a man who could be bribed," Rachel demurred.

"Baby—*anybody* will go for the price. Just a matter of making it big enough!"

Ben's report lifted their spirits, it seemed, but that afternoon, an unpleasant incident occurred. For several days Vince had been watching Candi carefully. She had been a source of masculine pride for him, something he had to have. Now she obviously avoided him, and it ate away at him.

After three, he found her sitting on the couch, reading

a book. He sat down at once and put his arm around her, complaining, "Candi, you been hiding from old Vince."

She looked up and shook her head. "I guess I've been down in the dumps, Vince. This place is gettin' to me."

"Why, you just need a little happy time." He grinned. "And you know I can make you happy, don't you, honey?"

Ordinarily Candi would have brightened up and joined in his mood, but today she refused his smile. "I just want to be left alone." She tried to leave, but he held her down. She struggled vainly against his iron strength and cried out shrilly, "Vince, let me go!"

He looked around and saw Bix and Rosie sitting at the table across the room and cursed them. Rosie shook his head and remained seated, but Bix rose just as Ben and Karl came out of the sleeping quarters, followed by Betty and Rachel. Dani was in the kitchen, making a pie, and Lonnie was chipping away at the floor but came to see what the noise was about.

Vince's face reddened, and the violence that lurked constantly under the surface broke out. He cursed them all and ended by saying, "Get out of my sight!" In his anger he gave a brutal squeeze to Candi's arm, and she cried out in pain.

At once Rachel marched across the floor and, with anger blazing in her dark eyes, yelled, "You filthy scum! You're a big man, aren't you? If I were a man, I'd . . . !"

Her words broke off when Vince suddenly stood and aimed a backhanded blow at her. Rachel dodged it easily, but Bix ran across the room to help her. "You shouldn't hit a woman, Vince." he said.

Vince grinned, and he said, "All right, I'll hit *you*, hip-

175

pie!" He took a step forward and drove his fist into the boy's mouth, driving him backward as if he'd been hit by a piston. Vince picked Bix up, struck him brutally in the face, three times, then let him fall to the floor in an unconscious heap.

Dani had stood there, stunned by her first experience of the raw power of violence. She wanted to go to Bix, but seemed rooted to the spot.

Karen, however, was not. Ignoring Vince, who stood over Bix, she knelt by the boy's side. She pulled one eyelid back, then said calmly, "Ben, you and Rosie help me get him on the couch."

Vince glared at the two men. "You want to take it up, acrobat? I'm a little harder than climbing a rope."

Savage paused, seeming small next to Canelli's burly form. He stood there, looking up at Vince, then answered, "No," and bent to help Rosie get Bix off the floor. Vince looked around for someone to attack, cursed loudly, and stalked away. Throwing himself down at a table, he began dealing solitaire.

Bix was not badly hurt, but he was shaken in spirit. As Karen cleaned his face, he said in a shaky voice, "He's a killer! Did you see his eyes?"

"I expect that's right, Bix," Karen said evenly. She left him and went to Candi, who had fled to her bunk and dissolved in hysterical weeping.

Dani found herself standing by Rosie. She tried to cover the trembling in her hands, sat down abruptly, and commented in an unsteady voice, "That was a bad scene, Rosie."

"Yes, ma'am, it purely was," he agreed. "I seen lots of

bad men in my business—but I reckon Canelli is as rough as any."

"I was surprised at Ben. I didn't think he'd be afraid of Vince, even if he is smaller."

"Miss Dani," Rosie said, shaking his head, "don't you make no mistake. Ben Savage ain't afraid of Canelli or nobody else! He just don't take on useless battles, that's what."

Dani dropped her head onto her hands, leaning on the table. "Oh, Rosie! I'm so *tired*! Is this ever going to end?"

The thin, dark face of Rosie Smith grew sober. He was an alien, cut off by his race from the others, yet his inner strength shone forth clearly.

"Why, God ain't forgot us, Miss Dani," he said simply. "I learned a long time ago that it's up to us to believe the Lord God to help us when we're in trouble, but we have to leave the *when* and the *how* up to Him!" He touched her shoulder and asked gently, "Can you say *amen* to that, Miss Dani?"

She lifted her head, and the sight of his thin face with the slight smile touched her. She put her hand out, and he took it, holding it warmly. "Amen, Rosie! And amen!" The burden lifted from her, and she sat there thinking how strange it was that an uneducated black man twice her age had such an ability to lift her spirits. As she had many times over the past weeks she thought: *Some things can't be learned from a book!*

Karen came to the rec room early. She had lain awake for a long time, listening to Candi sob and to Dani, who tried to comfort her. Empty from the lack of sleep, she busied herself making coffee.

"Hey, Doc, how about giving me some?" She looked up, startled, and saw nobody. Then her eyes caught a movement up high, and she spotted Savage up at the vent. She took a cup to him as he slid down.

"Pretty morning outside," he commented as he sipped the steaming brew. "How's Candi and Rachel?"

"Candi's hysterical, and Rachel's ready to kill," Karen answered wearily. "It's getting pretty hard, Ben."

They talked about small things, and finally Karen said, "Tell me about the outside."

He glanced at her. "Why don't you take a look for yourself?"

She shook her head. "I'm no acrobat, Ben."

He grinned rashly. "If you've got the nerve, you can look out all you want to." He shook his head as she stared at him, then put down the coffee cup, saying, "Come on. I'll show you."

Karen followed him to the rope. He took the end, quickly formed a loop, and nodded. "When I get up, put this loop under your arms. I'll haul you up, and we can enjoy a good view together."

"Why, you can't do that!" she answered, but he turned and ascended the rope. When he got to the top, he put his foot in the noose, then bent over and expertly formed another bowline just below it. He slipped his foot out of the original noose, put it in the lower one, then looked down and said, "Elevator going up!"

Karen stood there uncertainly.

"Come on, Karen. You can trust me. And it's time you started trusting men, I guess," Ben called down.

Angered by the words, she put the loop under her arms and said defiantly, "All right—do your stuff." Looking up, she saw him reach down and take a hitch on the rope, then lift; she gasped as her feet left the floor. She shut her eyes as she went up a foot and a half at a time, but opened them to look up. He was grinning at her. No sign of strain appeared on his face, but the muscles in his forearms swelled as he hauled her smoothly along.

Once she looked down, and the floor looked far, far away. Just then her shoulder bumped his foot, and he said, "Top floor—just slip your foot into that loop." She did as he commanded, and he said, "Now, trust in that loop and in ol' Ben Savage, who never dropped a woman yet."

She put her weight on the loop, and felt his arms pulling at her. He swung behind her, put his arms around her and said, "Take a look."

Karen gripped the bottom edge of the vent hole, bracing her lower arms against the wall, and drank in the sights. Mist was creeping along the feet of the huge pines that grew in a solid wall a hundred yards away, but the sun, a huge orb of yellow, sent heavy, slanted beams down through the branches of the trees—brilliant slabs of sunshine forming glittering gold prisms. The sky seemed bluer than she thought possible. It made her want to cry, and she whispered, "Oh, Ben, it's so beautiful!"

"Look over to your left, Doc," he directed. She turned her head, and he said, "See him?"

A big bird sat on a high limb of a dead pine. "What is it?" she asked.

"Red-tailed hawk. Keep watching, and you'll see him get his lunch." Finally the hawk swooped down and nabbed a mouse, then rose to carry it back to the limb. "I

179

think his nest is in that tree," Ben said. "He's a beauty, isn't he?"

She stayed up for ten minutes, then complained, "Ben! I'm getting a cramp in my leg!"

He swung her around. "Hold on tight. . . ." Loosing one hand, then the other, Ben said, "Going down," and she descended to the floor in a series of easy movements. Her feet felt numb, and she almost fell, but she was smiling as he came down and stood beside her.

"Thanks a lot," she said with a nod. "That was heavenly!"

"Savage's Aerial View Service—we never close," he said lightly. He slipped the rope off, and both saw that Dani was sitting at one of the tables. She was not looking at them, but raised her head when Karen called out, "Dani, come here! You've got to see the outside!"

Dani looked up at the vent and shrugged. "No, I don't think so."

"Oh, you've got to!" Karen insisted. Then she hesitated. "Are you afraid of falling?"

"No!" Dani answered sharply, but then added peevishly, "But I'm not a little thing like you, Karen."

"One hundred and thirty-four pounds," Ben piped up. "Still size twelve, I see."

A flush rose to Dani's cheeks. She lifted her head and commented, "I don't like to be treated like a yo-yo."

"Ah, you liberated types are all alike, boss," Ben said sadly. "You sure do miss a lot of fun." When the anger that he had provoked came, he said, "Course, it is *dangerous*. No sense taking a chance, I guess."

Dani said, "You are an insufferable male chauvinist! I can go up that rope as well as Karen!"

He said innocently, with a sly wink at Karen, "Why, I thought you could," and at once took the rope and pulled himself aloft.

Karen handed her the loop. "Just slip this under your arms."

Dani obeyed. Suddenly the rope cut into her chest as Ben called out, "Alley oop!" and she felt like a fool dangling there helplessly. She wore a dress, not slacks, like Karen. Suddenly she thought of the impossibility of modesty. If the men came out now . . . !

But she was soon at the opening, having been handled like a baby, and like Karen, was struck speechless by the view. She was a little afraid of heights, but with his arms around her like steel bands, she gave herself up to the pleasure of the sights of the outside world.

Finally she sighed and said, "I feel like Dorothy in *The Wizard of Oz*. Remember? Everything was gray and dark—then she got to Oz, and everything was in beautiful color!"

Ben showed her the hawk, and she even got to see him swoop down on a small snake. That seemed to be a miracle to her, though he felt her shiver slightly at the kill. Then she stiffened and said, "Look!"

He glanced over her shoulder and saw a large white-tailed deer, a buck with a handsome set of horns, step out of the woods and advance into the open. Two does followed him, and Ben felt Dani's flesh grow tense as she watched. Something must have alarmed the deer, for they suddenly floated away in a long, impossible jumps.

She slumped back against him, saying, "I've never seen wild deer!"

Finally her leg grew strained, and he said, "Turn around, and hold on to me." She turned awkwardly, and for one moment she was in his arms. He was watching her, his eyes inches away, and their bodies were pressed together. Dani flushed and tried to draw back, but that was impossible. A silence came over them, and in that moment, she forgot everything. Her arms were around his neck for support, and he held her waist with one arm, the other grasping the rope. Her breath grew short, and her lips parted slightly as she watched him.

Then he simply moved his head forward and kissed her on the lips. It was not a long kiss, nor did it demand anything. It was, in fact more of a salute than a kiss, and he grinned and said, "Good morning, boss!"

She blinked and felt strange, as if she would like to return the salute. Instead she gave her shoulders an angry shake and whispered, "Let me down from here!"

He stared at her, then said, "Sure." Taking her rope in one hand, said, "You can let go now." She avoided his gaze, but turned loose, and as she was lowered to the floor, anger and shame began to rise in her. Dani had always despised those who played games with their employees, and she felt cheap. As soon as she reached the floor and removed the rope, she mastered herself; but when Ben stood before her, studying her with his shrewd eyes, she said, "I think that will be enough sight-seeing for me." Then she added spitefully, "I'm sure you can find others to maul."

He nodded and seemed more interested than anything else. From the moment he had met Dani, he had sensed her pride. No woman, he knew, could have so much of it without having, somewhere, the power of great emotions. In her eyes and lips lay carefully controlled flexible capacities, as though she feared revealing herself. Now he had a view of the undertow of her spirit, as she looked at him with her angry eyes.

"Well, now, Miss Danielle Ross," he said evenly, but with a hard edge in his tone. "Somewhere under all that education and ability lies a real woman that a man would be lucky to get. You're standing there, though, ashamed because for one moment up there, you felt like a *real* woman."

She stared at him, then shook her head. "Savage, you don't know what's in me! Don't try to pretend that pass you just made at me was somehow noble and grand. Because it wasn't!" Her voice was unsteady, and she forced herself to wait, before saying, "It's my fault that you're in here, and I'm sorry for it. But don't ever touch me again. You hear me?"

He nodded slowly. "Sure, Miss Ross, I hear you." He made a tough shape before her, his eyes half closed. He said no more, but stood there, watching her until she wheeled and left, forcing herself to walk slowly across the floor out of the rec room.

After breakfast, the strain that lay over them was evident. Rachel glared at Vince, who ignored her, but he did make a half apology to Bix: "Sorry about that sock in the mouth, kid." He shrugged. "I've got a bad temper; got me into a lot of trouble, I tell you." Bix was anxious to make the matter up, and soon a game of Monopoly was going, with Sid and Rosie joining Vince and Bix. After Sid won, they all joined in a game called Trivial Pursuit, based on a knowledge of trivia. Ben was amused that Lonnie was unbeatable on sports, Candi on entertainment, and Karen on science.

There were surprises, for Lonnie correctly answered,

"What's the capital of Iceland?" with "Reykjavík." When Ben asked how he knew, he just shrugged. "I look at maps a lot." He evidently did, for he seldom missed on a geography question.

Rachel missed the question, "What country has the port of Haifa?"

"You don't know Haifa is in Israel?" Karl asked in surprise, but she refused to argue with him.

Bix never missed a single question on the movies or music and never answered one correctly on science. "I'm a specialist," he explained loftily, to which Lonnie grunted, "You're an ignoramus is what you are!"

Dani was the best, of course, and had to resort to lying to look bad. Ben caught her at it and whispered, "It's pretty bad when you have to pretend to be dumb just to be a part of the gang, ain't it, boss? Now, me, I never have that trouble!"

Karen knew almost nothing about entertainment. Sid, to everyone's amazement, flawlessly shot out answers to history questions. "Nothing much to read in the prison library but history books." He shrugged.

The noise level rose, and at ten everybody was hungry, so they had a mountain of sandwiches and a cake that Betty had been saving for the next day. They drank huge amounts of milk, coffee, tea, and punch. Then they went back to their games, switching partners, and continuing to play until nearly midnight. All except Rosie, Betty, and Dani, who had all come in last in their games and had to clean up, went to bed. The place was a mess.

"What time is it?" Betty asked finally.

Dani looked at her watch. "Twelve fifteen."

"You go on to bed," Betty said. "I'm going to cut up the chickens for tomorrow, then I'm going myself."

Dani didn't argue, but turned to go. Rosie had retired to one of the easy chairs and was reading. "Good night, Rosie," she called out. "I'll see you in the morning."

"Sure enough," he responded, giving her a wave and a smile. "I'll see you in the morning, Miss Danielle."

Dani slept like a log until six in the morning. She rose and took her shower, dressed, and went to the kitchen. Betty was not there, so Dani started to fix the coffee—then stopped.

"Why, Rosie—!" she turned to go over to where he sat with his head back on the chair. The Bible he'd been reading had fallen off his lap to the floor. "You'll be stiff as a board, sleeping with your neck bent, Rosie! Come on, now . . ." she said cheerfully.

She reached out and shook his shoulder. He tilted slowly to his left, then fell to the floor, his head striking the concrete with a dull sound.

"Rosie . . . !" Dani screamed. "What's the matter?"

As soon as she touched the cold flesh, she knew Rosie was dead. Dani knelt there, paralyzed by shock. Terror shook her nerves, and she lurched to her feet, trying to cry out. But before a syllable could pass her lips, a voice came from the doorway, and she wheeled to see Holtz advancing toward her.

10
Inquiry

Dani finally gasped, "It's Rosie, Karl! He's dead!" She rose, and ran blindly out of the room, back into the sleeping quarters.

"Dani, what is it?" Rachel cried out.

Dani lurched through the door of the bathroom, where she threw up violently. A few minutes later, as she washed her face in cold water, voices came from the men's side. On rubbery legs she walked back to the rec room. Her face had become so white that her eyes seemed like dark stains against the pallor.

They had moved the body to the couch, she saw with relief, and those who watched blocked her view of Karen examining the body. Holtz turned, and his own face was pale. "You found him like this?"

"Y-yes," Dani said haltingly. "I got up a little early—and at first I didn't see him."

Holtz considered that, then shot a look at Karen. "How long would you say he's been dead?"

Karen turned from her examination. "I don't know for sure. Rigor mortis hasn't set in, so it can't have been too long ago." She gave them a grim look. "I've got to examine him. If any of you feel squeamish, you'd better get out."

All of them turned at once to leave. Pale faced, Betty offered, "I'll fix some coffee." Candi said with a quiver in her voice, "I—I guess I'll get dressed."

It was something to do, to get away from that still form, and most of them walked away. Rachel shrugged and said to Karen, "What difference does it make what we wear? Nobody's going anywhere." She moved back to the kitchen and began mixing some hot chocolate, adding glumly, "If the killer keeps on knocking us off, there won't be enough of us left to have breakfast!"

When Dani and Candi returned, they found the others all assembled, most of them seated at the tables. Both sat down at a table with Holtz, and Betty brought them coffee, which neither could drink.

"Who saw him alive last?" Ben asked.

"Why, I suppose I did." Betty stopped on her way back to the stove with the coffeepot. She blinked her eyes rapidly, adding, "Dani and Rosie and I did the cleanup after the rest of you went to bed. But Dani left while I was cutting up the chickens."

"What did Rosie do after I left?" Dani asked.

"Why, nothing!" Betty shrugged and added, "He was in that chair, reading, and he never got out of it. Never even said good night when I left."

Vince said suddenly, "One thing is sure. It wasn't Stone who killed Rosie! One of us did the job!"

Silence blanketed the room, until Bix piped up, "Poor

guy! He was always talking about his kids and his grand-children and what he'd do when he got out of here!" Something came into his eyes, and he cast a calculating glance at Lonnie, who was sitting silently, his head bowed as he stared at his hands. "You won't grieve too much, Lonnie," he said bitterly.

Lonnie's head jerked up, and his voice was shrill. "What's *that* supposed to mean? That *I* killed him?"

Bix raised his voice, answering angrily, "I didn't say that, but you can't deny you hated him."

"I ain't so keen on *you*, either, punk!" Lonnie spat out. "You just keep workin' your mouth, and you might be next!"

"Both of you shut up!" Vince took a step toward the pair, halting as Karen suddenly walked up. "What was it, Doc?" he asked.

Karen's lips were turned down in a bitter expression, and her eyes were cold as she bit out: "Three wounds. Two of them he might have survived, but not the one that went right to his heart. He also had a lump on the back of his head, which could have been caused by a blow."

"How terrible!" Betty whispered. "The poor man!"

Ben suddenly got to his feet, directing, "Two of you come along with me. We'll check the kitchen knives." Holtz and Vince joined him in the kitchen as he added, "Betty, show us the hardware."

Betty opened the drawer, looked in, then stepped back. "There's only three knives—and they're all here. A paring knife, a butcher knife, and a bread knife."

Ben picked them all up, and the rest followed him back to the tables. He held them out toward Karen. "What about it, Doc? Could it have been any of these?"

Karen examined them, then shook her head. "I don't think so, Ben. It would take a heavier blade than a paring knife, and the slicing knife wouldn't do. Maybe the butcher knife, but I doubt it."

"Got to be here somewhere," Vince said. "Guess we better have a shakedown."

"Exactly!" Holtz said. "But in *pairs*." Grimly he added, "Our assassin, whoever he is, would love to search for the weapon alone! Ben, you've been a policeman; why don't you organize this thing?"

"I'd say half of us search the sleeping areas, the other half in here." He divided them up into pairs, and in ten minutes the searchers were poking into every possible hiding place.

Ben had paired off with Rachel, and as the two were pulling the bedding off the women's bunks, she asked curiously, "Do you think we'll find it, Ben?"

"I'd be surprised," he answered briefly. "There are plenty of hiding places in this silo." He was correct, for after two hours of thorough searching, they were forced to give up.

Betty cooked breakfast, and some of them ate a little, but Dani found it all she could do to force herself to drink some hot chocolate. As they all sat around, she suddenly said, "It had to be a man who killed him!"

Valentine threw her a wicked look and slammed his first on the table, snarling, "I've known plenty of broads who could use a shiv! Matter of fact, I've got a nice little memento right here—" He pulled up his left sleeve and pointed to a ragged scar, "From a dizzy blond in Chicago!"

"I don't doubt that a woman would stab a man." Dani

nodded. "But I've been wondering why he didn't call out for help." She looked at Karen and asked, "He didn't die *instantly*, did he?"

Karen stared at her, then shook her head. "I'd say not. Those first two cuts took at least a few seconds. He'd have had time to call for help, I'd think. But he'd have called, no matter *who* was attacking him."

"Only if he *could* call for help," Dani said. "I don't think he was able to. I think the murderer knew he wouldn't cry out."

"How could he be sure of that?" Rachel demanded.

Dani said slowly, "Only one way that I can think of. If somebody very strong grabbed him from the rear, around the neck, with one arm, so that he couldn't scream, and stabbed him with the other hand . . . ?" She left the question in the air.

"That makes me a prime suspect," Ben chimed in. "We were all trained to do exactly that in the Rangers." He smiled grimly, adding, "I was the best man in the company at the job."

"Clever of you to mention it, Savage, before one of us pointed it out!" Vince said in a suspicious voice. Then he looked around and gave a short laugh. "I wasn't in the army, but where I grew up, we had basic training, too. I know a hundred guys who can do a stunt like this—including me and Sid here."

Sid yelped, "You can leave me out—!"

"Shut up, Sid." Vince grinned wolfishly. "You shouldn't have told me all the tales about the big house—especially how you made a shiv out of a file and sliced that guy up!" He gave Bix a contemptuous look. "Even a punk like you could do an old guy like Rosie in, Bentley. So it could have been any one of us."

"It could have been a woman, too," Ben remarked. "She could have slipped up behind him, hit him on the head, and stabbed him after he was dead. Or she could have slipped him some kind of dope that put him out, then done the job."

They stared at him, then he shrugged. "One thing is pretty sure: Don't trust anybody! Best way of life, I've found."

"You don't think he'll try again?" Karen exclaimed. "Not now that we know he's in our midst!"

Dani answered slowly, "I think he will." She licked her lips, and a slight shiver went over her. "I think that's what he's here for—to kill us, if we don't do what Maxwell Stone wants."

Dani wrote the note saying that Rosie was dead, and slipped it through the slot. Late that afternoon, they heard the whine of the winch. Once again they formed into a group, and Dani read the Bible then spoke a few words. She spoke of Rosie's gentle spirit and his willingness to serve others. After mentioning his faith, she ended, "He was a simple man, Roosevelt Smith. His name was never in the papers, and he will not be remembered by many people. But *I* will remember him as long as I live, for to me he was a member of my family." She paused and seemed to struggle for a moment. When she lifted her head toward the darkness overhead, they all saw that tears rolled down her cheeks, but she was smiling. "We're part of the family of God, and I will see him again one day. The last thing he said to me was 'See you in the morning.' " She bowed her head, said a prayer, and the earthly part of Rosie Smith slowly rose and was swallowed up.

Bix whispered, "He was a good dude, that Rosie was!"

The next morning, Rachel found Bix chopping away listlessly at the concrete. He looked up and gave her a wan smile, muttering, "Waste of time! What gets me is that the killer knows about this crazy plan to escape. Matter of fact," he said as a thought struck him, "the dirty dog has been *working* on it!"

Rachel looked startled. She nodded slowly, saying, "I guess that's right, Bix." She squatted down and peered at the hole. "Funny—you said 'the killer' just as we'd say 'the repairman.' I can't really believe it, can you? Two people have been murdered!" Her dark eyes looked tragic, and she suddenly cocked her head and stared at him. "Did *you* do it, Bix? You look like such a nice boy, but I have to put you in the same category as Sid and Vince."

"You don't really think that!"

She appeared not to hear, only whispering, "It could be Savage. He's hard!" Then her eyes narrowed, and she said in a stubborn tone, "I think it's Holtz!"

"Aw, come on, Rachel . . . !" he protested.

"He's a Nazi, Bix, and they've never changed! He's just broadened his field—killing others besides Jews." Then she tried to laugh and rose, saying, "I'm going crazy, Bix. I think we all are, so it doesn't matter much, does it? On the whole, I'd rather die than lose my mind." She stared at him, then shook her head, her heavy, black hair swinging. "Don't trust anyone, Bix—not even the women!"

Bix stared at her, his open face filled with confusion. "You think it could be one of them? No, I don't believe it!"

She gave him a sad smile. "I hope you can keep your simple faith in people, Bix, but I don't think you will." She left him, and he sat there, staring at the hole for a few moments. Throwing the chisel down, he left the kitchen and passed through the rec room, noticing that Savage was again peering out the vent. He found Holtz lying on his bunk and burst out, "I'm not working on that stupid hole anymore! We're never going to get out of this thing alive!"

Holtz had been staring up at the ceiling; now he turned to look carefully at Bix. Noting the clenched hands and the angry, worried expression, he swung his feet to the floor and sat there quietly for a moment. Finally he said, "Bix, once I said the same thing. We were under heavy depth-charge attack, our batteries were practically dead, and there was no place to run. I had no hope at all, but my young lieutenant—Schwartz was his name—kept making plans, doing useless things while the rest of us just waited for the end. I thought he was a fool! There we were, a hundred fathoms deeper than the boat was supposed to *ever* go, with water pouring in and depth charges going off all around us. And this young fellow just kept on working, trying switches, patching up holes—while the rest of us sat there waiting for the end."

He stopped, and when Bix saw that he was not going to speak again, he asked curiously, "How'd you get away?"

"Why, I don't know, Bix." Holtz shrugged. "Maybe they ran out of charges. Maybe they got a call to go to another spot." He smiled gently at the boy and continued, "But ever since then, I've learned one thing, my boy: Never give up! That's what Churchill told the English. And that's why they won the war, I suppose." Before he left, Holtz put his hand on Bix's shoulder. "If you give up on that hole, Bix, you're finished!"

"The old bird's right, I guess." Startled, Bix looked over and saw Vince Canelli, in the door to the bathroom, with a look of reluctant admiration on his tough face. "Once you quit, you *are* finished!"

Holtz also noticed Savage staring out of the vent, when he passed through the rec room. As he left, Karen went to stand beside the rope. "Savage Aerial View Service open today?" she asked.

Ben looked down at her and nodded, "Like I said, we never close." He drew the rope up, tied a bowline in the end, and in a few minutes she was looking out of the vent. A blast of frigid air struck her, and she gasped, "That's cold, Ben!"

"Might get worse," he commented. "They get some pretty bitter winters in this part of Arkansas, Lonnie says." He held her while she scanned the horizon. Finally he asked, "You sure it's safe to be alone with me up here? I might let you fall."

Suddenly her body grew tense, and she turned awkwardly to look at him. Ben thought that her mind was as hard and angular as her body was soft and yielding, for her blue eyes calculated his face with a clinical precision. Her lips made a long, wistful curve paralleling the smoothness of her jaw, but the barriers were up, and he remained still as she looked into his eyes.

Karen noted the usually half-closed hazel eyes were fully open, regarding her with a frank curiosity. She became intensely aware of Ben's masculinity, not only the strength of his arm and the rounded muscles of his neck and chest, but the rich virility imposed on his face.

Finally he grinned, and asked, "Well, what's the verdict?"

Karen studied him for one moment, then a smile broke through. "I guess you've got as much right to suspect me, Ben." Turning to look back out the vent, she added, "I don't trust my judgment, anyway. I've not had a great deal of success with it."

He felt her grow tense. "What is it, Karen?"

"You haven't looked down at the ground, I guess." She pulled her head back and quietly explained, "The knife is down there—right under this window."

He stared at her, then ordered, "Go on down." Once he'd lowered her, Ben stepped into the higher noose and peered down. As he returned to Karen, he said, "Yes, it's there. Come on, let's tell the others."

"Wait until after dinner. Then we can see what kind of reaction we'll get."

Following dinner Ben announced, "We've found the murder weapon—Karen did, that is." Dani and Karl both looked excited, but most of the others just seemed surprised. "It's on the ground just under the vent."

Sid broke the ensuing silence, "That sort of points to you, don't it Savage? You're the only one can shinny up that rope."

"You don't know that, Sid," Holtz protested. "All we know is that Ben is the only one who *has* done it."

"Aw, get *real*, Holtz!" Vince snorted. "You know you couldn't go up that blasted rope! You're too old, and I'm too heavy. I can pump iron, but that kind of trick takes a little guy."

Dani said, "Maybe the killer didn't climb the rope. He could have *thrown* it through the vent."

Lonnie broke in instantly, "No way! Don't you remember how long it took us to get that piece of steel in, to make that rope fast? And he'd have to be in a hurry. Besides, if he missed, the knife would make a racket when it hit the floor."

"Haven't you all forgotten something?" Dani lashed out angrily. "Ben came here looking for *me!* He wasn't waylaid like the rest of us. He's one of my employees!"

Rachel asked quietly, "But how long have you known him, Dani?"

"Well, actually, not over a month," she stammered.

"Well, that's not long," Betty spoke up. "Stone is clever! We all know that. He knew you were going to be here, so why couldn't he have sent this man to join you, all the time planning to have him show up later?"

Dani opened her mouth to argue, but paused. She suddenly cast a look at Ben, who was regarding her carefully. He said nothing, and finally Vince argued, "Look, Reverend, I know you like the guy and all that, but he's a good candidate for our hit man. You've worked for the law. Now if you didn't really know Savage and somebody handed you the *facts*, wouldn't you put him at the top of the list of suspects?"

They were all looking at Dani, and her certainty about Ben seemed suddenly to weaken. Vince could be *right.* She thought, *But Dom Costello recommended him!* Her whirling mind balanced that against *No one else could have climbed the rope and thrown the knife out.*

She took a deep breath, then responded, "It does look bad for Ben, but it's all circumstantial. For all you know, *I* may be able to climb a rope! Or Bix there. I want to try something. Karl has tried to get us to look at ourselves ever since I've been here, and some of you haven't done it. I think it's about the only chance we have, so I'm asking you to try it."

"Try what?" Betty demanded.

"We all know, more or less, who we *say* we are," Dani said intensely. "But one of us isn't who he says he is. He's a liar as well as a murderer, put here by Stone to be his paid assassin. I think he came in with a false identity—and I say we've got to test each other until we find someone who's lying."

"How do we do that?" Vince asked quickly.

"I'll show you, if you just do as I ask."

They wavered, and there were loud protests from Sid and Betty, but finally they were brought into line by Vince, who said, "All right, we'll all go along. What's the plan, Reverend?"

Dani said, "First, we all write a biography." She held up her hand as Bix cried out, "I'm no writer!" "I simply mean one sheet of paper, with the basic facts. Where you were born, your education, all the jobs you've had, your hobbies. I'll make out a form so that all you have to do is fill it out."

After a vast amount of grumbling, they all agreed. "All right," Dani said. "Commander, I want you to help me—and you, Karen—and Ben." She shook her head when Sid protested against her choice of Savage. "He's had training at this sort of thing—and the rest of us will monitor him," Dani pointed out.

In less than an hour, the four came up with a form.

"I've been trying to get this done for a long time." Holtz shook his head. "And now *you* do it, Dani!"

They gathered the others, and Dani read out the items they had to include.

The next hour was very quiet. Dani filled out her own list quickly, then watched the others. Vince finished first and grinned as he handed it to her. "Strictly X rated, Reverend. Hope you won't be too shocked." One by one they all finished, with Lonnie trailing in with a much-erased paper.

Dani explained, "All right, we'll go over every biography. The person we're examining will have to answer *all* questions. If he's told the truth on this sheet, his answers ought to be right. But if he's lied about something, one of us may pick up on it." She smiled and said, "For example, it says on my sheet, that I've lived in Boston for a few years. Some of you have probably been in Boston. You ought to ask me about it: Where is the city hall? What's the name of the zoo? Who's the mayor? That sort of thing. Try to catch me in a lie."

"Sounds about as bad as Stone's idea about confessions," Rachel said sharply. She looked unhappy, but then shrugged and said, "Still, it's something to try. Who's first?"

"I say Savage," Sid replied, and Vince nodded at once.

"All right," Dani looked at Ben. "Any objections?"

"No." Ben leaned back in his chair and glanced around the room. "Fire away."

"All right." Dani read Ben's paper aloud, then explained, "Anybody can ask a question about any of these items."

"I have one," Bix began. "My brother's in the marines. You say you were, too, Ben. In which battle were the most marines killed—ever?"

"Iwo Jima."

Rachel asked suddenly, "Who was Al Schmidt?"

"A marine who was blinded in the Big One, but they made a movie out of that one, so I could have seen it."

"Well, they didn't make no movie about this one," Bix said. "Who's the commander of the corps?"

"General Al Gray."

"What color's the dome of the Capitol in Denver?" Candi asked.

"Gold."

"That's right!" she said. Then she asked, "What's the name of the burlesque on Tenth and Elm?"

Ben shrugged. "Don't know."

"*I* know!" Vince said with a grin. "It's the Majestic." He laughed and said, "But I guess Ben here is above such things."

They bounced questions off Ben for an hour, and he answered them readily. Finally Karl said, "The circuses in America are tawdry things, not like in Europe. I went many times there. You say you were a performer. What was your specialty?"

"Flyer on the trapeze," Savage answered.

Holtz leaned back and studied him. "Who was the first man to do a trapeze act?"

Ben looked at him in surprise, but said at once, "A Frenchman named Leotard invented it. That's where the name of the costume comes from. That was in 1859. He was swimming one day in Toulouse, and he noticed the cords that opened the overhead windows hanging down over the pool. He got the idea of tying a bar on two of them, and he learned to swing out over the pool and drop in."

Candi was staring at Ben, and she asked, "You really did that, Ben? It always scares me to death just to watch! What's it like?"

"It's about as free as anyone ever gets, Candi," Ben said slowly. He ducked his head, and they could see that he was remembering. When he spoke again, his voice was so soft that he seemed to be talking to himself. "We spend our lives fighting earth. Learning to walk, then falling down. Getting from one place to another. Always being pulled back to earth. Closest we come to forgetting gravity is swimming, I guess."

He stopped, seeming to have forgotten that they were there. "You come out of your dressing room, and everything is pretty grubby. The lights hit your face, and you start up the rope. Then you get to the platform, and somehow everything fades away. The crowd's still making a lot of noise, but it seems far off. You're up there away from it all, just the clean cut of ropes falling away in straight lines and the gleaming bars of the traps.

"Then you watch as your catcher, across from you, starts swinging, and the pulse of the whole circus, the whole world, is beating in your head. You put your hands on your bar, exactly eight inches apart. Then you slip off the platform, and the old earth catches you, and down you go! You hit the bottom and give the best kick you've got, trying to drive yourselves through the top of the tent. Up to the top of the forward swing, and there's that one split second when you're just floating. You know the world's going to pull you back, but for that one moment, you're free and loose and out of everything!"

The room was quiet, and Dani was staring at Ben, her eyes wide.

"Down you go, and you follow through, kicking back, straining to get every inch of height. All the time the beat is going. It's in your catcher, in you, in the band. And if you don't have that beat going, you'd better stay off the traps and learn to sell shoes.

"But the beat is there, and you're at the top of your last backswing. Then you drop, and as you go up, the beat is going—and it says *now*—and you turn loose of the bar and fire out into pure space!

"All the other acts have a wire or a pole somewhere. The flyer has nothing, just space. As you clear the bar, you double and make a spinning ball out of your body, and you go spinning through space, way up there over the world."

He stopped suddenly and looked around. For the first time since Dani had known him, his face seemed vulnerable.

"How do you know when to stop spinning and get your hands out?" Holtz asked.

Ben laughed shortly. "Most people don't."

"Who was the best?" Dani asked suddenly.

"Alfredo Codona."

"What made him so good?" Bix asked.

"He did a triple," Ben said quietly.

"Is a triple that hard?" Vince wanted to know.

"Back in his day, it was a sure way to die. That was in 1917, when Codona was in Havana. At that time three men had done a triple somersault, none of them French. An American named Gayton, a man named Hobbes, in London, and another named Dutton. But Codona canceled all his appearances and took three years off—and he got it."

"It looks impossible," Karen said, shaking her head.

Ben said, "When you leave your bar, you're traveling at a speed of sixty-two miles an hour. At that speed, you've got to turn completely over three times in a space of not more than seven feet. At that exact instant you have to break out and land in the hands of your catcher—who's got to be in exactly the right spot at exactly the right time."

The room was very quiet, and Dani saw that they had all forgotten the purpose of their activity. She asked softly, "Did you ever fall, Ben?"

He jerked his head toward her, and his voice was strained. "Everybody falls," he whispered.

Remembering the name he had called when he had first arrived, Dani asked, "Who was Florrie, Ben?"

The question has been softly put, but Savage's reaction was galvanic! His head went back, and he stiffened as though an electric current had shocked his body. He shook his head and said nothing.

At once Holtz attacked, "You must answer the question! Who was Florrie?"

Ben got to his feet and started to walk out of the room. When he was halfway to the door to the sleeping quarters, Dani called out desperately, "Ben, answer the question! You must know how this makes you look!"

He stopped and for one moment stood with his back to them. Then he turned, and his mouth had a hard, bitter line. Ben's eyes penetrated Dani, seeming to ignore the others. In a clipped voice, not at all like his own, he barked out, "I don't guess we have to have Maxwell Stone to dig out our private griefs. You're just as good at it as he is, Miss Ross." After scanning the room, looking into each face, his eyes came back to Dani, and he said quietly,

"Who was Florrie? Why, she was a girl I knew once." As he disappeared into the sleeping quarters, they all stared with shock at the empty door.

Rachel asked Dani cynically, "Where does *that* get us, detective?"

Dani sat there, stunned. Her heart told her that Ben was no murderer, but his refusal to speak about his past looked bad. She looked to Holtz, who was regarding her, and her eyes pleaded for help.

He shook his head, his face lined with strain. "We must not make too little of this. It looks bad for Ben. But we must also not make too much."

"There's still that knife under the vent, Commander," Betty broke in sharply. "And he's had the training to kill a man just the way Rosie was killed."

"Yes. As I say, it looks bad. But let us not take any vote tonight. It may be that Ben is our assassin, but I will not turn my back on *any* of you yet. Now, it is late. We will have more of this tomorrow."

They broke up, and Dani went to bed wearing so many clothes and covering herself with so many blankets that she could hardly turn over. She was more upset than she had shown the others. Ben Savage had been the *one* person in the absurd tragedy she had believed in without reservation. Now she felt as if someone had jerked a ladder out from under her, and she had nothing to cling to.

That night the winds that moaned through the vents were no sadder or more ominous than Dani's dreams.

11
"Is It Just for Good People?"

"Doc, I feel rotten!" Vince caught Karen as she came out of the sleeping quarters. He shivered in the icy air and tried to smile, but it didn't come off. "Guess I've got the grandpappy of all bad colds."

Karen's quick glance took in the uncontrollable shaking. When he broke out into a spasm of coughing, she said, "Sit down, Vince, and I'll check your temperature." While he sat with the thermometer between his lips, she took his pulse. She took out the thermometer, glanced at it, then ordered, "Unbutton your shirt, Vince." He flinched as the cold metal of her stethoscope touched his chest.

"Whatcha think, Doc?"

"Take two of these aspirin every four hours, and I want you to stay in bed for a couple of days." She ignored his protests, and after he ate a little breakfast, he went back to bed.

She sat at the table with Ben, Rachel, and Holtz, and Rachel asked, "What's the matter with Vince?"

"I think it's the flu—but he's been spitting up a little blood. Could easily develop into pneumonia."

"Wonder we don't all get it!" Rachel said. Her dark eyes showed a trace of humor, and she laughed. "Wouldn't it be a big joke on Mr. Maxwell Stone if we all died of natural causes instead of being murdered according to his little plan?"

Karen stared at her, then shook her head. "It's too serious to joke about, Rachel. This is no place to take care of a sick man. I've seen epidemics of this lay everybody out; and in this freezing prison, it'd be deadly. This cold—it's terrible!"

"I've been thinking about that," Ben said. Surprisingly, his bitterness of the previous night seemed to be gone.

He's hurt inside, though. Karen thought. *He's covering it up well, but something about that girl stays with him all the time!*

"The heat from the stoves is going right up," he said, gesturing toward the lofty area above. "If we had some sort of canvas and some rope, we could rig a canopy overhead that'd hold the heat in."

At once they all saw what he meant, and Holtz slapped the table. "Exactly! Sort of a tent, you mean? Yes!" He pulled a notebook out of his pocket and asked, "How much canvas, Ben? And what kind?"

Savage looked up, then across the room, calculating, "Take at least a thousand square yards, I think. Nylon, maybe, or some kind of tenting material. Have to have several spools of three-eighth-inch nylon rope." He shook his head as Holtz wrote this down and said, "Nothing to anchor to on the walls. Only way I can think of is to drill some holes; then you'd need some clips or eye bolts to anchor the ropes to the holes."

"You don't think Stone will give us all that?" Rachel scoffed.

"We won't know until we ask," Holtz pointed out. He questioned Ben carefully. Once he'd dropped the paper through the slot, Holtz said, "It's in the hands of God now."

"No, it's in the hands of Maxwell Stone!" Rachel corrected him, but she smiled unexpectedly and glanced toward Dani, "But I guess you'd say that Stone was in the hands of God, wouldn't you?"

"We are all in God's hands, Rachel," Dani answered. "I know some of you don't like to hear sermons, but I'd like to have our service now—here around the table. Would that be all right?"

Rachel stared across at her, then said, "Sure, if you'll let *me* pick the sermon. I'd like to hear an explanation about why all this has happened. Two people dead, the rest of us pretty fair candidates for the same. Where's your God in all this, Dani?"

Dani stood, knowing that Rachel was taunting her. She prayed quickly for guidance, then began slowly, arranging her thoughts as she spoke.

"You're not the first person to ask that question, Rachel. As a matter of fact, one of your own people asked it a lot more strongly than you just put it. You'll find it in the book of Job. Let me read you the first two chapters." She read the ancient story carefully, then looked around at them. "Job lost everything—his money, his home, his family—even his health. And he was so overcome by the terrible losses, that in chapter three he cursed the day of his birth. He longed for death, and his faith in God seemed to be gone, for in the last two verses he cried out, 'I have no peace, no quietness; I have no rest but only turmoil,' and in chapter seven, he asked the same question that you've asked, Rachel—and the same question, I believe, that everyone asks at one time or another. This is the way it reads in the New International Version." She quoted from her memory:

"Will you never look away from me,
  or let me alone even for an instant?
If I have sinned, what have I done to you,
  O watcher of men?
Why have you made me your target?
  Have I become a burden to you?
Why do you not pardon my offenses
  and forgive my sins?
For I will soon lie down in the dust;
  you will search for me, but I will be no more.

" 'Why have you made me your target?' " Dani smiled faintly as she said, "That's what we all feel at some time or other when life is falling apart—*Why are you doing this to me, God?* To the ancient Jews it was indisputable that God is almighty, that He is just, and that no human being is innocent in His sight. That's why, when Job's three friends came to reason with him, after he lost everything, circumstances made them think that Job was suffering because he had done wrong. That's the problem that Job and his friends grapple with—why do the righteous suffer?"

"Yeah, how about that!" Lonnie broke in suddenly. "My oldest sister never hurt nobody. She worked herself to death, raising us eight kids. Then when she was only thirty-seven years old, she got sick and died." Lonnie's round face turned hard and, with a bitter edge to his voice, he added, "She didn't go easy, either. Took her a year to die, and she hurt something awful the whole time. Why'd God let that happen?"

A sense of frustration swept over Dani, for she saw that not only Lonnie, but all the others were reacting with a stubbornness based on doubt. Her hands trembled as she clutched her Bible, longing to give up. But her stubborn streak held Dani in place.

"I don't have the answer to that, Lonnie. Job didn't get any answer, either. At times he became almost bitter against God. Once he cried out, 'Tell me what charges you have against me. Does it please you to oppress me, to spurn the work of your hands, while you smile on the schemes of the wicked?' But Job never gave up on God! In chapter thirteen he says, 'Though he slay me, yet will I hope in him!' "

Holtz asked quietly, "I have never understood that book, though I have read it often. How could a man who had been almost destroyed still have hope?" He looked around at the faces of his fellow prisoners, seeking for an answer, then shrugged. "I suppose he was a saint. But I am not a saint, Danielle—so it's difficult for me to look at this terrible thing we're caught up in and have much hope."

Candi's voice sounded thin and reedy, and her face was tense as she said, "Dani, that's in a book, but this prison ain't something made up! And I'm *scared!*" Her mouth trembled, and she tried to say more, but could not.

Dani said quietly, "I'm scared, too, Candi. I think we all are. I think Job must have been at times. But Job had one hope. He knew that God was just—he *knew* that! The ancient Jews never believed anything else. So Job kept saying, 'If I could just find God! He'd help me, He'd understand!' That's why in chapter twenty-three, verse three, he says:

> "If only I knew where to find him;
> If only I could go to his dwelling!
> I would state my case before him
> and fill my mouth with arguments.
> I would find out what he would answer me
> and consider what he would say.
> Would he oppose me with great power?
> No, he would not press charges against
> me.
> There an upright man could present
> his case before him,
> and I would be delivered forever
> from my judge.

"Job wants to find a merciful God; he says so over and over again," Dani said. "And he is *absolutely* sure that such a God exists. He says 'I know that my Redeemer lives, and that in the end he will stand upon the earth.' But who is this redeemer?"

Dani began to chronicle man's efforts to find peace throughout the history of the world. Finally she said, "Man has been suffering since the beginning of time, and he has cried out, 'Where is the one who can deliver us? Where is the strong one who is able to destroy our enemies of fear, of hatred, of famine—of all the plagues of the human heart?'"

Dani opened her Bible, looked at it for what seemed a long time, and when she spoke there were tears in her eyes. "When the deliverer came, he didn't come with pomp and ceremony, and he didn't come as a king to sweep evil away with a flashing sword. Let me read to you how He did come."

But she didn't read from the open Bible. She began to quote from the Bible version she had memorized as a child, and the quiet words seemed to hover in the cold air.

> "And Joseph also went up from Galilee, out of the city of Nazareth, into Judaea, unto the city of David, which is called Bethlehem . . . To be taxed with Mary his espoused wife, being great with child. And so it was, that, while they were there, the days were accomplished that she should be delivered. And she brought forth her firstborn son, and wrapped him in swaddling clothes, and laid him in a manger; because there was no room for them in the inn."

She blinked the tears away, and her lips softened as she said, "I always cry over that—to think that the deliverer of mankind was born in a stable!" Then she dashed the tears away quickly and quoted again:

> "And there were in the same country shepherds abiding in the field, keeping watch over their flock by night. And, lo, the angel of the Lord came upon them, and the glory of the Lord shone round about them: and they were sore afraid. And the angel said unto them, Fear not: for . . . I bring you good tidings of great joy, which shall be to all people. For unto you is born this day in the City of David a Saviour, which is Christ the Lord."

She closed her Bible and looked around. Sid was looking down, so she could not see his face, and Candi was weeping freely, her tears leaving marks down her cheeks.

"One week from tomorrow will be December twenty-fifth—Christmas. For most people, it's tinsel and Santa Claus. But for me, it's for that baby who was born: God's only begotten Son.

"But he's not a baby in a manger now," she said, and her voice rose. "He grew up, became the only perfect man the world ever saw. And when he was thirty-three years old, he was taken out and crucified. The Bible says that Jesus didn't die for His own sins. He died for our sins, for the sins of the world. And that's what Job meant when he said, 'I know that my redeemer lives. . . .' "

She quoted some New Testament Scriptures and ended, "We may die in this prison, but even if we get out, we'll die someday. For me, Jesus Christ is the answer. If I die in this place, I'll die trusting God!"

After Dani sat down, the others got up and went about other things, and despair gathered in her breast. *What good is it?* she thought bitterly. *They don't care—even with death at our elbows, they don't care!* Bowed down with a sense of futility, she blamed herself. *God, I'm no preacher. I can't do this again! I won't!* She got up, and the cold, bleak air of the silo seemed to creep into her spirit.

All morning she went over the information sheets with Holtz, and finally, after a bowl of soup at noon, doggedly returned to the task. Once she said, "This job is just about as useless as pecking away at that concrete!"

Holtz placed his hand over hers. "You are tired and a little discouraged." His grip was strong, and he squeezed her hand firmly. "Why don't you go take a nap? You'll feel better."

She put her own hand on top of his, noting how strong he was, despite his age. "All right, Karl," she answered wanly. "At least I'll get *warm!*" She went to her bunk, noting that Candi was buried under her small mountain of blankets. The air was so cold it hurt her lungs, so she burrowed deep under her blankets. After a while she grew warm and dropped off into a fitful sleep.

Awakening with a start when hands touched her, fear shot through Dani. "What . . . !" She shut off her startled cry, when, burrowing out from under her blankets, she found Candi kneeling beside her, weeping and shivering in the cold air. "Candi! What's wrong?"

"I—I don't know!" Candi unsuccessfully tried to stop the convulsive sobs that racked her.

"Are you sick? Can I get Karen?"

"No! I ain't sick. I'm just scared!"

At once Dani knew what was troubling the woman. She looked around and, seeing that the other women were gone, offered gently, "Candi, sit with me. We'll cover up and stay warm while we talk." Then she pulled Candi close and, under the covers, felt her quaking frame. Wrapping her arms around the other woman, Dani said, "Candi, Jesus loves you!"

Instantly Candi collapsed against Dani, emitting great sobbing cries. Finally she grew still, and Dani said, "Let me tell you how to have peace, Candi—" She began to speak softly, quoting Scriptures, answering questions, and finally she asked, "Would you like to have Jesus Christ in your heart, Candi?"

"Oh, Dani! You don't *know* what I've done!" she wailed. "You've been good, but I can't even *say* the things I've done!"

"Why, Candi, don't you know that they called Jesus 'the friend of sinners?' He didn't die for the good—because there are none! He died for sinners like you and me."

Dani prayed constantly that none of the others would come in. After a long time Dani said, "I'll pray for you, Candi. You just tell Jesus that you've been wrong, then ask Him to forgive you and to give you peace." She began to pray at once. The other woman's body tensed, but finally Candi gave a muffled cry, drew back, and stared at Dani with wide-open eyes.

"Oh, Dani!" she whispered, and her whole face was alight with a joy that made Dani rejoice. "I feel so—so— *peaceful!*" she exclaimed. "It's like a big load just dropped off my back!" She dashed the tears away from her eyes and whispered, "Is this what you feel?"

"Yes!" Dani was crying, too, and some of the joy that bubbled up in Candi seemed to be rising in her. She had never felt anything quite like it. "Jesus is the prince of peace, Candi!"

"Will it always be this way?"

"Well—" Dani hesitated, then nodded firmly. "He said one time, ' . . . My peace I give unto you. Not as the world giveth. . . .' I guess the world takes away what it gives— and He doesn't."

When Dani mentioned the terrible danger that faced them, Candi nodded. "Sure, I know. But it's not so bad now." Her face grew serious, and she was silent. Finally she nodded as if she had settled something and smiled at Dani, saying, "You know what? No matter how this thing turns out, I'm ahead of the game. I mean, if I'd stayed outside, how much chance would there have been for me to get saved? Not much! Not too many preachers in a strip joint! So if I do make it, one thing is sure—I'm never going back to that life!"

When Rachel called them to dinner, Candi said hurriedly, "And if I *don't* make it, why that's all right, too!" She squeezed Dani, threw off the blankets, and said as she got out of the bunk, "I'm like you now, Dani. If I die in this place, I'll die trusting Jesus!" She suddenly wheeled and ran out of the room.

Rachel stared after her. "What's with her?" she asked Dani.

"Why, I think she's just met up with one of your countrymen, Rachel."

"What's that you say?" Rachel asked suspiciously.

"Why, she's just met a man from Nazareth—Jesus by name."

Rachel's smooth face was marred with anger that turned her mouth cruelly down. "Leave *me* alone!" Then she wheeled and went to the bathroom, slamming the door and snapping the lock bolt home, as if she were shutting herself up in another world. She always locked herself in for the long showers she loved. But this time the expression on her face was a harder denial than the steel bolt on the door.

Dani shook her head sadly, wondering how she would ever be able to break through Rachel's wall. As she put on her shoes, Dani thought, *Rachel may be harder even than Vince or Sid.* As she passed out of the room she whispered, "But Candi was hard, too!"

At breakfast, Lonnie looked up from his eggs to ask, "What's with you, Candi?" Then he shot a quick glance at Dani and nodded. "Oh—you hit the glory trail, I reckon."

Candi smiled, and a flush touched her cheeks. "Sure, that's it, Lonnie. A little late—" She faltered, but caught Dani's encouraging smile, and it brought her head up. "A little late, but let me tell you, it's the best thing that ever happened to me."

Karen smiled briefly. "I'm glad for you, Candi." She pushed her plate back, saying soberly, "I guess you all know that Vince is worse."

"He coughed all night." Betty nodded. "And it's one of those hollow, dry coughs, too, the worst kind!"

"Yes, I'm afraid so. And Rachel has a temperature."

"I'll be all right," Rachel protested, but her cheeks were flushed and she looked little better than Vince.

"Vince's lungs aren't good. I think he has pneumonia. I don't want to take chances; I'm putting you both on the strongest antibiotic I've got," Karen added. "It'll make you sleepy, but that's what you need anyway."

At ten o'clock the supplies were lowered, and as usual everyone gathered to see what was sent.

"Look!" Karen cried out as the basket came to eye level, "It's filled with the canvas you asked for!"

Holtz pulled at the light-blue nylon cloth and turned to Ben, asking, "Will this do?"

"Yes." Ben nodded, and his face seemed less bleak than before. "There'll be more, I guess." As they quickly unloaded and the basket ascended, he commented, "I was pretty sure we wouldn't get this stuff."

"So was I," Bix agreed. "Maybe our luck's going to change."

The supply box was lowered twice, the last load containing a heavy drill motor and several bits. Just as they got them all unloaded, Maxwell Stone's voice came so unexpectedly that all of them started.

"Now, you are aware that I am not the monster you have made me out to be." A trace of self-satisfaction had entered his voice. "You have the material you requested to insulate your quarters. I must warn you, however, that if you attempt to use the drill for any other purpose, you will be severely punished."

Karen said quickly, "We have a very sick man on our hands. He needs to be in a hospital."

"That is out of the question. You may have whatever medicine you desire, Dr. Sanderson, but at the risk of being repetitious, I must remind you that the key to your release is in *your* hands, not mine! As the poet Milton said, 'The mind is it's own place, and in itself Can make a Heaven of Hell—a Hell of Heaven.' So you must make your own destiny." He paused, then asked, "Have any of you decided to rid yourself of the guilt we've so often spoken of?"

"What guilt?" Rachel suddenly stepped forward and lifted her face defiantly toward the camera. "Stone, everything you say is insane! Why, your words are like 'a tale Told by an idiot, full of sound and fury'!" She lifted her fist and shook it at the camera, shouting, "I confess that you are a lunatic! I confess that if I ever get the chance, I'll cut your throat!" Suddenly taken by a fit of coughing, she was forced to stop.

Angered Sid yelled, "She's right, Stone! *You're* the one who should be confessing! Them two people you killed—Rosie and Alex—was worth a hundred of you!"

"And how much were the people worth whom *you* killed, Valentine?" Stone shot back instantly. "How many were there? At least five—including two women—were there not?" Stone began to reel out a series of charges and convictions, along with dates, and each one seemed a club that struck Sid with telling force. When Stone finally came to an end, he asked caustically, "How many lives are *you* worth? You should have been executed years ago! But in this day it's very difficult for a man to be punished for his crime! Instead of handing out death sentences, our courts are handing out candy to murderers! But that will change, oh, yes! All will be level in our government, I promise you!"

Holtz suddenly cried out, "Don't think us all fools, Stone! Government? We know very well what *your* government will be!"

"It will be quite unlike the government that made *you*, Herr Holtz!" Stone shot back. "The degenerates of the Third Reich produced a race of killers. The government of my own country has gone in the opposite direction, so that criminals rule the streets and honest men and women huddle in fear. Men chase after women like dogs! There is no honor among them—and the women have the moral standards of Cleopatra, that harlot of the Nile who debauched the rulers of her day!" He ranted on wildly, ending, "You have been given the opportunity to confess your errors—an opportunity, I might add, that you have not always given to others! But you must act for yourselves, for I will not force you."

The speaker went dead. Sid's face had turned white, and he looked around with a hangdog expression, as if he expected someone to accuse him. When no one did, he wiped his brow, turned, and walked away.

Dani went at once to Holtz's desk and began writing. She was just finishing a page when she became aware that someone had come to stand beside her. Looking up quickly, she was shocked to find Ben gazing down at her.

"Sit down, Ben." She tossed the pen on the desk. "I'm sorry about asking you about—about the girl."

"You haven't forgotten her name, have you?" he asked. "*Florrie* was her name. But that's part of the deal, isn't it? Get everything out in the open?"

Dani moved uneasily, unable to read his face. "I—I don't know if that's such a good idea," she murmured. "I know you aren't the killer. You got into this trying to help me, and now I've done something to you. Something I regret very much!"

He studied her then shrugged. "Don't worry about it," he said. "I want to tell you something. Then maybe I'd like to ask you a question."

"All right."

"It's about Sid. He never knew his father. His mother was a prostitute. She threw him out when he was nine years old. He grew up on the streets. He got his first conviction when he was ten and constantly went in and out of reform school."

He paused, and Dani looked up uncertainly. There was little expression on his face, but she knew he was leading up to something. Ben went on slowly, telling her Valentine's totally bleak story. Finally he said, "Sid has been all that Stone said, I guess. He's thirty-nine years old, and half of his life has been spent behind bars. He's a thief and a murderer—and just about everything else you'd care to name."

When Dani saw that he was finished, she shook her head. "How terrible, Ben!"

"Sure," he nodded. "Now, about the question, boss."

"What is it?" she had no idea where he was going.

"Well, I've been watching you. We all have. You've been doing a lot of preaching. I guess I was pretty impressed the way you jumped in and gave Morrow some kind of comfort." He gave her a level stare. "And I like the way you've helped Candi. I can see she's in better shape today."

Suddenly he shook his head and touched the scar on his forehead. He sat staring at her so long that Dani finally said, "Well, Ben, come out with it."

"All right." He dropped his hand. "I haven't seen you talking to Sid—or to Vince. So here's my question: This brand of religion you've got, is it just for *good* people?"

"Of course not!" she snapped, and a flush touched her cheeks. "If it were, I wouldn't have talked to Candi!"

"Come on," Ben said in a hard voice. "Candi's not like those two, and you know it! If they are, what's kept you from trying to convert them? You ever talk to them like you did to Morrow or to Candi—one on one?"

"Well, no." Dani tried to speak, to explain, but could not find the words. As she struggled, to her discomfort, she realized he was *right*. She *had* excluded Sid and Vince because she had little compassion for them. Her exhilaration over Candi's conversion faded, and the bitter doubt that came from his words caused her to lose her temper.

"I think you're being very unfair!" she said through clenched teeth. "Those two aren't my responsibility!"

Savage got to his feet and looked down at her with a thoughtful expression. "Oh?" he said quietly. "Guess I was wrong." He cocked his head and murmured, "I always thought we were supposed to be our brothers' keepers . . . ?"

Then he walked away, and Dani bent over the desk, not knowing if the tears that came were produced by anger or guilt.

12
A Private Ghost

"Hey, you know this game is gettin' sort of interesting!" Bix looked up from where he sat across from Dani. The two of them had been going over Karl's endless lists, trying to find connections. "But I don't see that this is ever going to get us anywhere. Look here, for example, Dani. According to this list, all of us have been in a hospital at least once. Well, so what? Almost everybody's been in a hospital, right?"

"That's the way investigations work, Bix. It would be nice if all you had to sort through was the *relevant* material, but the trouble is, you don't *know* what's relevant until you look at it." Dani leaned back, put her hands behind her head, and stretched. "If we'd found that we'd all been in the *same* hospital, that would be important. But so far we've only come up with five things that all of us have in common."

"Yeah? What are they?"

Dani smiled as she recited them. "We all own cars, have

been in a courtroom for some reason, own a television set, have seen *Gone With the Wind*, and have owned or now own a pet."

Bix seemed disappointed. "Well, what about that being in court? Maybe some crazy judge is mad at us—trying to knock off a bunch of people he couldn't nail in the courtroom."

"Nope. We were all in different courts, for different reasons. Some were just witnesses or doing jury duty." She looked over to where Ben and Lonnie were installing the canopy and asked, "Do you think that thing will keep some heat in?"

"What? Oh, sure, I guess so." Bix was looking down at the stack of papers, still thinking about them. "How else are you and the commander sorting these things out?"

"Oh, we've got them categorized another way. How many things have all of us except *one* done? For example, all of us except Lonnie have been outside the country at least once; and all of us except Rachel have been to Dallas." She suddenly shook her head in a gesture of weariness. "It's a pretty long shot, Bix, but it's the only game in town." She rose, saying, "Think I'll see if Vince wants some lemonade."

Is it just for good people? As she brought Vince the drink Ben's question floated again into Dani's thoughts, and the unfairness of it pushed against her mind. Unconsciously she shook her head defiantly. *What does he know? I can't please everyone!* Though she tried to push away her anger, it would not leave.

"Hello." She looked down, startled to find Vince was awake. He was looking at her with feverish eyes, and his voice sounded hollow and thin.

"Why, hello, Vince." She smiled at him. "Could you drink some nice cold lemonade?"

"Guess so," he murmured and struggled to sit up. Dani helped him and pushed an extra pillow behind his back for support. He took the glass and drank thirstily, she noticed that his hand trembled. "Thanks a lot." His mouth turned up in a weak smile, and he shook his head. "Never been sick before. Sure is a drag, ain't it, Dani?"

"You'll feel better soon," she said. "When they get that canopy up, it'll be warmer."

He nodded and suddenly broke out into a spasm of coughing that left him breathless.

Dani could only sit there helplessly, watching him shiver. *Why, he's whipped!* she realized with a sense of shock. *He thinks he's going to die!* It came to her that the sickness was worse for him, because he'd never experienced anything like it. He was a man of great physical strength, strength he'd used to get the things he wanted.

"Karen's a good doctor," she comforted, making her voice as hopeful as she could. "It takes time for antibiotics to work, but by tomorrow, you'll feel better." She forced herself to smile, reached out with her free hand, and grasped the clasped hands of the sick man, adding, "It's rough, Vince, but you've been in rough spots before, I'd say."

He looked up at her, his eyes dulled by fever. "Yeah, sure I had a few bumps—but nothin' like *this!* Always before I could fight my way out of a spot, but what's a guy to do with a thing like *this?*" He bit his heavy underlip and dropped his eyes to her hand, then looked back at her, something in his expression that she couldn't read.

"All these 'confessions' that Stone's been looking for

give me a pain! But I guess I can make one right now, Dani—not to him, but to *you*." She shook her head, but he continued, "I ain't never been scared before, and I could tell you about a few times I was sure my number was up. But I'm scared now. I'm so scared I can't see straight."

She tightened her grip on his hands, saying urgently, "Oh, Vince, we're *all* scared. *Anybody* in a terrible trap like this would be scared. It's just human. Nothing to be ashamed of."

"Savage ain't scared," Vince contradicted her quickly. "Neither is Holtz or Rachel. They're pretty hard, those three—and I thought I was as tough as them, but that was before I went down." He suddenly gave his big shoulders a shake and blinked his eyes. "Now don't you come at me with your preaching, Dani, you hear me? I may have done a lot of bad things, but I'm not a whiner! Pretty small to live like the devil all your life, then go crawling to God when your number's up," he stated, trying to look tough. "Gimme some more of that lemonade and tell me what's going on—but no preaching!"

"All right, Vince." While he sipped the lemonade, she described their efforts to find a common denominator that would furnish a key to their mystery. It helped him to have someone there, she saw, so she entertained him with a few of the blind alleys she had followed with their efforts, such as discovering that none of them had ever been in North Dakota. "Maybe the chamber of commerce there is out to get us for ignoring their great state!" She laughed. "If they'd let me out, I'd be *happy* to visit them!"

She sat with him for over an hour, until Karen came in. "Time for your medicine, Vince." Karen gave him two pills, took his pulse, and nodded. "It'll be warm tomorrow, Ben says. You can get up and walk around some."

"Yeah, if I *can* walk—blasted legs are made of rubber!" He lay back and looked up at the two women, a thought stirring in his eyes. "One good thing about this—if anybody else gets knocked off, I'll be clear!"

He closed his eyes and seemed to go to sleep at once. When the two women had walked outside, Dani asked, "How is he?"

"Worse than he looks," Karen said. "His lungs are closing up. I'd put him on oxygen right now, if I had him in a hospital. Let's go ask Ben when he's going to get the roof on." She led the way to where Savage was balancing precariously on top of two tables topped with a chair. "Good thing we have an acrobat with us, Ben," she called up to him. "Anybody else would break his neck on a thing like that!"

He looked down and gave her a slight grin. "Come on up, Doc. I can use a helper."

"No, thanks. When's that thing going to be finished? We're all going to be down with something, if we don't get warm." She looked around the room and asked, "Couldn't you fix the sleeping quarters first? We can manage, but I want Vince out of this cold."

He nodded and put the drill down. "Sure. I should have done that first." He stood up and without warning stepped off into space. Both women gasped, and Dani cried out, "Ben . . . !" But he landed lightly on his feet, seemed to collapse and roll into a ball, and came to his feet lightly.

"Don't *do* that!" Karen said angrily. "All we need is for you to break both your legs!"

He looked at her with surprise then grinned shamefacedly. "Well, it's my only talent, Doc—and anyway, it's safer than trying to climb down that shaky mess." He pulled the cord, caught the drill as it fell, then said, "I was trying to get all the drilling done first, but we can put the canvas up in the other room now, then finish this one tomorrow. Come on, Sid. We'll have to move these tables."

Dani and Karen offered to help but were refused. They got coffee and sat down to watch the two men move the table. "Rachel seems about the same," Karen volunteered. "She's not nearly as sick as Vince—but a thing like that can change fast." They sat there, speaking quietly, and as Ben and Sid carried the last table into the sleeping area, Karen nodded, "I'm glad Ben thought of that. It might save some lives. He's a pretty handy fellow."

"Yes."

Dani's spare speech caused Karen to look at her sharply. "You two have a fight?"

"No. Not a fight, but he—" Dani suddenly found that she could not tell the other woman. She shook her head, saying only, "I'm just edgy today, Karen. For one thing, I keep thinking that our killer hasn't gone on vacation. He's still here, and there's no way we can defend ourselves. We can't sit around in a circle and just *watch* one another all the time, can we?"

"We only have *one* to watch, if you ask me!" Dani and Karen looked up to where Betty was rolling out dough on the serving table. With her head she motioned toward the sleeping area and continued sharply, "That Savage—he's the one, I tell you!"

Candi was watching her closely. She had asked the older woman to teach her to cook and had made but little progress. Now she shook her head. "Oh, Betty, I don't think so! He was the one who thought of putting that tent up. If he wanted to hurt us, he wouldn't have done that."

"Just a cover-up! He's the only one who could climb that rope to get rid of that knife, and he's learned to kill people in the marines. We ought to tie him up before he murders all of us in our beds!"

Dani smiled slightly at this. "If he's as deadly as you say, Betty, I doubt that all the rest of us put together could do that job."

Betty snorted, but Candi looked at her with a strange expression. "Betty, I spent most of my life hating people. Look what it got me." She dropped her head, then raised it suddenly, and the smile on her lips was matched by the light in her eyes. "Being brought to this place was the best thing that ever happened to me. Like I told Dani, even if I don't make it, I've found out there's something better than what I had—better than anything I ever even dreamed of."

Karen gave her a steady look, then commented, "You've changed, Candi. I've never seen anyone change so fast."

Candi laughed self-consciously. "I've hated God most of my life—and now I come to find out that He loves me. Ain't that something? Jesus loves me."

As the three women watched, their reactions differed. Dani felt a warm glow of satisfaction. Karen was glad, but with some reservations. Betty looked at Candi with a look of pure skepticism, but said only, "Well, the proof's in the pudding, I always say. The Bible says the saved are those that hold out to the end."

"But, Betty, it's Jesus who holds onto *us*—that's why I feel so—so *safe!*" Candi suddenly put her arm around the cook and squeezed her, giving a happy laugh. "All my life, I've tried to hold on to things, and I lost everything I ever wanted! Now I've lost everything, but I *know* somehow Jesus is holding on to me, and I don't care about the rest!" Suddenly she gave an embarrassed laugh, then turned and left the kitchen, saying, "I'll see if Rachel wants anything."

Karen grunted. "She'd better not try to spread Christian cheer around Rachel. Might get her head knocked off." She looked at Dani and said with a trace of concern, "Now don't *you* get this bug, Dani! *I* might be the killer, but you're not."

"How do you know that?"

"Too squeamish." Karen nodded wisely. "You threw up after just one look at poor Rosie's head! Nope, it's not you, so you stay well and take care of the rest of us prime suspects." Then she sobered, asking directly, "Dani, do you have *any* ideas at all about who it is?"

"No. I'm a flop on my biggest case, Karen. Sherlock Holmes would have had this thing sewn up by now!" She got up and took a final sip of coffee, saying wearily, "They never told us it'd be like this in Miss Wing's Finishing School for Girls!"

By ten o'clock the men had strung all the ropes in the sleeping quarters then installed the nylon over it.

"I can tell the difference right off!" Lonnie exclaimed joyfully. "Now maybe I'll thaw out!"

They were all tired, and most of them went to bed at once. Ben claimed the shower, since he'd done most of the work, and Karen said, "I'll take my bath tomorrow." The rest of them agreed, but Dani commented, "Everybody will be lined up tomorrow. I'll take my shower after Ben is finished."

She left the sleeping area, noting as soon as she entered the rec room that Lonnie was right—the insulated ceiling *had* made a difference. She fixed a cup of steaming tea, carried it over to the desk, and tried to work, but the frigid air numbed her fingers, so she moved to the couch. She tucked her feet under, pulled a woolly blanket up to her ears, and lay back to wait. The hot tea had warmed her, and she lay there, thinking, until she drifted off into a fitful sleep.

Restlessly she moved as the thoughts became dreams—mostly about her family. At first, they were just memories, but gradually they became terribly real. She dreamed that they were sinking into the earth and calling for her to help. She saw her parents, Rob, and Allison, their faces contorted with fear and pain. Beginning to whimper, trying to get to them, she seemed to be trapped, unable to move. With a violent movement, she attempted to break loose and gave a helpless cry—

"Dani! Wake up!"

She felt someone touching her shoulder and came awake instantly. The dream's fear clung to her, and at first she tried to break away, fighting at the hand.

"You okay?" Ben's face was sober, and only his strong hand kept her from falling off the couch.

"Y-yes," she stammered and sat up suddenly. He stood there watching her, and she tried to smile. "Bad dream," she explained. "I was dreaming about my family."

He nodded, saying, "Yeah, I know. I've thought a lot about them, myself. If I'd handled this thing better—"

"Oh, don't start on that, Ben!" She got up and found

that her feet were asleep, for she pitched forward help-lessly. He caught her and helped her to sit down. Con-scious of his hands, suddenly Dani felt a wave of embarrassment sweep over her. She swallowed hard. "Ben, sit down. I—want to tell you something."

He regarded her suspiciously but sat down and turned to watch her. Watchfulness sparked his hazel eyes, and she thought it would be impossible to break through his tough facade, but she had to try. "I've been having a hard time with what you asked me yesterday—" she began, and haltingly she told him about her anger. She shook her head. "It's been like a dagger, what you said, *'Is it only for good people?'* But I should have been angry at myself, Ben, not you. Because I guess that's what I've been doing, try-ing to stay with the 'good' people. Avoiding the tough ones, because they might hurt my feelings. So I'm sorry that I got angry with you."

He said suddenly, "I had a talk with Vince today. It meant a lot to him, the way you sat and talked to him."

She shook her head, and her mouth was firm. "That's not the same thing, Ben. Vince is no threat to me. He's so sick he's pitiful. But you've made me see what I've been doing. I—I'm going to work on it some, and you'll have to understand, God isn't finished with me yet."

"Better than me." He shrugged. "He hasn't even *started* with me yet!" He asked, "You hungry?"

"Why, I guess I am." She tried her feet, ignored the prickling sensation, and said, "Let's fix a midnight sup-per. What would you like?"

"I'd *like* a spicy Mexican dinner, but I'd settle for just about anything."

They went to the kitchen and made something that came

close to eggs Benedict. Ben fixed coffee and fried bacon, and they sat down and ate with gusto.

As they washed the dishes, Ben said, "Think I'll look at some of the stuff the commander has put together."

"I'll show you what we've got." After collecting mugs of coffee and the papers, they sat on the couch and began to go over the lists. It grew cold, and Dani shivered, so she said, "Let's cover up with that blanket." She tucked it around herself, and he gave her an odd look, then shrugged and did the same.

Soon Dani began to talk about her dream, which led her to speak of how worried she'd been about her family. He listened to her fears for Rob and Allison, then as she spoke about her parents, especially about her father. "He's too sick to do much," she said, "but he won't rest—not him! He'll be at the office, killing himself!" Her hands pulled nervously at the rough blanket.

After a moment, Ben said, "I hope it turns out right for them."

She lifted her head, hearing sadness in his tone. "What about your people, Ben? Won't they be worried?"

"No." He shrugged. "My father died before I was born. My mother's in a mental institution in West Virginia. She hasn't known me for the last five years. I have one brother in prison, but I haven't seen him in a long time. And I've got a sister named *Ruth* somewhere. The Savage family is about played out, I guess."

He turned to face her. Dani saw that his lips were tense, and when he spoke his voice held a terse quality. "I don't care what the others think, but I want to tell you about Florrie."

"Oh, Ben—!"

He shook his head, interrupting her almost brusquely. "It doesn't matter much, I guess. It all happened a long time ago, and it can't have anything to do with Maxwell Stone—but I'd like you to know."

Dani nodded. "If that's what you want, Ben."

Staring across the room, he began, "After my mother was put in the institution, I didn't have a place. They put my brother, Sean, and me in a foster home, but it wasn't good. I stood it as long as I could, but I ran away after a couple of months, not long after my twelfth birthday. Sean was three years younger, so he couldn't go. I bummed around, and three months later I'd just about had it. I knew sooner or later I'd get picked up and sent to a home, but one night I went to a circus."

His face was turned, but Dani saw that the memory made him smile. "I sneaked in, but got caught. They'd have chucked me out, but a family there, Tony and Anna Rudolpho, took me in."

"Were they performers, Ben?" she asked as he paused for a long moment.

"Performers? They were the Flying Rudolphos! The kings and queens of the big top! It was a new life to me. I'd been pretty much pushed around up until then, and they were—kind people. They'd never had any children of their own, so they sort of adopted me.

"I loved the circus and I made up my mind to be a performer—a flyer. They all laughed at me at first. When I told him my plan, Tony said 'A flyer? My boy, you start training for that when you are two years old—you're too old!' He put me on a trampoline and said, 'Turn a back flip—we've got four-year-old girls here who can do that, Ben!' Of course he did it just to scare me off, but I'd done

231

some diving, so I gave it a try. I bounced around to get the feel of it. When it felt right, I did a front somersault—and it was so easy that when I hit again, I did a back one. Anna and Tony stared at me. I told them I'd never even *been* on a trampoline, and they didn't believe me. 'Try a double,' Tony said. Anna argued, but I tried it and made it—not much of one. Meanwhile Tony stared at me and said, 'Never on a trampoline—and he does a double!'

"Well, that was the beginning. I lived for nothing but getting up on the trapeze, and it took two years. I had a lot of natural ability, the best trainers in the world, and nothing but time. So eventually it was Hugo, my catcher, and me doing the flying—and Florrie."

He paused slightly, then went on quickly, as if he wanted to get it all out: "She was a little thing, all steel wire and nerves, a niece of the Rudolphos. We grew up together, along with Hugo. There were other girls, but none of them meant anything to me. It was Florrie from the beginning. She always wore white, with sequins forming a rose. Because she was only nine when I came, I never thought of her as a woman—until one day I caught her as she came out of Hugo's hands. She looked at me without a word. But I loved her from that moment.

"I must have been blind not to see it, but Hugo loved her, too. He was older, and for a long time, I dreamed along, thinking about how it would be when Florrie and I married. All I cared about was her and the flying. Then one day Tony took me aside and told me, 'Everybody knows it but you, Ben. Hugo and Florrie are in love.' "

The silence in the room was almost palpable. Dani sensed the agony that Ben covered up with his tight voice. He said, "It kept eating at me, and I tried to leave, but I didn't. I hated Florrie—and Hugo, too—but I never showed it. Somehow I tried to think it would change, that she'd see how I loved her, and she'd leave Hugo—but that never happened."

He moved slightly, and Dani could see that his features were no longer steady. Slowly, controlling his voice with effort, he continued, "Everything went on. One day Hugo said, 'Florrie and I are getting married next month, Ben. I hope you'll come to the wedding.' I said, 'Sure, I'll come.' But something happened to me. I turned to ice inside. And that night—"

Suddenly he broke off, and his hands were trembling as he put his face in them. His shoulders began to heave, and when Dani heard the choking sobs that gathered in his throat, she put her arms around him, saying, "Ben, what happened?"

"We—were ready to do the last pass. Hugo would be holding Florrie; I'd do a double; and Florrie would pass under me as I came out of it. It looked dangerous, but it really wasn't. That night, as I was at the top of my back-swing, I saw Hugo! And—and I hated him! Something happened to me—something went wrong with the timing. I came at the two of them—her in his hands, before they were ready, and—" He could not finish. Dani drew him close, as she would have drawn a hurt child, pulling his head down to her shoulder. "I hit them like a cannonball!" He cried out, "We all three fell, and Florrie and I hit the net, but Hugo—Hugo caught just the edge of it! He—he tried to stop himself, but he couldn't. He hit the floor, and—" Ben shook his head, and his eyes were wide with shock. "He broke his back! And he died a week later!"

Dani felt his body convulse with the force of his sobs.

His tears felt warm on her own face as she held him tightly. She crooned meaningless words of comfort, and slowly his body relaxed. Finally he pulled back. His arms had been clinging to her, and now their faces were only inches apart.

"It was an accident!" she whispered, and her eyes were enormous in the dim light. She was soft and there was something gentle in her lips as she said, "It wasn't your fault, Ben. You can't punish yourself forever."

He seemed hypnotized by her, and now that the terrible sobs had ceased, he was robbed of his natural defenses. The wall had fallen down, and now she held him in her arms, and without purposing such a thing, he slowly leaned forward and kissed her.

Dani could not seem to move. She had never seen a strong man broken as Ben had been; and he had become more of a child than a man. She had put her arms around him to comfort him, simply drawn by the desire to help assuage the agony of grief that tore him apart.

But Ben was not a child, and his lips had fallen on hers and lingered long enough for her to feel a stirring that caused her to pull him closer. As his arms tightened, she sudden became aware of her own weakness. She pulled away sharply, drawing back, and at once he released her. She threw back the blanket and rose. He did the same.

"I—I'm glad you told me about it, Ben," she said, hesitantly.

He was looking at her strangely, but said only, "I never told anyone else about Florrie and Hugo. I guess maybe I should have. I feel—like something's been taken off me."

"I'm glad, Ben! I'm very glad."

"You're pretty good with people, boss. I don't think

anyone else would have been able to get me to tell about that part of my life. But about that kiss—" He saw her drop her eyes, and then asked, "Was that part of the treatment? Or did you really mean it?"

Dani closed her eyes. Her nerves still tingled, but she shook her head. "It was just a kiss, Ben. I—I felt so bad for you!" Then she lifted her eyes, and he saw that they were filled with some sort of apprehension—almost a fear—that he didn't understand. "Don't make anything of it," she whispered.

He nodded but still didn't move. Finally he said, "I think it *did* mean something—" He gave a small nod, and turned to leave.

But he paused long enough to say, "I think it meant something that you don't want to talk about, but I guess you've got your own private ghosts, Miss Ross, just like the rest of us!"

13
Candi

Snow began to fall on Thursday morning, drifting out of an iron-gray sky—heavy, damp flakes almost as large as dimes. Gusts of cold wind drove small clusters of them through the vents. They danced wildly around each other, settling heavily to the floor.

One fell on Dani's cheek, and she slapped at the burning sensation with a startled motion, then glanced up to see flakes whirling like motes as they hustled through the narrow apertures. She smiled, turning to Bix and Betty, who were standing together at the serving table. "Looks as if we'll have a white Christmas."

Both looked at her, then glanced upward.

Betty worried, "I hope they get that thing up soon—it's hard enough to cook in this place without sloshing around in snow!"

Bix shook his head dubiously. He had been working with Sid and Ben all morning, trying to get the guy ropes in place for the canopy. "Not as easy as in the other room,"

236

he said. "There's no center wall to support the canopy. Have to have more anchors, or the thing will sag so much the canvas won't stay in place—and if it's got to hold some snow, that'll be even harder."

Dani looked over to where Ben balanced precariously on the pyramid of tables, joining the ropes that crisscrossed the space. "It's a lot like making a spiderweb," she mused. "Except Ben's no spider." All morning he had moved from spot to spot, tying the ropes, and since there was no other way to get that high—and no one else would volunteer to mount the shaky affair—it was a slow process. She shook her head. "I'll be glad when Ben doesn't have to risk his neck on that thing."

Shortly before twelve, Ben came down, saying, "That's all the network—we can put the canvas on after lunch."

"Karen, I promised Vince he could come out and eat with us if I got the canopy in," Dani reminded the doctor.

"It's not on yet," Karen said. "He doesn't need to get too cold."

"Oh, but he's so *tired* of that cot!" Candi cried. "We can move one of the big chairs over and wrap him up!"

"Yeah, give him a break," Sid urged, and when Karen nodded, he gave a rare smile and dashed off, calling back, "Somebody get the chair ready, and I'll give him a hand."

By the time Vince came out, wrapped in a heavy coat and leaning heavily on Sid, everything was ready. A cheer went up, along with a burst of applause as Sid steered him to the chair and he collapsed into it. Vince's face was pale, and he had lost weight; but he looked around, and some of his old cockiness appeared as he waved a hand, saying, "Aw, come on, you guys—let's chow down!"

Dani helped serve the food, stopping to ask Rachel, "How are you feeling? Any better?"

Rachel nodded and attempted a small smile. "Yes—a little. I'm just so weak!" She shook her head, adding in despair, "It's that medicine Karen keeps giving me. It just knocks me out!"

"That's the way it hits some people, Rachel," Karen said. "But you need lots of sleep, so you stay on it for at least another day."

Betty had fixed two lunches, a light soup for Vince and Rachel and fried chicken and mashed potatoes for the rest of them. Lonnie took a huge bite out of a leg, chewed it thoughtfully, then said, "Hey, Betty, I thought you was a good ol' southern girl?"

Betty gave him a startled look, then snapped, "I *am!*"

Lonnie shook his head, "Aw, come on now! I may be dumb, but one thing I do know is fried chicken. I et all kinds, and you can always tell where you are in this country by the way they do chicken." He took another bite and shook his head. "I ain't sayin' it's bad—it just ain't southern."

Betty muttered, "You eat so fast you never taste anything, Lonnie Gibbs. I guess I ought to know where I come from!" She turned abruptly to Ben, demanding, "Well, are you going to get that cover over us today or not?"

"Won't take more than two or three hours, Betty," he said. Ben sat there, eating slowly and listening to Bix argue with Karl about music. Once he caught Dani's glance and she seemed embarrassed, dropping her eyes. When Karen left their table, he said, "You ought to be arrested, boss."

She looked up, a startled expression in her eyes. "Arrested?"

"For practicing without a license." Idly he pushed his potatoes around with a spoon, and when he looked at her suddenly, there was a touch of wonder in his eyes. "I never had much use for psychiatry, but I guess they must have something going. All that stuff about lying on a couch and telling everything—I thought it was nutty." He shook his head slowly. "I've been pretty locked up inside for a long time. Maybe that's why, ever since I left the circus, I tried every dangerous thing I could find—like the Rangers. Maybe the shrinks would say I was trying to off myself—and they might not be far wrong. But last night, after I did what I've *never* done—squalled like a hurt puppy!—something changed."

Dani stared at him. "What do you think it is, Ben?"

"Don't know," he said, folding his square hands into fists. "All I know is, I slept last night like a baby. No dreams at all. And when I woke up this morning, I—I could think about Florrie and Hugo for the first time since the accident without wanting to jump off a bridge." His face was intensely sober as he added, "I owe you one for that, boss."

His steady gaze flustered Dani. She felt her face glowing and said quickly, "I don't think it was anything I did, Ben. *You* managed to speak about Florrie and Hugo. Psychiatrists are right in line with the Bible in one way: They all agree that confession has to come before a man or a woman can be set free. Why, there's even a verse in the Bible that says, 'Confess your faults one to another.' "

"Yeah, but I've got the idea that if you hadn't been in the right place, at the right time, I'd never have been able to say it to anyone." He gave her a peculiar glance and added, "You know, I've been waiting for something ever since I met you."

"Why, waiting for what?"

"Why, waiting for you to start preaching at me."

A faint color touched Dani's cheek; she tried to smile. "I—I've wanted to, Ben. You'd be surprised if you knew how many nights I've been kept awake thinking about you."

He grinned suddenly, his lips broad and touched with a rare humor. "That right, boss?"

The color in her cheeks deepened, and she lifted her head, giving him a steady look. "Not like that. I want to see you find Jesus Christ. But I know you've got this big wall built up. So—I'll have to wait until something knocks that wall down, Ben."

He started to speak, but at that moment Karen returned, saying, "Come along Rachel—you, too, Vince. Time for your medicine."

Rachel groaned, "I *hate* that stuff, don't you, Vince?"

The big man shrugged as he got up and moved slowly toward the sleeping area. "It makes me sleep—and that's better than staring at the ceiling." Then he stopped and gave a sheepish grin. "Hey, it's great to be back in the world again!"

They all called out a cheery word. Ben broke in, "Come on, you guys, let's get this thing done before we all freeze!"

Betty said shortly, "The kitchen is *filthy!* I want every inch of it scrubbed!"

The two crews went to work at once. Ben, Karl, and Bix scurried around busily, moving the makeshift scaffold from one place to another. Constant scraping sounds and Ben's loud commands as the other two maneuvered the material up to him echoed through the room. Sid left to go work on the Jericho Project, and the chunk of the chisel came faintly to the kitchen crew, composed of Betty, Dani, Karen, and Candi.

Finally Betty pronounced the room clean, but she added firmly, "I've got to organize the meals for next week—and somebody has to peel potatoes and wash all the dishes."

Candi pleaded, "Oh, Betty, I'm so *grimy!*" She had done a great deal of the rough cleaning and was covered with old grease.

"You go take a shower," Dani said quickly. "Karen and I will take care of the rest of it."

After a quick look at Betty, who nodded, Candi gave Dani a hug. "You saved my life, Dani!" she cried and dashed out of the kitchen, calling out to the men as she ran, "Have that thing done by the time I've showered, you hear me?"

"She's a new person," Karen murmured as the three of them went to work. "Not at all what she was like when she first came." She and Dani worked on the potatoes and the dishes, while Betty sat in a chair and pored over her recipes.

Finally Betty looked up, "Oh, for crying out loud! I left some of my recipes under my bed." Soon she came back with the recipes in her hand. "Karen, Rachel's having some kind of spell—tossing and having a nightmare, I reckon," she worried.

"Maybe I'd better go take a look." Karen tossed silverware into a drawer, and threw over her shoulder, "I'll finish the dishes after I have a look at Rachel and Vince."

Dani finished peeling the potatoes and moved over to see what Betty was planning. "Oh, Betty, not spaghetti *again!*" she moaned.

"Well, if you think you can do better, sit down here and help." Dani pulled up a chair, and soon the two were engrossed in planning the meals. Once Betty gave Dani a quick glance and asked, "What Lonnie said about my not being from the South—that was crazy, wasn't it?"

"Oh, he was just showing off."

"Well, he'd better be careful." Betty sniffed. "With all these lists and things going around, I'm afraid to say anything!"

Dani and the older woman were just finishing when Karen came to finish the dishes. "How were they?" Dani asked.

"Why, Rachel was out like a light," she answered. "Betty, what did you say she was doing?"

Betty looked flustered. In an offended voice, she said loudly, "I said she was thrashing around and crying—and that's what she was doing!"

Karen and Dani exchanged quick glances, and Karen said, "Why, I don't doubt it—"

"You do so!" Betty cried out, and her face twisted up in what looked like the beginnings of a crying jag. Her hands trembled as she pulled a worn, well-used handkerchief out of her pocket and put it to her face. "You might as well come right out and call me a liar! Just like that Lonnie!"

Then she did burst out crying, and both Dani and Karen went to her side, mystified. Over and over Karen assured her that she had meant nothing by her remark, and Dani made equal assurances that Lonnie's remark was innocent enough.

When Betty's shoulders finally stopped shaking, she turned a tearstained face up to them. "I don't know what's the matter with me!" she exclaimed. "I've never acted like this in my whole life."

"Well, you've never had the pressures you've got now, Betty." Dani put her arm around the woman's thin shoulders. "You've done so much for all of us! You've worked like a slave, cooking and taking care of us—and I haven't even taken time to tell you how much I appreciate it—or how much I love you."

At the words *I love you*, Betty started to cry again. Finally, Karen nodded slightly over her head toward Dani. "Come along, dear. Let me give you something to make you rest. Dani and I will take care of supper, and—"

"Candi! What's wrong?"

At Bix's shout, all three women whirled to see Candi staggering across the room, her eyes wildly rolling in her head. Betty leaped to her feet, but Karen led the way, running toward Candi.

"What is it?" Karen called out. She reached Candi's side just as the woman fell in a helpless sprawl facedown on the floor. Karen pulled her over, and Dani saw that Candi was dead white and that her lungs were heaving. "She can't breathe, Karen!" Dani cried.

The others stood over them, and Karen shouted, "Get my bag, someone. Help me get her off the floor!" In a flurry of activity Betty raced off to get Karen's bag and Savage scooped the unconscious woman off the floor and placed her on two tables that Sid had shoved together.

"What is it, Karen?" Karl asked anxiously. "Is it a stroke?"

"She's been poisoned!" Bix shouted. "Just like Alex!"

Staring down at Candi, Dani saw the helpless twitching
in her limbs and her gaping mouth, trying, or so it seemed,
to take in air. She was wearing only a bathrobe and a pair
of slippers. Her raspy breathing scraped against Dani's
nerves, and Dani's hands tightened into fists as she
watched her friend's struggles.

Karen said in a tight voice. "Her breathing—
something's wrong with her breathing!" She looked up,
strain showing on her face, and said, "It must be poison!
But it's not the same as Alex."

"Can't we get her to throw up?" Dani asked.

"No, she'd drown if we tried to get anything down her
throat." The helpless look about Karen frightened the others. "I don't know what it is—"

Karen suddenly broke off and pulled back the collar of
Candi's robe. "Look!" She cried out. "She's had some sort
of injection! See these two marks!"

Lonnie said hoarsely, "That's a snakebite! I've seen lots
of 'em!"

"Impossible!" Karl snapped. "There's no snake in this
place!"

"I'll look in the bathroom!" Bix cried at once. "That
murderer may have sneaked one in and put it in there."

He disappeared, but no one saw him go; all watched
Candi's struggle to live. Her breathing became more shal-
low with each breath, and Sid asked in a frightened voice,
"Can't we give her some kind of artificial respiration, Doc?
We gotta do *something!*"

"That wouldn't help," Karen shook her head and spoke
in a voice that wasn't quite steady, "If it's what I think it
is, there's no hope."

"Karen—What?" Dani whispered.

"I believe she's been injected with a poison that works like the venom of some snakes—it may even *be* snake venom."

"I been bit by a rattler and a cottonmouth!" Lonnie said. "And it didn't do nothing like this to me!"

Karen moved Candi's head, trying to make the breathing easier, but it did not help. She kept her eyes fixed on the pale face as she answered, "No, the venom of those snakes are a hemotoxin. It attacks the blood, and that takes time. But some snakes have a venom that attacks the nervous system—neurotoxin. It's—very quick! The green mamba is one. The natives of South America call it the Two-stepper—because if one of them bites you, you only have two steps to get help—or you die."

Fear such as she had not even known existed overcame Dani. Her limbs trembled, and she had a terrifying impulse to yank her hair, throw herself on the floor, curl into a fetal position, and scream and scream—!

Nothing had prepared her for this, and it took every shred of strength she could muster to remain where she was when every nerve cried for her to flee from this horrible sight. She took a wild look around, and saw that others were as hard hit as she was; then she closed her eyes and fought the nausea that crept into her throat.

"Dani! Look, she sees you!"

Dani opened her eyes.

Candi's eyes seemed to plead for something, and her back arched as she fought for breath. "She's trying to tell you something," Karen whispered.

Dani leaned her head down until Candi's lips almost brushed her ear. After a terrible struggle, the lips moved, and Dani heard the faint whisper. She kept her place, listening with all her might, and slowly straightened up.

Candi slowly raised one hand, pointed in a strange gesture—and for a moment her strained features relaxed. A gentle smile touched her lips, and the pain was gone.

Then the arm fell back, and the labored breathing stopped so abruptly that it seemed like a blow.

Karen felt for a pulse, then shook her head. "She's gone."

Karl asked quietly, "What did she say, Dani? Could you make anything of it?"

Dani still held Candi's hand; now she put it on her cheek, and her hot, quick tears ran over the still palm. "Yes, I heard her," she whispered. Her voice was not steady, but a bright victory filled her eyes as she told them: "She said, *'Dani . . . I see Him—I see Jesus!'* " Then Dani kissed the pale hand, put in on the still breast, and turned blindly away.

14
Bix's Plan

Candi's still form lay under a tan blanket on the couch beside the wall. Karen, Dani, and Betty had taken her into the women's quarters, where they had fixed her hair and dressed her. Ben and Lonnie had carried her back, placing her gently down. Then all of them had gathered into a small knot around the serving table. It was as if they wanted to get as far away from that eloquent shape as possible.

Betty slumped down on a chair, her face twisted into a mask. "We're all going to die!" she moaned.

Ben looked at her, his face grim, and he shook his head. "All but one of us, I guess, if we don't do something."

Karen looked up from where she was kneeling beside the still form. "Do *what?*" she demanded. "We couldn't stop him from killing Candi."

"What do you mean *him?* It could have been any of you women!" Lonnie snapped.

Betty jerked her head up and opened her mouth, but

Dani interrupted quickly, "We don't have time for arguments!" Preparing Candi's body had sapped her strength and drawn her nerves as tense as a piano wire, but she straightened her back and her voice was firm as she stated, "Ben is right. We've got to do two things. First, we've got to try to figure out who the killer is. Second, until we do that, we've got to police one another."

"I think Dani is right." Karl nodded. His eyes went around the circle, and he shook his shoulders. "We have to suspect everyone."

Dani asked, "Karen, assuming that you're right about the cause of death, do you have any idea at all how fast the poison would have acted?"

"I'm no expert," Karen shrugged. "But from what little I remember, the venom of some vipers can paralyze in as little as two or three minutes."

Dani's expression changed, and she shook her head. "That means that the murderer must have—" Suddenly she broke off, and her lips twisted into a grimace. "That bathroom door!" she exclaimed. "Candi would have locked the men's door!"

"Why, that means that none of us men could have done it!" Lonnie exclaimed.

"No, it doesn't!" Bix said abruptly. They all turned to stare at him, and he nodded emphatically. "When I ran back to see if there was a snake in there, I noticed that the men's door was unlocked."

Dani considered him skeptically, asking, "You noticed a little thing like that, Bix? With a woman dead and with the possibility that there was a venomous snake in there?"

Something slipped in Bix's expression. As his eyes

darted from face to face, seeing the doubt in every eye, he exclaimed, "I'm not lying—You're all against me!"

Dani met Ben's eyes and saw him give a shake, indicating his lack of belief. "Come now, Bix," Dani urged. "We're not accusing you, but we only have your word that the door was unlocked. And I've heard you say that you're afraid of snakes. Yet you ran to that bathroom with no fear at all."

"Sounds like you were pretty sure there wouldn't be no snake there," Sid said triumphantly. "Nobody in his right mind would go charging into a spot like that, unless he *knew* there wasn't nothin' to be afraid of."

Bix's face paled, but Dani shook her head, then looked at Karen. "It could have been you, Karen," she said evenly. "Obviously there's no snake. That's just a sick game Stone's dreamed up—or his paid killer. That wound on Candi's neck has to be the result of hypodermic shots, and you went into the room to see about Rachel."

"And I'm the expert with the needle?" Karen answered. Her face was pale and her lips tight, but she looked straight at Dani. "Anyone can give a shot, Dani—even you. As a matter of fact, it would be *easier* for you than for anyone."

"Why do you say that?" Dani asked.

"Because Candi trusted you more than she did anyone else! We all know that. She'd be completely off her guard with you."

Dani blinked, but then nodded. "All right—was it me? It couldn't have been, because I never left the kitchen. You and Betty know that."

Karen shrugged. "Betty may know it, but I don't. We were all milling around. I left once to go to the refrigerator, and Bix came over wanting some ice. We sat down and drank some tea. How long did we talk, Bix?"

"Why, it must have been at least five minutes, I guess," Bix said, giving Dani an uncertain glance.

"And I wasn't watching you the whole time, either!" Betty said. "Like Karen says, it was so busy and noisy. I remember looking around once for you, and I didn't see you."

"Then any one of the three of us could have left long enough to kill her," Dani said evenly. "What about Rachel?"

Karen shook her head. "She's very susceptible to the drugs. I don't think she would have been able to *walk*, much less overpower Candi."

"She woke up when we were getting Candi ready," Dani suggested.

"But you saw how groggy she was." Karen shrugged. "Even now I don't think she understands that Candi's been killed. She's been like that for two days. You all have seen her, but it's *possible*. If she's the killer, she'd have been acting like that just to throw us off."

"Would a woman be strong enough to hold someone down and give those shots, Karen?" Ben asked.

"Maybe. It could have been very quick, if the killer caught her off guard."

"But it would have taken at least a minute or two, wouldn't it?" he persisted. "She was almost dead when she got out to us. I think he must have held her until she passed out—then he could come back unnoticed. Maybe he even intended for us to find her in the bathroom, but she got the strength to get up and stagger out here."

Karen shook her head slowly. "It sounds as if I'm trying

to throw this off on a man, but it seems unlikely that the killer could have given those shots without Candi putting up a struggle. As soon as she saw the needle, she'd know what it meant." She looked around the circle, adding, "Whoever did it must have grabbed her, given her the shots, and held her—probably with a hand over her mouth—until she lost consciousness."

"That'd take a right strong woman," Lonnie said. He looked over toward the door and shook his head. "If I was the killer, I wouldn't have took the chance of going right through the women's side. Rachel was there, and anybody could have seen a guy goin' in there!"

"He didn't have to go through the women's quarters," Ben said. When every eye turned to him, he said, "I checked the bathroom right after Bix did. Not for snakes. I wanted to check the door." He shrugged and looked at Dani. "The door *was* unlocked," he said.

"But Bix could have unlocked it!" Karl insisted.

"Maybe so—maybe not," Ben said. "So could Betty or Karen."

"How many of the men could have slipped into the bathroom from the men's side—and how did the door get unlocked?" Dani asked quickly.

"Don't know about the door," Ben said. "If it was one of you three women, it'd make sense to unlock it and throw suspicion on the men. About the other—" He paused and thought hard, his gaze shifting from one man to the other. Finally he said, "I was pretty busy, going up and down that pile of tables. Karl, I remember telling you that Bix was all the help I needed. You went over to the desk, didn't you?"

"Why, yes," Karl nodded. "I was there until Betty came out."

"No, you wasn't!" Sid turned to look at the tall German, and his small eyes were filled with suspicion. "I come out once from where I was chippin' away on that dumb concrete, and Bix was talkin' to Karen at the table. Savage was up on them tables, but you wasn't at the desk. I thought you'd maybe gone to check on Vince."

"Why, that's right!" Karl said quickly, and a flush tinged his cheeks. "I—I *did* leave for just a moment."

"To go where?" Karen demanded.

"Just to my bed to get a notebook. I'd been reading it earlier, and left it there." The silence, in addition to the steady gaze of Savage and the others, irritated him. "Well, don't *stare* at me! You could have gone into that bathroom yourself, Sid!" he said loudly. "I saw you go in the men's section."

"Is that right, Sid?" Dani asked.

"Sure it's right—and that bathroom door was *locked!*" he said defiantly. "I tried it."

"Why'd you do that?" Dani demanded. "You weren't going to take a shower."

"I dunno—" Sid's voice trailed off, and he muttered, "I just did, that's all."

His defense was so weak that Bix shook his head, saying, "It could have been you, Sid—and it could have been Ben or me, for that matter. I wasn't keeping track of you, and I don't think you were keeping track of me."

No one said anything, and Dani commented carefully, "It goes back to the fact that no one can *prove* he or she is innocent—even Vince and Rachel. So I say in this case, we'd better reverse the law."

"Reverse the law?" Karl asked, a puzzled frown on his face. "What does that mean?"

"It means," Dani said in a hard-edged tone, "we're all guilty—until we're proven innocent."

Ben Savage uttered a terse laugh. "Only way to do that," he nodded, "is to get knocked off yourself!"

"Vince's pneumonia has gotten worse."

Karen returned to join Dani, Bix, and Ben, who were sitting around a table, drinking coffee. Strain etched her face, and she slumped in a chair wearily, saying no more. The night had finally dragged itself out, though there was no sense of morning; only by their watches were any of them aware of the passage of time.

Dani rose. She set a cup of coffee down in front of Karen, asking quietly, "Is he going to make it, Karen?"

The tall, blond woman took a sip of the bitter brew, looked down inside the cup, then shook her head. "In a hospital, I'd say yes. But in this place. . . ." Doubt pulled her mouth down into a bitter scowl, and she added, "You can cross Vince off your list of suspects. He couldn't whip a sick kitten!" To the others' surprise, tears rose unexpectedly in her eyes, and she dropped her head.

Ben reached out impulsively, putting his hand over hers. "It's tough, Karen. You've got the worst of it."

Dani blinked, thinking how unlike Ben it was to make such a gesture. When Karen lifted her head and smiled at him, Dani sat back and studied them, saying nothing; but there was a calculating expression on her face.

Suddenly Bix said, "There it is!" They all got to their feet at once, and the sound of the winch drew the others to the spot. Bix and Ben shoved the tables together, and Ben mounted swiftly, loosening a section of canvas he had fastened only on one edge. This allowed the box to come down through the canopy, and Dani turned at once to face the camera's gleaming red eye.

"Stone," she said, "We have another of your victims— which will come as no surprise to you."

Stone answered instantly, "I did *not* know of such a thing."

"We have no time for you just now," Dani commented. "We'll have a service for our friend. I invite you to join us."

There was a strong irony in her voice, but Dani had long ago learned that the man had no sense of humor. She went to stand beside Candi's body. Pulling the blanket back gently, she looked at the still face, then turned and said, "Candi had a bad life. You all know how little happiness was in it. And you know, as well, that if she had not come to this place, there would have been even less joy in the rest of her life. But something happened to Candi—something beautiful in a dreadful place. It is much like an incident related in Luke's gospel, the seventh chapter: 'And, behold, a woman in the city, which was a sinner, when she knew that Jesus sat at meat in the Pharisee's house, brought an alabaster box of ointment. And stood at his feet behind him, weeping, and began to wash his feet with tears, and did wipe them with the hairs of her head, and kissed his feet, and anointed them with the ointment.'"

Dani looked down again at Candi's face now eloquently peaceful, and said, "Candi found this passage. She brought her Bible to me and pointed it out, and she said, 'Dani! That's like *me!*' And she was right, for Jesus did for her the same as He did for the woman in the story—" She read again from the Bible: " 'And he said unto her, Thy sins are forgiven. . . . Thy faith hath saved thee; go in peace.'

"I'm grieved that Candi will never have the new earthly life she so wanted to live. But I am filled with joy, for I know she has done exactly what that woman who washed the feet of Jesus did—she has gone in peace!"

Dani read a few more Scriptures and said a prayer; then the men put the body in a box, and as before, all of them felt the strange sensation.

"Which of us'll be next?" Sid whispered under his breath.

Stone waited until the winch ground to a halt, and they all watched as the rectangle of light appeared as the basket cleared the opening. When the lid slammed in place with a clanging noise, he said, " 'This fell sergeant, death, is strict in his arrest.' We all must die, and for one in the bloom of youth to be struck down is doubly painful."

"You like quotations, Stone," Dani interrupted him. "Well, let me give *you* one—and from your favorite author: 'Murder most foul, as in the best it is; But this most foul, strange and unnatural.' "

A brief silence followed her ringing accusation, and then Stone said, "Ah, *Hamlet*, I think, Miss Ross? But completely out of context, completely! Surely you can see that the murder of Hamlet's father has *nothing* in common with the death of this woman?"

The anger that had been building up in Dani for days suddenly boiled over, and she raised her fist in a gesture of defiance, crying out in a clear voice, "Maxwell Stone, you are exactly what I have said—a foul murderer! You have killed three people, and you will kill the rest of us, I feel sure. You are always spouting about freedom and liberty, yet you are a tyrant no different from Nero or Stalin! No better than they, and God will have you before His bar of justice!"

"Miss Ross! For one of your intelligence you show little awareness of the signs of the times!" Stone lifted his voice into what they had learned to recognize as his oratorical style, and for the next twenty minutes quoted from a dozen different historical figures. His use of their words was usually out of context, and his tone was that of a man who was so totally convinced that his course was right that Dani saw at once the futility of reasoning with him. She listened carefully, filing his words away.

"The country is full of bleeding-heart liberals, trying to find some sort of Betty Crocker recipe, some nice, sweet chocolate cake that will cure all our ills, but it will not be done without shedding of blood! And you, Miss Ross, in that book you're so fond of, there's a verse that reminds me of the tribulation that's got to come to America! And it will come! Those fools who continue to destroy our nation from within must go!"

"What verse in the Bible do you mean?" Dani asked.

" 'In Rama was there a voice heard, lamentation, and weeping, and great mourning, Rachel weeping for her children, and would not be comforted, because they are not!' " Stone shouted, "There it is, Miss Dani Ross! Even in the Bible there was a need for purging!"

Dani exclaimed, "Stone! Don't you see you condemn yourself with that verse? It refers to Herod, when he slaughtered the children of Bethlehem in his mad attempt to kill Jesus Christ! Herod—the most despicable tyrant of his time!"

But it was as if her words made no impact on him. " 'So young, and so untender?' " he cried out. "You have a 'voice . . . soft, Gentle, and low, an excellent thing in a woman,' Miss Ross, but you have been brainwashed by the criminals in charge at Washington." He raged on, as usual, about the leadership of the country.

When he had finished, Holtz spoke up. "I am an old man, Stone, and so are you. Our lives lie behind us. But these young people have done nothing. Three people are dead. Let these go; do with me what you will."

Stone said in an insulted voice, "You have learned nothing! It is not for *my* pleasure I keep you here—as I have told you repeatedly. Your own stubborn pride, that is what must give! And my patience grows short! If you are wise, you will not continue in your rebellious attitudes! That is all I have to say!"

The speakers fell suddenly silent, and Savage said, "Merry Christmas to you, too, Maxie!"

When they moved away toward the kitchen, Karl said heavily, "I've got bad news." They all stared at him, and he added, "You can forget the Jericho Project. I got through the concrete just before Stone's little talk." He lifted his hands in a hopeless gesture. "Solid steel beneath the concrete. No hope."

Bix exclaimed in outrage, "All that work for nothing?" His face was much thinner than it had been when he had first come, and his eyes were wide and staring. Dani didn't like the wildness that shone out of Bix's sunken eyes. He lowered his voice, saying, "Well, maybe that didn't work, but I've been thinking, and I've got a plan to get out of this place."

Holtz caught Dani's nod and moved closer to Bix. "Bix, my boy, we've been over—"

"There's only *one* way out of this grave—and it's up there!" Bix pointed upward, and a crafty look swept his face. "I been thinking about this for a long time, and it comes down to this: If somebody don't do something, Vince is gonna die! We all are!"

"But there's no way to get up there, Bix," Dani argued gently.

"There's *one* way," he insisted. He lowered his voice. "I don't know if he can hear us or not—but here's what I'm going to do. The next time that box goes up, I'm going up with it!"

They all stared at him, and Holtz said, "Why, Bix, don't you know that we've *all* thought of that? It was the *first* thing I thought of, and the others as well. But there's no chance—no chance at all! The camera stays on until we unload the box and send it back. They're watching, Bix, just to see we *don't* come up on the box."

"What I'll do," Bix went on as if Holtz had not spoken, "is to rig some sort of harness. They'll be looking down *inside* the box, but I'll be underneath, see? They won't be able to see me. You guys can make some kind of a scene— take Stone's attention off the box. Maybe knock the camera sideways. When the box gets to the top, I'll jump out and get 'em!"

"With what?" Sid demanded. "Them guys is bound to be packing iron! You don't even have a shiv!"

"Sid's right." Ben nodded. "We don't even know how many are up there, but I'd guess more than one. Even if they didn't have guns, they're probably pretty tough dudes. They'd throw you down just for laughs, Bix."

Bix stood there with his head bowed, his face frozen into a stubborn expression as they all tried to talk him out of it. Finally he said, "You can stay down here until you get picked off, if you want. Me—I'd rather take a chance—even if it ain't much of one."

Sid examined Bix's face, then nodded. "Kid's got something, but he ain't the one to go up." He nodded toward Ben, saying shrewdly, "You're the karate expert—the big marine fighter. You'd have a whale of a lot more chance than Bix here."

Ben's face didn't change. "That's partly right, Sid—but there's one little thing you don't know."

"What's that?"

Ben spoke quietly, but a pressure on his cheeks drew them in as he answered. "I—I had a bad fall once. From the trapeze. Ever since that time, I can't go up."

"Why, you go up that rope all the time!" Bix cried.

"Sure, thirty feet—and holding onto a rope that's set," Ben nodded. "But I can't stand *space* under me! You think I didn't try? I went up twenty times, and as long as I was on the platform, I was fine—but I could never shove off!" He shook his head and added, "I could go up *inside* the box, but not underneath!"

For a moment, no one spoke. Suddenly Sid gave a tight grin. "Probably won't work, anyway, Ben," he said.

Bix nodded. "Sure, Ben, I understand."

Holtz stood quietly, watching as the others agreed, then he said, "One thing has happened to us—we have learned to have compassion on one another. I think if this situation had come up earlier, we would not have been so ready to accept Ben's handicap." He lifted his lips in a broad smile and added, "A shame that people have to die to learn how to live!"

Savage was unable to speak, for he had fully expected nothing but condemnation for what he himself saw as cowardice. He looked at Dani, who smiled at him, then at Karl and Bix, who were doing the same.

Lonnie said, "Aw, hoss, don't get in a dither about all this!" Karen's eyes were bright as they met his. Finally Betty sniffed and said tartly, "Well, maybe we're all getting a little understanding, but *one* of us is still a murderer. And I don't want for one minute to turn my back on any of you!"

A very faint smile touched her faded lips, and she nodded at Ben. With a reluctant grace she added, "But all the same, I'd appreciate it, Savage, if you'd use all that fighting you learned in the marines on anybody you see sneaking up behind me! And I guess I'm going to let you pray for me, Dani Ross!"

Dani smiled and said, "I haven't waited for your permission, Betty."

15
Caught in the Act

Candi's death seemed to paralyze all of them. None had realized how her recent cheerfulness had served to break up the cold gloom of the silo, but her absence and the silence left by it pulled down their spirits.

"I can't believe she's gone," Rachel said woefully. Early Friday morning she had come out of her drugged sleep, and the shock of the murder had shaken her visibly.

"You didn't hear or see anything, Rachel?" Dani asked.

Rachel thought hard, then sighed. "I remember a few things, but they're all mixed up. I was having some kind of nightmare, and someone came in—I think it was Karen—and asked me something. Then later I heard a lot of shouting, and the lights came on. I guess that's when it happened. But that dope just lays me out, and I'm not taking any more of it, Karen!"

"You're better now, Rachel." Karen nodded. "We'll see how you do for a day or two. But Vince is no better."

They were all lethargically sitting around the tables—all except Betty, who was sitting with Vince.

"We've got to stir ourselves," Dani said, attempting to put some life into her voice. "We act as if we're whipped, and that's just what Stone wants."

Lonnie lifted his haggard face, and his natural animal spirits were burning low. "Well, we *are* whipped," he muttered. "All the time I been thinkin' *somehow* we're gonna get out of this dump. But what's the use of kidding ourselves?"

Holtz said, "There's always hope, Lonnie." He had lost weight, so his neck looked stringy, an old man's neck, and his eyes had retreated into his skull. There was still a faint gleam of defiance in them, but Dani knew he was reaching the end of his rope.

"No, that's wrong," Rachel spoke up. She stared across the table at Holtz, her antagonism for the man written clearly on her pale face. "The men and women and children who went to the ovens at Buchenwald and Belsen— what hope did they have, Holtz? None at all!"

The German turned his face to her, and there was no anger in him, only an air of resigned compassion. "Rachel, it must be clear to you that we are living on the razor's edge. Any of us may die—this very day. Why do you hang on to your anger and bitterness, when all they do is destroy your own spirit? Do you want to face God with that on your soul?"

"There's something in what Karl says, Rachel," Dani said. "Those who violated God's law by bringing on the Holocaust will have to stand in judgment, but that's no reason for you to let hatred for them burn all love out of your own life."

An angry look flashed across Rachel's face. "I don't want any of your Christian religion! Look what it got Candi!"

Dani shook her head, saying, "But your own people have seen what that hatred of the Nazis can do. The *chalutzim* came to agree that it was a waste."

"What's that—calootsim?" Bix asked.

"Tell them, Rachel," Dani urged. "I know you're proud of that part of your people's history."

Rachel looked confused, then responded angrily, "I gave up all that religious part of being a Jew!"

Dani studied her, then shrugged, saying, "The pioneers who live on the kibbutz are called *chalutzim*. They've won the world's respect for their courage and perseverance for the way they live."

Rachel got up suddenly. "I've got to have a shower," she announced and left without another word.

The others watched her go, and Bix shook his head. "She's a tough one. Most women would have a little problem with taking a shower in there, where another woman was just murdered." He shrugged and looked around, "I got one thing figured out—about going up. There's always a bunch of arguing going on. I mean with Stone spoutin' his nutty philosophy and some of you getting back at him. Next time, Karl, you get him into a big argument, and the rest of you move around until you're between the camera and the box. Way I see it, he'll be too busy arguing to notice anything."

"It just won't work, Bix," Lonnie warned. "They'll eat your lunch—even if you *do* make it up there."

"I got this," Bix said and pulled out the chisel Ben had made. "If it'll chip concrete, it'll work on a skull." Dani began to plead with him, but he shook his head stubbornly. "It may be only one chance in a thousand but that's better than waiting around to get butchered!"

The day wore on. After supper Betty stopped by to whisper to Dani, "I got something to tell you."

Dani looked at her with surprise. "What is it, Betty?"

"Not *now!*" she hissed. "After everyone has gone to bed. I'll stay up late. Wait until everyone's asleep. Then get up and come out here. Don't tell anybody about it!"

There was such a tense expression on Betty's face that for one fleeting instant, Dani thought: *She's the killer, and she'll kill me if I come out alone with her!* Then the impossible thought passed. "All right," she murmured and said no more.

Everyone went to bed early, and for a long time Dani tried to stay awake. Ordinarily she had trouble dropping off to sleep, but for some reason she felt very drowsy. She dozed off several times, coming awake with a start, but each time she heard Rachel or Karen tossing restlessly, so she lay there, waiting.

Finally she dropped into a more sound sleep but was awakened by a noise that came from the other room. It was someone calling, but the voice was so hollow that she could not recognize it. Suddenly she remembered her promise and sprang out of bed, stumbling across the dimly lit room. As she passed through the door between the two sections at once she saw a terrifying sight. Simultaneously Ben came up behind her, pushed her to one side, and dashed across the room.

Dani saw Betty hanging by her neck from the rope that dangled from the vent, her hands tied and her face turned dark crimson. Karl was holding her up and saying, "Help me!" He had both hands around Betty and could not do more, but Ben at once slipped the noose from Betty's neck and took her from Karl's arms.

"Get Karen, Dani!" he yelled, and she ran to the door, calling loudly. Both Karen and Rachel leaped from their beds, and throwing on their robes, came quickly into the rec room, as did Sid and Lonnie. All of them were babbling, trying to find out what happened.

At first Dani assumed that Betty was dead.

"She's all right," Karen said quickly, examining Betty. Then Dani heard the hoarse gulps as the injured woman sucked air into her lungs. "Another few seconds, and it would have been too late." She looked up with a light of excitement in her eyes and cried, "The killer didn't make it, this time!"

"Who did it, Betty?" Bix asked.

"Give her a minute," Karen snapped. She drew Betty up into a sitting position and looked at her carefully. "Betty, don't talk until you want to—but as soon as you can, we need to know who tried to kill you."

They all froze as Betty struggled to speak. She put her hands on her throat, twisted her neck and said, "It was him!"

She pointed at Karl, who at once objected, "No! I found her hanging!—and I saw someone leave."

"It was *him*, I tell you!" Betty insisted. She seemed to be gathering strength and sat up straighter, though still leaning on Karen. "I knew it was him, even before he grabbed me."

"No mistake, Betty?" Dani asked sharply. "He grabbed you and put the noose on your neck?"

"Well, he come up from behind," Betty admitted. "Kept his hand over my mouth so I couldn't scream, and he hit me right here—" She touched her temple and winced at the pain. "Almost knocked me out, so I couldn't see much—but it was him."

"Karl?" Dani asked, giving him a straight look. "When I came in you were at her side—no one else was in the room."

He looked around the room, his eyes wide. "I—I heard something, and when I came to see what it was, I saw her hanging by the rope, so I ran over and held her up. She was still alive, but I couldn't hold her and get the rope off. You saw it, Dani!"

"All I saw was that you were here with her alone and that she was dying," Dani remarked tersely. "Ben, you were right with me as I came in—did you see anybody else?"

"No. Karl was alone."

"Can I have a drink of water?" Betty sat there fingering the red mark on her thin neck, and when Karen brought her a glass, she drank it, saying, "It hurts!" Then she looked at Dani and said, "You remember I asked you to meet me here in the kitchen after everyone went to sleep?"

"Yes, Betty?"

"Well, I found something, but I was afraid to tell it, because you'd think I was lying."

"What did you find?" Dani asked.

Betty rubbed her neck, then nodded. "Yesterday I was sitting with Vince, and he was wringing wet with fever. I looked for a handkerchief to mop his brow, but he didn't have any. So I went to one of the other men's bunks and tried to find one." She paused and said, "I want *two* of you to go to *his* bunk—" She pointed at Karl and finished, "Get the little leather case on the shelf by his bed."

Karl stared at her incredulously, but Dani ordered instantly, "Ben, you and Karen go get it."

They left at once as Karl began to protest, "I don't know what this crazy woman is trying to do, but you all know she's never liked me."

Dani shook her head. "Let's wait and see, Karl." When the pair returned, Karen handed Dani a small, brown leather case. "That's an old shaving bag," Karl said instantly. "I haven't used it for weeks!"

"Look inside!" Betty cried out. "Look under the bottom."

Dani zipped the case open and, looking inside, saw that it was empty. The bottom seemed loose, so she reached inside and pulled back a piece of stiff cardboard. Something bright caught her eye, and she slowly pulled out an object and held it up for all of them to see.

"It's the weapon that killed Candi," she said slowly. The others crowded in close to see that she had a pair of hypodermic needles. "They're wired together—see? Even the plungers are wired so that they work in tandem."

"Clever!" Karen nodded. "It'd be easy to make a double mark, like a snake's fangs, and it'd put twice the amount of poison into the system." She looked at the device carefully, then shook her head. "Not the same kind as those in the medical kit. And none of mine have been missing anyway."

Dani said reluctantly, "Karl, we're going to have to think of you as the killer. We may be wrong, but the evidence against you is heavy."

"Anyone could have put that thing in my kit!" he objected angrily. "And if I *were* the killer, do you think I'd be stupid enough to *keep* the murder weapon around?"

"You might want to use it again," Dani explained, and she pulled a small plastic bottle from the bottom of the kit. Holding it up to the light, she said, "I don't want to test it on anyone, but it's pretty certain that this is the same poison that killed Candi." Putting the case down, she stood there with her eyes fixed on Karl and began to speak.

"You could have killed Alex easily. I never thought for a second that the *eggs* had the poison in them. That's too haphazard for our man—doesn't fit his method. Karen fixed the eggs, but *you* were standing right by her side, weren't you? She left the stove to come over and get the milk out of the icebox, and while she was gone, you were standing right beside those eggs. It would have been easy for you to poison them, Karl."

"But I didn't!"

"As for Rosie, you have no alibi. You're strong enough to have done it, and you had the opportunity."

"But, Dani," Karl protested, "you know I could never have climbed up that rope to get rid of the knife—I'm no acrobat!"

"I agree." Dani nodded, and an expression of distaste covered her face, for she had admired Holtz, and it went against her nature to pile up the evidence. "But there's another way that knife could have gotten under the window."

"How?" Holtz demanded.

"Through the slot, where we put the orders for our supplies."

Ben's face revealed the shock that ran through him at her words. "Sure!" he nodded. "It would fit through easy enough."

"But how would it get from there to under the window?" Lonnie asked, puzzled.

"The killer has been in contact with Stone all the time, or so I think." Dani shrugged. "I believe there's some way to get things in from the outside, if we could find it, but all he'd have to do is include a note telling Stone to put the knife under the window. That'd put the suspicion on Ben and take it off him."

She paused, then said, "That leaves Candi and Betty. As for Candi, you lied when you said you never left the rec room, didn't you?"

"I—I forgot. But that bathroom door was *locked!*"

"There's no way to prove that. But you were the *first* one in this place. If you are Stone's hired assassin, you could easily have had that lock fixed so that you could open it from the men's side. We'll take another look at it, but it wasn't locked when she was murdered or shortly after, because Ben checked it, and so did Betty."

"She's probably the killer herself!" Karl cried. "She's trying to pin it on me because she's guilty."

"Did she hang herself and try to frame you for that?" Rachel demanded, and his face fell. "He's guilty!" she spat out. "Just another Nazi!"

"I wouldn't take your word for it, Rachel," Dani said quickly. "You're too filled up with prejudice. But you and Karen and I were together when Betty was attacked. I was dozing off and on, and when I heard her cry out, I didn't take time to look for you. Did you two notice *any* of the others being gone?"

"Rachel was right in front of me when we jumped up and came out," Karen said. "And since Ben bumped into you going through the door, that leaves Vince, Bix, and Lonnie."

"And they all came out *after* we got there," Ben said.

"The killer would have to have overcome Betty, put her on the rope, and gone back to bed. *Then* Karl would have to have gotten up, come into this room, and tried to get her down." He shook his head. "Karl, I like you a lot—but it would take of lot of faith to accept that."

"The evidence is strong against you, Karl," Dani said. "It's all circumstantial and would never convict you in a court of law. But we're in our own cosmos now. So you can speak for yourself."

Karl stood, his face sagging and his shoulders drooping. Looking around he said, "You have made up your minds. Any one of you could be accused on evidence no stronger than this, but you have decided. You are wrong, however, and that is my only plea."

Dani stared at him, bit her lip, then shaking her head, stated firmly, "Is that all, Karl? Well, it's not enough."

A strange look crossed Holtz's face, a trace of a smile. He looked at Rachel and spoke quietly, "Well, my dear, you are about to have your dearest hope come to pass. You are going to have the opportunity to execute a Nazi."

"Oh, don't be ridiculous!" Dani said. "No one will touch you—except to keep you tied up."

"That'll settle the thing!" Ben commented caustically. "If Karl is the killer, we'll all be safe. Probably die of old age in this place."

Dani did not give Maxwell Stone much of a chance when the supplies came down and the red light blinked on. It was late afternoon, and they all gathered at once, this time with some sort of heady excitement, although Ben said wryly to Karen, "Can't see it makes much difference. Either Stone will admit it's Karl, or he won't. Either way we'll still be in here."

"You have—"

"Just a minute, Stone!" Dani called out loudly. She motioned to where Karl was standing between Ben and Lonnie. "We've captured your paid assassin."

Silence ran on for several seconds and then: "Indeed? I congratulate you. Are you quite sure Herr Holtz is the man?"

"We feel he is."

"I see. And what do you propose?"

"That you let us out of here in exchange for his life."

Stone suddenly laughed and questioned, "And if I do not, will you kill him?"

Dani's resolute expression faded. She tried to think of some way to pressure Stone, but there was nothing.

"You will not?" Stone asked again. "No, certainly not. That is your weakness. Have you learned *nothing* from all that I've said?"

"I know what *you* would do!" Dani exclaimed angrily. "You'd kill him out of hand, if it would benefit you in any way!"

" 'There are more things in heaven and earth,' Miss Ross, 'than are dreamt of in *your* philosophy,' " Stone stated. "One of them is that the individual is not as important as the state."

"You are wrong there, Stone!" Dani said firmly, looking up into the camera. "Every state, every nation, every civilization passes away—but the soul of every human being is immortal, therefore the individual is of infinitely more worth than the state."

"Very clever! 'A Daniel come to judgement!' " Stone

exclaimed. "If you were only able to see the light, my dear, I could predict that you'd do great things. I could use you in my organization. You have beauty and brains, which is a rare combination, indeed! However, you have not learned to live with the world of reality. As I have pointed out more than once, we do not live in ordinary times; therefore we cannot use ordinary means. How does the bard put it? Oh, yes! 'Diseases desperate grown By desperate appliance are relieved, Or not at all.' That's what you and your friends can never seem to see, Miss Ross. Our world does not have a simple headache. It is dying of a terminal sickness, and only radical surgery will save it. 'There's a divinity that shapes our ends. . . .' "

"Move over in front of me," Bix whispered to Rachel, and she looked at him in surprise. He put his finger on his lips, saying, "Be quiet, but when the box goes up, try to get the old buzzard's attention."

Rachel stared at him, but he ducked and pulled some sort of device out of a bag at his feet. It seemed to be a rope with some hooks, and she watched while he carefully moved to the supply box, attached them to the sides, then stood back. Sid was watching, and he gave Bix a warning shake of his head and mouthed the words, *Don't do it, Bix!* But the boy merely gave him a stubborn look and stood there, waiting.

Stone said finally, "I am out of patience with all of you! Your fate is on your own heads. Do you want me to send the box down for my hired assassin, as you call Herr Holtz?"

The winch started to whine, and at once Rachel moved forward, to the center of the group. She lifted her head and cried out, "If I had my way, Stone we'd pull his fingernails out, one at a time! But you'd never let us go, even if we gave him to you, would you? You dirty butcher—Holtz is bad enough, but you're worse . . . !"

As Rachel continued her tirade, they all watched her with interest. Then Dani heard Ben whisper urgently: "Kid! Don't try it!" She turned her head to see Bix dangling from the bottom of the box! It was already fifteen feet in the air, and she wanted to scream for him to let go, but even as she watched, the box cleared the canopy, and Bix's dangling feet disappeared.

Rachel continued her outraged speech, but suddenly the whining of the winch motor stopped. The silence seemed to cut off her words.

Stone said, "Our young friend has gotten himself in considerable trouble, has he not?"

Dani ran to look up through the gap in the canopy, and the others joined her. It was very dark, but they could see by the dim light that filtered upward that Bix was kicking his feet wildly and struggling to clamber up into the box.

"He'll be killed if he falls from there!" Dani cried. Running to the camera, she pleaded. "Please, let him down!"

"Oh, he'll come down," Stone said. "Everything that goes up must come down. So I bid you good night. 'Sweets to the sweet: farewell!' "

"He's gonna fall!" Lonnie groaned. "Look out!"

When Bix's hands let go of the ropes, and he plunged toward the hard concrete, Sid, Lonnie, Karen, and Dani jumped backward out of pure reflex action. But without thought Ben Savage jumped under Bix's body. After a sickening sound of flesh on flesh, Ben was driven to the floor, where he lay sprawling with Bix on top of him, still screaming.

16
A Nice, Warm Bath

D‍ani leaped forward with a cry: "Ben! Ben!" At the same time Karen called out, "Be careful, don't jerk them around!" Dani stood back, and Betty put an arm around her as they watched Karen examine the two men.

Bix spoke up in a high-pitched, cracked voice, "I—I thought I was a goner!"

"You *were!*" Karen snapped. "Now shut your mouth and raise this arm. Now this one." After a moment she opined, "You've got the luck of the Irish! Not a single broken bone." Then she turned to Ben, who was beginning to stir, saying quietly, "Don't move, Ben."

Dani discovered her legs were trembling so violently that she could hardly stand up, but she forced herself to stay, ashamed that she had jumped back with the rest, leaving Ben to take the full impact. Many times she had almost hated him, but she knew she'd never be able to forget that sight!

Then his eyelids fluttered, and he began to move. He

mumbled something, the eyes opened, and he blinked rapidly before asking, "How's Bix?"

"Better than you!" Karen said. "You've got a bump the size of a baseball on your head! Now be still and let me check you over."

In the final analysis, Karen could find nothing more than a terribly bruised left shoulder and a bump on the head, for Ben, and a tender knee joint and a twisted wrist, for Bix. She stood up and helped Ben to his feet. "By rights you ought to have at least a concussion! Come sit down!"

Shakily Ben walked to one of the chairs and sat down gingerly. Bix came and stood in front of him, his face working. He tried to speak but could only swallow. Ben looked up at him and said with a grin, "Bix, you and I have got to stop meeting like this!"

Bix made a pitiful attempt at returning the grin. He took a deep breath. "I was dead meat, Ben! All I could think of was getting all busted up and dying by inches in this place." He bit his lip, then suddenly turned and walked away.

Karen pulled back Ben's shirt, shook her head and directed, "Go get in the tub and soak for an hour. Make the water as hot as you can stand it." She shooed them all away, and Ben marched off slowly but obediently.

"I'd better go check on Vince," Karen announced.

Lonnie got up at once. "I'll tell him about what the kid tried to pull off." The two left, and Betty went to the kitchen, leaving Sid, Rachel, and Dani sitting, with Karl standing stiffly back away from them.

He looked very lonely, and Sid said, "Aw, come on and sit down, Holtz. You ain't likely to knock anybody off in a crowd."

Dani said, "We're all pretty washed out, Karl. Come and join us." She watched as he held himself stiffly at attention; then slowly his shoulders bowed, and he came and wordlessly sat down. Rachel stared at him bitterly, but Sid, who was sitting close to him, suddenly slapped his shoulder, saying, "That was sure something—the way Savage stepped under the kid!"

Karl nodded. "Yes. It took a very brave man to do that." Then he faced Dani and asked quietly, "I assume you want to tie me to my bed tonight?"

"Karl—" Dani said.

But he interrupted her, "I am not complaining. In your place I should do the same."

"Or *worse!*" Rachel snapped.

Karl got up slowly. "Is it all right if I go lie down? I'm not feeling too good."

"Of course, Karl." Dani watched him leave the room and turned to Rachel. "Don't you have any pity at all for him?"

"No!" Rachel got up and looked down at Dani, pausing, "You just don't know what it's like, being a Jew. If you did, you'd hate the ones who killed your people, just as I do."

Dani thought for a moment, then said softly, "Jesus was a Jew. But as He died, He prayed for the ones who were killing Him. He had what your people called *rachmones.*" She paused to look upward into Rachel's face, but saw no sign of pity there. "That means 'pity,' " she explained to Sid, who was taking it all in.

Rachel shook her head, and her lips thinned. "Dani," she said slowly, "I'm not going to change. You'll never make a convert out of me."

She walked away, and Sid put his hand on Dani's arm.

"Don't feel bad," he comforted her. "I doubt if an angel could convert that one."

Dani turned to him and put her hand over his. It was the first time she'd ever touched Sid, and she saw his eyes fly open in surprise. He tried to pull his hand back, but she tightened her grip, looking into his face. The silo had planed him down, as it had everyone else. The sleek, black hair had become lusterless and shaggy, and the usually sharp black eyes had dulled. He was wearing a black jacket that was far too large for him, and it made him look like a beggar.

"What about you, Sid?" Dani asked suddenly. "What would it take to convert you?"

"Me!" he asked, astounded. "You mean *me*?"

"What's so surprising about that?" She smiled. "Jesus loves you as much as He loves anyone else."

Sid stared at her, gave a rough laugh, and pulled his hand back. But there was something in his face that had not been there before, and for half an hour Dani quoted Bible verses to him—those that spoke of the love of God.

Finally, at dinnertime, Dani asked, "Can I talk to you again about this, Sid?"

"Don't see why not," he mumbled. He ducked his head and shuffled off, but he was occupied with his thoughts all during the meal. After dinner, Dani said, "It's Christmas Eve. I'd like to read the Christmas story before we go to bed."

"Forgot to hang up my stocking." Lonnie grinned. "So let's have the story."

"Karen, could we go back and gather around Vince?"

"Might do him good." Karen nodded. "He's pretty low."

So they all filed back and took up stations around

Vince's bed. He was so weak that it was all he could do to lift a hand, but his eyes were fixed on Dani as she led them in a few carols. Karl sat on his bunk, saying nothing, but he joined in when they sang "Silent Night," and even Rachel came to stand beside Lonnie and join in.

Then Dani read the story from Luke, of the trip, long ago, from Nazareth to Bethlehem. Vince's ragged breathing was the only sound besides her own. "And she brought forth her firstborn son, and wrapped him in swaddling clothes, and laid him in a manger; because there was no room for them in the inn."

She paused and said, "I guess that's the epitaph for the whole world. God loves the world, sends His Son to die for their sins—and there's no room for Him! And ever since that day," she said gently, "Jesus has come again and again to the world—to every man and woman and child. And most people find they don't have enough room for Him. But that's what Christmas means: God has suddenly decided to step out on the stage and become part of the play. He came by birth, the same as every one of us. It wasn't the kings and princes who welcomed him, but the simple people, the shepherds."

She closed her Bible and said, "We have no gifts for one another, do we? If we were outside, we'd probably have a pile of presents, all wrapped in foil. But not here. Yet I do have a gift, for each one of you—the only thing I have that hasn't been stripped away. So may I give it to you now?"

Dani moved to Vince's bedside, stooped down, and kissed his cheek, whispering, "I love you, Vince!" When she straightened up, they all saw that two tears were rolling down the sick man's cheeks, and his lips were quivering. Then Dani turned to Rachel, who crossed her arms and stared at her. Dani kissed her softly, and said, "And I love you, Rachel—very much!"

Finally she made the full circle and stood there, her gray-green eyes luminous. "I haven't been able to do that sort of thing very much," she said very quietly. "It's been hard for me to say what I feel. But I wanted all of you to know that God has given me a great love for each one of you."

She turned and walked away. Ben sat down beside Vince, and when the others had left, except for Karl, Vince said in a thin voice, "Savage, what *is* that dame? I never seen nothing like her!"

Ben shook his head, his eyes hooded as he looked down at the big man. "I don't know, Vince. But a man wouldn't get bored around her, would he now?"

"Come with me, Ben. I want to talk to you."

"Sure." Ben got up, and the two of them went over to a pair of upholstered chairs. He waited for Dani to sit, took the other chair, and waited for her to speak.

"I want to tell you three things," she said. They were sitting at right angles to each other, and he could see her profile clearly. The sheer sweep of her cheek was intensely feminine, and there was a fragility about her, despite her tall stature.

"First, I want to say, I never saw anything like what you did. Saving Bix, I mean." She gave a slight shudder at the thought, adding, "The rest of us were cowards!"

"Why, no—you just never were a part of a circus." Ben moved his head in a circle, testing it, then drew her gaze. "Somebody's always falling in the circus. Gets to be a habit to step in and break the fall. I saw the Bandinos fall once—five of them. They were riding cycles on the high wire, with no net. Something went wrong, and they all came down. Everybody beneath jumped to get under them—*and* that's taking the cycles, too!"

She listened to him, then shook her head. "I guess that's so, but it made me feel terrible, Ben. Bix would be dead or mangled if you'd acted like the rest of us."

He was uncomfortable and asked quickly, "What's the second thing?"

"It's—more personal," she said, and he saw that her hands were nervously pulling at her sweater. Curiosity caught him, and he waited until she finally spoke. "You—kissed me once—and when I pulled away, you said something I can't shake out of my mind. Do you remember what it was?"

"I remember the kiss, but not what I said."

"You said, 'You've got your own private ghosts.' " She turned and looked at him suddenly, her eyes fully open. Her lips were soft and vulnerable, and there was a pleading look in her expression. "You think I'm afraid of men, don't you, Ben?"

"The thought did cross my mind," he admitted slowly. "There's some sort of wall around you. Don't know what it is, but it's high and tough."

"That's what I want to tell you about. I never thought I'd be saying this, Ben, because, because I never thought my—my feelings for you would be important. I thought we'd just go along, and you'd keep on thinking I was a hard-boiled woman without much heart, and I'd think you were just a tough hooligan with no heart at all! Well, I was wrong about you," she said evenly. "You're more than a hooligan."

"Maybe I am—maybe not." He slipped lower in his chair and asked, "What's the wall for, Dani?"

"It's there because I can't afford to fall in love with any man," she said quickly, as if afraid that she'd never get it out. "I don't have the *right* to do that."

"Why not?"

"Because I've got something to do—and love and men can't get in the way." She took a deep breath, then began to speak rapidly. "A few years ago, Ben, I was all set. I had my CPA and a great career going with the attorney general. I started law school part-time, and I met a man who was in Hayworth Divinity School. His name was Jerry Hunt. He was a Christian, and I tried not to fall in love with him. But I couldn't help myself! He was—" She ducked her head and was silent, then lifted her face to him.

"He was a good man. More fun than any man I'd ever known, but at the same time, more dedicated. Good-looking, too, though I didn't care about that. We worked very hard to keep from falling in love. I wasn't going his way. He was a missionary volunteer to Africa. I was on the way to big money and big things. Well, somewhere along the line we fought each other to a standstill. I agreed to drop out of law school and go to seminary, so that I could marry him and go to Africa."

She paused and looked across the room, where the others huddled around a table. Lonnie and Bix were playing cards with Sid and Rachel, while Betty looked on. When she turned back, a strange quality filled her eyes, a regret that made her look vulnerable. "We loved each other, but we fought all the time! And I was always in the wrong. Always! Because he wanted nothing but to serve God—while I still wanted the things I'd given up.

"So I'd get angry, and he'd never fight back. That made me feel just that much worse." Memories came back to her, and she shook her head. "I never should have agreed to marry him, but I did. Almost a year after we met, we had a frightful quarrel, and this time Jerry did get upset. We'd been driving out on the freeway, and it just seemed to blow up in our faces. We found ourselves yelling at each other, and I told him he was nothing but a pious hypocrite. He turned white and began to tell me how wrong I was. So I yelled, 'Stop the car!' He didn't, of course, so I reached over and turned the key off. That *did* make him mad. When the car stopped and I got out, he yelled at me—the only time he ever did! He went roaring off—driving like a madman and leaving me alone beside the freeway."

Suddenly she began to cry almost silently.

"What happened?" Ben asked.

"He had a—a head-on collision with a big truck!" Dani sobbed. "He died instantly!"

He sat there, watching her as she bowed and put her face in her hands, sobbing helplessly. Finally she stopped and looked over at the group, but they had not noticed. "I'm sorry," she said. "I thought I could speak about it without crying. Anyway, I nearly died myself—or wanted to. But when the first grief was gone, I knew what I had to do." She faced him and said urgently, "I knew I had to take his place. That's what I'm going to do, Ben—or was, until I wound up here. If I get out, I'm going to take Jerry's place."

Ben stared at her. "Is that allowed? I mean, does God let people do that? I sort of thought that each one of us was special—that nobody *could* take another's place?"

"Oh, I don't know about the theology," she said wearily. "But there's one less missionary in Africa because of me, I know *that!* So that's why I didn't like what happened to me when you kissed me. I can't let you or any other man in my life. It belongs to God. I *owe* it to Him."

Ben sat there, looking at her, and she became restless under the hazel eyes that seemed to see beneath the surface. Finally he shook his head. "I'm just a roughneck, Dani. You've got all the fancy education; you've read all the books—but I think you're all wrong. And if this guy could talk to you, he'd probably say the same thing I'd say: 'Live your own life, Dani Ross.' Because that's all any of us can do."

She watched him, then stubbornly shook her head. Her mane of heavy hair glinted reddish as it moved, and she said, "I've got to do it, Ben. Not that there's much chance of it now, but I wanted you to know."

He shrugged and asked. "What's the third thing?"

She pushed her hair back from her face with a nervous gesture, then looked straight into his eyes.

"The third thing is, I know who the next victim is going to be."

A nerve twitched in Ben's face, and he sat up suddenly. "What?"

"Yes, I know." Certainty rang in her voice like steel, and she warned him, "And I *think I know* who'll be doing it, but the next victim will be—me!" She smiled at his expression, then sobered. "Listen carefully, Ben. . . ." For the next ten minutes, she spoke steadily.

Finally he shook his head adamantly. "No!" But she continued to speak, and finally he found himself nodding. "All right—maybe it'll work, but it's risky!"

"So is living, Ben." Her long lips turned down suddenly, and she added, "So is love—but I guess we're all going to keep on doing both!" She rose, paused, then held out her hand. He took it with a look of surprise, and she said, "I've never been able to thank you for coming into this place, trying to get me out. I guess I never will—but what I said in the other room, I meant it, Ben. Good-bye!"

She turned and walked away quickly. Stopping by the card players, she announced, "You can take all the baths you want—until eleven. Then I'm going to soak for *two hours*—so get your bathing done before that." They all agreed, for most of them went to bed earlier. She sat down and took a hand, and finally Ben came over and joined the party.

One by one, they all left. When Dani was alone, she looked toward the sleeping area, her eyes dark with a strange emotion. At eleven-thirty, she turned the lights out and went into the sleeping quarters. The other women were breathing steadily as she picked up her gown and robe, then moved into the bathroom.

The shadowy figure's feet made no sound as they moved lightly across the floor. Once, when a sleeper shifted, the figure froze until the regular breathing resumed. With catlike steps the stalker moved across the floor and placed one hand on the doorknob, pausing long enough to heft a short length of metal that was firmly grasped in the right hand.

The door opened noiselessly, and with one quick, soundless motion the dark-clad intruder stepped inside and closed the door. A swift look at the other door, then a few steps on rubber-soled deck shoes. *The shower curtains are around the tub—I didn't think the wench would be so modest!*

Three more steps—and a careful grasp on the shower curtain.

She's quiet, maybe asleep—
That would make it easier—
Got to get her quiet, then hold her under for no more than a few minutes.

The water was not on, nor was there any movement.
She's dozing in the tub!
Now! Yank the shower curtain, and—

Suddenly the killer stopped dead still, one hand still on the curtain, the other lifting the steel pipe, frozen into instant immobility, for it was not the woman, Dani Ross, inside, lying in a tub of hot water!

Instead, Ben Savage was standing there, his hazel eyes bright and his mouth curved in a wide smile—and beside him, fully dressed, was Dani Ross!

"Hi, Rachel," Ben said. "We've been waiting for you."

Ben's little speech nearly cost him his life, for with a movement faster than a striking snake, Rachel slashed at his head; the steel grazed his temple before it crashed into the wall behind him.

The blow, light as it was, sent an explosion of stars dancing through his brain. Sheer instinct made him counter with a slashing one of his own; the hard edge of his left hand caught Rachel a glancing blow in the temple, driving her to one side. Instantly Ben leaped out of the tub and halted just in time to avoid another slashing blow that would have crushed his throat, if it had landed.

"You're pretty good, Rachel." Ben nodded. He lurched back as her foot came off the floor in a flash, catching him on the outside of his thigh. He grunted and countered with a feint at her face, but she drew back at once. He fell into the classic position, knees bent, knuckles ready at the end of his weaving arms, and twice she made a pass at him, which he warded off.

"But I'm better," he jibed.

She cursed and fell into a defensive position, but even as she did, Ben whipped his foot up, catching her on the wrist holding the steel. The chisel flew through the air, striking the wall, and Dani, who had scrambled out of the tub, made a grab at it. She retrieved it then backed away to the left.

Rachel wheeled and, almost quicker than Dani's eyes could follow, threw a straight jab at Ben's eyes. He moved his head to one side, caught her wrist, and with a quick movement flipped her over. Her back struck the floor with a dull thud, and her breath whistled out, but she at once rolled over, and her foot caught him in the stomach. Instantly she was on her feet and made a feint. As he followed it she stepped to the side and threw her arm around his neck, her forearm instantly cutting off his wind. He reached back over his head, but she was too wily for that and ducked.

The pair careened around the room until the lights started going out for Ben and a curtain of red descended as his lungs cried out for oxygen. Dani saw his face beginning to turn crimson and leaped forward, lifting the chisel. Rachel sensed her movement and managed to twist around. Releasing one hand, she delivered a stunning blow to the side of Dani's neck, which drove her against the wall. Rachel tried to recapture her hold on Savage, but the diversion had enabled him to recover. He reached up, pulled her arm away, then gave a great twisting lunge that threw her to one side.

He was off balance, and she sent a powerful kick at his groin, but Ben took the blow on his thigh and in return lashed a fierce backhand. The hard edge of his hand caught her on the forehead, and she went down instantly, her eyes dulled.

Ben reached down and put a come-along hold on her right fingers, and she rose up with a cry of pain as he applied the pressure. "You're good, sweetheart," he said in his best imitation of Humphrey Bogart. "You're *real* good!"

Dani was getting to her feet, holding her neck painfully. "Ben, are you all right?"

"Yeah. Little Miss Muffet here finally found a spider, but she couldn't run away."

Rachel cursed and tried to pull away, but he lifted her with the come-along grip, and her voice was cut off sharply. Ben reached into his pocket and tied her hands together with a piece of wire, then stepped back.

The room was suddenly crowded, and Dani held up her hand, saying, "Everyone into the rec room."

When they were there, Ben said, "You were right on the nose, boss. Real good sleuthing." He told the crowd, who were staring at Rachel, how the capture had been made. "Dani knew she was the next victim, and she knew the killer would drown her in the tub—if he could. So I agreed to take her place. She opened the men's door, and I slipped in."

"How'd you know that stuff, Dani?" Sid asked in awe.

"Sit down, and I'll tell you about it." They each took a seat, and Dani smiled as she continued, "I didn't know for sure who the killer was, but I knew I was next, and I knew it had to be in the bathroom." Her face grew sad, and she said quietly, "If I'd been smart enough, I could have saved Candi's life—maybe even Rosie's.

"The key was in those wild speeches Stone makes. They're all filled up with a lot of junk, but I've studied them for days, trying to find out something. There was something odd about them—and I just couldn't *get* it! Until last night, in his speech, it all fell together. Strange how simple complicated things are when you have the key!"

"What was it, Dani?" Karl asked.

"Two things," she answered. "In every speech he mentioned the name of the person who was going to be the next victim. It was usually buried in a lot of other meaningless material, but it was always there."

"I don't remember his mentioning Alex's name," Karen said.

"He didn't exactly—but he said, 'Unlike *Alexander*, who grieved because he had no worlds to conquer. . . .' I'd never have remembered it, if I hadn't transcribed the speech and gone over it again and again."

"What was the other clue, Dani?" Bix asked. He was staring at Rachel with an unbelieving stare, but turned his face toward the speaker.

"In every speech he told us how the next victim would be murdered. I know that sounds impossible, but he did it by using quotes from Shakespeare's tragedies. He used lines from a play, and then the victim was murdered as a character in that play was murdered! For example, in the speech naming Alex, he used two lines from Romeo and Juliet, 'He jests at scars that never felt a wound,' and 'What's in a name?' and he also used the name of Romeo. And Romeo," she said slowly, "died of poison."

Karen whispered, "What a terrible thing! He played a *game* with us!"

"How'd they get it all together?" Karl asked. "I mean, the clues to who would be murdered were so complex. How did Rachel know how to apply them?"

"He had some way of getting word to her." Dani shrugged. "Isn't that right, Rachel?"

"Sure it is!" Rachel said defiantly. She laughed harshly, adding, "You searched this place a dozen times and didn't find it—and it was right under your noses! Right behind the medicine cabinet in the bathroom! That's where I got the poison."

Karen stared at Rachel. "But—how did she get the poison in the omelet? She never even came near while I mixed it, and Karl took it to the table."

"There was never any poison in that omelet," Dani said calmly.

"What?" Karl demanded. "But there *had* to be! It was all Alex ate that night."

Dani reminded him, "There was one other place he could have gotten it. And we all knew about it, because he took it after every meal."

"The Maalox!" Ben caught on instantly.

"Yes, the Maalox." She nodded. "We all knew about it, didn't we?"

"But how did she poison the bottle?" Bix demanded.

"She left the table, for just a few minutes, while we were all eating," Dani said. "It was the one time when it would be safe for her to go through the bathroom, into the men's side, and put the poison into Alex's medicine. I also suspect she had some sort of drug to raise her temperature so she could pretend to be sick. She used it later on, I'd guess, pretending to be sick like Vince. That's what you did, isn't it, Rachel?"

"You're the great detective," Rachel snarled. "Figure it out!"

Karen said slowly, "There are a number of ways to raise a temperature. She must have used some drug."

Rachel gave her a sour look, but couldn't resist. "Sure I did. I had a reaction once to Imferon. Ran my temperature up. So all I had to do was take a little every time I wanted to fool you dumb clucks. All those pills you stuck in my mouth that were supposed to knock me out? I never swallowed any of them! Just hid them under my tongue and spit them out later!"

"Sure." Ben nodded. "Maxwell made his fortune in medicines. He'd know all about that."

"I think she's probably a quick thinker," Dani said clinically. "She was there when the omelet was brought up, and she saw a chance to throw suspicion on Betty and Karl—and even Karen—and at the same time put herself in the clear by pretending to be poisoned with the same dish."

"What kind of person would plan such a terrible thing?"

"Well, Maxwell's clinically insane, Karen." Dani shrugged. "We all know that. But I rather think that Rachel's just a plain murderer—though she'll probably claim temporary insanity in court."

"You'll never get me in court!" Rachel said defiantly.

Dani regarded her for only a moment. "And poor Rosie! Stone didn't call him by his nickname, but he did mention *Roosevelt*—which was Rosie's full name. He also mentioned *Julius Caesar*. And he did quote several lines, such as 'Cowards die many times before their deaths; the valiant never taste of death but once.' And then a real giveaway, the last words Caesar ever spoke before he was stabbed to death: *'Et tu, Brute!'* "

"You and your employer are very artistic, aren't you,

Rachel?" Holtz asked, looking to where she stood, her head up and her eyes defiant. "All that about the Jews and the Nazis—I suppose that was part of your act?"

"You believed it, too!" Rachel's eyes glowed with anger, not remorse, as she glared around the room. "You've got me, but you won't kill me! We all know that!"

"Don't be too sure," Sid said. He moved closer to Rachel, with a gleam in his black eyes. "All of us ain't as gentle as Dani," he murmured. "Just give me two minutes with her—"

"Keep him away from me!" Rachel yelled, trying to back away.

"Let's hear the rest, boss," Ben said. "What about Candi? Same thing?"

"I had a hard time with that one, Ben," Dani admitted. "Especially naming the victim. He slipped that into a phrase so cleverly I missed it for a long time. He said, 'Instead of handing out death sentences, our courts are handing out candy to murderers.' *Candi.*" She shrugged. "And then he mentioned the 'harlot of the Nile that debauched the rulers of her day.' "

"Cleopatra!" Holtz breathed.

"Yes—and all that business about the snake was because Cleopatra died of the bite of a deadly viper."

"She had a good shot at the poor child," Holtz said. "It must have been easy, since she was alone with her."

"What about me?" Betty demanded. "Did he have me in any of his old speeches?"

"He said something about Betty Crocker. And he gave some pretty broad hints, such as when he told me, 'You have a "voice . . . soft, Gentle, and low, an excellent thing in a woman." ' " Dani grimaced, adding, "I ought to have caught that one! It is said of Lear's daughter Cordelia—and I once acted that role in college! He even dared to use another phrase which Lear said to Cordelia—'so young, and so untender?' " And of course, Cordelia is hanged at the end of the play. Why didn't I *see* it?"

"Don't feel bad, Dani!" Lonnie cried out. "I don't see how you ever remembered any of his stuff."

"It is a marvelous gift," Karen said with admiration. "But what about the last clues—the ones that trapped Rachel?"

"Oh, once you have the pattern, it's simple. He said, 'A *Daniel* come to judgement,' and I knew I was next. Then he started using lines from *Hamlet:* 'There's a divinity that shapes our ends,' and 'Diseases desperate grown . . . ,' and when he used the phrase, 'Sweets to the sweet: farewell!'—the lines spoken about Ophelia, at her funeral—I knew I was going to be murdered."

"How'd she die—in the play, I mean?" Betty asked.

"She was drowned. Where else could anyone be drowned, except in the bathtub?" Then Dani said wearily, "That's the way I discovered how Stone chose his victims and how he planned to kill them."

"But how'd Rachel *do* it?" Sid asked in bewilderment. "We've thought all along that a woman wouldn't be strong enough to handle some of the killings."

Dani studied Rachel curiously, then turned to ask, "Ben, how about that? She almost got the best of you in that free-for-all in the bathroom."

"She's very good," he observed. "Faster than anyone I've ever tackled. I'd say she's a black belt. And very strong, too."

"Rosie was a little guy," Lonnie reminded everyone.

"And Betty here won't weigh a hundred pounds, soaking wet."

"Sure," Ben agreed. "Be no trouble for a tough cookie like Rachel to handle either of them."

"I could have taken *you*, too, Savage," Rachel snapped. "If your lady friend hadn't been there to give you a hand!"

"Not only an expert in karate, but in murder," Holtz said slowly. "I take it you slashed poor Rosie, then went up the rope and got rid of the knife to throw suspicion on Ben?"

"A piece of cake!"

"You also planted the hypodermic needles in my case." He nodded. "And that *was* you I got a glimpse of just after you'd hanged Betty!"

"Sure it was!"

Betty looked at Karl. Her hand flew to her mouth. "Oh, dear! You saved my life! And I was *awful* to you!"

Holtz came up with a small smile, "Well, you can make me one of those fine apple pies, Betty, and we'll call it square."

"Why has all this happened? Why are we all here?"

They all looked at Rachel, but she merely shrugged. "I don't know. Mr. Stone don't confide in me. He just pays me."

Dani startled them all by breaking in, "Oh, I can tell you that."

"What?" "Dani, tell us!" half a dozen other cries met her astonishing statement.

"Do you really know, boss?" Ben asked curiously.

"Oh, yes. It was simple once I got all the facts and had time to think about them!"

"You missed a great chance to say, 'Elementary, my dear Watson!' " Ben said. "Well, let's have it!"

17
The Only Hope

Dani looked around at the faces fixed on her in shock and shrugged. "It's just like discovering the pattern using Shakespeare's quotations and giving the name of the victim. If there's a pattern to something, no matter how complex, once you have the key, it's easy to open the door."

"Well, I've been going over those confounded lists for *weeks*," Karl said. "And I haven't been able to make a thing of it! What's the key?"

"It's been buried there under my nose all the time, because Rachel lied about her background," Dani said, looking directly toward Rachel.

"Sure I lied!" Rachel snarled. "Stone made up a story for me, but I lied about most things on those lists."

"That's what made the difference." Dani nodded. "You all know how hard we worked to find things we'd all done—and only came up with five?"

"Sure." Bix nodded. "Stuff like we've all seen *Gone With the Wind* and we've all had some kind of pet."

"Right! But when I found out that Rachel was lying, that meant that there were more constants."

"How'd you find out she was lying?" Sid asked.

"One of our 'all but one lists'—lists of things all of us but one had done—was a list of cities we had visited." She looked around the room, and her face was careful as she said, "Rachel said she'd never been to Dallas."

"And she really had?" Karen asked.

"Once she let it slip that she'd attended one of the home games of the Cowboys—and she'd be unlikely to do that *without* passing through Dallas, wouldn't she?"

Karl was staring at her, his face suddenly filled with dread. "Dallas! It's Dallas that ties us all together, Dani?"

Dani nodded slowly, then looked around. "And I could make a new list now, that *all* of us would be on." She paused, then asked slowly, "How many of you have ever been to the Mayfair Hotel in Dallas?"

"That girl!" Karl lifted his hands suddenly, and his voice cracked with emotion. "It's that Williams girl!"

"But *we* had nothing to do with her death!" Karen protested.

"Stone thinks we did," Dani said. "He blames us all for not getting help for her."

She looked at each face, and every one except Ben had the same expression—a mixture of fear, anger, and guilt. Betty suddenly sat down and buried her face in her hands, moaning, "I *knew* I'd have to answer for that someday!"

"Don't talk like that, Betty," Karen said quickly. "What could you have done?"

"The same as the rest of you—I could have gotten the police!"

Her words sank into the group as a stone drops into a

still pond. They hit each person as hard as the truth had hit Dani when it had burst through.

Only moments after the terrific fight in the bathroom, it had leaped into Dani's mind in the form of a logical proposition: *Rachel is the murderer, therefore everything she has said may be a lie. She said she'd never been to Dallas, so she probably has been to Dallas: Therefore all of us have been to Dallas.*

Dani had thought of the time she had been attending a professional meeting—which was being held in Dallas's Mayfair Hotel.

It was the only time she had ever seen a person murdered!

As soon as she made the connection, the whole terrible scene flashed through Dani's mind, with the clarity as of the view from her third-story hotel window.

She remembered word for word what she had said to the policeman who had questioned her the next day: "I saw a man and woman—and she was on the pavement, trying to get up. When she did, he hit her and knocked her down again. They weren't right beneath my window, so I had to lean out to see it. He kept hitting her, knocking her down, and she would get up and try to run away. I—I could see the blood on her mouth, where he'd hurt her."

When the policeman had asked if she heard the woman call for help, she had said, "Y-yes, she called out, 'Please help me! O my God—he's killing me! Please—somebody help me!' "

That cry had echoed in Dani's mind for weeks, waking her up at night and keeping her in a state of despair over her failure to respond to the young woman.

Now, looking around at the others, she said unsteadily, "I guess you all had interviews with the police. When they asked me why I hadn't called them, I said it never oc-curred to me that *somebody* hadn't already done it." Bitter-ness touched her lips, and she gave her shoulders an angry shake. "But nobody else *did* call. We all just watched and let a man murder a woman."

Betty's face was dull with shock, and her voice a faint whisper, "I thought it was all over! But a thing like that's never over." She looked around, fear scrawled across her face, and added, "For six months after it happened, I didn't sleep. Finally I had a breakdown. That's why I lied about where I come from. When I got out of the asylum, I moved and changed my name. I'd lived in Pennsylvania all my life, but I didn't want to stay where anybody knew me, so I moved to Saint Louis."

Holtz had been staring at the floor, but now he looked up. "Death was a familiar figure to me during the war. I saw the young woman being attacked, but I was not a citizen then. I didn't want to get involved in a criminal matter, so I said nothing. I thought—as all of you thought, I suppose—that the police would get a dozen phone calls. The whole thing happened in front of dozens of wit-nesses."

"You're right, Karl." Karen nodded. "I was in Dallas for a vacation." Irony sharpened her voice, and she shook her head. "I'd just gotten back from Six Flags when I looked out the window and saw the thing. I started to call the police, but I thought the same as you and Dani did."

"Sure, we all thought that," Bix said woodenly. "I was playing a gig with a group at the Mayfair. The cops found out I'd seen it and kept me talking about it for two hours: Why *hadn't* I done something, they wanted to know. I was down on the world then, and I told them I wasn't getting paid to protect the broad—it was *their* job." He made a futile gesture with his hands. "I *could* have done something, too. That's what got to me after it was over. Maybe I couldn't have gone out and taken the guy—but I could have called."

"It was that story in the paper that got me!" Sid said. "Way it was wrote up, we didn't *care* about the girl!"

"Yeah, I almost looked up that reporter and busted his nose!" Lonnie agreed sourly. "I never even seen the thing, not really. I was delivering some booze to the hotel and just passed by. I saw this guy was hasslin' this girl, sure, but how was I to know he was going to knock her off? I said to my boss, as soon as I got back to the warehouse, 'Seen some guy pushing a dame around outside the Mayfair,' and next thing I know, the cops is there, pumping me!" He gave his head an angry shake. "I finally hadda get out of Dallas and go back home over that mess!"

"But what does Maxwell Stone have to do with that woman?" Karen asked.

"*Williams* was her married name," Dani spoke up. "She was getting a divorce, I remember. I'm wondering if her maiden name might have been *Stone*." She stopped, bit her lip, then said slowly, "I've never forgiven myself for not doing *something!*"

Silence fell across the group, until Sid broke it by saying, "Stone must have gotten our names from the papers."

"No," Ben said. "The papers never listed your names. But Stone had connections and money. He could have gotten it from the police records. Lots of people have access to those reports, and some of them have been known to be on the take."

"Did they ever catch the guy who killed her?" Sid asked.

"He got life without parole, I read." Lonnie spoke

thoughtfully. "But there was a little piece in the Little Rock paper about him. He'd only been in prison for four months when he got killed in some kind of rumble."

"Wouldn't be hard for a rich guy like Stone to arrange that." Sid shrugged. "With enough coin, you could get *anybody* burned."

Dani looked around, then said quietly, "Well, we've come a long way today. We've got our killer, and we know why we're in this place, but I'm afraid it doesn't mean a lot."

"I think you're right," Karl said. "With the kind of mind Stone's got, even if we all confessed and said we were sorry, he still wouldn't let us go."

"Can't afford to." Ben nodded. "Multiple kidnappings and three murders? He'll *never* let us go."

His words expressed everyone's thoughts, and Sid gave Rachel a hard look. "Maybe if we give him this doll's fingers, one at a time, he'll reconsider."

Rachel paled, but shook her head. "Wrong there. He'd let me run through a meat grinder before he'd change his mind."

"The thing that bothers me," Dani said slowly, "is that he might panic, now that we got his assassin put away. He may just decide to let us starve—get rid of us any way he can, so he can bury all the evidence."

"The 'evidence,' " Karen said sharply, then gave a humorless laugh. "That's *us*, I take it. But you're right, Dani. Haven't you sensed that he's getting tired of his game with us? Things are happening faster, and he can't risk having us around. I think he'll kill us soon, especially now that he doesn't have Rachel to pick us off."

"But—he doesn't *know* we have her," Ben mused.

Dani stared at him, noting the intense look on the lean face. "Well, he'll know soon enough, Ben."

"Maybe not."

"You have an idea, Ben?" Bix asked hopefully.

Ben stood there, thinking hard, while the others said nothing. Finally he lifted his head, then slowly faced them. His hazel eyes were half closed, but they could sense that his mind was working rapidly. "Maybe, I do," he said finally. "But it's a long shot."

"Anything's better than nothing, Ben," Karen urged. "What is it?"

"Well, Bix was right about busting out of here. The only shot is through that opening up there. Night after night I've thought, until my head aches, about some way to get through that hole, and I guess you have, too.

"There's one time when nobody can see under the box," Ben said thoughtfully. "From the time the box goes up from the floor, the camera can pick it up, but as soon as it gets twenty feet or so up, it's out of the camera range. And the guys topside can't see what's going on, I'd guess, until the box gets to them."

Dani frowned. "But what does that mean?" She stared up toward the canopy, then back to him. "How could anyone get to the box *after* it's left the floor?"

Ben looked up briefly. "Karl, you've always said that nobody could climb up out of this place, but I think it can be done."

"You are not a fly, Ben." Karl smiled faintly.

"Don't have to be. Come and look at this." They all followed him to the side of the silo. Ben reached up to touch a shapeless piece of steel that protruded slightly. "These were the supports for a steel ladder that used to go all the way to the top. Stone had them cut off with a torch. Down here, close to the floor, there's not much left of them, but I've gotten a glimpse of the ones higher up, and the welders weren't so careful. Some stick out half an inch or even more."

"But you couldn't climb up on such a small thing!" Dani exclaimed.

"Mountain climbers do—on even less."

"But what good would it do, even if you got to the top? You know a guy as careful as Stone wouldn't leave an open door. He'd weld it shut," Bix objected.

"Who knows?" Ben shrugged. "Every case I ever worked on, somebody left something out. Maybe he *did* leave a door—but even if he didn't it's a chance to use the box to get through that opening."

"I still don't see it, Ben!" Bix protested. "How could you get from the *wall* over to that box as it's going up?"

A thought wrote itself on Ben's face, and he didn't answer Bix's question. Instead he said, "Let's take a break. I need to think a little about this thing. Sid, you and Lonnie hang on to Rachel."

"She ain't goin' nowhere," Sid grunted.

The others moved away, but Ben said, "Dani . . . ?"

"Yes, Ben?"

"Got to ask you something." He led the way to a couch but didn't sit down. He turned to face her, and she couldn't read the expression on his face. "I wanted to ask you something, but not in front of the others."

Mystified by his look, she asked, "What is it?"

"Well, there's only one way I can think of to fool Stone. First thing in the morning, we give him the notice that you've been killed. Then—"

"Then I go up in the box as a corpse?" Dani said swiftly.

He stared at her. "You think too much and too fast," he said. "Man who marries you won't have a chance! You'll read through his little schemes before he even gets them off the ground!"

"Maybe not," she shot back, a small dimple appearing in her right cheek. "I've seen some women so crazy about men, they couldn't even think of their own names. Maybe I'll be like that."

He studied her with a jaundiced eye. "Yeah? Well, it'd be good for you, I guess."

She grew nervous under his examination and said quickly, "I'm the corpse in the play. But I can't see how that will help."

"You sure you want to do it, boss?" he asked carefully. "No telling what we'll find up there. Maybe five guys with machine guns, and Stone might be mad enough to have them toss you down right then."

She threw her head back and looked him in the face, her eyes wide open. "I'll do it, Ben. But what about you?"

"Come along, I'll have to experiment a little."

She followed him into the kitchen, and he came out with a pair of pliers. "Be right back," he said, disappearing into the men's quarters.

"What's he up to, Dani?" Karen asked.

"I don't know, except that we're not going to tell Stone that Rachel missed. We're going to have my funeral, and then I go up—just like the others."

Lonnie stared at her, then shook his head. "I wouldn't want to be at *my* funeral!" he exclaimed. "But what'll that get us?"

Dani shook her head, and they waited until Ben came through the door, some Romex wire in his hands.

"I had to pull out some wiring, so we won't have some of our lights, but if this works, we won't need them," he said. He put down the wire, pulled the pliers out of his pocket, and carefully measured his own height, then cut off a length. "Get the butcher knife and strip these ends, will you, Bix? Lay them back about eight inches—and Lonnie, get the rest of the nylon rope we used for the canopy." By the time Bix returned, he had cut three lengths of the heavy wire. They all watched him make a knot in one end, so that he had a loop about five inches in diameter; then he folded the stripped copper wires to fashion a three-inch loop. He finished all three pieces of wire, then said, "Measure me off some of that rope—three times across the room at the widest part."

Karen held one end of the rope while Dani walked it off, and soon they had the three lengths. He came over and looked at the remainder of the thin cord. "That'll be enough, I guess."

"Enough for *what?*" Dani asked.

"Well, here's the plan," Ben said, taking a deep breath. "Tomorrow morning, Dani goes up in the box—as a corpse. I won't be in sight, Karl, so you have your usual confab with Stone, and put in it that I've got some broken bones from catching Bix. Tell him you have to have splints. Karen, you can insist on that. And listen, have a *short* funeral!"

"Why short?" Dani asked.

"Because if you sneeze, the whole thing's blown!" he grinned, sobered, and said, "These old ladder stubs are out of the camera's line of view, so Stone can't see what's going on. I'll be going up a rope all the way to the top of this silo."

They all stared at him, and he said with a shrug, "We'll know pretty soon whether or not that's going to work. First we have to make a thick rope out of these strands—as thick as we can. We may even have to take some of the rope we used for the canopy. If you've ever noticed the ropes that fliers climb up, they're very thick—makes it easier to grasp. So let's work on that. Then I'll have a shot at the Matterhorn."

"How long does it have to be?" Karl asked quickly.

"A hundred feet ought to do it."

"Then I will show you what a sailor can do with a few pieces of rope!" Karl took over, and after making a sample out of four strands, asked, "Will this do?"

Ben grasped it and looked up with a startled expression. "Hey, this is *great*, Karl!" he exclaimed. "Even better than the real thing!"

"Good! Now I will work." He measured off several equal segments and sat down in a chair, his hands weaving a thick rope out of the single strands. In less than half an hour he held up the end, saying, "Here is your rope, Ben."

"Can you weave these copper wires into the end, so they won't slip?"

"Of course." He worked intently for a few minutes, then said, "I'd risk my reputation on this work!"

"And I'm risking my neck, but it looks good." He took the rope, coiled it up, then placed it around his neck. After retrieving the three lengths of wire, he walked to the steel fragments of stubs and turned to say, "Now, all I have to do is climb to the top, fasten this rope to something, and then tomorrow I'll be all set."

He turned to go, but Dani said quickly, "Ben, could I say a prayer before you go?"

Though he had turned, now he glanced toward her. His face was set, but he nodded slightly. "Go ahead. I need all the help I can get, boss."

She said in a very low tone, "You have said it all, Ben. But we all know this is *very* dangerous! Once you're up thirty feet, you'll be in the dark, just feeling your way. And if something goes wrong. . . ." She faltered, adding in a voice that wasn't entirely steady. "There's no safety net, is there, Ben?"

"No net." His voice was spare, but he was ignoring the others, looking at her in an unusual manner. "Only line of Shakespeare I know came from some movie I saw. Somebody said, 'We owe God a death . . . he that dies this year is quit for the next.' "

Dani nodded. The second part of "Henry the Fourth." A lump came into her throat, and she bowed her head quickly and began to pray. Though she didn't see, all followed her example, except Rachel, who stared at the group contemptuously.

"Lord, we have no hope except in You," she prayed simply. "Give Ben strength, guide his hands, keep him in the hollow of your strong hand. In the high places, take away his fear. He does this, Lord, not for his sake, but for all of us, so I ask you to bring him back safely. In the name of Jesus, I ask it—amen."

"Amen," several murmured, and Ben said, "Thanks, boss." Then he turned and reached up with one of the short lengths of wire. He looped it over a stub four feet over his head, put his foot in the loop hanging down, and pulled himself upright. "Onward and upward," he said cheerfully, then took another section of wire and carefully fed it up to another extension. This one was somewhat longer, they could all see, and the loop slid over it with a comfortable margin. Ben put his other foot in the loop of that wire, lifted himself up, then carefully lifted the first strand from its position and, reaching upward, tried for another hold. Both braces seemed to be too short, so as they all watched, he chose the third wire, which was longer, and carefully pushed it upward. Obviously, the longer the wire, the more it would give and sway; he had difficulty looping the next stub, but finally he did it.

When he moved up, Dani expelled her breath, not aware that she had been holding it.

"That's going to be a *long* climb!" Bix whispered. "Especially in the dark!"

They all watched until he disappeared through the canopy—and Dani found out that it was even *worse* not being able to see him. *If he falls, nobody will know until he hits the floor—nobody could try to stand under him as he did for Bix!* Then she asked herself, *Would I jump under him, if he fell?* Finding no assurance, she stood there with the others, listening for the tiny noises that filtered down, until finally he moved out of the range of their ears.

Although they thought about Ben, he was not thinking of *them*. Long ago he had learned to close his thoughts to crowds, to think only of the task at hand. He had succeeded in doing this on the trapeze, so that he never heard the applause or any crowd noise at all. Now he slipped off into that silent world, thinking only of capturing the next stub.

By the time he had climbed ten feet above the canopy, there was almost no light, just the dim rays that filtered through the hole left for the supply box to pass through. It was enough for him to see the stubs for another twenty feet, and he realized that he had been right about the welders—they *had* been more careless with their work as they went higher. The fractured supports were sometimes two or three inches long and rough besides, which made them hold tighter to the polished wires.

When the time came that he could not see the next support, he leaned the wire against the wall and pushed it up until it touched something. Then he lifted it and almost at once felt the noose slide over a projection. He breathed a sigh of relief, but as he put his foot in the loop, the thought came, *Maybe it's just a fragment—maybe it'll pull loose as soon as I put my weight on it.*

So what? his mind answered. *You don't have any choice anyway, because you can't go down this thing backward.* He grinned in the darkness, then put his weight on the noose and pulled himself up. It held, and he forced himself to ignore the thoughts of falling.

His arms grew tired, but there was no point in resting. Twice he had to use the longest wire, and even then it was difficult, for it kept trying to collapse. He had no idea how far he was from the top, for the door, of course, was closed. *Be a fine mess if I rammed my head into the ceiling and shook myself off!* he thought once, but he realized he'd touch the ceiling with the wire first.

All the time he had been telling his mind that he was only six feet off the ground, as he had been taught in the circus. But finally that became impossible, for without warning, while he was in mid step, the whole wire suddenly slipped about half an inch! That fraction triggered a fear that went off like a fire alarm in his brain, and he looked down without thinking.

He was *not* six feet off the ground, but almost a hundred. There, far below, he saw the floor through the hole in the canopy and even caught a glimpse of Dani and Lonnie standing there, looking up. They seemed very small!

Ben clung to the wire, expecting at any moment to feel it all let go, and he'd go plummeting to his death on the concrete. He had been in danger of his life more than once, but never in such silence. Before there had always been violent noise and the clash of action, but now he could only hang there in the silence and wait.

He found himself thinking of the prayer Dani had said just before he left, and the words came back to him very softly, almost as if someone were speaking them inside his skull. *In the high places, take away his fear.*

Peace came over him, and Ben simply reached up with the wire, anchored it almost at once, and pulled himself up.

The rest of the climb took only a few minutes. He groped in the darkness, trying for the next stub, and when he could not find one, he reached out to find the outline of a door under his hands! It was a steel door, with a sill for his feet and a large steel handle on which to anchor the rope. Ben suspected that it was welded on the other side, for it did not give a fraction when he banged it with his fist.

"It would have been nice," he muttered, but reached up, caught the end of his rope with the wire noose, and attached it firmly to the handle. Then he dropped the rope, and when it hit the canopy far below, somebody cried out, so he shouted, "Stand clear!"

He looped the rope around his leg and rapeled down the side of the cold steel, in what amounted to a controlled fall, stopping himself when he approached the canopy. He ducked under it, and as he came down the last twenty feet, he was aware that all the others were cheering.

His feet had barely hit the floor before they were on him, Dani, Karen, and even Betty with their arms around his neck, and the men beating him on the back.

He stood there, surrounded, and felt Dani's cheek on his. Hot tears touched his face, but she whispered in his ear, "You may turn out to be a louse sometimes, but right now you're a hero!"

He grinned and finally interjected, "Well, now that you've slobbered all over me, let me point out a few difficulties! But I need a drink first."

They all moved to the kitchen, and Betty served them big glasses of iced tea. Ben drank it down, took a second, then stared around him. "I guess we'd better go over this thing carefully, because I figure it's our last shot. First, we have to convince Stone that Rachel has done the job. She *has* to be pretty visible, and she can't be allowed to give any sign to Stone—none at all."

"Lemme take care of that, Ben!" Sid glared at Rachel then walked over to where she was standing. Suddenly he pulled out the butcher knife that had been used to strip the wires and stepped behind her. She screamed and tried to move, but he reached out and caught her by the hair. Jerking her back, he put the knife to the back of her neck and remarked clinically, "Some of the hit men in the Chicago area found out a real smart way to carry out contracts—and not have no murder weapon that could be traced. They found out that you take an ice pick and ram it into a guy's neck, way up high, and it kills him right off." He looked at Karen and nodded, "That's right, ain't it, Doc?"

"Yes," Karen answered instantly. "If it were placed exactly right, it would do just that."

"Well, I didn't get no instruction, like those guys did, but it got to be pretty big." Sid nodded. "I mean, you buy an ice pick in any hardware store, and after the job, it's just an ice pick, like a million others, right?" Then he pulled Rachel's head back and put the point of the knife on her neck. "So tomorrow I stand right here with this shiv on your pretty little neck. Lonnie stands where he can see your face. If you even *blink* at that camera, you'll be dead meat, doll!"

Ben grinned. "Good! Now you'll have to be perfectly still, boss. And let's have a *short* funeral service!"

"But once the box is on the way up, how do you get to it?" Holtz demanded. "You'll be on the wall, a hundred feet in the air and at least twenty feet away."

"Twenty feet's not a lot," Ben said. "I've made jumps a lot farther than that."

They all stared at him, and Dani put their thoughts in words, "Ben, you can't do that! It'd be suicide!"

He shook his head, "Here's what we'll do. Karl will make something like a small cargo net. We'll put it under you, Dani, and as soon as you get out of view of the camera, you'll fasten it to the sides of the box. It'll need to be pretty strong, and the only thing I can think of to anchor it with is some sort of hooks. Anyway, while you're still down low, you get that net out, then lie down again. They'll pull you up through the door, and as soon as the box is in the hole, I'll jump, catch the net and go up under the box."

Appalled at the idea, Dani cried out, "Ben! It'll be *dark* when the box goes through the opening!"

"You won't even be able to see the net, Ben," Karen argued.

"That's why we'll use a net," he explained. "A rope would be easy to miss, but all I have to do is hit the net with any part of my body, and I can grab it and scramble up."

That began a long debate, for all of them felt that it was an impossible task. But it came to an end when Ben stubbornly shook his head, and finally said, "It's the only hope we've got, and you all know it."

They finally scattered, but Dani stayed long enough to say quietly, "You left one thing out, Ben." She came close and put a hesitant hand on his arm. "You've not been able to let go of your hold when you're up high."

Her hand on his arm was light, but he was acutely aware of the pressure. He let the silence run on, and both of them were thinking of the last time they'd touched, when he'd kissed her. He murmured, "I guess it's time I laid my personal ghost to rest, Dani." He examined her through half-shut eyes and asked, almost idly, "How about *your* ghost? You think you'll ever be able to get it to leave you alone?"

She shook her head, and at once the moment was broken. "I don't know what's ahead—for me or for you, Ben. All I know is, if I have any chance at all, if any of us do, it's because of you. I know how hard this is for you—so while we're alone, I—I want to thank you for what you're risking for us."

"It's for me, too." He shrugged. Then turned and walked away, leaving her alone, and she felt somehow that she had not said what she should have. As she walked across the room, the futile, empty feelings of lostness increased. Unexpectedly, tears rose to Dani's eyes, and she dashed them away quickly as she moved toward the others.

18
Mr. Maxwell Stone

After Holtz put the message saying that Dani Ross was dead into the slot, there wasn't much to do but wait. Dani had to stay in the women's quarters, in case the camera came on unexpectedly, and the minutes seemed to crawl by. Karen brought her breakfast, but Dani only nibbled at the French toast, though she drank all the orange juice and asked for more.

At ten thirty Karen brought her a small pitcher of the beverage. "Throat a little dry?" she asked sympathetically, sitting beside her on the bunk. "Well, nobody can blame you for that, I guess." She waited until Dani had drained her glass, then filled it up again. "How much chance do we have, Dani? On the level."

"A better chance than the average person has of winning the big lottery prize," Dani answered dryly. She didn't want to talk any more about odds or chances, so she asked, "Did you see the net Karl made?" She got up and picked up what looked like a mass of loose rope, but when she held it up by one end, it became a net with one-foot squares. "The commander sure knows his knots!" she exclaimed. "These won't slip—I tried to jerk them out of place on purpose. And it ought to be plenty long enough—about ten feet."

"How do you keep Stone from seeing it? And how does it fasten to the supply box?"

"Lonnie's going to carry me out all wrapped up in a blanket, and this will be under it. As soon as I clear the canopy, I snap these hooks onto the ropes that hold the box," she pointed out. "Lonnie and Sid tore up part of the stove to make the hooks." She smiled briefly, her mind not on what she was saying, "Betty raised the roof—until she realized that if this thing doesn't work, *nobody* will be using the stove for long."

Karen's eyes grew sober. "That's right. But if—" Suddenly she lifted her head, then both women got to their feet. "There goes the winch," she said nervously. Suddenly she threw her arms around Dani, and the two women clung to each other for a brief moment. Then Karen pulled away and ran out of the room.

Dani felt weak and unsteady, but she walked quickly to the door. Staying well back, so that she could not be seen, she waited until the sound of the winch broke off. She could hear Stone's voice clearly, when he said, "Once more, you people bear the responsibility for what has happened!"

"You've convinced yourself of that," Holtz said. "Though you cannot really believe it. But I will not argue with you. We have lost our finest, and I am beyond such arguments. Lonnie, go get Danielle, and we will have a brief service."

Dani went back at once to pick up the net. Lonnie came in, and when he got to her, she saw that his face was working nervously. "I—I guess this is it, Dani," he said hoarsely. "Sure do hope—" He broke off and shook his head sharply, then mumbled, "Well, God's gonna take care of you. I prayed all night for you."

Dani stared at him, then patted his thick shoulder. "Keep right on praying, Lonnie!" She stepped to the bunk, lay down on the blanket, and arranged the net over her lower body, carefully holding onto the hooks. "I'm ready now."

Lonnie folded the blanket over her as she had instructed him, leaving her face out but the rest of her body well covered. Then he picked her up, one hand under her knees and the other supporting her back and head. Dani closed her eyes, concentrating on not moving a muscle. She felt the difference as he stepped into the rec room and let her head bob slightly with the motion of his steps. He stopped and carefully placed her in what she knew was the supply box. Her head bumped as he put her down, and one of the wooden braces on the bottom bit uncomfortably into her shoulder blades, but she willed herself to relax, not moving a muscle. *God, don't let me cough or sneeze,* she prayed.

"This woman was Your handmaiden, God," Karl said. "She was, of all of us, the closest to You, so the words I say this morning will not be to You, but to those of us who remain—"

Dani dared not open her eyes for a glimpse of Ben, though she knew he would be starting up the rope for his long climb. Her hands were trembling, and an empty feeling filled her stomach. Willing herself to think of something else, she let her mind go up, trying to picture what would take place when the box she lay in passed through the opening high over her head.

What a fearful thing for Ben! she thought. *His own private ghost, that's what he called it. He'll be in the darkness, with a concrete floor a hundred feet down and no net. He'll have to turn loose and leap out into that darkness, not even able to see the net, and if he misses—!*

Dani tried to pray, but discovered that she was unable to do much. Then she remembered a seminary lecture on the Great Awakening. The professor stressed how that tremendous move of God had been brought on by intense prayer. His words came to her as she lay there in the cold: *They prayed all night—often for many nights. They prayed, it is reported, until they finally got through to God, and people commonly asked, "Have you prayed through?" This meant, "Have you prayed so long and so fervently that you've heard from God, that He's given you His assurance so firmly that you don't need to pray anymore on the matter—you're 'prayed up!'"*

As Karl said, "I will read a few verses from the book she loved so well . . . ," Dani realized that she *was* "prayed up." All night long she had wrestled with God, feeling lost and lonely, but now a strange peace filled her. As Karl finished reading the verses, she addressed God in her spirit, saying, *Now, Lord, Thy will be done.* Then the winch started, and the box suddenly moved, coming clear of the floor and swaying slightly as it rose.

She kept her eyes nearly shut. When the light grew dim, she knew the box had passed through the canopy. Opening her eyes, she saw the rectangle of light in the ceiling and quickly threw back the folds of the blanket and sat up. The swaying of the box was like a pendulum as she picked up the net and threw it over the side, then secured the hooks on the two ropes that supported the left-hand side of the supply box. She gave the net a shake, to be sure it was hanging free. Just as the bright beam of a powerful flashlight came on, she lay back, arranged the blanket in folds over herself as best she could, and closed her eyes.

Savage had taken a station beside the rope, after a light breakfast. It was out of camera view, and at some point that morning everyone came by to spend a few moments with him. Karen had brought him some coffee, and he'd asked about Vince.

"Touch and go." She shrugged. "He's nearly in a coma—wakes up for a few seconds, then falls back. Even with hospital care, it'd be tricky." She was wearing no makeup, and her oval face was tense. "I talked to Dani," she said.

"How's she doing?"

"Better than I am!" Karen laughed shortly. She pushed her hair back, shook it so that it fell down her back, then added, "She's worried about you, Ben. We all are."

"I've done harder stunts."

She took a deep breath, then shook her head. "You're a hard nut. I've never known anyone tougher, so you can face this thing because you're tough. And Dani can face it because she's got faith in God. But the rest of us—" She hesitated, and there was a frail quality in her face as she put her hand on his arm and said, "You're in God's hands, Dani says, but all of us, Ben, we're in *your* hands!"

She got up and left quickly, and Ben sat there sipping coffee until Lonnie and Sid came over. "Who's watching Rachel?" Ben asked.

"I wired her to the table," Sid explained. He stood there ill at ease, then pulled something out of his pocket. "Merry Christmas, Ben." A slight smile touched his thin lips.

Ben took the object, looked at it, then grinned. It was the chisel he'd made to drill through the floor; Sid had wrapped the handle with black friction tape and tied a bright-red bow around it.

"Gee, Sid, and I didn't get you *anything!*" Ben grinned, hefting the weapon.

"Get us all outta here." Sid nodded. "That'll make this the best Christmas any of us ever had."

"Yeah, Ben," Lonnie put in. "And don't try to be a hero when you get up there," he advised. He shook his heavy head, his jaw stubborn. "This ain't no time for tennis rules, Ben. Put those birds down any way you can."

"Don't worry about that," Ben said. "I'd drop a bomb on them, if I could!"

Bix had come by, trying to be cheerful, but he finally said, "I hate to admit it, Ben, but I'm scared sick! And I ain't got to do nothing but *wait* down here." He suddenly put his hand out and said sheepishly, "Aw, Ben, what can I say? You pulled my potatoes out of the fire once, and now you're risking your life to do it again."

"Bix, I've got an interest here myself," Ben reminded him. He smiled and struck the boy a short blow on the shoulder. "Remember what that great American philosopher once said, 'The opera ain't over until the fat lady sings!' "

Bix grinned, then ducked his head and moved away, just as Betty came with more coffee and a piece of cake. "Thanks, Betty," Ben said. Although he wasn't hungry, he took a small bite of the cake, then shook his head.

"You're the best cook ever, Betty. When we get out of here, I'm going to hire you."

Summoning up a smile, she mumbled, "God help you, Ben!" Just as she started to speak again, the winch began to whine, and she hurried away, her eyes wide with fear.

As soon as the winch started to lower the box, Ben walked over to the rope and put his hand on it but made no attempt to climb. He had decided it would be too much strain to hold on up at the top for such a long period, so he waited until he heard Karl give the agreed-upon signal— the words *I will read a few verses from the book she loved so well.* As he heard it, Ben grasped the rope and began climbing. He walked up the wall, not pausing until he had gone past the canopy about twenty feet. His arms grew tired, and he looped the rope around his leg, letting it take the strain while he rested his arms. He could hear Karl reading slowly and hoped they hadn't cut the time too short.

As he began climbing again he looked up once, noting the bright rectangle of light that marked the opening. For the first time he thought, *What if they happen to look at the side of this silo and see me?* But even if he'd thought of it earlier, he'd still have had no choice.

He rested twice more; on the last rest Ben heard the winch start, and he hastened to the top of the ladder. It took less than five minutes for the box to journey from the floor to the top, so he had plenty of time to adjust his feet on the sill of the door.

Too much time, because there was nothing to do now. He remembered the thousand jumps he'd made through the air, but there'd always been Hugo there, with strong, sure hands. And there'd always been a net below, just in case.

What if it happens again? What if I freeze here until it's too late—until the box goes through? He shook his head and looked down, for a strong beam of light had shattered the darkness in an inverted cone, and he instantly saw Dani's still face in the box. The sight seemed to give him some sort of strength, for he thought no more about himself.

The humming of the winch sounded very loud in the silence, and the box rose, twisting slowly. Ben kept his eyes on it until it was only twenty feet away from the top, and he saw Dani's absolutely motionless face. Even with the fearsome leap just seconds away, he had time to think of what a beautiful woman she was. He had come to distrust attractive women, for many of them lacked inward beauty, but ever since he'd met this woman, he'd been aware that she was like no other he'd ever met. They had been abrasive with each other, and he now regretted the times he'd deliberately provoked her, trying her to see if he could find the weakness he suspected lay beneath her face.

Then the box was at his level, and he saw the dangling net and gathered his legs under him. There was a banging noise as the box hit the sides of the opening, and then it slid through, shutting off almost all the light. That was the exact moment he'd waited for.

Everything was shut out of his mind, except that the net was now invisible in the darkness, but he launched himself away from the wall, putting every ounce of his strength into it—arms straight out, legs straight back.

Only twenty feet, but gravity was a giant hand pulling him down. Could he go twenty feet horizontally before that giant pulled him down ten feet?

He opened his fingers wide, every nerve crying out to feel the rough touch of just *one* rope!

Missed! I missed it! With that exquisite sense of timing, he knew that he'd dropped quickly; failure raked across his nerves.

But at that instant his fingers brushed against something, and he went into the net. Neither hand caught a strand of the webbing, but both hands and arms went through. Even as his weight hit the net, Ben pulled one arm back, managed to free it, and grabbed the net firmly. As he swung wildly under the box, from the effects of his velocity, he freed his other arm, aware that the sudden pressure on the box had driven it against the sides of the opening. He thought grimly, *They won't miss that!*

A crack of light marked the outline of the box, and he heard somebody say, "What's going on?"

The gap spread to at least a foot, and Ben waited no longer. He spotted a pair of legs to the right and rolled his legs back, then shoved them forward, coming out from under the box with a twisting force that drove him against the legs of a man, who was instantly knocked down.

"Hey! Watch out!" he cried out.

Ben blinked as the sudden brightness of the sky and the snow half blinded him. He rolled to his feet, yanked the chisel out of his pocket, and struck out as hard as he could. Ben's hand tingled as the weapon caught the man on top of the head and instantly shut off his cry. He dropped at once, but Ben sensed rather than saw another man coming up on his left. He threw himself to one side, but not in time, for something struck him on the temple.

He went down with a myriad of flashing lights in front of his eyes, but he was not out. Acutely aware that he lay very close to the trap door and that the supply box had continued to rise, Ben thought, *He'll try to shove me into that door!* At once he felt strong hands grip him, forcing him backward. Still confused by the blow, suddenly Ben felt an emptiness under his back and knew that he was right over the hole.

"Put him down, French!" a voice said, and the hands pushed him with an inexorable force. *Too strong for me!* Ben thought, and with almost half his body over the opening, he suddenly drew back and struck the man in the head, using the chisel. It was not enough to put him out, but the blow addled his assailant. Ben shoved the dazed man off to one side and mercilessly struck him again, driving him to the floor.

The winch had shut off, and the supply box was swaying slightly, but Ben had no time for that. One man stood between him and death—and he well knew that this man was more dangerous than any he'd ever faced.

"Well, Savage," Lovelace said evenly. "I must congratulate you." He looked large and dangerous, standing there with his hands in his pockets. His light-blue eyes focused on Ben steadily, and there was no sign of fear or even of apprehension on his smooth face. "Mr. Stone and I designed this prison, and we agreed there was no way any human being could get out. Of course, we never anticipated having an acrobat as one of our inmates. A mistake of ours, but it doesn't matter."

He had not pulled a gun, and Ben watched him carefully, almost certain that he had one. As if he had read Ben's mind, Lovelace smiled and pulled a Luger from his overcoat pocket. "It's almost a shame, Savage," he said, shaking his head in a mocking gesture. "To come so close and yet still lose."

Ben moved a step closer, thinking, *If I can get near enough, maybe I can kick the gun away.*

But Lovelace lifted the gun and said with a smile, "No, I would prefer you to stand there, if you don't mind, Mr. Savage. I know you would like to get close enough to use your skill at karate on me, but I really can't permit it."

"Looks like you've got the best of the argument." Ben shrugged. "What's next? Throw me down the shaft?"

"Why, no," Lovelace said. "You'll simply take a ride back down in the box."

"Why not shove me down, like I did with your friend?" Ben taunted. "You're going to kill us all anyway."

"Mr. Stone prefers it this way. I have no more time for you." He moved to a switch and lowered the box to floor level. Then he moved beside it and said, "I'll take care of Miss Ross, Savage, but it's back into the hole for you."

Ben watched helplessly as Lovelace shifted the Luger to his left hand, then reached over to put his arm under Dani. Lovelace merely glanced at what he thought was a corpse, keeping his eyes fixed carefully on Ben, but a flash of movement came one split second too late.

"What the devil!" he exclaimed and let out a cry of pain as the gun exploded, shaking the still air.

Dani had come out of the box and thrown herself at Lovelace's gun hand, catching his arm, dragging it downward, and sinking her teeth into the flesh of his wrist.

Ben sprang instantly forward just as Lovelace jerked the gun free and caught Dani across the temple with a grazing blow. But even as she fell, Ben was on him like a cat. Raising his right arm, he brought it down with a clublike blow that caught Lovelace right on the neck, driving him to his knees.

It would have broken the neck of a lesser man, but the thick muscles of Lovelace's neck cushioned the shock, and even as he fell stunned, he kept his grip on the Luger. His back was to Ben, who knew that the man was down but already recovering from the blow. Ben swung his foot in a vicious kick that caught Lovelace in the kidney and caused him to cry out in pain. The force of the kick threw Ben off balance, and he went down hard, almost on top of his enemy.

They were under a framework of steel, with a corrugated roof, but the blinding snow still bothered Ben. He saw the Luger still held tightly in Lovelace's grasp and made a stabbing grab at it, succeeding in getting both hands on the man's wrist. At once Ben knew he had made a mistake, for he could not hope to match Lovelace's animallike brutality.

Knowing that he had no hope to outmuscle the man, Ben threw caution to the winds, dropped his grip on the man's thick wrist, and stabbed, with his fingers spread wide, straight at the man's eyes. Lovelace turned his head, but Ben got a glancing blow at the right eye, and no man can stand that without reflex action. Lovelace threw up both arms in agony and backed away until he was standing out from under the shed. For that one second he stood there off his guard.

His left hand covered his face, and the other held the Luger at waist level. Ben instantly kicked upward, knowing that if he missed, he would be out of position and would certainly take a bullet.

His toe struck Lovelace's fist, and the power of the kick

sent the gun spinning high. Both men watched the parabola of its passage through the cold air. Scrambling through the foot of snow that covered the flat roof, each tried to knock the other off balance. The Luger fell with a soft *plop*, within a foot of the edge, and in their frantic haste to get it, Ben and Lovelace staggered and fought. The two men gave tremendous lunges as they came within a few feet of it.

At the same time both realized they were going to slide off the roof!

Ben heard Lovelace utter a wordless cry of terror as he tried to stop, but could not. He himself rolled backward and made a wild grab, catching the built-up metal flange that ran around the edge of the roof, constructed to keep the hot-tar roof from dripping. It was only two inches high, but Ben's hands gripped it like steel talons.

A grunt caused him to see that Lovelace had done the same. Together they dangled by their fingertips, a hundred feet in the air. Lovelace's eyes were wild with fear, and his feet were scratching and clawing at the wall, but heavy as he was, he made no progress.

Ben looked down at the ground, then turned his face toward Lovelace. "You should have run away and joined the circus, like I did, pal." He grinned. "Watch *this!*"

Ben began swinging his body, pendulum fashion, from side to side as the other watched. Two swings provided momentum, on the third Ben gave a powerful kick that drove his feet up as high as Lovelace's shoulders and firmly hooked them there. Lovelace opened his mouth and moaned as the extra weight dragged him down, but at once Ben put one foot on the ledge; with this leverage he was able to draw himself up, so that he came up to the roof and then sat there, legs dangling.

"Help me!" Lovelace begged, his eyes pleading.

Ben considered the man and said, "I'm thinking right now of a good man named Rosie—and another one named Alex. I'm thinking of a girl named Candi." He paused and stared down with blazing hazel eyes, then shook his head. "Can't think of any reason to let you live."

Lovelace seemed to shrivel, and the manhood ran out of him. He began to weep, and finally Ben got up and found the Luger. He reached down and caught hold of the man's collar, complaining, "I'll hate myself for this! Pull yourself up."

Lovelace strained and with Ben's help came scrambling up, to crawl on the snow, expelling his breath in huge sobs. When Ben said, "Put your hands behind you," he obeyed at once. Ben drew the short wires out of his pocket and tied the big wrists together as tightly as he could. Then he got up and ran to the shed.

Dani came out to meet him, and announced, "Ben, I'm glad you didn't kill him." As she smiled tremulously her gray-green eyes reflected his face. One hand touched his cheek, and she said softly, "We're going to be all right."

"Sure." He nodded. A little reluctantly he added, "Thanks to you. If you hadn't gotten his attention, we'd both be on death row."

She put her hand on his arm. "I guess we make a pretty good team, don't we, Ben?"

"Beauty and the beast." He grinned and looked around quickly. "We're still in the lion's den, though. Let me be sure our friend here stays put, and we'll move along."

He secured the two men who were still out, then wired

Lovelace to a steel support, after ordering him to take off his heavy overcoat. Slipping into it, he looked around. "That's the other way out," he said, pointing to a roughly built structure under the same roof as the supply door. There was a platform built of steel angle irons, and he motioned to the large electric motor that served as a winch for both elevator and supply box. "They brought us all up in this elevator and take the bodies out this way."

"Come along," he got into the makeshift elevator, and when Dani was in, Ben threw the switch, and the elevator started down. "I figure Stone is down at the bottom of this silo," he said. "He'll be looking for Lovelace, not us, but just to be safe, you lie down."

The elevator moved slowly down. Leaning over, Ben saw a man standing beside a desk, staring into the monitor before him and talking loudly. "Maxwell Stone's last speech," Ben murmured softly; he turned sideways as the elevator dropped and came to a jolting halt.

Ben caught a glimpse of Stone when the man turned to glance at the elevator. Certain he would be detected, Ben tightened his grip on the Luger. But people see what they expect to see, and Stone, who had not stopped speaking, merely turned back to the monitor.

Ben stepped out of the elevator and stood right behind Stone, who shouted, "You have proven yourselves to be beyond rehabilitation! I have tried, but you refuse to admit what you are—therefore, I leave you to your fate!"

Ben placed the cold muzzle of the Luger on Stone's wrinkled neck, saying, "It's time for a word from our sponsor, Maxie."

The mild words jolted Stone, and he wheeled at once, his face twisted in disbelief. He was below middle height and past middle age. His droopy face had the tired flesh of the old, and he had combed his thin hair over a bare skull.

Stone stared at Ben. As Dani appeared at Ben's side he swallowed and wavered, as if shaken by a blow. But he replied, "Ah, Mr. Savage! I see that you are a man of force and initiative! And Miss Ross—such a woman as yourself is not to be wasted." He smiled, but it was like the silver on a coffin, for both Ben and Dani sensed the death that lay beneath the man's surface.

"You're going to offer us a job with your outfit, Stone?" Ben inquired.

"No! Not a *job!*" He shook his head so violently that his thin neck seemed too tiny for it. "No, I've been looking all over this country for people like you. I can promise you—!"

"What are you offering for the three people you've killed, Stone?" Dani asked quietly.

His mouth gaped and with sudden compassion Dani asked, "Was the girl who was killed your daughter?"

"Yes!" Stone's anger boiled over instantly. His eyes bulged, and he began to scream.

"Tie him up, Ben!" Dani picked up the microphone and stared into the screen.

On the small screen Karen stood holding on to Betty. Bix and Lonnie, Sid and Karl stared up at the camera, their faces all frozen.

"We made it!" she cried out.

All six broke into a wild dance, crying and shouting. She let them have their holiday before directing, "We've still got to have help, so just hang tight." A thought struck her, and she glanced at Ben, saying, "The investigative firm of Ross and Savage has things in hand!"

Ben blinked, then returned her grin. "I always wanted to be your superior, but I guess being equal is good enough."

They wired Stone to a sturdy steel shaft, and he screamed at them insanely as they left.

It was a beautiful day, and the heady feeling of freedom caught them. But the most beautiful thing was the new Jeep parked outside. "If it's got a telephone," Dani said, "we're home free!"

She peered inside, then turned to give Ben a brilliant smile. "Bingo!" After a few tense moments, her head went back and she said thickly, "Dad? It's Dani! Yes, I'm all right, but you've got work to do. Call the FBI. . . ." She spoke rapidly, sketching the situation, including Vince's condition. "Dad, better hurry. Stone's got a young army around here," she warned. "Yes, yes, I will. What? Yes, Ben's right here with me. He's all right."

She hung up the phone, took a deep breath, then got out. She started to speak but somehow couldn't.

Ben glanced at her white face. "Sometimes the shock hits you after the trouble's over. We'd better get inside; some of Stone's army might spot us." Inside he went to the mike and told the others what was happening. "Just have to wait," he said finally. "I expect it'll be five or six hours before the cavalry shows up. But we can get the rest of you out one at a time."

For the next hour he worked the winch, bringing them up to the roof, then down to the control room. Vince was placed gently onto the bed beside the desk. He was conscious and able to whisper, when Dani bent over and put her ear to his lips, "Knew—you'd do it!"

She patted his hand and nodded, but he became unconscious almost at once.

Three hours after Dani made the call, Ben said suddenly, "I hear something!" They all ran to the door, peering around one another. Ben glanced up and said, "Look—army helicopters!"

They all stepped outside as a flight of clumsy-looking choppers swooped down. The first hovered over the roof, while others circled, with guns bristling. One touched down fifty yards from where the prisoners stood; a door opened, spilling out a squad of riflemen with weapons at their shoulders.

Soon they were all in the helicopter, rising above the silo, higher and higher, until the one-time prison shrank to the size of a small box. The chopper lurched, changed directions, and the silo vanished as they skimmed over the icy tops of the firs. The sparkling snow below, dotted with the deep-green trees, stirred something in Dani, and she leaned over Ben's shoulder, saying quietly, "Merry Christmas, Ben!" She took a deep breath and repeated her words with a fervency that amounted to a deep-seated prayer: "Merry Christmas."

He turned toward her and said nothing for a moment. Finally he smiled and answered, "And God bless us—every one!"

19
"Maybe We Can Make Something of Each Other!"

"Happy New Year, Daughter."

Startled at the unusual formality in his voice, Dani looked quickly at her father. The family had been seated around the antique claw-footed oak table, nibbling at snacks and waiting for midnight. When the rockets began bursting in the sky and the faint rattling sound of firecrackers came from down the road, the rest of them had gone to the bay window.

She studied his face, thin and pale from the lack of sun, but somehow stronger than ever, for his illness had planed away just enough flesh to reveal the strength of the bone structure and throw his essential steadiness into prominence.

"Happy New Year, Dad." She smiled and kissed his cheek. He held her hand, looked up at her, and confessed quietly, "For a while it looked as if it wouldn't be so happy for any of us."

Dani nodded. For a week the media had besieged her and her family. Reporters from newspapers, journals, television anchormen, agents looking for first rights, like locusts they had descended both on the office and the house.

From the moment Maxwell Stone had been indicted for conspiracy to murder, the entire country could not get enough details. The bizarre setting of the strange prison, the collapse of Stone's military "empire," the story of the survivors, and most of all the dramatic escape captivated the world! Lovelace, Rachel and Stone's pictures became familiar to America as the three were trotted off to jail to await trials.

Dani had tried to go to the office, but discovered that she had no hope of conducting business as usual until the white-hot interest of the press and the public died down. "Well, Dad," she'd said later, "if we ever are able to get down to business, we'll have plenty! Angie's got a list two feet long of clients who've just *got* to have Ross Investigations work for them!" However, as soon as the ephemeral interest of the public was drawn elsewhere, both expected that most of those sensation-seeking clients would vanish.

"It's been a hard week," Daniel's words drew her back to the present. He looked down at her hand, studied the strong, lean fingers, then suddenly looked up. "We thought we'd lost you, but God is faithful!"

"Hey, come on over here and look at the fireworks!" Rob called. He came over to where Dani stood, noted the grip his father had on her, and pulled her away. "Aw, come on, Dad, let's not have any sticky sentimentality around here—okay?"

Allison came over and pinched his arm, and with a sly grin interjected, "You mean like the kind *you* showed, Rob? You know, when Dani first came home and you slobbered all over her? Disgusting, that's what it was!"

His lean face flushed, and he turned and grabbed her. Despite her screams of protest, Rob threw her over his shoulder. "That's it for you! I'm starting the new year by tossing you in the fishpond!" He carried her off, ignoring her kicking and screaming, and the others smiled as the sounds grew faint, then were cut off by the slamming of the front door.

"I hope he doesn't really *do* it," Dani worried. "It's pretty cold tonight."

"He won't." Daniel got to his feet, went to the window, and looked out. Allison ran by, screaming, hotly pursued by Rob, and Dani said quietly, "I guess I spent more time in the silo thinking about those two than anything else. They both need so much love and assurance, and I began thinking that maybe I'd never be around to give it to them."

Her mother put her arm around Dani's waist. "They grew up quite a bit during all this—both of them. Oh, they're still going to have some growing pains, but it brought them both up pretty short."

"I worried about you, too," Dani said. "One thing kept coming to me: I thought about how I never really told you how much I love you." She put her arms around them both, gave a healthy squeeze, then laughed. "So if I 'slobber' over you—as Allison so delicately puts it!—just mark it down to belated loving behavior."

Daniel said fondly, "You've always been a fine daughter, Dani. Never given us any trouble." Then his tone changed and he asked, "What are you going to do now?"

"Why—go back to the office!"

"Maybe you shouldn't," he suggested. "I know you hated to leave seminary, Dani. You long to go to Africa." He shook his head. "That's your dream, and I don't want to stand between anyone and what she really wants—especially when it's a call from God."

Dani let his words die away, and for a long moment she stood there, lost in a private world. Then she shook her head, her long hair swinging freely over her shoulders. When she spoke, it was with a determination that both her parents had learned to respect. "I know what you're telling me, Dad. You don't want to be a burden, and all that, but it really isn't like that. There wasn't a great deal to *do* in the silo, so I spent a lot of time thinking—about what I'd done, what I'd become, and what I'd do if I ever got the chance. It was like being in a religious order, in a way. All cut off from the world, with lots of time to pray! And I thought some things out."

"What kind of things?" Daniel asked at once.

"Well, about the mission field. Someday I may go to Africa, but I'm not ready for a thing like that now. I'll probably do some more seminary work, study some more. But I discovered one thing: I knew a lot *about* God, but I didn't know God Himself very well!"

She broke off to relate her experiences on the plane, coming home from seminary. She spoke of her difficulty ministering to the passenger with a terminal disease, then of the other times in Stone's prison when she had failed.

"We all fail like that!" her father protested.

"I suppose, but finally what I knew God was saying didn't come in an audible voice, but just—just *seeped* into my heart!" She broke into a laugh that lit up her face, and said, "My professors would have a fit if they heard me say that—*seeped into my heart!* They'd want me to say, something like 'An epiphany broke through and fragmented the ground of my being'!"

"What is God leading you to do?" her mother asked.

"To be still and know that He is God," Dani said simply. "And that means settling down to work. To make Ross Investigations the best agency in America. The verse that kept coming to me over and over was: '. . . Whatsoever ye do, do all to the glory of God.' I think God was telling me there's nothing 'sacred' about going to Africa. Just putting on a pair of shorts and a pith helmet and calling yourself a missionary won't put you on good terms with God. So no pith helmet for Dani!"

"It's going to be a trenchcoat and a slouch hat over the eyes, eh?" Her father smiled. "A private eye for the glory of God?"

"Sounds like an oxymoron, doesn't it?" Dani said, but her eyes were very serious. "I think God has said in effect, 'Dani, you be an investigator. Be a detective for My glory. Help those who are helpless. Keep your hands clean. Serve Me by being a servant to people who need help.' "

"Sounds as if it's not going to pay too well," Ellen said, but she was smiling. "It'll be something new. What do you get when you cross a seminary student with a private eye? *Dani Ross!*"

"Dad, it's what I want to do, what I believe God wants me to do. But it's your business, and if I operate it on this plane, I could kill it dead."

Her father gave her a sudden smile, reached out, and

hugged her. "Daughter, 'blessed are the dead which die in the Lord!' "

They were all suddenly very excited, and for a few minutes spoke of the possibilities that lay ahead. Then Daniel asked, "Dani, what about Ben? Will he be working for you?"

The question took her off guard, and she bit her lip somewhat nervously. "I don't know."

"Didn't he *say* anything about what he was going to do?" Daniel questioned. "Except for that one time, he's kept himself mighty scarce." Savage had made a single visit to their house, the day after the escape. He had come in with Dani but stayed only briefly.

Ellen said, "I think he fled our gratitude. We practically smothered the poor man!"

"Maybe so," Daniel said thoughtfully. "But that's no reason for staying gone forever. Do you know where he is?"

"Not really," Dani admitted uncertainly. She drew her lips together into a determined line, and her jaw took on a stubborn aspect. "I guess if I'm any kind of detective at all I can turn up one man!"

Two days later, however, Dani was beginning to think she had boasted prematurely. After returning to the agency, she had spent every spare moment trying to turn up some trace of Ben, all absolutely fruitless. Al Overmile had observed this with a jaundiced eye. "The guy has skipped," he had stated with a shake of his heavy head. "You don't need him anyway, Dani. We can handle this agency."

Angie had observed Dani's intense expression and had

little difficulty determining the cause. She put in some time of her own and finally ferreted out Ben.

"I've found him," she announced triumphantly the first thing on Tuesday morning. Dani had come in looking tired, but she brightened at Angie's words.

"Where?" she demanded.

Angie tapped her chin slowly with one forefinger. "I've been thinking, Miss Ross, about a raise. I mean, if I'm going to have to do all the investigations *and* the typing, I'll have to have more money!"

"Angie—you beast!" Dani cried and came around to shake the smaller woman by the shoulders, but her smile was evidence of her mood. "Where is that sorry imitation of a detective?"

"He's in Shreveport."

"Shreveport? What's he doing there? And how'd you ever turn him up?"

Angie answered the last question first. "I called the FBI. It came to me that they'd want to know where he is, since he'll be one of the star witnesses against Stone."

"But what's he doing in *Shreveport*, of all places?"

"He was flying his plane back from Arkansas and had engine trouble. He had to land there, and I'd guess he's too broke to get it fixed. At least that's what the man who runs the airport thought. He said Ben was trying to fix the engine with bailing wire!"

Dani took a deep breath. "I'm going to Shreveport, Angie. Get me some kind of flight."

"May have to be a private plane." Angie shook her head. "I don't know if any of the major airlines go there."

"Whatever." Dani nodded absently. She picked up her purse and walked out of the room, leaving Angie to stare after her. A smile came to Angie and she murmured, "Watch out, Savage! The hunt is on!" Then she picked up the telephone and began to dial.

The two men sitting in the small office heard a plane land, but remained too engrossed in their card game to look outside. They looked up at once, however, when the door opened and a cool feminine voice said, "I'm looking for Ben Savage."

The older of the two men, a short, muscular type, removed his cigar from his mouth and stared at her, as did the other—a tall thin man wearing a mechanic's boiler suit covered with grease. They blinked at the tall, well-dressed woman as if she were an outer-space alien.

L. D. Hoover, the manager, got to his feet, his eyes running over Dani. Using his cigar as a pointer, he indicated a green door to his left. "Why, sure. He's back in the storeroom—asleep I guess. Maybe I can help you?"

Ignoring the question, Dani walked across the floor with a motion that drew both men's eyes.

"Hey—!" Hoover yelped, "He might not be dressed, he was up all night, working on that old crate of his—!" But the closing door cut off his words. Hoover slowly replaced the evil-smelling cigar and, without taking his eyes off the door, shook his head slowly. "Can you imagine being woke up by a broad like *that*, Joe?"

"Guess Savage's got hidden charms!"

Dani stepped into a room with one window. By the golden bars of light filtering through the worn blind, she saw that shelves crowded with boxes and equipment took up most of the space. A desk and chair were wedged into one corner, and right under the window lay Ben Savage

337

on a black vinyl couch patched at critical locations, with silver duct tape.

He was lying on his back, sound asleep, but unlike most people, he slept with his mouth tightly closed. *How like him!* Dani thought as she stepped closer. *Afraid he might actually say a few words too many.* He needed a shave, and something about his face remained alert even though he was sound asleep.

"Ben . . . ?"

At the sound of her voice, his eyes flew open, and he rolled off the couch, his hands spread wide in a defensive gesture. He stared at her for one brief moment, then his hands dropped, and he nodded. "Hello."

"That's *all* you've got to say!" she cried angrily. "I've left the agency and come all the way up here to find you, and all you can say is 'hello'?"

He stared at her. "What are you doing here?"

She gave an exasperated shake of her head. "Ben Savage, where have you been?" She had no way of knowing how attractive she was, standing in the sunlight, her eyes flashing and every line of her body intensely feminine.

On the way there she had decided to plunge right into the matter, avoiding any sentimentality. She had told her father before she left, "He's a good man, Dad, and we need him. So I'm going to Shreveport and drag him back any way I can."

Her father had lifted his eyebrows at that, suggesting that a little tact and a softer line might be more effective. "After all, Dani, you two went through a lot together. There's more here than just a business agreement."

She had snapped instantly, "No! That's what it is, Dad—a business deal! No more!"

Now, standing in front of Ben, she spoke rapidly, not allowing any sentiment to come into her voice. "You've had your vacation. Now it's time to come back to work."

He studied her carefully, then shook his head. "Can't do it right now."

"I suppose it's because of that plane? How much would it cost to fix it?"

"Three hundred and forty-seven dollars and sixteen cents."

She began to rummage through her purse, pulled out a checkbook, and asked, "How long will it take? I suppose you'll have to order the parts?"

"They're down at the express office."

She wrote a check. "There's five hundred. Will that be enough for gas and everything you need to get you home?"

The word *home* brought a flicker of interest into his eyes, but he merely stared at the check. "Thanks for the offer, but I guess not."

She reached out and stuffed the check into his pocket. "Don't be silly! It's *your* money, Ben. After I made a fool out of myself and fired you, you never got your last pay-check."

Up until then her words had been businesslike, her tone crisp. Suddenly softness touched her mouth, and she smiled. "Go get your parts and fix the plane. How long will it take?"

He stood there, a solid shape in the barred sunlight, and she knew his mind weighed her in the balances. He had often looked at her like that, judging her in his private courtroom. Now he came to a quick decision. "If Hoover

339

will let me use the pickup to get the parts, it'll take about two hours."

"I'll go with you," she said. Dani walked back into the small office where the two men were waiting. "Mr. Savage will require the use of your truck." She smiled. "Will that be all right, Mr. Hoover?"

Her smile caught him, and without thinking, he nodded, saying hastily, "Oh, sure! Take your time, Ben!"

Ben took the key and led her to a green El Camino. As he started the engine and pulled away from the curb, she began speaking very quickly, as if to avoid some unpleasant subject. "Vince got out of the hospital yesterday. He told me you'd been to see him before you left town."

"Yeah. He was in pretty bad shape, but I guess he's coming around." He gave her a sideways glance, adding, "You've given him a new point of view—about women, that is."

"Oh, he was so sick he'd have clung to any woman who paid him any attention."

"Nope. Not Canelli." With easy skill, Ben dodged in and out between two huge eighteen-wheelers. "Karen was there the last time I went to see him."

"Oh, yes, we had lunch together before she went back to Minnesota." It was Dani's turn to give Ben a quizzical look. "Talking about a hit parade, Karen thinks you're special." When he didn't answer, she probed a little more. "Matter of fact, I got the distinct impression that she was hoping to see more of you."

"No point in that." He shrugged. "She's too intellectual for me."

Dani blinked, wondering if his remark was some sort of personal snub, but he seemed to mean nothing by it, for he added, "She'll find somebody, but she doesn't need me."

They talked about the others, Dani giving Ben the news that Bix had *almost* decided to give up his career as a rebel. She smiled, commenting, "It was really funny, Ben. Bix took such pride in that role! But the last thing he said was, 'Guess I'll have to find a new life-style. Maybe I'll become a yuppie.' And he was so *serious* about it!"

Ben relaxed and said, "Lonnie went back to Arkansas with me. He flew with me in my plane." As he turned down a side street, he added, "I've had to change my judgment about rednecks. Lonnie's rough, but I wouldn't mind having him at my back, if things got hairy."

"That's right." Dani nodded. "Poor Betty! She didn't know what to do! But she finally decided to go back to Pennsylvania, to her old hometown. Said after being in that silo with a murderer, even *that* place didn't seem so bad."

"I guess the silo changed us all," Ben agreed. He pulled up to the curb, turned off the engine, then sat there, staring out the windshield. "I guess that fall I took years ago finally came to an end in that place. I'd gone about as far and as long a man ought to."

"What about Florrie and Hugo? Any more bad dreams?"

"No, just some bad memories," he said, then turned to give her a crooked smile. "But I guess all of us have a few of those, don't we?"

Dani knew he was referring to Jerry's death. She diverted him quickly, "Well that leaves Sid and Karl. Karl went back to Germany. I think he wanted to get America out of his system. He'll be all right. But what about Sid? What'll happen to him, Ben?"

"Up to him, I guess. Lots of prisoners go back the second time. Crime is the only thing they know, and it's hard to break into a straight society. I told Sid we'd stay in touch. Gave him a name or two." He opened the door. Just before he got out, he added, "I guess each of us has his own pint of dirt to eat. And if Sid wants it bad enough, he'll make it." Quietly he added, "That's the role call, isn't it? But it doesn't count Alex and Rosie and Candi. Three good guys!"

He got out, and while he was inside, getting the parts, Dani went over the conversation, analyzing his words. How could she break down his resistance?

When they returned to the airport, Ben led her to a small building to the left of the others. Inside she stopped when she saw an old biplane, a two-seater, the type once used for crop dusting as well as for flying-circus acrobatics.

He saw her reaction and smiled. "Won't take long. Better sit over on that chair, so you won't get grease all over you." As he worked, he became more voluble, telling her about the plane. "Bought it for five hundred dollars. Fellow who owned it hit a wire. It flipped over twice and broke both his legs. The plane was in about six million pieces. Took me a couple of years to put it back together."

She listened, saying little, and finally he slammed the cowling shut, and said, "All ready. Want a ride?"

Dani stared at the plane. "I've only ridden in airliners," she said doubtfully. But the amusement in his eyes angered her, so she shot out, "I'm ready if you are."

He leaned back against the plane, studied her, and shook his head. "You hate to have someone else be better than you," he observed. "You don't like not being able to do something that others can do. Right now you're scared spitless to go up in this crate, but you're too stubborn to admit it."

She glared at him, then snapped, "If you're finished with your armchair psychology, Savage, I need to get back to work!"

He grinned, and it made him look much younger. "All right, let me go settle up with Hoover for the gas."

While he was gone, she looked at the old plane, swallowed, and thought, *What am I doing going up in this thing? It just proves he's right about me!* But she showed none of her thoughts in her face when he returned carrying a small bag which he stowed in the backseat.

Ben turned to her and said innocently, "It's going to be quite a trick to climb into this thing with that tight skirt on."

Gritting her teeth and struggling with the skirt, she managed to get into the front seat. He came alongside her, squatted on the wing, and handed her a soft leather helmet with huge goggles. While she struggled to put it over her heavy masses of hair, he strapped her in firmly. Giving her a small headset, he explained, "We can talk through this."

Then he got into his own seat, and she heard his voice, tinny and mechanical, ask, "You sure you want to do this?"

"Yes!"

He started the engine, and Dani, accustomed to the quiet, distant hissing of jet engines, nearly leaped out of her skin at the roaring explosion! Ben ran the engines briefly; then slowly the plane moved out of the large doorway. It took only a few moments to taxi out on the runway. Then he offered, "Still time to change your mind."

"No. Let's go."

The plane trembled as Ben revved up the engine, and they went bumping along clumsily for what seemed like a long time. Then he said, "Here we go," and suddenly there was no roughness. Looking out over the side, Dani saw the ground fall away, and she gripped the sides of her seat convulsively, expecting to fall at any second.

But they rose steadily, and soon Ben said, "We'll fly along at this altitude for a while." He said no more, but five minutes later he asked, "You all right, boss?"

His use of the old name warmed her. "Yes! It's *fun!*" After the first fear left, Dani had begun to enjoy the sensation. It was nothing like being inside a large 747; after the initial takeoff, that was like being on a train or a bus. But this! She felt the wind as it pushed the plane around constantly and knew that Ben's constant control overcame that force. The air was cold but invigorating and fresh.

He began to point out the rivers and the swamps that stretched out beneath them, and he dropped low enough for her to see one small lake so filled with white egrets it looked like snow! Ben flew very carefully, and she knew that was for her benefit.

Finally he said, "New Orleans right over there." She looked to see the skyline of the city, in the close embrace of a crescent curve of the Mississippi. "Be down in ten minutes."

He brought the plane in so lightly that there was little sensation and came to a halt in front of several other light planes. When he had chocked the wheels, he came to her, his face reflecting the evening shadows.

"Thanks for the ride," she said. "It was wonderful."

"Sure." He hesitated, then said abruptly, "I'm not coming back to work for you."

Her eyes opened wide, and she moved away from the plane to stand close to him. "Why not? Is it money?"

"No, it's you."

She stared at him, and a streak of anger ran through her. "I knew that! I've always known you resented me, and I know why—it's because I'm a woman!"

He touched the scar over his eye, stared down at his feet, then shook his head. A flare of resentment touched his hazel eyes. "I don't give a hang if you're a woman!"

"Yes, you *do!* You've got this—this *thing* about women," she tossed out. "You'd never admit it, but you think a woman's place is in the home, keeping house and changing diapers!"

"That system's worked pretty well for a few thousand years," he shot back. "And all this guff about feminist rights isn't going to give us anything better."

"You don't really care about that, Ben," Dani said heatedly. The argument had flared up so suddenly that she had spoken more freely than usual. "You're just afraid that I'm *better* than you are at some things!"

"I'm not such a fool as that," he said instantly. "You're smarter than I am. I never said you weren't. That means you're a better cop than me in some ways—and I don't deny that. You're an intellectual, and I'm a hooligan. You're better at a lot of things than I am." He shrugged.

She stared at him, and the anger drained out of her. "Oh, Ben!" she said quickly. Her eyes grew softer. "Don't talk like that!" She stood there, trying to find words that would tell him how she felt, but she knew she never would, for she didn't know that herself. Finally she shook her head, saying, "What good did being an *intellectual* do us when we were in Stone's hands? *You* got us out of that awful mess!" She took a deep breath. "Ben, I'm right about this, aren't I? You resent the fact that I'm a woman. You won't let yourself trust *any* woman because of what Florrie did to you!"

The thoughtless words slipped out, and instantly she regretted them. He stared at her, then nodded as he said in a hard-edged voice, "Maybe that's so, but since we're putting all our cards on the table, Miss Dani Ross, I'll just tell you the truth. You want to know the *real* reason why I won't work for you?"

Dani hesitated and nodded slightly. "Yes, I'd like to know."

The quarrel had touched him, and she saw the rashness buried beneath his cool exterior. "You're bound and determined to be somebody you're not," he said. "You want to be an old-fashioned type of woman, gentle and soft—but you can't, because no private eye can be that. So you try to be tough and hard. Someday," he added, "you're going to find out which woman you *really* want to be."

She blinked suddenly and said, "That's my private life!"

"Yeah? Well, so was Florrie my private life—but you're right, it's your business. Only I don't have to stay around and watch it."

He turned to go, but she caught at his arm, and when he came to face her, she said, "We can be a good team, Ben. All I'm asking is that we *work* together."

"You keep out of my life, and I'll keep out of yours," he said roughly. Anger boiling over, he put his arms around her and drew her close before she could move. She instantly placed her hands on his chest and tried to pull back. He watched her struggle, then said, "I wouldn't mind working for a woman, Dani," he said. "But you're not a woman—you're some kind of *cause!*"

"Let me go!" she cried out, for the touch of his hands wrecked her ideas of putting their relationship on a purely business footing. "You don't know what you're talking about!"

"Sure, I'm just a roughneck, no sensitivity," he jibed and pulled her even closer. "But let me tell you something. That time I kissed you, in the silo. . . ." He paused, seemed to struggle for words, then said in a quiet voice, "I—I saw something in you, Dani, and it was real for me. For the first time since—since Florrie. But then you looked at me like I was something that'd crawled up out of the sewer!"

"Ben, I didn't mean it like that!" Dani whispered.

He dropped his arms, his face grim. "Look, this is no good. What are we? I'm a roughneck, and you're brainy. I think women ought to be feminine, and you're trying to be a man. I can't trust a woman because one of them let me down. And you can't be a woman because you've decided to become a nun and spend the rest of your life in a convent!"

Dani stood there, and his words struck her hard. She stared at him, trying to escape, but could not. Against her will she thought of their days together—and the time he'd kissed her. She struggled to summon arguments to offset his charges, but none came.

She could only say, "Ben, don't run away. We can work it out." She had to struggle to get the next words out, and they came with a breathless quality. "I—I need you, Ben." Without willing it, she threw her arms around his neck.

347

"And I think you need me." She was trembling in his arms, but courage filled her eyes.

"We'd drive each other crazy in a month!" he muttered.

Dani had never liked to beg—not for anything. But now she felt as if she was about to lose something priceless. She looked into his eyes and pleaded, "Ben, don't leave! If you don't like what I am, help me to change."

His arms went out, and he pulled her close. She pulled his head down and kissed him fully on the lips. For one moment she clung to him, letting him see what she was— a woman beautiful and shaped by life and longing for all that she had never had. Then she stepped back.

"Will you stay?" she asked.

Shaken by the kiss, he looked at her, then nodded slowly, and a smile came to him—an easy smile, drawn from the real humor interwoven with his spirit. "Always wanted to have a hand in making a woman into what she ought to be."

She laughed, took his arm and swung into step with him. "Funny you should say that, Ben, because I've always thought I could make something out of *you*, if I had the chance!"

He grinned at her with something in his eyes that she couldn't read then made one more comment: "Well, maybe we can make something of each other, boss!"